At the Edge

Of

The World

C J Bessell

Books by C J Bessell

This Series
Jacob's Mob
Currency Girl
At the Edge of the World

Copper Road Series
Pioneers of Burra
For the Love of Family

Margaret Chambers Series
Margaret
Burnt Bridge

ISBN: 978-0-6451051-8-6

Breathing life into family history

Prologue

Norfolk Island 1838

As soon as Jessie stepped from the launch she felt like she'd come home. The warm breeze caressed her skin like a lover's embrace and she couldn't stop the wide grin that spread across her face. Aaron slipped his arm around her waist and nuzzled her neck. She tilted her head to one side inviting him to place a kiss on her cheek, which he obliged.

"Are ye happy, Mrs Price?" he whispered in her ear.

She turned her face and brushed her lips against his. "I am, Mr Price."

He grinned and released her. "Come then." He picked up their bags, handing her the smallest one. "We have quite a walk ahead of us."

Jessie didn't mind. It was a warm day with barely a cloud in the sky and the walk to Orange Vale would stretch out her unused muscles. They had only gone a hundred yards or more when Captain Bordes called out to Aaron.

"Price. Wait up."

Aaron stopped and turned while the Captain hurried to catch up to them. He doffed his hat in Jessie's direction. "Mrs Price."

"Captain," she murmured. She only knew Captain Bordes by sight and had never been introduced to him. He was an unremarkable man in all respects except for his startling green eyes, which were now perusing her from head to foot.

"I believe congratulations are in order," he said grinning.

"Thank ye," said Aaron shifting one of the bags to his other arm. "How can I help ye, Captain?"

"Ah, tis not ye that can help me, Mr Price, but rather the other way around," he said shifting his gaze to Aaron. "Major Anderson's arranged accommodation for ye and Mrs Price in Kingston."

Jessie arched one brow and looked at Aaron to see how he would react to the news. His expression remained unchanged as he nodded. "I'm most obliged to the Commandant."

"Rightly so," said Captain Bordes. "Not everyone receives such indulgences as ye."

The Captain didn't bother to hide the disapproval in his voice and Jessie glanced at her husband. Aaron's expression remained one of open friendliness, but Jessie saw the subtle shift in his eyes. His clenched jaw would've been unnoticed by the unobservant. Jessie wondered how attentive the Captain was to such things. She thought it would pay him to keep his thoughts to himself and her husband on side.

Jessie licked her lips and waited while the silence stretched between them. Aaron shifted his weight and appeared to be doing his utmost to let the Captain's words wash over him.

"So, tell me, Captain," he said with a sigh. "Will ye be showing us to our new lodgings?"

"Private Harris will be along in a moment. He'll show ye. I have other matters to attend." He doffed his hat once again. "Good day, Mrs Price."

"Captain," said Jessie inclining her head.

As soon as Captain Bordes was out of earshot, Aaron spat on the ground. "Twat."

Jessie suppressed a smile and sighed. She hoped Private Harris would be along soon, it was getting quite warm standing out in the sun. She wasn't entirely surprised and was most grateful that they would be residing in Kingston. The only people out at Orange Vale were prisoners and she would've been the only woman. Yes, she was most grateful to the Commandant for providing lodgings in the main settlement.

She swallowed. Of course, that would make it impossible to avoid Mrs Sharpe. She knew she'd have to face her, but it would seem that would happen sooner rather than later. There was nothing she or anyone could do - she and Aaron were married and that was that.

Private Harris came panting up the road and stopped beside them. "Mrs Price," he said tipping his hat in Jessie's direction. He sucked in a large lungful of air and turned his attention to Aaron. "If ye'll follow me."

Without waiting for a response he continued marching down the road. Jessie and Aaron hurried after him. Jessie knew there was no love lost between her husband and the military, but it would seem their feelings towards him had deteriorated in his absence. She hoped Aaron would ignore them and their petty squabbles.

Private Harris led them to a small wooden house on the outskirts of Kingston. It was typical of the other houses that dotted the hillside. A large yard to one side of the cottage was occupied by several vegetable plots which were now overgrown. Private Harris opened the gate and stood aside while Aaron and Jessie walked down the path.

"Well, I'll leave ye to it," he said eyeing Jessie as she passed him. "Lieutenant Hamilton will expect ye as soon as you're settled."

"Aye," said Aaron over his shoulder.

Jessie had thought Aaron would at least be given today to settle in, but obviously, this was not to be the case. She followed Aaron into the house and dropped the bag she was carrying onto the nearest chair.

"Go, Aaron. I'll get us settled in."

He dropped the bags he was carrying and turned to face her. "Hamilton can wait."

He took a step towards her and gathered her into his arms. She drew him close and breathed in his familiar masculine scent.

"I doubt he'll wait too long," she said tilting her face upwards and standing on tiptoes. Aaron obliged by lowering his face towards hers and kissing her. It was a long slow kiss full of promise, and Jessie groaned when their lips parted.

"Aye, he won't wait that long." He placed another brief kiss on her lips before letting her go. "If ye don't mind, I'll go see Hamilton now," he said running his hand down her spine to the top of her hip. "And then later, we can take all the time we want." She squealed with delight when his hand moved lower and squeezed her bottom. He grinned. "Until later then."

She smiled as she watched him. He reached the door in two strides and opened it. A shiver went through her when he looked over his shoulder at her. He didn't try to hide his desire and it thrilled her.

Jessie spent the rest of the day cleaning and getting their new home in order. It was a simple three-roomed house with an out-kitchen and washhouse. It was simply furnished, but adequate. Jessie couldn't have cared less either way. It was hers. Hers and Aaron's and she couldn't believe that she finally had a place to call home.

She spent the following morning out in the garden. She was intent on weeding as many of the plots as she could. She was pleased to discover there were salvageable crops hiding amongst the weeds. Her pail was nearly full of weeds and she stood and stretched her back before picking it up. She was still admiring her work when she heard a familiar voice.

“I heard you were back.”

She looked up to see Mrs Sharpe opening the gate. She smiled as she watched her come towards her. Her face was unreadable and a nervous knot formed in Jessie’s stomach.

“Mrs Sharpe,” she said dropping her pail of weeds.

“Oh, Jessie.” Mrs Sharpe stopped and looked at her, and then she wrapped her arms around her and placed an affectionate kiss on her cheek. “It’s so good to see you.” She let her go and smiled.

“Likewise.”

Mrs Sharpe stood staring at her for several seconds before shaking her head. “So you married him then?”

Jessie nodded. “Yes.” She felt the muscles down her spine tense as Mrs Sharpe continued to appraise her. She swallowed and sucked in a breath. Whatever Mrs Sharpe had to say, she reminded herself, it would make no difference.

She reached out and placed her hand on Jessie's arm. "Tom was perhaps more surprised than I was. He was sure your grandmother would stop you from throwing your life away on Mr Price."

Jessie grimaced as a pang of guilt went through her. "She wanted to." She would write to her grandmother and beg her forgiveness.

"Ah I see," said Mrs Sharpe with a knowing smile. "Does she know you've married?"

"She will by now," said Jessie shifting her weight to the other foot. "My brother, George took me to Sydney and he would've told her when he returned. I'm sure she'll give me her blessing eventually."

"I hope so." Mrs Sharpe glanced around the garden that Jessie had started to get into order and nodded her approval. "Well," she said returning her gaze to Jessie. "Congratulations, my dear."

"Thank you," said Jessie heaving a sigh of relief as the tension left her. "I had hoped you and the Reverend wouldn't be too upset with me."

"Well…we are a bit disappointed…but I'm delighted you've returned." She smiled and tucked a wisp of hair behind her ear. "Now that you're the wife of a prominent Overseer, I think we should give you a proper introduction to the people of Kingston."

Jessie's brow arched upwards and she stared at Mrs Sharpe. "A proper introduction?" She knew many of the people of Kingston already. After all, she'd been living on the island for over a year now.

"Yes," said Mrs Sharpe. "How about I host an afternoon tea in your honour and introduce you to the ladies? I think that would be most appropriate."

It took a moment for her words to sink in and for Jessie to realise that her station had changed. She was no longer a servant, but rather the wife of Aaron Price, and that made all the difference.

***

Chapter 1

Norfolk Island December 1840

The sight of sails on the horizon always evoked excitement among the residents of Kingston, but today, it brought dread for Jessie. Her dear friend, Ellison Sharpe would be on board when the Governor Phillip sailed in ten days. She would likely never see her again and she could already feel the void she was going to leave in her heart.

How it had come to this she still didn't know. The Reverend had had more than one disagreement with the new Commandant, and last month he'd demanded the Reverend and his wife leave. Jessie had hoped Captain Maconochie would relent and change his mind, but that hadn't eventuated, and tomorrow the brig Governor Phillip would be moored off the island.

She sighed as she finished off her sewing and admired the blanket she'd finished edging. Her baby would be coming soon – she had that same feeling in her lower back like right before Ellen was born. Her belly was protruding to the point where she could no longer see her feet. They felt tight in her shoes and she imagined her ankles had swollen to the size of melons.

She cocked her head to the side and absently ran her hand over her stomach as she listened for any sound that Ellen was awake. All was quiet. She folded the blanket and set it aside before struggling to her feet. She made her way out the back door and stood on the porch which led to the out-kitchen. She breathed in the fresh air – the smell of rain hitting dry earth was on the breeze. Dark clouds were gathering and no doubt a downpour would soon ensue. She opened the kitchen door and the aroma of pork stew cooking assaulted her. Hmm, it smelled good as she lifted the lid and gave it a good stir. It would be cooking for hours yet, but it was already making her stomach grumble.

She pushed the kettle over the hearth and reached for the tea caddy. It felt rather light and she shook it before lifting the lid. It was nearly empty but there was bound to be a chest of tea on board the Governor Phillip. She would have to ask Mr Foster to put some aside for her.

"Jess. Jess are you there?" came a voice. This was followed by the kitchen door opening and Ellison Sharpe came bustling in. "Hmm, something smells good."

Jessie swung around and smiled. "Good afternoon. Yes, that would be your famous pork stew."

"I thought I recognised it." She laughed as she lifted the lid on the pot and breathed in the aroma. "It looks good."

"Thank you," said Jessie. "I was about to make a pot of tea. Will you stay for a cup?"

"Yes," she said plopping herself down at the kitchen table. "I suppose you heard. The Governor Phillip's been sighted." Her voice trailed off with a note of despair. "I don't want to leave." She put her head in her hands briefly. "If only Tom hadn't argued with Captain Maconochie."

Jessie put her hand on her friend's shoulder. "I know. I don't want you to go either, but the Commandant isn't likely to change his mind now."

Ellison placed her hand over Jessie's and sighed. "No. Not likely at all."

"Where will you go?" said Jessie filling the teapot with boiling water. She took two cups and saucers from the shelf and placed them on the table.

"I don't know," said Ellison with a shake of her head. "Tom will first have to present himself before the Lord Bishop in Sydney and explain himself."

"Will he have to pay some sort of penance do you think?" said Jessie pouring a cup of tea for Ellison and pushing it towards her.

She hated the idea that the Reverend might be punished in some way just because he disagreed with the Commandant. She poured a cup for herself and sat down. Still, perhaps the Reverend should've kept his thoughts on the treatment of the prisoners to himself. From what she understood, Captain Maconochie was trying to improve the situation for them and they were being treated more humanely than before.

Ellison sipped her tea and tears welled in her eyes. "I don't know. I hope not."

Jessie's heart clenched at the despair in her friend's voice. She reached out and squeezed her arm. "I hope not too."

The sound of big raindrops on the roof and the clash of thunder in the distance heralded the arrival of a summer storm. Jessie put her cup down and looked at the ceiling. "I'll just go and check on Ellen."

Ellison nodded. “It’ll pass quickly I expect.”

Jessie agreed. These summer downpours tended to be short-lived, and the sun would be peeking through the clouds again in no time. She made her way into the house and even before she reached Ellen’s room she could hear her wailing. She’d turned one year old earlier in the month and had taken her first tentative steps just a few weeks ago. Jessie was glad she’d started walking before the new baby came.

Jessie entered Ellen’s room and found her standing up in her crib with large tears rolling down her cheeks. Her mop of nut-brown hair was sticking out in all directions, and at the sight of her mother, she started bobbing up and down on her chubby legs.

“Hush my darling,” said Jessie lifting her from the crib. She placed a kiss on her forehead before putting her down on the floor. She had no hope of carrying her with her large pregnant belly. “Come with Mamma,” she said taking her by the hand.

The two of them slowly made their way through the house to the back door. The rain was pouring over the roof of the porch in a torrent, and splashing onto the stone pavers.

Sometimes if the rain was heavy the porch would flood – she hoped that wasn't going to happen today. A loud clap of thunder overhead made her jump, Ellen squealed in fright and Jessie felt a dampness between her thighs. It was time – her water had broken. She instinctively put her hand under her stomach and sucked in a deep breath.

"Come on sweetheart. Aunty Elli's here to see you."

She opened the kitchen door and ushered Ellen inside.

"Hello sweetie," said Ellison holding her arms out in invitation to Ellen. She grinned and toddled over to her and collapsed into her outstretched arms. Ellison swept her onto her knee and placed a kiss on top of her head.

Jessie grabbed the back of a chair and leaned against it. "My water just broke," she said looking at Ellison. "I'm sorry to ask – it's still pouring out there…but could you go and fetch Mrs Fletcher for me? She'll be expecting me to call on her."

Ellison leapt to her feet and put Ellen on the chair. "Yes, of course. Are you alright?"

"Yes," said Jessie forcing a smile. "I'll be fine, just as soon as Mrs Fletcher gets here."

"I'll be as fast as I can," said Ellison over her shoulder as she rushed out the door.

Jessie heaved a sigh and ran her hand down her spine as she stretched her back. She eyed Ellen who was sitting watching her with her fist shoved in her mouth. Jessie had to get them both back into the house. She had no intention of having her baby on the kitchen floor. "Come to Mamma," she said holding out her hand to her daughter. "There's a good girl."

After a moment's hesitation, Ellen rolled onto her stomach and lowered herself from the chair. She toddled over to Jessie and grasped her hand. Jessie smiled. "Good girl, Ellen."

She stepped out onto the porch with Ellen by the hand. The rain hadn't eased one whit and water was starting to pool around the stone pavers. She ignored it and led Ellen back into the house. Ellen let go of her hand as soon as she spied her rag doll which she'd tossed into the corner this morning. Jessie let her go and gasped as a contraction went through her. Sucking in a breath she eased herself into the nearest chair. Her baby didn't appear to be in a hurry to be born, but she hoped Mrs Fletcher and Ellison were hurrying back to her. She was more than a little scared at the prospect of giving birth alone.

***

Aaron paced the small sitting room. He could hear Jessie's groans through the thin wall as she laboured to bring their child into the world. He would like nothing better than to be somewhere else – anywhere. Anywhere where he didn't have to hear her low moans and the occasional grunts. He felt helpless, and he knew that was fuelling his desire to be somewhere else.

The bedroom door opened and Ellison Sharpe stepped into the sitting room. She looked harassed with several straw blonde tendrils hanging loose around her face. She swept them aside as she grinned at him.

"It's a boy. You have a fine and healthy son."

Relief surged through his veins as the tension left him. "I do. And Jess?"

"Rather exhausted, but Mrs Fletcher is attending to her. She's fine."

"Can I see her?"

"Not yet," she said with a shake of her head. "But I'll bring your son out to see you if you like?"

He nodded. A son. It seemed surreal to him to think he now had a son of his own. A year ago he would never have dared to imagine such a thing. Ellison Sharpe disappeared back through the door.

He sighed as he waited for her to reappear with his son bundled in her arms. He should take his family to Sydney. He'd been granted a ticket for New South Wales earlier in the year, but Jessie had insisted on staying on the island. At the time he'd agreed with her. Along with the ticket had come a promotion to Principal Overseer in the Engineers Department. They had a good life here and a part of him was more than a little afraid to leave the safety of the island.

Ellison reappeared and handed the small bundle to him. He was so tiny and his head was covered in dark hair which took Aaron by surprise. He had expected him to be fair like Ellen was when she was born.

"What will you name him?" said Ellison peering at the baby.

Aaron looked up at her. "Aaron. We'll name him for me."

"Oh," she said smiling. "I thought you might've named him for your father."

Aaron's jaw clenched and he breathed in loudly through his nostrils. "My father doesn't deserve such an honour." His words carried more venom than he'd intended. In reality, he hadn't thought about his father in many years. He'd disowned Aaron following his arrest back in Oxford and Aaron had vowed to be a better man than he ever was.

He said it with such finality that Ellison's brow raised and she took a step back. "I'm sorry…I."

"No. It is I that is sorry, Ellison. Ye were not to know of my feelings for my father. Please accept my apology."

"None is needed," she said.

A loud groan followed by a long dragged-out scream took them both by surprise and Ellison turned and hurried back into the bedroom. Aaron's heart had leapt into his throat at the sound of Jessie's cry. It was over, the baby was born – what could cause her to scream like that? Several more moans emitted from the bedroom and he stood rooted to the spot with fear. Something was very wrong.

He hoped Ellison would return in a moment to tell him what was happening, but no one appeared, and Jessie continued to moan. A viper of fear squirmed in his belly as he looked down at his tiny son lying in his arms. What if something happened to Jess? He swallowed as he began pacing the small sitting room again. He felt so helpless as the minutes ticked by until everything went quiet. He stopped and stared at the bedroom door, willing it to open. Was she dead?

He couldn't say how long he stood there willing the door to open, but when it finally did his heart leapt into his throat. Ellison bid him with a wave of her hand to come inside. He swallowed and stared at her for a moment before his legs began to work. He walked tentatively into the bedroom – half afraid of what he might find. But he needn't have been afraid. Jessie was sitting up in bed holding a swaddled bundle in her arms. Her untidy damp hair clung to her and she looked exhausted, but she was glowing.

"You have twin boys," said Ellison beaming at him.

"Twins?" He walked over to the bed and placed his small bundle beside Jessie before kneeling. "I was so scared. Are ye alright?" He leant forward and kissed her cheek which was moist with the sweat of her labours.

Jessie smiled. "I'm fine now," she said looking down at her newborn son. "I would've been terrified if it wasn't for Elli and Mrs Fletcher."

Aaron turned his head to look at the two women. Ellison also looked tired but was smiling at Jessie and her sons. Mrs Fletcher inclined her head in Aaron's direction. "I can't thank ye both enough," he said with genuine relief.

"Yer welcome, Mr Price," said Mrs Fletcher gathering her shawl around her shoulders. "Tis a wonderful day when we welcome two wee babes." She walked to the door and turned before leaving. "I'll call in on ye in a day or two, Mrs Price."

"Thank you, Mrs Fletcher," said Jessie as she handed her son to Ellison.

"I don't know how you'll tell them apart," said Ellison gazing down at the baby in her arms. "They're so alike." She put him down in the crib before picking up baby Aaron and placing him beside his brother.

“They’re like two peas,” said Aaron eyeing his sons with awe. He now had two sons. He could hardly believe how his life had changed since meeting Jess, and she just kept on giving him more than he deserved. He turned to his wife with words of love on his lips, but she was already asleep – breathing softly in and out.

***

Chapter 2

Hudson and Atkinson

Aaron grinned as he walked down the road to the barracks. It was a mild morning for July with the promise of a fine day to come. He expected to get the first load of stone hauled up to the build site today, and he was excited at the prospect. His thoughts returned briefly to his wife and children still tucked in their beds. His twin sons, Aaron and Moses were growing like weeds. Since their birth, his thoughts had gone more and more toward leaving the island for good. He was becoming obsessed with the idea of taking his family to Sydney.

When he'd first been granted his ticket for New South Wales neither he nor Jessie had wanted to leave. Life was good here. He had a well-paid position and everything they could want, but now…he stopped walking and listened. The odd noise he thought he'd heard was muffled but distinct and appeared to be coming from some nearby shrubs. He moved quietly towards the cluster of guava trees. Kneeling, he peered through the leaves for any sign of what or who was concealed and making the noise. The sound of panting and grunting continued and he crept around the shrubs and down a small incline.

He reached the other side of the ditch before he saw them. Two men half concealed by a large boulder were obviously in the middle of amorous congress. One had his bare arse hanging out of his breeches and was thrusting and panting while the other one moaned in obvious pleasure. Aaron swallowed the bile that rose up the back of his throat. Of course, he'd seen it before – it had been common on board ship and in the prison here on the island. No matter how often he saw or heard the obvious sounds of men fucking one another he never got used to it.

There'd been more than once in his life when he'd beaten off men who'd tried to use him like that. But this didn't appear to be an assault, rather both were eager participants. Aaron sucked in a breath before rising to his full height.

"Oi," he yelled as he leapt from the ditch and reached for the nearest man. He grabbed him by the collar and wrenched him to his feet.

"Fuck. Get off me," the man yelled as he twisted around and stared into Aaron's determined face. His eyes bulged as he tried to wrench Aaron's fingers from his collar.

Aaron knew him. His name was John Hudson and he didn't think this was the first time he'd been involved in buggery. He let him go and Hudson fumbled with his breeches which had pooled around his ankles. Aaron turned his attention to the other man who was hauling up his breeches and preparing to run. He seized him by the shoulders and spun him around. The young freckled face of Henry Atkinson stared back at him with his mouth agape. He looked terrified but wasted no time in grabbing Aaron by the ears and head-butting him.

"Aargh ye bloody bastard," yelled Aaron as Atkinson's head slammed into his brow. He staggered backwards before landing in the dirt. His head was ringing and his brow above his right eye was already throbbing. The rest of his senses didn't appear to be working as he sat there feeling numb and dazed. He tentatively felt his brow with his right hand. He didn't think it was split open, but it sure as hell hurt - his whole head was pounding.

He sat there for a few minutes before getting his feet under him and stumbling after the two, who had scarpered through the bush back towards the road. He took the ditch in one stride and scrambled up the other side. Sweeping the branches of the guava tree aside he staggered after them. By the time he reached the road, there was no sign of them. He glanced up and down – it wasn't likely that they'd have run down the road. If they'd gone into the bushes on the other side then they'd probably headed for Anson Bay.

Aaron put his hand to his forehead and winced as his fingers explored the new lump on his head. *Shit.* He felt that familiar feeling around his jaw as the contents of his stomach soured. His mouth filled with saliva and he groaned as his breakfast was expelled beside the nearest bush. He sucked in several deep breaths and wiped his mouth on his sleeve.

He stood up and stared at the bush where he thought the two had gone before deciding not to pursue them. They couldn't go too far. Instead, he staggered down the road to the military barracks. He was going to be late getting to the quarry and he hoped Lieutenant Hamilton would get his gang to work.

He was nearly at the barracks when he spied Captain Bordes accompanied by two privates coming down the road towards him. He hastened his step.

"Captain," he called when he got close enough.

Captain Bordes eyed Aaron as he came to a halt. "What's amiss then?"

"A couple of sodomites. I caught them in the act, but one of them head-butted me and they took off toward Anson Bay."

The Captain's unconcerned expression changed immediately. "Do ye know who they were?" He peered at Aaron and grinned. "You've got a nice egg on your head."

Aaron ignored his comment, but couldn't resist the urge to run his hand over his brow again. "Aye. Hudson and young Atkinson."

"We'll track them down," he said looking out towards the bay. "Ye should go and see Doctor Harnett."

"I'll be fine," said Aaron dismissing the Captain's concerns. His head was pounding but he had no intention of telling Captain Bordes that.

"Suit yeself…come," said Captain Bordes to his companions. Without another word to Aaron, the three started down the road in the direction of the bay.

Aaron watched them for a moment before turning his attention to the tasks he had to do today. It was only a short walk down to the beach and along to the small loading pier. Aaron was anxious to get there. He passed several work gangs on the way, but none of them were his. He hoped they'd already be at the quarry and loading the first lot of stone. He could feel the adrenaline beginning to surge through his veins as his anxiety grew. It only escalated when he reached the pier and found there was no boat to take him out to Nepean Island.

"Shit," he said out loud as he removed his cap and ran his fingers through his hair. He could see the launch – it looked like it was coming towards him. He wasn't sure. After pacing up and down a few times he began waving his arms in the air in the hope of attracting the boatswain's attention.

The minutes ticked by in agonising slowness until he thought he saw someone from the launch waving at him. He sighed with relief but wished the damned thing would hurry. Five minutes later the launch bumped against the pier and young Bobby stared at him.

"What happened to ye?"

"Never mind," said Aaron leaping into the launch. "I need ye to get me out there as fast as ye can. Has the punt arrived yet?"

"No," he said pushing off and picking up the oars.

Nepean Island was only about half a mile off shore, but today it seemed to take forever to get there. Aaron picked up the other oars and joined in the rowing in the hope of getting there as soon as possible. It probably took no more than ten minutes before the launch was secured at the bar on the east side of the island.

"Thank ye," said Aaron over his shoulder as he climbed out and headed up the track.

By the time he caught sight of the quarry, he was breathing heavily, and not just from the exertion of rowing. Relief flooded him when he arrived and saw his gang. They already had the cart half loaded with the stone they'd been quarrying and cutting for weeks. He saw Lieutenant Hamilton give them some instructions before walking towards Aaron.

"Good morning," he said staring down his rather long nose at him."What happened to you?"

Aaron absently ran his hand over his brow. "Young Henry Atkinson."

The Lieutenant's brows raised as he surveyed Aaron with a look of expectancy. "Nothing too serious I hope."

"It's serious," said Aaron keeping his gaze on the Lieutenant. "I came across him and John Hudson in an act of amorous congress. He head-butted me and they both took off. Captain Bordes has gone to track them down."

His eyes widened and then he peered at Aaron's forehead. "I'm sure the good Captain will apprehend them soon enough. You should go to the hospital and have your head checked."

"It's fine," said Aaron.

"That wasn't a request," said Lieutenant Hamilton. "I'll handle the transportation of the stone up to the site. I'll meet you there tomorrow morning." With a nod, he turned and walked back to the gang loading the dray.

"Aye," said Aaron under his breath. Left with no other choice he turned on his heel and began the walk back to the launch. His head was still pounding but he was sure it was nothing.

***

Jessie sighed as she tiptoed out of the bedroom and quietly closed the door. Ellen and the twins were finally down for an afternoon nap and she might now get five minutes to herself. Well, not exactly to herself. She'd get the vegetables done for supper and maybe bring in and fold the washing if she had time.

She'd just stepped out the backdoor when Aaron appeared from around the side of the house. She gasped at the sight of him. Not only because she wasn't expecting him at this hour, but because he looked like he'd been hit in the head with a sledgehammer. He had a large lump above his right eye and a black bruise halfway down his face. He gave her a lopsided grin.

"My God, Aaron," she said staring at him. "What happened?"

He shook his head. "I got headbutted…I'm alright," he hastened to add. "Doctor Harnett says I'm fine."

Jessie winced as she looked at his poor face. “Who did that?” No matter who did it, she knew there’d be serious repercussions for them. She didn’t want to know about that. The thought of men being flogged always made her queasy.

He sighed. “I came across John Hudson and young Henry Atkinson involved in some amorous conduct. Atkinson headbutted me before they both took off. Captain Bordes’s gone after them.”

Jessie paled. They would be more than flogged for that. “What will happen to them?” She didn’t really want to know what awful price they would pay, but she also knew sodomy was a serious offence.

“I expect they’ll go to trial. Don’t worry,” said Aaron putting his arms around her and hugging her close. “They’ll be caught soon enough.”

Jessie embraced her husband and relished being in his protective arms. He would keep her safe, she knew he would, but what if Atkinson and Hudson came here? They were now desperate men with nothing to lose and they may seek revenge on Aaron – and her. She licked her lips as she pulled from Aaron’s embrace. “What if they come here?”

"They won't" He groaned as he ran his fingers through his hair. "I'll get some soldiers assigned to watch the house if ye like."

Jessie nodded. "Yes please." She knew Aaron. He'd said they won't come here, but he didn't really believe that. He was just trying to make her feel better. The look in his eyes belied his words and she was grateful he'd suggested assigning soldiers to keep watch until the two were captured.

***

Jessie spent a nervous two weeks. She jumped at every noise, always expecting Hudson and Atkinson to appear at any moment. Two Privates patrolled her yard every day, but it hadn't eased her concerns. She was convinced the two would seek revenge against Aaron, and no matter how hard she tried she couldn't shake the feeling.

The attack on Aaron was the talk of Kingston, and several ladies had come calling in the last two weeks. Of course, she'd expected her good friend Mary Vowell to come calling. Her husband, Richard was the Superintendent of Convicts.

"I just can't believe how brazen they were," said Mary Vowell sipping her tea. "Don't ye worry Jess." She put down her cup and leaned forward to pat Jessie's arm. "They'll be caught any day now."

Jessie smiled. "I do hope so."

"I heard they've sent more soldiers to look for them," said Mrs Fletcher taking a slice of cake from the tray. "I wouldn't like to be them when they're caught."

Jessie thought she sounded pleased at the idea of them being punished. She knew they would be – of course. An attack on Aaron couldn't go unpunished, it was just that Jessie didn't like to think about it. She put down her cup and walked over to where the children were playing.

"Stop that this instant," she said smacking Moses on the back of his hand. He had Aaron by the hair and was pulling on it with all his might. Aaron was squealing and now Moses was as well as she grabbed him and scooped him into her arms. He kicked his legs and screamed in outrage, but Jessie kept a firm hold of him and slapped him on his leg for his trouble. "Stop it. You naughty boy."

"They're quite a handful," said Mary eyeing the screaming seven-month-old Moses. "Girls are so much easier don't ye think?"

"Yes," said Jessie sitting down with Moses on her knee.

Ellen and Mary's daughter Hannah were playing happily with their rag dolls, quite unperturbed by the racket the boys were causing. Aaron's squeals subsided as soon as Jessie removed Moses and his hair pulling. She sighed as she tried to calm Moses, who was now the only one still making an awful noise. "Hush now, hush," she crooned as she jiggled him on her knee. "Come now, be a good boy for Mamma."

"Do ye think they'll hang them?" said Mrs Fletcher looking from Jessie to Mary. "They certainly deserve it."

Mary shrugged. "I don't know. If they do I hope they send them to Sydney. I don't like the idea of having to watch a hanging."

Jessie swallowed. "We wouldn't have to watch would we?"

"No, but surely ye'd want to?" said Mrs Fletcher looking surprised.

Jessie was saved from having to reply when the front door opened and Aaron strode in. He smiled and nodded.

"Good afternoon, ladies," he said before turning his attention to his wife. "They've caught them. Ye don't have to worry anymore."

Relief flooded through her as she stood and placed Moses on the floor. "Oh thank God." Aaron was safe and so was she. She walked over to Aaron and wrapped her arms around his shoulders. "Thank God we're all safe now," she said placing an affectionate kiss on his cheek.

He smiled down at her. "Aye."

***

Chapter 3

Sydney October 1841

Aaron stood at the ship's rail perusing the docks. There was an unexpected nervousness in his stomach and a pulse of adrenaline in his veins. He breathed in and out steadily as he watched the soldiers disembark. They were escorting two men in chains, no doubt to be secured at the gaol until their trial. One of them glanced over his shoulder at him with a look of hatred in his eyes. It was Hudson, and Aaron stared unflinchingly back.

He waited until they'd cleared the docks before swinging his bag over his shoulder and heading for the gangplank. The uneasy feeling persisted and he swallowed as he stepped onto the plank and walked off the ship. Stepping foot for the first time in Sydney as a free man was more than a little strange. It had been more than fifteen years since he'd been free to go where he pleased and it felt surreal that no one was stopping him now.

"Wait up, Mr Price."

Aaron turned and waited while Captain Bordes marched down the plank towards him. He'd half expected the Captain to seek him out. They would both be giving evidence in the upcoming trial, but Aaron had hoped to avoid spending any time with the man. He made no secret of his disdain for convict overseers and his dislike for the likes of Aaron. As a ticket of leave Principal Overseer, Aaron was his superior and it clearly rankled the Captain.

"Captain," said Aaron inclining his head when he reached his side.

Captain Bordes tipped his hat. "I thought I might accompany ye to the barracks. After all, we've been thrown together with this business."

"Aye," said Aaron with a wry smile. "I welcome your company, Captain." It was a lie, but it was better to keep the man on side than to antagonise him. They would be spending several weeks together before returning to the island, and Aaron had no desire to give him reason to complain.

"Excellent," he said coming into step beside Aaron as the two began walking to the barracks.

In truth, Aaron was happy for the company. It was his first visit to Sydney and he didn't know his way around. Of course, he would've found the barracks on his own. Sydney wasn't so large that he could get lost – at any rate, the military barracks were only a ten-minute walk up George Street.

***

Norfolk Island

Jessie finished kneading the dough and set it aside. She drew in several breaths and wiped the sweat from her brow on her apron before taking it off and hanging it on the hook. The day was already warm and promising to get warmer.

"Come, sweetheart, we'll go and see what those boys are up to," she said holding her hand out to Ellen.

She obediently slid from the chair and took her mother's hand. Jessie smiled as the two left the kitchen. She was such a sweet child and nothing at all like her rambunctious younger brothers. They were probably causing havoc having been left to their own devices.

Jessie stood on the porch for a moment lifting her face to the fresh sea breeze. She closed her eyes and sighed as her hot skin cooled. She hoped Aaron was alright.

Thoughts of him had been invading her mind more and more in recent days. Was the trial over? What had happened to Hudson and Atkinson? What if they sent them back to the island? She opened her eyes and sucked in a breath as she pushed all thoughts of them aside. She would not live in fear.

She opened the back door and ushered Ellen ahead of her as they went into the house. All was quiet which sent a bolt of panic through her. “Aaron, Moses,” she called as she hurried through to their bedroom. A quick glance told her they weren’t there. She rushed back into the sitting room. “Aaron, Moses,” she called again as she hurried into her bedroom.

There they were the pair of them sitting on the floor with a box of chalks. Moses was busy crushing one into the floorboards with a wooden block. Aaron had used his to scribble all over the place. Jessie sighed. It could’ve been worse – chalk was easily cleaned and apart from half of the chalk being ruined, there was no harm done.

“You naughty boys, you know you shouldn’t have them.” She knelt and gathered the chalks back into the box and snapped the lid shut. Moses was already crawling away as fast as he could, while Aaron was doing his best to rub the crushed chalk into the floor. Jessie scooped him into her arms and followed Moses out into the sitting room.

"You stay here," she said putting Aaron on the floor beside his brother. He looked at her with his big hazel eyes so like his father's. Her heart melted at the sight of him and she leaned down and placed a kiss on his forehead. "Be good."

She was just finishing cleaning the chalk from the floor when there was a knock on the door, followed by Mary and her two-year-old daughter, Hannah. "Hello, Jess. Are you there?"

Jessie got to her feet and poked her head out of the bedroom door and smiled. "In here. The boys decided to do some decorating."

"What little treasures," she said surveying what was left of their handiwork.

"Yes," said Jessie wiping the last of the chalk from the floor. She straightened and gave Mary a brief hug. "I'm so glad you could come."

"I'm happy too," she said stepping back into the sitting room

"I promise I'll be as quick as I can be," said Jessie removing her apron and hanging it over a chair. "Do you need anything from Foster's?"

"No. And take your time. I'll manage."

Mary really was the best friend. Jessie didn't know how she'd cope without getting a break from the children on occasion. "Thank you." Jess placed a warm kiss on Mary's cheek before grabbing her basket and hurrying out the door.

Mr Foster ran the Commissariat Store which was only built about five years ago after the original store down at the waterfront was flooded. The new building was three stories high and located opposite the civil officer's houses. They were a row of lovely stone cottages. Jessie paused briefly at the end of the row where a gang of convicts were busy working on a new cottage. She wondered if they were Aaron's gang. He'd told her he was building one of the new cottages and she thought it was that one. After a moment she turned and headed up the hill to the store. She went up the stairs and opened the door. The first floor was mainly divided into offices and

Jessie ignored them and proceeded down the stairs to the basement.

She spied Mr Foster immediately. He was sitting behind his counter with a large ledger open in front of him. He was only a young man but he sported the bushiest red beard. He looked up as she entered and smiled.

"Good morning, Mrs Price," he said returning his attention to the ledger. "I'll be but a moment."

"Take your time," said Jessie sauntering over to the counter and leaning on it. She perused the shelves behind Mr Foster. They were well stocked and cluttered with boxes and casks and she was relieved to see a chest labelled tea. She was nearly out and hoped Mr Foster would let her have a full caddy.

"Now, Mrs Price how can I help ye?" he said pushing the ledger aside and turning his brown eyes in her direction.

"Ah, well I have a list," she said reaching into her pocket and handing it to him. "But I hoped you might let me have some tea and butter if you can spare it."

"Aye," he said scanning her list of provisions. "I can let ye have a bag of tea and we've plenty of butter."

"Thank you so much."

He put the list down on the counter and proceeded to lift the lid on the chest of tea. "Hobson," he called as he scooped the leaves into a brown paper bag until it was about half full. He replaced the lid and put the bag of tea on the counter.

An older man appeared from behind the shelves. "Aye, Mr Foster?"

"Go fetch a pat of butter for Mrs Price."

"Aye."

He disappeared again behind the shelves. Jessie smiled as she put the tea in her basket.

"I can have the rest of your order delivered tomorrow afternoon," said Mr Foster going back to his ledger.

"Perfect. Thank you."

Hobson returned a few minutes later with a pat of butter wrapped in an oilcloth. Jessie thanked him and put it safely in her basket. She made her way back upstairs and had just reached the top when Lieutenant Hamilton stepped through the main door.

He removed his hat and smiled. “What a lovely surprise, Mrs Price. How are you?”

“Well thank you,” said Jessie smiling in return. Her heart started thumping against her rib cage and she swallowed. She didn’t know the Lieutenant that well. She’d met him once or twice, but she was very conscious that he was Aaron’s superior. “And you?”

“Most fine thank you,” he replied. “Did you see the cottage we’re building for Mr Seller? Your husband’s gang is making excellent progress in his absence.”

“I did notice it, yes. I wasn’t sure if that was the one Aaron was building. It’s going to be a very fine house,” said Jessie reaching for the door.

Lieutenant Hamilton beat her to it and held it open for her. “It is indeed.”

“Well, good day,” said Jessie inclining her head.

“Ma’am.”

Jessie breathed a sigh of relief as the door closed behind her. She was so afraid she was going to say something silly to the Lieutenant.

***

Chapter 4

Sydney October 1841

Aaron was relieved as he left the court. The last time he'd been in there he'd been sentenced to hang, and the place unnerved him - even now. He was also pleased to put the business of Hudson and Atkinson behind him. It was over. He grimaced as he began walking up the street. Well not quite. The pair would hang on Friday morning and he would be expected to attend. He took no pleasure in it.

He'd just turned the corner into George Street when a very familiar figure crossed the road and stepped in front of him. He smiled widely in recognition.

"Aaron Price," said Reverend Tom Sharpe obviously delighted to have run into him.

Aaron was equally surprised and pleased to see Tom Sharpe. Since his marriage to Jessie, the Sharpes' attitude towards him had softened considerably. He would almost go so far as to say they were supporters of his. "Tom. What a delightful surprise."

"Likewise. Likewise," he said nodding. "What brings you to Sydney? Is Jessie with you?" He craned his neck looking behind Aaron as though he expected Jessie to appear out of thin air.

"No, Jess isn't with me. I'm here giving evidence in a rather nasty business."

The Reverend's brows shot upwards as he returned his gaze to Aaron. "Ah. Not the Hudson and Atkinson matter?"

"Aye. How do ye know about that?"

Tom sighed. "I'm Chaplain of the gaol, and I attended on the pair before the trial today. I wasn't aware you were involved."

"I wish I wasn't, but aye it was me who discovered the pair. Anyway, enough of that awful business. How's Ellison?"

"Well, very well. You must come and join us for supper."

"I wouldn't like to intrude."

"Nonsense," said Tom with a wave of his hand. "I would get the rounds of the kitchen if I didn't bring you home with me. Please you must come or else be responsible for my marriage."

Aaron grinned. "Well, in that case, I'd be delighted to join ye."

"Excellent. We're just around the corner in Cleveland Street."

The two fell into step as they began walking up George Street together. Aaron felt himself relaxing in Tom Sharpe's company. After weeks in Sydney on his own, he welcomed the company of a familiar face. It was only a short walk to Cleveland Street and the two-story Georgian house that the Sharpes called home.

"Welcome to our home," said Tom as he opened the front door. "Ellison. Elli," he called as he made his way through the parlour.

Aaron followed him inside and closed the door behind him. He found himself in a large parlour sparsely furnished with shabby furniture that had seen better days. Aaron was surprised. He remembered their house on the island had been well-furnished, and not at all shabby.

"What's all the fuss, Tom, I'm here," said Elli wiping her hands on her apron as she entered the parlour. Her eyes widened at the sight of their guest. "Aaron. What an unexpected surprise." She embraced him and smiled. "You're alone?"

"Aye. I'm here on Government business."

"I've invited him for supper," said Tom removing his hat and hanging it on the nearest hook. "I hope we've got enough to spare."

"Of course we have," said Elli giving her husband a sideways glance. "You two get yourselves settled at the table while I get your supper." She bustled out of the room leaving the two men to make their way to the dining room.

"Do you smoke?" said Tom retrieving his pipe from his pocket.

"No, but please by all means," said Aaron gesturing.

Tom nodded as he lit his pipe and blew a puff of smoke. "Come then."

He followed Tom from the parlour through double glass doors to the dining room. It was a large room furnished with a small table and chairs and a buffet. It was decidedly bare without even a rug on the floor. The table looked like it had been hastily set for three and Aaron, following Tom's lead, seated himself.

"You must excuse our surrounds," said Tom taking another puff of his pipe. "Our circumstances are somewhat reduced since arriving in Sydney. I'm hopeful the Lord

Bishop will see his way clear to giving me a proper post in the not too distant future."

Aaron nodded. He knew the Reverend had been expelled from the island under less than ideal circumstances. Still, it saddened him to see them living so frugally.

"I expect he will when he thinks I've paid my penance," said Tom standing and walking over to the buffet. "Wine?"

"Aye, I'll join ye."

"I do miss having a congregation of parishioners to attend to," said Tom pouring three glasses of red wine. He placed one in front of Aaron and one in the place where Ellison would be sitting. He snuffed out his pipe and joined Aaron at the table with his glass of wine in hand. "Our situation isn't quite as dire as it might appear. We still have funds from the sale of our house at Milkmaid's Reach, but we're being very careful with it. We're hopeful of purchasing another property when we finally get settled."

Aaron raised his glass. "Well, to getting settled and ye own church, Tom. I wish ye the best of luck."

"Thank you," said Tom raising his glass and clinking it against Aarons.

Aaron took a sip of his wine. It tasted full-bodied with overtones of berries. It was rather delicious.

"Oh good, I see you two are settled," said Ellison coming into the dining room carrying a laden tray. She placed it on the buffet before placing the plates on the table in front of the men. Aaron breathed in the aroma and smiled. He remembered Ellison was a good cook and the cottage pie she'd placed in front of him made his mouth water.

He waited while Ellison seated herself and bowed his head while Tom recited grace. No sooner had he said amen, than Ellison launched the first barrage of questions at him.

"So, how are Jess and the children? Oh, I expect the twins have grown so much."

"Aye, they have. They're crawling and I think they'll be walking by Christmas." He put a mouthful of pie in his mouth before she could ask her next question.

"Oh my," said Ellison staring at him. "I can't imagine them so grown already. And Jess's well?"

"Oh, aye," he said hastily swallowing. "She's well, but the boys are a mischievous pair who keep her busy."

"I can only imagine."

Aaron couldn't help but notice a shadow of sadness cross her face as all the light left it. She gave him a tremulous smile and took a sip of wine. "We…that is Tom and me…we lost our dear sweet boy two months ago." Tears welled in her eyes but she swallowed and blinked them away.

Tom reached out and squeezed her hand. "Aye. We named him John Lambie Sharpe."

Ellison drew in a deep breath. "He came too soon and we only had him for three days. Our poor wee boy."

"I'm so sorry." He didn't know what else to say. The pain he saw in both their eyes made him want to turn away. He knew he was beyond lucky to have his daughter and sons, and he couldn't imagine the pain of losing any one of them.

"Thank you," said Tom releasing Elli's hand. "We're forever hopeful that God will answer our prayers and one day bless us with a child."

Aaron nodded and smiled. "I pray he will." He put another mouthful of pie in his mouth and savoured the delicious flavour. He thought time was running out for the Sharpes to be blessed with a family, but he hoped they would succeed.

"You're most kind," said Elli sipping her wine. "So you and Jess are not yet expecting another one?"

He shook his head. "Not that I know of."

The conversation turned to general concerns about the colony and life in Sydney. Aaron didn't have much to add about the island. Not much had changed since they'd left. Aaron promised to pass on their regards to Jess and departed at around ten o'clock. He'd thoroughly enjoyed his evening with the Sharpes and if he hadn't been returning to the island next week he would've invited them out to supper with him. As it was, he had the hanging to attend to and a present for Jess he was yet to collect. He expected the Governor Phillip would sail the following week once the business was at an end.

***

Friday dawned grey and overcast and Aaron couldn't wait for the day to be over. Attending a hanging was something he would never choose to do, but it was expected. He stepped out into the courtyard of the barracks and surveyed the day. It was warm and the earlier rain had turned the day sultry. He removed his jacket and slung it over his shoulder as he crossed the courtyard to the front gate.

He half expected Captain Bordes to be waiting for him but there was no sign of him. He went through the gate and began walking towards the gaol which was on the corner of Essex Street. He hadn't gone far when a man walking towards him made eye contact. He saw recognition in the man's eyes. Aaron thought he knew him but couldn't immediately remember who he was. He walked passed him and was about to dismiss the man from his mind when he called out to him.

"Yer Price aren't ye?" the man said with a snarl. "Yeah. Yer the bastard that give me a hundred lashes."

Aaron turned and faced the man. His heart began thumping against his rib cage as the adrenaline surged through his veins. He knew him. His name was Doyle or something like that and he was an old hand from the island. He couldn't remember exactly, but it was likely he was telling the truth. Aaron had caused many men to be flogged in his time as a Police Runner and later as Overseer. It was his job to bring them to justice and he had no qualms about it.

"Fuck off," said Aaron ignoring Doyle's threatening look.

He turned his back on him and took two steps before he was grabbed from behind. Doyle wrapped his arm around Aaron's throat forcing his head back as he held him in a tight grip. Aaron gasped and grabbed Doyle's arm with both hands as he tried to release the pressure against his windpipe.

"Ye won't be doin' it again ye bloody bastard," said Doyle as he strained to hold Aaron and choke him.

Aaron gagged and gulped in a lungful of air as he finally managed to twist free of Doyle's grasp. Doyle wasn't done. He pulled a knife from his belt and thrust it towards Aaron's neck. He saw the glint of the blade in time to grab Doyle's wrist and deflect the blade harmlessly away.

"Oi what's this then?" came a familiar voice.

Aaron didn't take his eyes off Doyle as he applied as much pressure as he could to his wrist until the blade slid from his numb fingers. His eyes bulged as he turned to see who had joined the fray. He wrestled free of Aaron's grasp and stumbled before getting his feet under him. He took off running down George Street.

Captain Bordes picked up the knife and turned it over in his hand. "Are ye alright?"

"Aye," said Aaron gasping for air as he massaged his throat.

"Good," he said handing him the knife and taking several strides in the direction of Doyle's disappearing back.

"Wait," yelled Aaron chasing after him he grabbed him by the shoulder. "Leave it."

"What? Ye can't let that piece of shit off with that."

Aaron nodded. "Let him go. There's no harm done." He wasn't afraid of chasing down Doyle but for some reason, he didn't want the confrontation. If he was honest, he was shaken by the attack. He'd made many enemies over the years but he'd never expected to be assaulted like that in broad daylight. It unnerved him.

Bordes eyed him with one brow arched and then he shrugged. "Well, alright if that's what ye want."

"It is."

***

Chapter 5

Norfolk Island November 1841

Jessie wasn't expecting visitors and so the knock on her front door surprised her. "Who is it?"

"It's me…Mary."

Jessie smiled as she opened the door. "What a lovely surprise, how are you?" She hugged her friend before standing aside to allow her and her daughter, Hannah to enter.

"Good thank ye," said Mary removing her bonnet and putting it on the sideboard. She smoothed her dark hair with her hand and smiled. "I don't suppose ye've heard…sails were spotted this morning."

Jessie felt her heart skip a beat. "Sails? No, I didn't," she said with a note of excitement in her voice which quickly died. "Oh, it's probably a whaler."

"No, I don't think so," said Mary with a shake of her head. "I overheard Mr Ormsby saying it was the Governor Phillip." Hannah was hanging onto her mother's skirt peering at Ellen and the twins. "Go and play," said Mary disentangling her daughter and urging her to join the other children.

She reluctantly let go and toddled over to join Ellen who was trying to build a tower of blocks, while Moses was intent on pulling it down.

Jessie felt her heartbeat quicken again as she thought of Aaron finally coming home. He'd been gone more than a month and she had missed him sorely. She prayed Hudson and Atkinson weren't on board – she didn't want to live in fear of them. Pushing all other thoughts aside a wide smile spread across her face. "Well, Mr Ormsby would surely know."

"Indeed I think so," said Mary smiling. "I expect your husband will be onboard, don't ye think?"

"Yes. I can hardly wait. I've missed him so."

Mary grinned. "Well, ye don't have long to wait."

Jessie sat down and picked up her sewing that she'd put aside. "Will you stay for tea?"

"No, I can't stay long." She sat down and leaned back in the chair. "Richard's at home in bed with a terrible headache. I only came by to tell ye the news."

"Well I appreciate it," said Jessie. She was housebound with the children right now. The boys were not yet walking and she couldn't very easily carry two of them. They'd gotten so big and heavy. If people didn't come to give her the news she'd never know what was going on. And she didn't know what she'd do without Mary.

***

Jessie was up early the following morning. She'd hardly slept as thoughts of Aaron had invaded her mind. Was he alright? What had happened to Hudson and Atkinson? God, she hoped they hadn't been sent back here.

The children were all still abed and she hoped they'd sleep for another hour. She stepped out the back door and paused as she breathed in the fresh morning air. Rain clouds were gathering which would only add to the humidity as the day warmed. She set to work in the kitchen stoking the hearth and preparing bread dough.

She expected Aaron would disembark before midday and her heart raced at the thought of seeing him. This had been their first time apart since they were married, and Jessie had missed him more than she would've imagined. She sprinkled a fine film of flour on the bench and upturned the dough from the bowl. She paused and drew in a deep breath. The wait to see him was going to be agonising. She could already feel a tight knot of anxiety in her stomach and the only thing that would release it was Aaron.

Midday came and went and still, there was no sign of him. By mid-afternoon, Jessie had convinced herself that Mary was wrong. It must've been a passing whaler. Even the children were subdued. It was as if they knew their mother was preoccupied and on edge.

After supper, she settled the children into bed and prepared for an early night. She was tired after having very little sleep the night before and a busy day with the children. She picked up the lamp and was heading for the bedroom when the front door opened. She turned, startled at the unexpected intrusion. Aaron grinned at her. His grey-flecked hair was windblown and his hazel eyes looked relieved to see her.

"Aaron." She gasped as she put the lamp down and threw herself into his arms. "I convinced myself it wasn't the Governor

Phillip." She buried her head into his shoulder and relaxed as his arms enfolded her and held her in their safe embrace.

"I've missed ye," he murmured as he nuzzled her neck and breathed in the scent of her.

He sighed when she tilted her face towards his and smiled. "I've missed you so much."

He lowered his head and their lips met in a passionate kiss. Jessie opened herself to him as his tongue explored. She moaned when their lips parted and Aaron grinned. "I see you've really missed me."

Jessie felt her cheeks warm under his intense gaze. She lowered her lashes and pulled free of his embrace. Why she felt so shy in her husband's arms was beyond her. She wanted to be held by him - wanted to be desired. "I have," she whispered.

He took her hand and brushed his lips across the back of it which sent a shiver through her. Without another word he led her to their bedroom, lifting the lamp from the sideboard as he went. Jessie's heart was thumping against her rib cage as her breathing quickened. She'd missed Aaron so much, but she had no intention of allowing him to rush their lovemaking tonight – no, and she wanted to know all about his trip to Sydney.

She pulled her hand free and closed the bedroom door behind them. Aaron arched a brow and she smiled. "I don't want to wake the children. They're going to be so excited to see you."

"Ah…good idea."

He placed the lamp on the bedside table and watched as Jessie unbuttoned her blouse and tossed it over the chair. She drew in a breath as she undid her skirt and petticoat and allowed them to fall and puddle at her feet. She could feel his eyes burning into her and she smiled. Stealing a glance she thrilled at the desire she saw in his eyes.

"Aren't you getting undressed?" she said loosening her stays and adding them to the pile of discarded clothes.

"Aye," he breathed, "but I'm currently otherwise occupied."

Jessie was now in nothing but her shift and she turned to face him as she began freeing her hair from its plait. "Really?"

He grinned as he removed his jacket and tossed it aside. "Aye."

Jessie turned her back on him and finished unplaiting her hair. She shook her head and her honey-blonde hair cascaded down her back. Ignoring the noises Aaron was making, she picked up her brush and began brushing out her hair which was crinkled from being in a plait all day.

Satisfied, she put down her brush and turned around only to find Aaron was already in bed. He smiled and turned back the sheet inviting her to join him. She needed no further encouragement. She untied the drawstring of her shift and allowed it to float to the floor before climbing into bed beside him. He gathered her into his arms and pressed his naked body against hers as he kissed her.

Jessie thrilled at the feel of his naked flesh against hers as she ran her hand down his back. His muscles rippled beneath her fingers and a soft moan escaped his lips when she squeezed his bottom. She smiled and pressed herself harder up against him until she could feel the whole length of him. She nuzzled his neck and kissed him before putting her hand on his chest and pushing him away. She threw her leg over him and continued to push against his chest until he rolled onto his back.

Aaron grasped her hips and settled her on top of him before running his fingers over her thighs. She gasped and arched her back when they explored her soft womanly cleft. Everything faded as the pleasure he was giving her became the only thing that mattered. After several minutes she groaned and pushed his hand aside and eased him into her. She could feel him trying to thrust beneath her, but she wanted to take it slowly and enjoy every second. She leaned forward and put her hands on his chest as she took control of the rhythm.

Aaron allowed her to take control for several minutes before his impatience took over. He groaned, and gripping her by the hips rolled them both over until she lay beneath him. Jessie was panting as their hips ground together. "Oh Aaron," she called out as she reached her crescendo. Spurred on by her cries of pleasure he thrust faster until he let out a groan of ecstasy. He lowered himself to the bed beside her and gathered her into his arms.

He kissed the top of her head and sighed. "I love ye."

Jessie lay panting in his arms with her bottom pressed into his hips. "I love you too."

"I hope we didn't wake the children," said Aaron.

Jessie lay still, listening for any sign that their offspring had awoken. All was quiet. "No."

She rolled over so she could see her husband, and ran her hand down his face before brushing her lips against his. "I missed you so much," she said with a sigh. "And I don't want to ruin the moment, but I must know what happened to Hudson and Atkinson. Did they send them back here?"

"No. Ye need not ever worry about them again."

"Oh." She knew what that meant and needed no further explanation. On the one hand, she was glad they couldn't threaten them anymore, but on the other – she swallowed. "Are you alright?"

"Aye. It's never a nice business, Jess, but I did what must be done." He squeezed her and kissed her forehead. "Ye'll never guess who I ran into."

"No, who?" she said with one brow arched.

"Tom Sharpe."

"Oh, did you see Elli too?"

"I did. They invited me to sup with them and so I spent a very pleasant evening in their home. They both send their love."

"Oh, I'm so jealous. Are they well?"

"Aye quite well. They're hoping Tom will get a posting soon."

Jessie snuggled into him and sighed. "Ah, so they're still paying their penance then?"

Aaron nodded. "I'm afraid so."

She prayed the Reverend would soon have a church full of parishioners to care for. He loved that and she was sure Elli would prefer not to be living in Sydney. "Perhaps I could come with you next time?"

"Perhaps," he murmured.

Jessie's heavy lids closed and she drifted off to sleep with thoughts of her dear friend uppermost in her mind.

***

Chapter 6

The Perambulator

The following day Aaron presented Jessie with the most fabulous gift he'd brought for her in Sydney – a pram. She ran her fingers over the wooden handle and grinned as she admired it. It was perfect - made of wicker and lined with blue satin with a foldable hood.

"Thank you so much," she said hugging him. "It's just wonderful."

He grinned. "I thought it might give ye more freedom to go out and about. I'm glad ye like it."

"Oh, I love it. And it's so thoughtful of you."

He kissed her briefly. "I must get going. Lieutenant Hamilton will be expecting me. Enjoy your day." With a smile, he left through the front door.

Jessie couldn't wait to get the children up and breakfasted so they could all go out. She'd been virtually housebound for a year except for quick trips to Mr Foster's store, or when Aaron had time to accompany her and the children. Now, for the very first time, she could go out whenever she pleased.

She put the twins into the pram together. It was a bit squishy and Aaron complained by screwing up his face. He held his arms up to her and big tears rolled down his face.

"Hush, hush sweetheart. You'll love it," said Jessie as she opened the door and wheeled the pram outside. "Come Ellen." She held her hand out for Ellen to take it and closed the door behind her.

It was a beautiful morning with a light sea breeze blowing. Jessie sighed as she began slowly walking down the road towards the main settlement. It was slow going with Ellen toddling along beside and she wished the pram had a seat for her. In no time Aaron quieted and shoved his fist in his mouth while Moses jiggled up and down in obvious delight. Jessie laughed at him as she pushed them down the road.

Her friend Mary lived in one of the lovely stone cottages. Jessie had only visited her once before the twins were born, but she was sure Mary's house was the second from the end. She hoped so as she knocked on the door and waited. Her heart rate had quickened, partly due to her nervousness at calling unannounced, and partly because she hoped she had the right house.

A moment later the door opened and Mary stared at her. “Jess.” Her attention quickly moved to the pram. “Oh my, wherever did ye get that?”

Jessie grinned. “It was a present from Aaron. Isn’t it just gorgeous?”

“It is,” she said running her fingers over the wicker. “Oh, it’s marvellous.” She grinned and wrapped her arms around Jessie and kissed her cheek. “And now ye can visit me. Come in. I’ve just made a fresh pot of tea.”

“Thank you,” said Jessie lifting Moses from the pram. “I was a bit worried coming unannounced.”

“Nonsense,” said Mary gathering Aaron into her arms. “Ye’re always welcome, and I could do with the company.”

Ten minutes later the two were enjoying a cup of tea while the children played happily at their feet. Mary had given them all a biscuit to keep them quiet while the two women swapped gossip.

“Did ye hear that young coxswain drowned?” said Mary putting down her cup.

"Ye know the one - he was in charge of the boat out to Phillip Island."

"I think I know who you mean. Was his name Johnny Butler?"

"Aye. Well, I heard he fell overboard and drowned last week. Poor man – he wasn't very old."

"He was a prisoner wasn't he?" said Jessie sipping her tea. "I heard Aaron speak of him a few times. Apparently, he used to be a marine."

"Really?" said Mary raising an eyebrow. "Speaking of marines, I hear Captain Bordes is leaving."

"Yes. He and his regiment are being relieved when the next ship comes in. I wonder who'll replace him?"

Mary shrugged. "Who knows? Just between ye and me, I was hoping Mr Ormsby would be replaced."

"Doesn't he work for your husband?" said Jessie.

"Aye…well he did, and he was always disagreeing with Richard. But now he's been appointed Superintendent of Agriculture as well as Assistant Superintendent."

"So doesn't he still work for him?"

"Not really, he's now his equal and he's quite horrid. And in his position as Magistrate, he loves to hand out floggings. I don't like him one bit," said Mary finishing her tirade. "Ye won't say anything will ye? It wouldn't pay to have my opinion bandied about."

"I won't say a word – not even to Aaron."

Mary smiled. "Thank ye."

After a lovely visit with Mary, Jessie bundled the boys back into the pram and began the slow walk home. She loved her newfound freedom and made a mental note to thank Aaron again for his thoughtfulness. She sighed as the wheels caught in a rut and she shoved it hard to get it out. If only the roads were in better shape she might even be able to take the children down to the beach.

***

Summer 1842

Jessie settled the children for the night and made her way to the kitchen. Aaron wasn't yet home and she was looking forward to having supper with him when he finally arrived. She'd been expecting him to talk about moving to Sydney ever since his return, but he hadn't. She suspected he'd changed his mind about moving but it could be that he'd been so busy over the last few months that he hadn't had a chance to think about it. Either way, she intended to raise the subject and find out what he was thinking.

She poured herself a glass of wine and left the bottle on the table. Ten minutes later Aaron came bursting through the kitchen door. His eyes lit on her sitting at the table sipping her wine. Without a word, she stood and poured a glass of wine and handed it to him. He took a sip before putting it on the table and gathering her into his arms.

"Something smells good," he said tilting her face to his and kissing her. "Hmm, and ye taste like good wine."

She grinned and pulled from his embrace. "Sit, and I'll dish up your supper."

"How was ye day?" he asked easing himself into a chair. He sighed and ran his fingers through his hair.

"Good. And yours?"

"Fine."

Jessie sliced a large helping of fish pie and slid it onto a plate for Aaron. Her stomach grumbled as the aroma hit her nostrils – it smelled delicious. She cut a smaller slice for herself and added a dollop of mashed sweet potatoes to each plate. She turned and placed the plates on the table before seating herself.

"I've been meaning to ask you ever since you got back from Sydney. What did you think of the place?"

"Not much," he said slicing the pie and taking a mouthful.

Jessie nodded. "Hmm." She dug her fork into the pie and sliced off a piece. "Have you changed your mind about us moving then?" She popped the pie into her mouth – it was creamy and fishy and the pastry was flaky and the whole thing was rather delicious. She was very pleased with her efforts.

Aaron's eyes rested on her for a moment and he shrugged. "Not right now." He took a sip of wine. "Anyway, we're happy here aren't we?"

"Of course we are." She couldn't help the feeling that something had changed and she didn't understand what. Aaron had been intent on giving their children a normal life, and moving to Sydney had been a big part of that plan. She drew in a breath and slowly let it out. "Did something happen to change your mind?"

There was no mistaking the shadow that crossed his face at her words. She reached out and squeezed his hand. "It's alright if you'd rather stay here." She smiled and removed her hand.

Aaron let out a sigh and put down his cutlery. "Aye, something did happen. I should've told ye at the time, but…"

Jessie swallowed a mouthful of pie and gulped down some wine. What could've happened she had no idea, but she hoped he was going to tell her. She gazed intently at her husband who was looking uncomfortable on the other side of the table.

"It was one morning. I was on my way to Court I think when this man accosted me on the street. He was one of the old hands – Doyle I think his name was. Anyway, he came at me with a knife and if not for Captain Bordes's interference I don't know how it may have ended."

"He tried to kill you?" Jessie's heart had leapt into her throat at the mention of a knife.

"Aye…well I suppose so," he said with a shrug. "Anyway, it wasn't the knife so much that unnerved me as his words. He hated me…said I'd caused him to be flogged."

Jessie stared open-mouthed. "Did you?"

Aaron shook his head and refilled his glass. "Probably, I don't know. That's the thing. I've given a great many men cause to hate me, Jess. And many of them are now in Sydney."

Realisation dawned on her – he was scared. That thought unnerved her more than anything. He was scared of nothing or so she thought. "Do you fear one of them may kill you if we go to Sydney?"

"God, no!" He waved his fork in the air. "No, I fear if I were to go to Sydney on my ticket I may lose it and end up back here without that protection." He swallowed another mouthful of pie and sighed. "Ye don't know what it was like for me back then."

He was right, she had no idea and she shuddered to think of him treated like the hundreds of other prisoners.

"I clawed my way out of that cesspool by doing the Commandant's dirty work. And that has earned me a lot of enemies," he said gulping down more wine. "If I ended up back there I would be a dead man and then what would happen to ye and the children? I can't afford for that to happen."

It broke her heart to see the anguish on his face. His hazel eyes bore into her like he could make her understand just by looking at her. She did understand and it didn't matter if they stayed here. "I like it here and I'm sure the children will be just fine."

"Do ye really think so?" he said as his eyes searched her face for some indication that she might be lying.

"I do," she said smiling. "It may be a bit unconventional but the children will accept the life they have here without question."

"I hope ye're right."

She smiled and nodded. "I am. You'll see."

***

Chapter 7

The Disappearing Canvas

Aaron nearly ran into Lieutenant Hamilton as soon as he entered the Commissariat. He hadn't been expecting anyone to be on the other side of the door.

"Ah, sorry," he said sidestepping the Lieutenant.

"Actually, Price you're just the man. Mr Foster's had a length of canvas disappear and I'd like you to find out what's amiss."

"Aye. A length of canvas ye say? I'll look into it."

"Good." He stepped outside and closed the door behind him.

Aaron immediately headed down to the basement to investigate Mr Foster's claims. Foster was leaning on the counter staring into space and only appeared to notice Aaron when he spoke.

"I believe ye're missing a length of canvas, Mr Foster."

"Aye," he said running his fingers through his beard. "I only noticed it was missing this morning, but it may have been gone for a few days."

"What makes ye think so?"

"Well, it was on a shelf down the back there and it was only when I had Hobson move the sacks in front that I noticed it was gone."

Aaron leaned over the counter and looked towards the back of the store. It was dark and shadowy and he couldn't see a thing. "How much was there?"

"A decent amount," said Mr Foster following Aaron's gaze. "At least three yards."

Aaron's eyes widened and he stared at the storekeeper. "And ye can't be sure when it disappeared?"

"No."

"Hmm. I gather ye didn't see anyone. What about ye assistant?"

"Hobson? Maybe," he said shrugging. "Hobson," he called over his shoulder.

A few moments later Hobson came shuffling down the aisle between the shelves. His gaze rested momentarily on Aaron before he turned his attention to his master. "Aye, Mr Foster."

"Mr Price here wants to talk to ye."

"Hrmph," he said casting his rheumy eyes in Aaron's direction once again.

"What do ye know about the missing canvas?" Aaron saw an unmistakable flicker of knowing in the old man's eyes. "Come and show me where it was."

"Aye."

Aaron lifted the wooden flap and went around the other side of the counter. He followed Hobson as he shuffled down the aisle to the rear of the store. He stopped beside some casks and pointed at the shelf.

"Here."

"Aye," said Aaron kneeling. "It's a bit dark back here."

"Aye," said Hobson shuffling his feet.

"So tell me what ye saw," said Aaron straightening.

Hobson cast his eyes in Mr Foster's direction before resting them on Aaron. "I saw the coxswain last week," he said in a low voice. "Where he shouldna been."

"Ye mean Butler? He drowned."

"Aye."

Aaron frowned as he tried to decipher what the old bugger was saying. He drew in a breath and slowly let it out. "Are ye saying ye saw Johnny Butler after that?"

Hobson cast his eyes towards Foster again before turning back to Aaron. "If I tells ye what I know ye'll put in a good word for me?"

So that was his game. Aaron didn't blame him. Why risk your neck if there was no reward? He nodded.

"I saw him sniffin' round the store after that."

"And ye think he stole the canvas?"

"Well, he disappeared didn't he?"

Aaron pressed his lips together as he weighed up the old man's words. "If ye lying to me."

"I ain't," he said with a belligerent stare. "I got no reason to lie to ye. But ye'll remember ye promised to put in a good word for me?"

Aaron nodded. "I'll remember."

He sauntered back down the aisle towards the counter. He hoped Hobson wasn't lying – and if Butler hadn't drowned he had to find him. Three yards of canvas…he stopped in his tracks…that could be enough to make some sort of raft. He proceeded to the counter and lifted the flap.

"Do ye have any linseed oil?" he asked Foster.

"I don't generally keep it. Ye can get it direct from Mr Ormsby if he's got any."

"Aye thank ye."

He left the store and headed for the loading pier and the quarry. If Butler wasn't dead and he'd stolen the canvas there were likely only two places he'd be. Out at Anson Bay which was remote and hardly visited, or he could be hiding in one of the many caves along the cliffs. He still wasn't sure he believed Hobson – he could be sending him on a fruitless search.

After a short trip out to Nepean Island, he met Hamilton at the quarry and filled him in on his theory. "I'll take a couple of men and go search," said Aaron rubbing his chin. "If ye see Ormsby can ye ask him if he's missing any linseed oil?"

Lieutenant Hamilton stared at Aaron down his long nose. "Ye think Butler will try and make a boat?"

He shrugged. "Why else would he steal a length of canvas?"

"You may be right," said Lieutenant Hamilton. "If I see Mr Ormsby I'll be sure and ask if he's missing any linseed…take Rob Jones and Will Lawrence with you."

"Aye, thank ye."

Aaron spent the rest of the day searching every inch of Anson Bay without finding any trace of Butler. He arrived home for supper frustrated and disgruntled. He was sure Hobson was lying but he had no idea why.

"Sit down and I'll fetch your supper," said Jessie urging him towards a chair.

As soon as he sat down she ran her hands over his shoulders, massaging the tight knot of muscles. "You're all wound up," she said placing a kiss on his cheek.

"I am." He ran his hands through his hair and down his face. "I'm not having any luck tracking down a missing prisoner."

"I'm sure you'll find them," she said sitting in the chair beside him and gazing at him. "I have news that may take your mind off your troubles."

"Aye, what's your news?"

"We're having another baby," she said grinning. "In the spring."

His eyes searched her face before a wide grin spread across his. He took her face in his hands and kissed her. "I don't deserve ye." He leaned forward and gathered her into his arms and pulled her onto his lap. His lips met hers again in a long kiss as his hands gripped her hips. “I love ye so much,” he said when the kiss ended.

Jessie smiled down at him. “I love ye too.”

“Ye know when I first met ye I was a desperate man, and now look at me - happy and free, and all because of ye.”

“Desperate? I don’t remember you being desperate. I do remember you being very frustrating.”

He laughed. “Ye didn’t know me very well back then. But I assure ye, I was desperate and ye were my only hope.” He meant those words. She’d been his only chance of having a wife and family and he felt a pang of guilt at how he’d pursued her. “I may have lied to ye back then, but not now. When I say I love ye and ye are the best thing that ever happened to me, I swear it’s true.”

“I believe ye,” she said staring down into his eyes. She straightened and then glanced down at him again. “If we’re telling truths, then perhaps it’s time I told you that I lied as well.”

His eyes widened and he stared at her. “Ye did? What did ye have to lie about?”

She giggled. “I was fourteen when you married me. I’m only now eighteen.”

"What?" He stared open-mouthed at her. "No, ye were not." Fourteen? He didn't believe her.

She giggled again. "Yes, I was. I didn't tell you the truth because I thought you'd lose interest in me."

He wrapped his arms around her and hugged her close. "I would never have lost interest in ye."

Their lips met in a passionate kiss that left him wanting more. She wriggled her bottom as she placed her hands on his face and he groaned. They had not yet eaten supper.

***

Aaron spent the following three days in a fruitless search for the missing canvas and Johnny Butler. He was convinced Hobson had lied and his frustration was reaching boiling point.

Rob Jones removed his cap and scratched his head. "What do ya reckon we search south of the rocks?"

Aaron glanced at Jones and then surveyed the rocks. It would be rough going, but they'd searched just about everywhere else. He nodded. "Good idea. We'll have to go back to Anson Bay and backtrack along the beach." He'd walked along the top of these cliffs before and he'd never found a way down. They presented an almost sheer drop to the rocks below.

"Aye," said Will Lawrence eyeing the cliffs. "I'm not goin' down that way."

The three men made their way along the cliffs until the ground levelled out and they were able to reach the beach. Aaron scanned the beach for any signs as they headed for the rocks on the point. There was no sign that anyone had recently traversed the sand.

The three men clambered over the rocks with care, stepping from one to the other. Aaron reached the point first and immediately spied what he thought was a small cave about ten feet up the cliff.

"Jones," he called over his shoulder. "Go check that out." He pointed to the small alcove and then continued to search the cliffs further along.

He hadn't gone far when Jones yelled out to him. "There's somethin' here. It looks like the canvas."

Aaron turned. "Don't touch anything."

William Lawrence and he clambered over the rocks as fast as they could and then climbed up the cliff to the cave. Aaron was panting and could feel the excitement of adrenaline coursing through him.

"Looky here," said Jones indicating to what looked like the framework of a makeshift boat.

Aaron knelt and inspected it. Canvas had been stretched over some branches which had been lashed together. He ran his finger over the canvas – it was wet and he brought his fingers up to his nose and inhaled. "Linseed," he said standing. "There must be a tin of it somewhere, but don't touch anything. We don't want Butler to know we've discovered his hideout."

"Ye still think it's Butler then?" said Lawrence arching a brow.

"I don't know, but I very much intend to find out."

Apart from the boat, there were signs that someone had been living in the cave. A still-warm fireplace and a few logs were against one wall. A blanket roll had been tossed to one side and what looked like some basic provisions wrapped in a cloth sat atop the logs.

"There's a tin back there," said Jones emerging from the back of the cave. "I'd say he's only put on one coat of linseed. The tin's still heavy."

"Good," said Aaron glancing down at the rocks. "We need to find somewhere to hide and keep a lookout for the bugger coming back. Come on."

They left the cave and scrambled back over the rocks. There was nowhere to hide, and Aaron's frustration threatened to derail him. He stopped and sucked in a deep breath while he tried to think calmly and logically. Whoever it was couldn't approach the cave from the south, they'd have to come from Anson Bay end. When he reached the beach he scanned the cliffs. He was confident no one could come down that way. They'd have to come the same way they did – which was down a narrow track where the cliffs levelled out.

"Lawrence, I want ye to head back to Kingston and grab some provisions and refill our water," said Aaron scanning the area for a suitable hiding spot. "Jones and I will conceal ourselves around here somewhere."

"Aye," said Lawrence taking the canteens and nodding. "I'll be as quick as I can."

"Good," said Aaron before turning his attention back to Jones. "Come on, those tussocks over there look like they may hide us."

Ten minutes later Aaron and Jones had found a good spot to conceal themselves behind a slight rise and a large clump of long grass. They had a fair view of the beach and the track as well as the road to Kingston. Aaron was confident they'd see anyone who was heading for the rocks and the small cave. The question was how long would they have to wait?

It was starting to get dark by the time Lawrence returned. He hadn't seen anyone on the road or nearby. He crouched down and handed each of them a refilled water canteen. "He might've seen me though and be wonderin' what I'm doin'."

It was possible, although Aaron thought he would've seen him. "Aye, maybe." They were going to have to give it up soon – they weren't going to be able to see in another half an hour. "Tell ye what. Go for a wander along the cliffs, gaze out to sea for a bit and then head for Kingston. If he has seen ye, he'll think ye've left and he might come out."

"Aye, alright."

Lawrence scrambled out from behind the tussocks and Aaron watched as he wandered along the cliffs. He stood for a minute or so and then he began walking back down the road towards Kingston. Aaron wasn't convinced that this was going to work and so was rather surprised when a few minutes later he saw a hunched-over figure hurrying along the top of the cliffs. He nudged Jones who turned and grinned.

Aaron put his hand on Jones's arm and held up his hand indicating they should wait. Jones nodded and they both watched as the figure scurried down the beach towards the rocks. Aaron's heart was beating hard against his ribs as the two crept out of their hiding spot.

"We'll follow at a distance," he said in a low voice. "I want to catch the bugger in the cave, ye understand?"

"Aye," said Jones nodding.

Without another word, Aaron walked slowly down to the beach. He was half crouched and his eyes didn't leave the dark shape of the man who was now climbing over the rocks. He swallowed as they stepped onto the beach, hugging the base of the cliffs as they made their way towards the rocks.

A minute later he breathed a sigh as the man they were following disappeared. He'd obviously made it back to his cave and he quickened his pace. When they reached the rocks he paused again. He wished Lawrence had come back – he could do with a third man just to make sure the bugger didn't escape.

"Ye stay at the bottom of the cliff," he whispered. "I'll go straight for the cave, ye be ready to grab him if he runs."

"Aye."

The two men slowly made their way over the rocks until they were at the base of the cave. They were well concealed by the fading light and the shadow cast by the cliff. A soft glow was emanating from the cave, which illuminated the opening. Taking a deep breath Aaron launched himself at the cliff and scrambled up as fast as he could. Without pausing he entered the cave.

A man was kneeling by a flickering fire and he looked up with alarm etched on his face. It was Johnny Butler and Aaron wasted no time in launching himself at him. He took him by surprise and Butler fell backwards onto his back with Aaron on top of him.

"It's Butler," yelled Aaron as he grabbed his arms and brought his hands together.

"Git off me," yelled Butler as he tried to wriggle out from under Aaron.

Holding him with one hand Aaron reached into his pocket for a length of rope, but in that split second Butler managed to wrest himself free and push Aaron from him. He got to his feet and backed up the cave as his eyes swivelled from Aaron to the cave opening. Before Aaron could launch himself at him again he ran for the entrance and straight into Jones's arms.

"Now where do ye think yer goin'," he said spinning him around and wrenching his arms up his back.

"Aargh, let me go."

"Not likely," said Aaron coming to his side and wrapping the rope tightly around his wrists and tying a knot. "Ye've given us a mighty run around."

He spat in Aaron's face and looked like he was going to ram him. If not for the firm grip Jones had on him Aaron thought he would've succeeded. He wiped the gob from his face with his sleeve. "Ye bastard," he said before smacking him across the face as hard as he could.

Butler's head reeled back and he let out a loud grunt.

"Let's get him out of here," said Aaron giving the cave a final look. "We'll come back tomorrow and clear all this stuff out."

"Aye," said Jones poking Butler in the back as he shoved him towards the cave opening.

Aaron followed the two. He was relieved to finally have Butler in custody. The bugger deserved all he had coming.

***

Chapter 8

Lynch and Brennan

Aaron shifted his weight as he stood in the courtyard of the barracks. It was early yet but the day was promising to be a warm one. His gaze rested on the triangle erected in the middle of the courtyard. He felt a ripple go down his spine. He well remembered the day he was flogged - his bowels contracted at the mere thought of it.

He moved his gaze to the man being led to the triangle. He was in chains and sobbing. The soldiers on either side of him appeared to be unmoved by his plight. They removed his chains and secured him before ripping the shirt from him, leaving his back bare and exposed. Aaron knew that would be bloody pulp before the lash was done.

Commandant Maconachie stepped forward from the crowd. "Fourteen men have been sentenced to be flogged this day. I urge each and every one of you to repent and devote yourselves to God's teachings." He paused and surveyed the thirteen men waiting for their punishment to be meted out. "Johnny

Butler, you've been sentenced to two hundred lashes as due punishment."

Aaron's stomach squirmed and he drew in a breath. Two hundred was a fairly standard punishment, but he had no intention of staying to watch the lash do its work. He didn't need to see another man flogged to within an inch of his life. Commandant Maconachie nodded to William Gallaher who was standing ready with the cat in his hand.

Aaron winced as the first stroke of the lash bit into Butler's back. He turned and walked from the yard, taking deliberate strides that were neither too slow nor too fast. He heard Butler call out *Oh, Jesus Christ* as he reached the door to the barracks.

Another blow and Butler howled in agonising pain. Aaron wished he could block out the man's screams as the memory of himself being flogged flashed before him. He entered the barracks and made his way to the front door, where he paused and drew in several deep breaths. He was glad he had other matters to attend to this morning and he wouldn't be missed.

He was walking towards the hospital when he saw four or five men carrying another man. He hurried over and opened the door to the hospital to allow them to take him inside. "What's happened?"

"There's been a quarrel," said the man closest to him. "Up there, on the road. They've taken Brennan to gaol. Lynch's dead."

"Aye," he said eyeing the dead man. He knew Patrick Lynch by sight and Stephen Brennan was well known to him. He hurried up the road to where the man had pointed. Two knives and a hammer were lying on the side of the road where an ominous bloody patch stained the ground. He picked them up before approaching several men who were milling about, including Will Forster the Superintendent of Convicts.

Aaron approached him. "What happened?"

"There was a scuffle and Brennan stabbed Lynch," said Will Forster looking at the hammer and knives in Aaron's hand. "He admitted it."

"Here take these," said Aaron to a young police runner who had just arrived on the scene. He handed him the knives and hammer. "Commandant Maconachie will no doubt want to see those."

"Aye," he said taking them.

"Has anyone informed the Commandant?" said Aaron to the general assembly.

A few men murmured and shuffled their feet.

"I will," said Will Forster. "I believe young George Chapman saw what happened. Would ye track him down and bring him to see Maconachie?"

"Aye I will," said Aaron before turning his attention to the men who were still standing about. "Get to your stations, and if ye saw what happened present yeself before the Commandant afore the day's out."

After a few grumbles, they obeyed and the crowd slowly dissipated.

"Ye best present yeself as well, Price," said Will Forster over his shoulder as he began heading towards the barracks.

"Aye, I will," Aaron called after him.

He waited until everyone had moved on before he turned his attention to finding young George Chapman. It was barely half past seven o'clock and he doubted the boy would yet be at school. He must've been on some errand though to have witnessed the murder. He had no idea what sort of errand a ten-year-old boy would be on at this hour.

He turned and headed back to the hospital. His father was the overseer of the hospital and would no doubt have some idea where his son would be. Anyway, he wanted to know how Lynch had died. He entered the hospital and following the sound of voices, he soon found the assistant surgeon and Patrick Lynch who was laid out on a table.

"Ah, Price," said Henry Graham looking up from his inspection of Lynch's body. "Terrible business."

"Aye it is," said Aaron averting his gaze from Lynch. "So do ye know how he died?"

"Oh yes. He's been stabbed in the heart…would've died almost instantly."

"Oh," said Aaron taking a step closer and peering at the small wound in Lynch's chest. "There wasn't much blood at the scene."

"Well, no I don't expect so. Most of the bleeding's internal."

Aaron nodded – surprised and interested in the surgeon's response. "I'm actually looking for Chapman. Have ye seen him?"

Graham straightened and looked thoughtful. “I haven’t. But I expect he’s in his office. Down the hall – last on the left.”

“Thank ye.”

He made his way down the corridor and knocked on what he thought was Chapman’s door. Hearing a muffled ‘come in’ he opened the door and went inside. Chapman was sitting at his desk and looked up when Aaron entered.

“I’m rather busy, so please make it quick if ye don’t mind.”

“I will. I’m looking for your son, George. He witnessed a murder this morning and I need to find him.”

Chapman’s round brown eyes looked frantic as he ran his hands down his face. “Good Lord.”

“Aye. Well, I presume he was out on some errand or other, to be out so early I mean.”

“Yes, yes. I sent him down to the dairy to fetch some butter. It was too early for the store to be open ye understand.”

“Right, well I’ll see if he’s still there. Good day.”

"Wait," said Chapman. His eyes bulged and he looked like he might have some sort of fit.

"Ye need not worry. I'll take care of ye son."

"Of course, thank ye. No, it's just that I should accompany him to the Commandant's office, but well…I suppose ye know I'm expecting a number of men." He rubbed his face again. "There're fourteen being kissed with the lash today and I'm needed here."

Aaron nodded. "Perhaps I could fetch Mrs Chapman?"

"God no!" He seemed to pale at the very thought. "It's best she doesn't know – at least not yet. She'll be hysterical."

If it was Jess she'd want to be there, but he presumed Chapman knew his wife better than he. "I promise I'll accompany him and be by his side while Maconachie questions him. If he's at all upset I'll end it."

"Thank ye."

"Ye're welcome." Aaron closed the door behind him and sucked in a breath. He was glad it wasn't one of his sons. He felt his heart quicken. The thought that he may not be able to protect them from the horrors of the island preyed on his mind, and this event had brought it into sharp focus. Chapman's lad couldn't be more than ten and he had no idea how one so young would react to seeing a man killed.

He pushed all thoughts of his children aside as he headed for the dairy. He hoped the lad was still there – perhaps old Swanny had consoled him. He wasn't in luck. There was no sign of him at the dairy and according to the men he hadn't been there this morning. Aaron groaned. Where had he gone? He hoped he hadn't gone home – but where else would he be? He walked back up the road towards the settlement – keeping an eye out for any signs of young George Chapman. There was none and he was left with no choice but to go to the Chapman house and hope Mr Chapman was wrong about his wife.

He saw him before he reached the house. A small hunched-over figure sitting on the front porch. He drew in a breath before approaching the boy.

"Good morning, George," he said kneeling beside the lad.

Two round tear-stained eyes met his. He wiped his nose with the back of his sleeve. "Good day, Mr Price."

"Ah, ye remember me – I wasn't sure if ye did." George nodded and Aaron smiled. "I know ye saw something terrible this morning on the road."

Fresh tears erupted and he nodded again. "I didn't tell anyone."

"Aye I know," said Aaron putting his hand on the boy's shoulder. "It's alright. Ye've done nothing wrong. I spoke with ye Pa earlier and he knows what happened."

George's round brown eyes became even rounder if that was possible. "Is he mad?"

"No, not at all." Aaron shook his head and did his best to reassure the lad with a friendly smile. "But ye know Mr Machonachie will want to talk to ye. He'll want to know what ye saw. Do ye think ye can do that?"

"Do I have to?"

"Aye, but ye need not worry, George. I'll tell the Commandant what I know and ye can do the same. We'll do it together."

"Did ye see it too?" said George brushing aside his tears.

"Well, no I didn't see the quarrel like ye did, but some others did. Ye need not worry that ye were the only one. And they'll be telling Mr Maconachie what they saw as well."

The boy nodded and pulled a dirty handkerchief from his pocket and proceeded to blow his nose. "Alright I'll do it."

"Good lad." Aaron straightened and heaved a sigh. He was thankful the lad wasn't too traumatised to tell his story. Although he'd reassured him there were others, he suspected George saw more than anyone else.

***

Chapter 9

Trials and Tribulations

The events of recent weeks had left the entire population of Kingston on edge. Murder was a nasty business and rumours had been rife ever since.

"I heard the two made a pact," said Mary looking at Jessie over the rim of her teacup. "I know it's dreadful to think of it, but it wouldn't be the first time."

Jessie paled at the thought. She'd heard the rumour and had dismissed it as that, pure rumour and gossip. She sipped her tea and then shook her head. "You don't truly believe that?"

"Well I don't know," said Mary putting down her cup. "Why else did they quarrel so publicly in the middle of the road? I heard they did it so there could be no doubt that one had murdered the other, and the other was guaranteed to be hung."

"Well if that's true they succeeded," said Jessie taking a slice of cake from the tray. "Brennan will surely hang for it."

"Hmm, I expect so. Do ye know when the trial will be? I suppose your husband will attend. I'm glad Richard wasn't involved if I'm honest."

Jessie smiled. She didn't blame her friend for that. "Yes Aaron will attend, but it's poor George Chapman I feel for. He's no more than ten years old."

"Surely his mother will go with him," said Mary glancing at her daughter who was playing happily at her feet with Ellen.

Jessie shook her head. "I don't think so. I went to see her shortly after the horrible event at Aaron's request. She was most upset."

"Do tell."

"Well, there's not much to tell." Jessie put her cup down and shrugged. "I was a bit nervous as I knocked on the door."

Mary leaned forward in her chair and was now giving Jessie her undivided attention. "I don't blame ye."

The door opened a moment later and Mrs Chapman stared at me. She was in a dishevelled state with her hair hanging around her face – she looked unkept and she'd been crying. She brushed her hair aside. "Mrs Price what an unexpected surprise. Won't ye come in?"

"Thank you," I said with a tremulous smile. "I hope you don't mind me coming unannounced, but after recent events, I wanted to make sure you were alright. Can I do anything for you?"

She grimaced and shook her head. "No one can do anything. I just want to take my children and leave this dreadful place, but I can't." She looked me up and down. "My husband's not free like yours. God knows why ye stay here when ye don't have to."

I didn't know what to say. I hadn't expected her to be so bitter or angry so I ignored her comments about us. The poor woman didn't mean it – she was distraught. "It's been a dreadful business, and I'm so sorry your young lad was involved. But surely your husband will go with him when the trial begins."

She shook her head. "Not likely. Like I said he's not free to go where he pleases."

"Well what about you, Mrs Chapman? You could attend with your son to ensure his safety."

She looked around the room and then back at me. "I've got other children to care for and I can't just go running off because one needs me." She rested her gaze back on me with a look of contempt. "If ye've got nothing else to offer I'll bid ye good day, Mrs Price."

"So that was that," said Jessie shaking her head. "I couldn't wait to get out of there, and I'd say there's little chance of poor George Chapman having any support from his family."

"Poor little lad," said Mary with genuine concern. "Your husband will surely look out for him if no one else does."

"Yes of course he will," said Jessie picking up her cup. "I think he's been rather concerned for the lad. It was he who took him to see Maconachie after it happened." She popped the last mouthful of cake in her mouth. It was a rather delicious lemon cake and she was pleased with her cake-making efforts.

"So, did ye say ye knew when the trial was going to be?"

Jessie grinned and licked her fingers. "They'll be going to Sydney for it when the Governor Phillip returns, and you'll never guess. Aaron has invited me to go with him."

"What? To Sydney. Oh, I'm so jealous. I haven't been anywhere in ages."

"Well, not Sydney exactly. He said he'd take me up to my grandmother's and come back and get me once the trial is done. I'm so excited."

"Oh Jess that's wonderful, and you so deserve to see your family after so long. I'm still jealous though." She turned down her mouth in a petulant pout. "I wish Richard would take us to Sydney for a visit. I haven't seen my sister in nearly two years."

"Ask him – surely he will."

***

A month later the sails of the Governor Phillip were spotted, and as usual, sent a wave of excitement through the settlement. Jessie was more excited than most knowing she would be sailing for Sydney in a matter of days. She packed one bag for the children and one for herself which was actually half full of clean clouts for the children. Having three children under three, none of whom were fully trained to use the privy meant she needed to be well prepared.

There were letters from her grandmother and Ellison Sharpe which she devoured. Grandma would be so surprised when she arrived on her doorstep, but there was no way to forewarn her. Jessie wasn't concerned. She'd be welcomed with open arms, she knew that.

Ellison had exciting news – Tom had finally been given a proper position in Bathurst. They'd be moving there as soon as arrangements were finalised. Jessie clasped the letter to her bosom – and Ellison was expecting another baby. She'd pray for her – surely this time they would be blessed with a child. She ran her hand over her slightly rounded belly and smiled. She'd write to Ellison and share her own baby news.

They boarded the ship three days later and settled into their shared cabin. Unlike the last time she'd been on the Governor Phillip, their cabin was more like a bunkroom than a cosy cabin for two. There was a bunk for Aaron and herself and three hammocks had been hung, one above the other in a three-tier arrangement for the children. It left just enough room to store their bags and that was all. No chair or table could possibly fit.

"Come with me," said Aaron coming into the cabin. "All of ye." He scooped the twins up, one under each arm. They giggled with glee as he marched out the door with them.

Jessie took Ellen by the hand and they followed Aaron. What he was so excited about she had no idea but anything that distracted and kept the children occupied was fine by her. At the end of the corridor, he put the twins down and opened a door before gesturing to Jessie to enter. She squeezed passed him and entered a large room that was occupied by several women and half a dozen or so children.

"This is my wife, Mrs Price - ye may know her," said Aaron arching a brow. "Either way, this is Mrs Friend, Mrs Hughes and Mrs Monaghan. These ladies are with the military and have most kindly invited ye to join them and their children."

Jessie gazed around the room and a wide smile spread across her face. Aaron and Moses had already made a beeline over to where two boys a bit older than them were playing with some wooden horses.

"Thank you, ladies. It's most kind of you to include us," said Jessie. She was feeling quite overwhelmed by their generosity. The next week on board the ship was going to be so much easier than she'd imagined. "I believe we've met Mrs Monaghan. At Mrs Vowell's house."

She stared at Jessie for a moment before smiling. "I believe you're right. You and she are good friends are you not?"

"We are," she said nodding before turning her attention to the other ladies. "I'm most pleased to meet you, Mrs Hughes and Mrs Friend."

"Well, I'll leave ye ladies. Good day," said Aaron tipping his cap as he departed through the open door.

Jessie and the children spent most of the afternoon with the soldier's wives and their children. The women chatted about people and matters that Jessie knew nothing about, but she didn't mind. The children were happy and occupied and that made her life so much easier.

That night she lay cradled in Aaron's arms. The children were in their hammocks which had wrapped around them like cocoons. They couldn't possibly get out of them or fall out – she hoped.

"Thank you for today," she whispered before brushing her lips against his. "It was most kind of you to introduce us to the ladies and their children."

He squeezed his arms tighter around her and smiled. “I had to find something for those little rascals to do. And you. I’m glad you’re happy with the arrangements.”

“I am. I have no idea how I would’ve survived a week stuck in this cabin with them.”

He chuckled softly. “Either ye or them wouldn’t have survived.”

The Governor Phillip docked in Sydney nine days later. It had been a longer voyage than usual due to some squalls and bad weather. Jessie had enjoyed the voyage as much as she possibly could, but she’d be glad to disembark. Unfortunately, they had to wait while Aaron made arrangements for their transport to the MacDonald River. The wait was agonising for Jessie. This was her first visit in four years and she was anxious to get there.

After an extra day and a half on board, they finally disembarked. Waiting for them on George Street was a covered wagon, driven by an old man with a white bushy beard and barely a hair on his head. He looked most peculiar.

“This is Jack,” said Aaron as a way of introduction. “He’s agreed to take us to the

MacDonald River, and he'll come back and get ye when it's time."

"Thank you, and pleased to meet you," said Jessie with a smile she hoped did not portray her true feelings. Jack was so thin and looked like a puff of wind would knock him over. He wasn't a good colour either. Jessie couldn't help but wonder if Aaron had not gone quite mad hiring this man.

Jack smiled showing Jessie a mouthful of missing teeth. Oh my – no wonder the man was so thin he probably couldn't eat a thing.

"Ma'am." After giving Jessie a cursory nod he slouched back in the driver's seat.

Aaron packed their bags in the back of the wagon before lifting the children in. "Sit there and get comfortable," he said as he waited for them to settle. "No, not there Moses – sit on the bag."

"Are you sure about this man?" Jessie whispered.

Aaron smiled. "Aye. He'll do a fine job ye'll see. Anyway, I'm coming with ye to make sure ye get there." He helped her climb into the back with the children. "I love ye." He stood on tiptoes and kissed her. "And I will not let anything happen to ye."

She smiled and kissed him in return. “I know.”

***

Chapter 10

The MacDonald River

Jessie was surprised that the trip to her grandmother's was uneventful. Aaron was right about Jack – he knew his business. He'd kept a steady pace for most of the day and had been most obliging – stopping whenever Jessie needed to.

"If you look you'll see Grandma's house around the next corner," said Jessie grinning at her children.

Her two sons were hanging out of the wagon as they did their best to see the house. Ellen was only slightly more subdued. She was sitting up front on her father's knee and Jessie could see her head swivelling in every direction. She remembered all too well her first visit to her grandmothers and how she'd craned her neck to be the first to spot the roof of the house. That seemed like a lifetime ago.

A few moments later Ellen exclaimed with joy, "I see it, Mamma. I see it."

"Yes darling, that's Grandma's." Jessie's heartbeat quickened at the sight of the familiar tin roof. The homestead came into view as they rounded the next bend. It looked exactly as she remembered it – with its wide veranda and twin gables. It had been too long.

Jessie had to restrain Aaron and Moses as soon as the wagon came to a stop they made to leap out of it. “Wait for your father.” She grabbed them both by their overall straps and gripped them tightly as they struggled to be free. “Wait I say.”

A minute later Aaron scooped them both into his arms and swung them around. They giggled with glee before being put down. He kissed the tops of their heads, “stay here. Wait for your Mamma and Ellen.”

“Thank you,” said Jessie reaching for Aaron. “Give me a hand please.”

He placed his hands on her waist and easily lifted her down from the back of the wagon. His hazel eyes held her gaze as he lowered his mouth to hers. It wasn’t a long kiss but it left Jessie wanting more. She drew in a breath when their lips parted. “I’ll go see who’s home.”

She couldn’t help the small smile that played on her lips as she passed Jack. He was already slumped in the driver’s seat with his hat pulled low over his eyes. He had turned out to be quite different from how he appeared. Jessie stepped onto the veranda and looked up and down. There was no sign of anyone so she knocked on the door. She wasn't too sure if anyone would hear her. Grandpa Joe and George were probably down in the paddock still. Will would be in the stables and Grandma…well she should hear her.

"Grandma, it's me," she said knocking on the door for a second time.

A few moments later she heard the thud of footsteps and a muffled. "Hold ye bloody 'orses I'm coming."

Jessie's brows raised to her hairline -. that didn't sound like Grandma. The door opened and a young woman wearing an apron and mob cap peered at her. Then a wide smile spread across her face as recognition dawned.

"Jessie. Is that ye?"

"Eliza!"

"Oh my Lord it is ye," said Eliza grabbing her and squeezing her in a tight hug. "Ye Grandma will be beside herself when she sees ye."

Jessie staggered when she let her go. "What are you doing here? Last I heard you'd gone to Wilberforce or somewhere."

"Aye, I did. And I met a man, Ned, who I married and we both came back here. Oh my," she said looking passed Jessie. "Don't tell me they're ye children?"

Jessie turned and smiled at her husband and children who were standing beside the wagon - waiting. "Yes, and my husband," she said turning her attention back to Eliza. "Where's my grandmother?"

Eliza dragged her eyes back to Jessie. "She's having a lie down. Go and see her, she'll be that excited to see ye."

"I will. Would you mind calling William to come and see to Jack and his horses?

"Aye," she said nodding.

Aaron stepped onto the veranda and smiled. "We'll wait here, Jess."

"No, Mrs Smith'll have me sacked for leaving ye out here," said Eliza looking alarmed at the suggestion. "Come in and sit in the parlour. I'll fetch William and then we'll get ye settled."

Jessie went inside leaving Eliza to organise Aaron and the children. The house appeared to be unchanged from the last time she'd been here - it was still cluttered with furniture. She wondered how well her grandmother could see now. She made her way down the hall to her grandmother's bedroom - and paused. A flutter of nerves started in the pit of her stomach as she knocked softly and opened the door.

Maggie was stretched out on the bed and waved a hand in the air. "Go away, Eliza. It can't be time for me to get up yet."

Jessie drew in a breath. "It's not Eliza. It's me, Grandma…Jess."

Maggie sat bolt upright and stared blindly. "Jessie? Truly..." Tears welled in her eyes as she beckoned her to come closer.

Jessie walked over to the bed and took her grandmother's hands in hers. "Yes…it's me," she whispered. "I'm so sorry, Grandma." Hot tears pricked her eyes and she blinked them away. "I hope you can forgive me for running off."

"There's naught to forgive child," she said taking her face in her gnarled hands. "I hope ye can forgive me for being an interfering old woman." She kissed her on each cheek. "I never thought I'd see ye again."

Jessie wiped her tears away with the back of her hand. "I know you had my best interests at heart, Grandma," she said taking her hands in hers again. “My husband’s with me and I hope you can be polite to him.”

Maggie smoothed her hair and swung her legs over the side of the bed. “Of course, I can…an’ the children? Are they with ye too?”

“Yes,” said Jessie helping her Grandma to her feet.

“Oh, Jess I’m so glad ye came.” She wrapped her arms around her and pulled her close, and then moments later she pushed her away. “Are ye expecting another baby?”

Jessie smiled. “Yes, I am. In the spring.”

“Good Lord, Jess. That’ll be four younguns under three years old. How will ye manage?”

She laughed. “I don’t know. I pray this one will be patient like Ellen.”

“I can’t wait to meet her an’ the twins,” said Maggie looping her arm in Jessie’s. “Be a dear an’ grab my stick.”

Jessie reached for the stick and put it in her grandmother’s hand. “Have you gone completely blind, Grandma?” She guided her out the door and into the hallway.

“Near enough,” said Maggie with a derisive scoff. “I can make out shapes is about all. I can’t see to read or write anymore…ye would've noticed my letters are not in my hand."

She had noticed and now she could see her grandmother gazing blindly ahead of her. It was obvious she couldn't see. She led her down the hall to the parlour where Aaron and the children were waiting. Aaron rose to his feet as soon as he saw them.

"It's a pleasure to finally meet ye, Mrs Smith," he said stepping forward.

"Likewise," said Maggie letting go of Jessie. She took Aaron's face in her hands and ran her thumbs over his cheeks. "Ye'll not be addressing me as Mrs Smith. Call me Maggie or Grandma – I care not which." She kissed him on each cheek. "Hmm, he's a good-looking one."

Jessie suppressed a giggle at the look of amusement on Aaron's face. The meeting had gone better than she'd imagined and she felt the knot in her stomach begin to unravel. Jessie pushed Ellen forward into her grandmother's reach and she kissed her forehead before doing the same to Moses and Aaron. They for once were rather subdued as they stared at the old woman who was their great-grandmother.

"It's so good to meet ye little ones. We'll have such fun together," she said hunching her shoulders and smiling. "Where's Eliza? We need some refreshments before supper."

"I asked her to fetch William to help Jack settle the horses for the night," said Jessie.

"Oh, well I'm she'll be along shortly. Why don't we get ye settled? How long are ye staying?"

"Aaron will only be staying tonight," said Jessie smiling at her husband.

"Aye. I've got business to attend to in Sydney," he said putting his arm around Jessie. He placed a kiss on her forehead. "I'll be back to collect Jess and the children in a week or so."

"Wonderful!" said Maggie clapping her hands together. "Come, we'll get ye settled. Which room do ye want Jess? The usual one for ye an' Aaron?"

She grinned at the thought of Aaron snuggled under the pink counterpane. "Perhaps not, Grandma. I'll need to be close to the children."

"Of course, come along then ye can have the two rooms further along the hall."

Half and hour later they'd inspected their accommodation and settled in for their stay. Jessie gave the children a quick flannel wash and dressed them in clean clothes before sending them off with their father. She would've loved a wash and change of clothes too, but that would have to wait for tomorrow. She was making her way back down the hallway when a tall young man accosted her.

"Jess." He wrapped his arms around her and crushed her to him in a bear-like hug.

When he let her go she stared up into his grinning face. "William?" He was no longer a little boy or even a gangly youth. His shoulders were broad and he'd filled out since she'd seen him last. "Oh my goodness I hardly recognised you."

"Ye've changed too," he said looking her up and down. "Ye look well."

She grinned. "I am well. Gosh, it's so good to see you. Has George come up to the house as well?"

He shook his head. "George isn't here. He's down at Uncle Joseph's in Pitt Town." Seeing the crestfallen look on her face he put his arm around her. "Don't fuss, he'll be back in a day or two. How long are ye staying?"

"At least a week," she said smiling. "Aaron's returning to Sydney tomorrow and leaving us to visit until he comes back."

"The children are with ye then?"

"Of course, what else would I do with them," she said laughing. "Come and meet them, Uncle William."

***

Chapter 11

Family Time is Too Short

Aaron left for Sydney the following morning and Jessie bid him goodbye with mixed feelings. She prayed the trial and subsequent hanging wouldn't pray too much on his mind. He was concerned for young George Chapman – he'd voiced his fears to her about the lad. What if it had been one of their sons who'd witnessed the grisly murder? She shuddered and pulled her shawl around her shoulders. It wasn't just the chill autumn air that sent a shiver down her spine.

She paced along the veranda towards the kitchen breathing in the fresh air. The day would begin in earnest soon, but for now, she had a few moments before the children were out of bed. A flock of cockatoos screeched overhead and she watched them as they disappeared above the trees. She'd missed being here more than she imagined.

She opened the kitchen door and was embraced by the warmth from the hearth. Eliza was at the table kneading dough and looked up with a wide smile when she saw her. Jessie was reminded of the first time she'd seen Eliza making bread and how fascinated she'd been.

"Good morning," she said grinning at Eliza. "This is like old times."

"Aye, it is. I've not long made a pot of tea – pour us one each why don't ye. I won't be long here."

"So how long have you been back here?" said Jessie fetching two cups from the dresser.

"About a year I think." She paused her kneading and looked thoughtful. "Aye, about a year. We were living down in Wilberforce and things went bad with Ned's job. So we started working our way up the river, stopping and looking for work and such – and we ended up here."

"And you and Ned are married then?" said Jessie pouring the tea.

"Aye. I wasn't about to settle down with him without getting married. Bugger that." She put the dough in a bowl and covered it before sitting down at the table with Jessie. "I've got a little boy – Teddy."

"How wonderful. How old is he?"

"He'll be two in September," she said picking up her cup and taking a mouthful.

"Oh, he's just a little bit older than the twins. They'll be two at the end of December."

"I bet they're a handful," said Eliza rolling her eyes. "Teddy's bad enough."

Jessie laughed. "Yes, they are." She sighed as she sipped her tea. She felt so comfortable sitting here with Eliza talking in familiar surroundings. She hadn't seen her in years and yet they'd picked up right where they'd left off. A pang of longing to return to the bosom of her family stabbed at her heart.

She finished her tea. "Well, I must be off. My darlings will be getting up soon and wanting breakfast."

"Aye," said Eliza gulping down the last of her tea. "I'll make a big pot of porridge and serve it in the dining room."

"Thank you," said Jessie rising and walking to the door. "And thank you for the tea and conversation. It was so nice."

"Aye it was," said Eliza smiling. "Like old times."

Jessie headed inside the house and down the hallway. She heard her boys squealing but it wasn't coming from their room. She stopped and listened. It sounded like they were outside in the rear garden.

Alarmed, she turned and ran towards the sound of their voices. She stepped outside and hurried down the steps to the garden before she spied them.

She stopped and grinned with her hands on her hips. William had hold of Moses and was swinging him around in a circle. He was laughing and Aaron was clapping his hands and squealing with delight along with another boy, who she presumed was Teddy.

"Me, me," squealed Teddy.

"Wait ye turn," said William coming to halt. He threw Moses into the air and caught him.

Jessie's heart leapt into her throat. "William," she yelled as she hurried towards her brother and sons. "Be careful you don't drop him."

William turned and grinned at her. "I won't." He tossed him into the air again and Moses squealed with glee. "Alright, who's next?" he said putting Moses down who staggered on his chubby legs but looked very pleased with himself.

"Good morning, sis," said William lifting Teddy into his arms.

"Good morning. I thought my sons were safely tucked in their beds."

He laughed as he began spinning Teddy around until his legs flew out into the air. "They were, but then I heard them as I was heading down the hall to see Grandpa Joe."

"Mamma," said Moses throwing himself at her legs.

She scooped him into her arms and kissed his smiling face. He was still in his pyjamas and greatly in need of a clean clout. "And so you thought you'd make them sick before breakfast?"

"Well, aye, something like that. Teddy loves it, so I thought Moses and Aaron would too." He tossed the boy into the air and caught him before putting him down.

It all seemed to make perfect sense to William, and Jessie sighed in exasperation. "Well, I suppose there's no harm done."

"Ye worry too much, Jess."

"Well, thank you I suppose. Come on, Aaron," she said holding her hand out to him. "You need to get dressed and have some breakfast." He dutifully took her hand and she turned to go back inside.

"I'll join ye in a bit," called William.

Half an hour later the children were changed and dressed for the day. Jessie settled them at the dining room table for breakfast under Grandma's watchful eye. She fetched bowls and cutlery from the dresser and placed them on the table.

"Will you have porridge, Grandma?" she asked poised to place a bowl and spoon in front of her.

"Aye, an' set a place in case George comes in."

Jessie arched a brow as she placed the bowl and went to fetch another. "Do you think he'll be home at this hour? It's a half-day ride from Pitt Town."

Maggie shrugged. "I expect he spent last night at the ferry."

"Why would he do that?"

"He's met a young woman an' I expect he would've visited her on his way home." She chuckled and put her finger to her pursed lips. "Shh, he doesn't think we know."

Jessie smiled. She was delighted to be part of the secret. "I won't say a word."

Eliza arrived carrying a large tureen which she placed at the end of the table. "William and Mr Smith have already had breakfast. Mr Smith asked me to tell ye that they'll be working down the back paddock."

"Thank ye, Eliza. A pot of tea?"

"Aye, I'll fetch it."

Jessie retrieved two cups and saucers from the dresser and placed them beside the tureen. Moses began thumping the table with his spoon and Jessie rolled her eyes. "Stop that this instant," she said removing the spoon from his chubby fist. "You know very well not to do that."

For one moment he looked like he was going to launch into a tantrum, but he thought better of it when Eliza returned. She placed the teapot and jug of milk on the table. "Anything else?"

"No that's all," said Maggie. "Will ye serve, Jess?"

"Yes, of course."

She filled the children's bowls with porridge and poured a little milk over before serving her grandmother and herself. She eyed Moses as he began eating his breakfast. He was her troublesome child, and she didn't entirely trust that he wouldn't start flicking porridge at his brother. He grinned at her and she nodded – for once he appeared to be behaving.

"I thought we might take the children down to see the cows," said Maggie running her fingers along the rim of her bowl. She dipped her spoon into the porridge and brought it neatly to her mouth.

"They'd love that," said Jessie picking up her spoon.

Maggie cocked her head as loud footsteps reverberated along the veranda. "Ah, that will be George."

A moment later he burst into the dining room and came to a halt as he took in the scene before him. "Jess."

"George. Oh George it's so good to see you." She rose to her feet and in two steps she was by his side. "It's been too long." She wrapped her arms around him and he did the same. It was so good to be engulfed in her brother's arms and tears came unbidden.

"What a surprise. When did ye get here?" he said letting her go.

"Yesterday," she said wiping her eyes.

"Is Aaron with ye?" he said looking at the dining table as though he might appear.

"No. He has business to attend to in Sydney. He'll be back in a few days to collect us."

"These are your children?" A wide grin spread across his face as he ran his fingers through his unruly hair. "Oh my God."

Jessie laughed. "Yes, I've been busy. And I'll be having another one in the spring."

"Good Lord, Jess," he said gaping at her. "Never mind. I want to hear all about your life on Norfolk Island. Are ye happy?" He sat down and reached for a bowl and helped himself to a large serving of porridge. "Morning, Grandma."

"Good morning, George," said Maggie

"We're very happy," said Jessie sitting back down. "What about you? What have you been up to?"

"Nothing much," he said shovelling a mouthful of porridge into his mouth. "I hear Aaron's free now."

And so the conversation settled on Jessie telling George every little detail about their life on the island. As she was recounting the last four years she realised one big thing had been missing, and she became acutely aware of the pain in her heart – her family.

***

The days slipped by and Jessie found herself praying Aaron wouldn't return too soon. The boys were running wild with William and Teddy and they fell into bed exhausted every night. She wasn't sure how they'd adjust to life back on the island. They were still only babies but William seemed to think they were old enough for just about anything. They were loving it and she was secretly pleased that her brother was taking them off her hands.

"Jess, will ye do me a favour?" said Maggie coming to a halt in front of her. "Will ye go an' tell Eliza we'll have luncheon on the veranda? Some of that cold beef would be nice if there's enough for us all."

Jessie put her mending aside and rose to her feet. "Of course, Grandma." She put her hand on her shoulder and placed a kiss on her cheek. "Are you alright?"

"Oh aye. I just can't get down those steps to the kitchen," she said putting her hand on Jessie's cheek. "I'll bring Ellen."

Jessie glanced at her daughter who was playing happily with her rag doll on the rug. She looked up at her with her big blue eyes. "Be good for Grandma."

She nodded. "Yes, Mamma."

The midday meal was a noisy affair, with three children and her two brothers competing to dominate the conversation.

Grandpa Joe finally interjected in a quiet voice that brought the table to immediate silence.

"So, Jessie when are ye and Aaron moving to Sydney? I hear tell he's got his ticket."

Jessie had been half expecting someone to ask this question all week, and she thought she was ready for it – until it was asked. She swallowed and smiled. "Well, it's true he has his ticket, but I don't think Aaron wants to leave the island."

George's brow shot up. "What? No, he never wanted to go back after ye were married. Has he changed his mind then?"

"Ah…well," she stammered while she played for time. How much did she want to tell them? She'd been careful not to tell George or Grandma about the enemies Aaron had made, although Grandma had probably guessed.

"What is it lass?" said Grandpa Joe putting down his knife and fork. "Whatever it is ye can tell us."

She cast her eyes around the table. All eyes were on her but they were full of love and concern and she sighed. They deserved to know the truth. "Well, it's not that simple.

Aaron…well last year he went to Sydney to give evidence in a trial…and,"

George reached out and put his large warm hand over hers and squeezed. "Are ye scared?"

Her clear blue eyes locked with his. She shook her head but her eyes filled with tears and she blinked several times in an effort to dispel them. "Not for myself."

Maggie straightened in her chair. "Out with it, Jess. What's got ye spooked girl."

"Aaron's made a lot of enemies," said Jessie drawing in a deep breath. "And when he was in Sydney last year a man tried to kill him. He was just walking down the street and he came at him with a knife, and if Captain Bordes hadn't come along I dread to think what would've happened."

"I presume the man was once a prisoner on the island?" said Grandpa Joe.

"Yes. And Aaron could see the hate in the man's eyes," said Jessie with a shudder. "He's not the only one. Many who have reason to hate Aaron have now gone to Sydney."

"Well there's a simple solution," said Maggie waving her hands in the air. "Don't go to Sydney, come up here. No one's going to come up here looking for him."

Jessie smiled. "Thank you, Grandma, but we couldn't live with you, and anyway, Aaron's no farmer."

"He wouldn't have to farm," said Grandpa Joe leaning his elbows on the table. "We could build ye a nice house down on the river. We've plenty of land. And your grandmother's right, no one would come here looking for him."

"Perfect," said George grinning. "Aaron could get work at Wiseman's Ferry and ye'd be safe here with us."

Jessie gaped at her family. She could tell by the earnest looks on their faces that they were serious. "We couldn't possibly."

"Why ever not?" put in William with a shrug. "It makes perfect sense to me."

"Twould seem ye outvoted, lass," said Grandpa Joe taking hold of Maggie's hand. He brought it to his lips and kissed the back of her hand before turning his eyes back on Jessie. "Think on it."

"I will…thank you…it's a wonderful idea but I'll have to talk to Aaron about it."

"Of course," said George grinning. "He'll be here in a day or two and we can all talk to him about it. I can't see why he'd say no."

This was such an unexpected turn of events and Jessie was feeling a little overwhelmed by the generosity of Grandma and Grandpa Joe. But, a little voice in the back of her mind thought the proposal was perfect. How she'd love to live here and raise her children by the river. All she had to do was convince Aaron that they would be safe.

***

Chapter 12

Supreme Court, Sydney

Aaron paused on the threshold of the courtroom – the doors were open and a busy clerk loaded with papers brushed passed him.

"Sorry," he mumbled.

Aaron barely acknowledged the man as he drew in a deep breath. His stomach was tied in knots and no matter how often he came here he always felt uncomfortable. He'd be glad when today was over. Steeling himself he entered the court and scanned the room. The lawyers were pouring over papers at a large bench, and several clerks were rushing about. The jurors had not yet arrived, but he noticed William Forster, Henry Graham and young George Chapman sitting at the back of the room.

He knew most of the witnesses being called were prisoners, and they'd no doubt be brought in one by one. He made his way to the back to join them.

"Good morning, Mr Price," said William Forster with a nod.

"Mr Price, tis good to see ye," said Henry Graham.

"Morning," said Aaron before sitting down beside the young lad. "How are ye, George?"

His round brown eyes looked anxious. "Alright, I s'pose. Mr Graham's been taking care of me on account of my Pa working at the hospital."

Aaron nodded. He was glad Henry was taking care of the lad. Of course, it made sense that his father would've asked the assistant surgeon to watch out for the boy. Probably better than his mother accompanying him - Mr Chapman had been right about his wife being somewhat hysterical. "Well, it'll be over soon."

"Aye."

The rumble of footsteps caught Aaron's attention as the jurors filed into the room. He didn't envy them their job today and he was glad he had little evidence to give.

"That's the jury," whispered Aaron in George's ear. "They're the ones who'll listen to what ye have to say and decide if ye telling the truth."

George's eyes rested on the twelve men for a moment. "Well, that's alright. I'll be telling the truth." He turned his scared brown eyes to Aaron. "What if I don't remember exactly?"

Aaron smiled. "Ye'll remember just fine when the time comes."

He nodded and turned his attention back to the jurors.

"All rise," said the clerk. "His Honour the Chief Justice."

Aaron stood and waited while the Chief Justice seated himself at the bench. Stephen Brennan was then brought in and secured in the dock. Aaron thought he looked defiant in the face of what he thought would be overwhelming evidence of murder. A man seated near the bench rose and addressed the jury.

"I, the Attorney-General present this case before you as one of the most atrocious, cold-blooded murders that ever a Jury had to consider." He paused before launching into the details of the case. "Stephen Brennan waylaid the deceased, and after coming at him from behind he struck him with a hammer on the head, which rendered him insensible. He then threw himself upon him and stabbed him to the heart with a knife." He paused once again. "Mr Callahan for the defence," he said before seating himself.

Mr Callahan stood and walked over to the witness stand. “The defence calls its first witness – George Chapman.”

Aaron felt the boy beside him stiffen before he slowly got to his feet.

“It’ll be alright,” said Henry Graham patting the boy's arm. “Would ye like me to accompany ye?”

He shook his head. “No, I can do it.”

Aaron watched as he slowly made his way to the witness stand. Mr Callahan then read out the statement that George had given previously. Aaron had heard theboy’s evidence before, but it still chilled him to the bone.

“Lynch was walking down the road and Brennan hit him two or three times with a hammer on the head – he hit him hard. He had his back to Brennan,” said Mr Callahan. He paused before continuing to read the disposition. “Lynch didn’t fall, he turned around and they started fighting with their fists. I think there was a sod of dirt in Lynch’s way and he tripped over. Brennan fell on him. I saw Lynch’s shirt covered with blood. The men took him to the hospital. Is this your statement, George? The one you made to Captain Maconachie?”

"Aye," said George in a tremulous voice.

"How close would you say you were to the two men, George?"

"Um, about fifty steps."

"So you could see them clearly? You knew who they were?"

"Aye, I know Stephen Brennan – he makes shoes. I also knew Patrick Lynch."

"Thank you, George. You may step down."

Aaron watched him as he made his way back to his seat. He'd done well and he could see relief etched on his young face. The next witness was called, and for the following two hours or so a stream of prisoners came forward and gave their evidence.

"I call Aaron Price, Principal Overseer at Norfolk Island to the stand," called Mr Callahan.

Aaron drew in a breath as he stood and walked to the stand.

"So, Mr Price you found the knives and a hammer at the scene. Can you please tell the Jury what you found?"

"Aye. I arrived five or so minutes after Lynch was taken to the hospital - he was dead. I went to the place where he fell and I found two knives and a hammer close to where the blood was."

"Can you please tell the court if these are those?" he said holding a hammer and two knives for Aaron to inspect.

"Aye."

"Thank you, Mr Price. I call William Forster, Superintendent of Convicts at Norfolk Island."

Aaron returned to his seat, relieved that his part in the trial was done. He patted George on the arm. "Are ye alright?"

"Aye," he said nodding. "It wasn't so bad."

Several more witnesses were called and Aaron hoped that was the last of them. His thoughts turned to Jessie and the children – he hoped she was enjoying her stay with her grandmother. He hadn't expected to be embraced by her family – after all, he'd taken her away, but they'd been so welcoming. He was actually looking forward to seeing her brother, William again, and he hoped he might have an opportunity to properly thank her brother, George. He was brought back to the present by the final words of Mr Callahan.

"And so that sums up the case for the defence, and I would impress upon the Jury to consider all of the evidence in this case."

"Thank you, Mr Callahan," said the Chief Justice looking over the top of his spectacles. "The Jury may now retire to consider their verdict."

"All stand," said the clerk.

Aaron stood and stretched while the Chief Justice left the chamber. He hoped the jury wouldn't consider their verdict for too long.

"Can we go now?" said George.

"We can go and wait in another room if ye like, but we can't leave yet," said Henry Graham.

Aaron looked down at the lad. "Ye have to wait until the Jury comes back with their answer. They won't be long."

"Oh," he said slumping back down in his seat.

Aaron felt for him, but there was nothing to be done but wait. He paced up and down and stretched his legs before sitting beside George again. He relaxed back in the seat and prepared to wait.

Twenty minutes later the head juror returned and consulted with the clerk. He nodded and then began walking towards where they were seated.

"Excuse me, George. The Jurors would like to ask you some further questions."

He looked at Henry who nodded. "It's alright. Go ahead."

Aaron watched as the small figure disappeared through the door to the juror's room. He was a brave lad but he couldn't help but wonder how this whole affair would affect him in the future. He returned ten minutes later and sat back down. He was quiet and kept his thoughts to himself.

Another half an hour ticked by before the clerk announced the return of the Jury and Chief Justice. Aaron was relieved it hadn't taken longer. Stephen Brennan was brought back in and then the Chief Justice returned.

"How say you?" said the Attorney General rising to his feet. "On the question of murder."

The head juror stood and spoke loudly. "Guilty."

"I pray the sentence of the Court upon the prisoner will be swift," said the Attorney General leaning against the bench. "I invite the prisoner, Stephen Brennan to address the court if he so wishes."

Brennan gazed around the court taking in everyone present, resting his eyes on young George Chapman for longer than necessary. "I care not for the end of a rope. If the evidence of a boy is to be believed before that of men who have defended me today, then perhaps it is time for a man to be hanged." He paused and addressed the Chief Justice directly. "If I'm to die then the sooner the better."

Aaron glanced sideways at George. Tears welled in his eyes and he sucked in his lip. Henry Graham had put his arm around the lad but Aaron didn't think he looked comforted. He was clearly terrified and his round brown eyes were glued to Brennan who was glaring openly at him.

"The sentence of this Court is that you will be publicly hanged," said the Chief Justice addressing Brennan directly. "It is my hope that it will be conducted as speedily as possible."

"All rise," said the clerk as the Chief Justice rose from the bench and left the court.

Aaron breathed a sigh. It was done and would soon be over. He prayed the execution would be swift. It did no good to prolong such things and he was anxious for it to be done for several reasons. Poor young George could relax in the knowledge that Brennan was dead and could cause no further harm. For Aaron, he was anxious to have his wife by his side. She brought calm and goodness to his life and he needed her.

***

The Hanging

The morning dawned grey and overcast and Aaron shivered in the cool autumn air. He estimated there were only a hundred or so people present in the gaol yard. He knew many more could be expected for a public hanging, but Brennan had been saved that humiliation at the eleventh hour. As the bell tolled nine o'clock Brennan was led to the scaffold, accompanied by the Reverend, a military guard and the executioner.

Aaron's eyes were glued to the prisoner. He walked purposely albeit pale – he appeared to be perfectly cool and collected. Aaron had been sentenced to hang twice in his life, so he knew what that sentence felt like. The last time he'd been ready to die, had welcomed it. He imagined Brennan felt the same way as he made his way to the scaffold.

On reaching the foot of the scaffold, Brennan knelt on the blanket which had been spread on the ground. He stared around the yard with a determined look. "I was sentenced to be publicly hanged but I was told this morning the inhabitants of Sydney would not be admitted, but it is no matter." He bowed his head and appeared to pray for several minutes. "My lads, I have been transported for seventeen years an' I have never had anything like this happen to me. I'm going to die, an' I declare that there was not one word of truth in all that was said by the boy Chapman. Many of ye here have known me a long time, an' ye know that I would not come up behind a man and murder him."

The guard motioned to Brennan to ascend the scaffold. He got to his feet and hurried up the steps and stamped his feet firmly on the platform as he looked at the assembled men with contempt. The executioner adjusted the rope around his neck and stepped aside to retrieve the hood.

"Do I look like a murderer now with the rope around my neck?"

Aaron felt admiration for the man. He was facing his end with more courage than most and maintaining his innocence until the end. Aaron couldn't believe that young George Chapman had lied –what possible reason would he have? No, Brennan was guilty and Aaron felt no pity for the man.

"Lord have mercy upon me," he said as the execution placed the hood over his head.

A second later the bolt was pulled and Brennan swung free of the scaffold. In less than a minute he was dead.

***

Chapter 13

Coming Home

The constant drizzly rain made the trip from Sydney to the MacDonald River miserable, but Aaron pushed his discomfort aside as soon as the homestead came into view. Jess was in there with his children and he was in sore need of seeing them and holding her in his arms.

As soon as Jack brought the wagon to a halt he leapt down. "Take it around to the stable, Jack. Ye remember where it is?"

"Aye," said Jack with a nod. He paused with the reins in hand. "Do ye think the cook might have more of that soup?"

Aaron grinned. "Ye can always head to the kitchen and find out."

"Aye, I'll do that."

Aaron grabbed his bag and in two strides was on the veranda. His heart quickened as he knocked on the door. He could hear muffled voices and a moment later the door swung open and Jessie threw herself into his arms. He dropped his bag and wrapped his arms around her.

"Jess, oh God I've missed ye," he whispered as he nuzzled her neck and breathed in her familiar scent.

She took his face in her hands and smiled. "I've missed you too."

He pressed his lips to hers and pulled her close until he could feel the full length of her hard up against him. Her round pregnant belly pressed into him and he released his grip, but still explored her with his tongue. She tasted so sweet and he groaned. They would not be alone for hours and the wait would be agony.

Their lips parted and he grinned. "The little one's grown."

Jessie laughed and ran her hand over her stomach. "He has."

"He?"

"Well, I don't know, but I've come to think of him as he."

"Aaron. I thought I heard ye voice," said George coming to halt in the doorway.

"George," said Aaron releasing Jessie and holding out his hand for George. The two shook hands and Aaron gave him a lopsided grin. "I never got the chance to thank ye properly," he said putting his arm around

Jessie's waist. "Thank ye for taking care of my wife and seeing her safe. We may never have married if not for ye."

George smiled and nodded. "It was my honour to get her to the church and see her safe. How else would I have gotten rid of her?"

"What?" said Jessie in mock horror slapping his arm.

George laughed and stepped back. "Are ye going to keep ye husband standing on the doorstep? Come in."

Aaron picked up his bag and followed George and Jess into the house. He could hear children's voices coming from the parlour and he made a beeline for them. The boys squealed and ran to him as soon as he entered. He scooped Aaron into his arms and snuggled him.

"I've missed ye rascals," he said putting him down and lifting Moses into the air. He giggled as his father nuzzled his neck and kissed him. Aaron grinned as he put his son down. "Where's my girl?"

Ellen had a wide smile on her face as she held her arms out to him. "Papa."

He obliged by lifting her into his arms. She wrapped her arms around his neck and kissed his cheek. His heart melted at the affection she showed him.

"Maggie, it's good to see ye again," he said putting Ellen down and walking over to where the old woman was sitting. "Thank ye for taking care of my family."

"Nonsense," she said with a wave of her hand. "Come closer, give me a kiss." Aaron obliged her and she grasped his face in her gnarled hands before kissing him on each cheek. "How long are ye staying?"

"Just the night," said Aaron straightening. "We need to be back in Sydney by tomorrow evening. The ship will likely sail on Saturday."

"So soon?" said Jessie from the doorway.

"Aye, I'm sorry it can't be longer."

"No mind," said George. "We have tonight."

After supper, the children were put to bed and Aaron retired to the parlour with Jessie, her brothers, Maggie and Joe. He was anxious to have her to himself, but it was her last night with her family and so he suppressed his impatience. When they finally retired to their room Jessie was yawning and looked exhausted.

She climbed into bed beside him and he gathered her into his arms. He wanted her but contented himself with holding her close and feeling her small solid form pressed up against him. He sighed and nuzzled her hair.

"There's something I would talk to you about," she said turning over to face him.

"What? Now?"

"Yes, I know it's late and we're both weary, but it's important."

"Alright, what is it?" He kissed her forehead before relaxing against the pillow.

"Well, Grandma and Grandpa Joe have offered to let us come and live here. They'd build us our own house, so we wouldn't actually be living with them. We'd be safe here."

It was not what Aaron had expected. He couldn't have said what he'd anticipated – but this wasn't it. "That's a very generous offer." He squeezed her and smiled. "And perhaps we'd be safe but what would I do? I'm no farmer, Jess."

She pushed herself into a sitting position and looked down at him. He could see the excited light in her eyes. "You wouldn't have to farm. You could get work at Wiseman's Ferry."

He shook his head. "I don't know. It's a big move and with just a ticket of leave we'd be risking everything." He reached up and squeezed her arm. "Be patient, Jess. We'll be free I promise ye. I want it more than ye can know."

"Then why not come here? Think of it, Aaron. No one from the island would ever come up here – we'd be safe – you'd be safe."

He sighed. "I can see that ye really want this."

"I do." She bent down and kissed him. "Think of the children. They love it here."

He'd thought of little else this past week. Ever since Brennan had been hanged and blamed young George Chapman for it. The thought of it being one of his had haunted him. He wanted desperately to take his family away from the island, but if he lost his ticket – that thought made him come out in a cold sweat. "Will it be enough for me to say I'll think on it?"

"Yes," she said snuggling back down under the quilt. She pressed herself against him and wrapped her arm around his waist. "Thank you."

***

There was no time for any further discussion the following morning. They were up early and packed and by eight o'clock were on the road and on their way to Sydney. The day was chill and overcast and Jessie prayed it would remain dry. Aaron had reserved accommodation at the Commercial Hotel in George Street for the night, and Jessie was thrilled to see a blazing fire had been set for them. She rubbed her frozen fingers together in front of the flames and sighed.

"I have a surprise for ye," said Aaron wrapping his arms around her and nuzzling her neck. "I think ye'll be rather pleased."

"A surprise? I'm not sure I like surprises." She couldn't recall ever experiencing a good surprise in her life. The surprise giver always thought they'd done something special when in reality it rarely worked out that way.

"Aye, ye'll love this one." He kissed her cheek and let her go. "I'll take the children downstairs and get them fed. Ye get changed and be ready to join me for supper when I return."

She rolled her eyes sideways at him – she was intrigued. "Alright."

It was nice to have half an hour to herself without having to worry about the children. She removed her cloak and tossed it over the back of a hard chair. She took her blue layered skirt from the bag and shook it out. It was crumpled but no one would likely notice. There was no hiding the crinkles in her blue jacket which she held up and eyed critically. It would be dimly lit in the dining room and anyway, it would have to suffice.

She stripped off her travelling costume and poured some water into the bowl. It was cold and she shivered as she wiped the flannel over her face and down her neck. That would have to do. She pulled her hair from its plait and brushed the crinkles out as best she could, before winding her long tresses into a bun and pinning it to the top of her head. A few tendrils refused to be tamed which she thought added a certain amount of allure.

Dressed and ready to accompany Aaron to supper she settled herself in the only comfortable chair by the fire. Her mind wandered as she tried to think of what sort of surprise Aaron might have for her. Maybe he'd decided to move to MacDonald River? He was going to surprise her by telling her over supper – just the two of them. He might even buy a bottle of champagne. Oh, that would be so wonderful.

Her reverie was interrupted as the door opened and Aaron entered. He had Aaron in his arms and Moses was dragging his feet as he came in the door. Ellen looked like she was about to collapse from exhaustion.

"They'll all be asleep afore we get downstairs," he said grinning.

"If not before," she said rising to her feet.

Ten minutes later the three children were in their sleep attire and tucked into their beds. Aaron and Moses were sleeping top to tail in a small trundle bed and Ellen was curled up in a quilt at the bottom of theirs. There was no need to tiptoe out of the room or close the door quietly – nothing would likely wake them until morning.

Aaron paused at the top of the stairs and offered her his arm. "Ye look beautiful." He kissed her and ran his fingers down her face. "I love ye."

"I love you too."

As she'd expected, the dining room was dimly lit and only half full of patrons. Aaron took her hand in his and led her over to a table that was already occupied.

"Jess!" said Ellison Sharpe leaping to her feet as soon as she saw her.

A moment later she was engulfed in a tight embrace. She pulled herself free and stared into the familiar face of her dearest friend. "Ellison. Oh my goodness. When Aaron said he had a surprise for me I never expected it was you."

"It's a spot of luck," said Tom Sharpe smiling. "We're moving to Bathurst next week, so it is most opportune."

"Yes, another week and we would've missed one another," said Ellison placing a kiss on Jessie's cheek. "It's so good to see you."

"Likewise," said Jessie shaking her head. "I can't believe you arranged this, Aaron …thank you." She kissed him and smiled.

"I'm glad ye weren't disappointed."

"Oh, how could I possibly be?"

"Sit down and I'll fetch us a bottle of wine to celebrate."

Jessie seated herself beside Ellison and smoothed her skirt. "And you're well?"

Ellison beamed and squeezed her husband's hand. "Yes. All is well with me and the baby, and we're praying our luck has turned. Tom has a new position, and with

God's blessing our son will be born healthy and well."

"I pray he will," said Jessie running her hand over her stomach. "And I pray our little one will be as well. So, tell me about Bathurst?"

"There's not much to tell," said Tom with a shrug. "Although, in truth, I'm beyond grateful to be having a church and parishioners to care for once again."

Aaron returned with a bottle of wine and four glasses. He poured and raised his glass. "To new beginnings."

"Aye, to new beginnings."

After a wonderful evening spent with the Sharpes and a long day of travel, Jessie fell into bed and went straight to sleep. The only thing that could've improved the day was if Aaron had agreed to move to the MacDonald River. She was sure he would – maybe tomorrow.

***

Chapter 14

Pardon Me

The return trip to the island was uneventful, apart from a few squalls and two days of solid rain. However, Jessie worried about how they were going to settle down once again to life on the small island. A month away had left her wanting more, and she had the feeling Aaron was equally unsettled.

He was quiet and withdrawn and she didn't quite know how to broach the subject with him. She waited a few weeks in the hopes he would come to her to unload whatever was preying on his mind. He didn't, and she could feel a chasm widening between them. He was quiet over supper and even when she asked him about his day he shrugged.

"We've started work on the hospital extension."

"Oh, that will make a difference I'm sure." Moses caught her attention out of the corner of her eye. "Stop playing with that." She reached over and scooped a spoonful of sweet potato and put it in his mouth. "Now eat."

After supper, once the children were abed she determined to find out what was on his mind. She left the children's room and closed the door. Aaron had his back to her putting another log on the fire. She drew in a deep breath and slowly let it out.

"What's wrong?" she said walking slowly towards him.

He glanced at her over his shoulder. "Nothing."

She sighed. "Yes, there is. You've hardly spoken to me in weeks. Is it something I've done?" Her clear blue eyes locked with his hazel ones and she saw something flit across his eyes. What was it? Guilt?

"No, ye've done nothing."

"Then please, what is it?" She closed the gap between them and embraced him. He paused for a moment before wrapping his arms around her.

"Ye must be so disappointed in me. I'm such a coward."

"What? No." She pulled away and stared into his anguished face. "What would make you think such a thing?"

He groaned and ran his fingers through his hair. "I know ye want to go to the

MacDonald River to be with ye family. But I can't."

"That's alright. It was only an idea." She couldn't believe that was all it was and he'd been bottling up his feelings about it.

"No," he said shaking his head. "It's not alright. It's a grand idea…but I'm a coward. I swear though, I'm doing something about it."

"You're not a coward – please stop saying that."

"I am. I'm too scared to go on my ticket. There it is - I've said it." He drew in a breath and she saw the despair in his eyes. "But, I've got an idea, one that I've written to Tom Sharpe about."

"What? Well, tell me. We're in this together, Aaron and it does no good to keep things from me."

"I know, and I'm so sorry," he said enveloping her in a tight embrace. He nuzzled her hair and kissed her forehead before releasing her. "I'm going to petition Maconachie for a conditional pardon. I've written to Tom Sharpe asking him for a character reference, and I've asked Lieutenant Hamilton as well. It might be enough to get Maconachie to recommend me."

Jessie could feel her heart beating against her ribcage. Was this even possible? "Do you think it might work?"

He shook his head. "I think so. I've served sixteen years here on this damned island, and I've done everything they've ever asked of me." He swept her into his arms. "When we married I promised ye we'd be free, and we will. I'm sorry I can't go until I've got more than a ticket."

"It's alright, I understand," she said tilting her upwards. "And you're not a coward for wanting it."

He pressed his lips to hers and she sighed.

***

August 1842

Her contractions started in the early hours of the morning and Aaron fetched Mrs Fletcher and Mary. She was relieved to have the two women by her side and surprised that Mrs Fletcher was right about her baby being impatient. It was only mid-morning when he came screaming into the world. She gazed down at the swaddled bundle in her arms with his brown fuzz and swarthy skin.

"Hello, Matthew," she cooed pulling the blanket aside so she could get a better look at her new son. His face was round and fat and he reminded her of the large satisfied cat that used to live next door to them in Launceston.

"Here, let me take him," said Mrs Fletcher reaching for him. "Ye need ye rest."

"Thank you," she said kissing the top of his head as he was whisked from her arms.

She settled down under the covers and sighed. Another son had not come as a complete surprise to her – she'd thought all along he would be a boy, and she wasn't disappointed. Her thoughts drifted to the ship that would be moored off the island by nightfall. Sails had been spotted yesterday and she prayed it would bring good news and a letter from the Reverend. She was anxious to hear news of Ellison, but more than that, she hoped he'd sent a letter for Aaron.

As it turned out the ship was a merchant vessel that had stopped at the island for repairs. There was nothing to do but wait and hope that the Governor Phillip would be making port soon. Aaron appeared to be equally anxious as they waited. He'd penned his letter to Captain Maconachie and Lieutenant Hamilton had provided him with a letter of recommendation. Although the Reverend wasn't popular with the Commandant, Jessie still thought his commendation could make a difference.

The Governor Phillip finally arrived at the beginning of September. A letter from Ellison and Grandma was accompanied by the letter from the Reverend. Jessie heaved a sigh of relief.

"When will you present the letters to the Commandant?" said Jessie running her fingers over the crisp envelope. This could be their ticket to freedom and she couldn't suppress the feeling of excitement that surged through her.

"Tomorrow. I see no point in delaying any further," said Aaron.

They both knew it would be months before they got a reply from the Convict Department in Sydney, but at least there was hope. Even if the wait was going to be agony.

***

Aaron ran his sweaty palms down his breeches while his eyes rested unblinking on the Captain sitting across from him. Maconachie's long face and deep-set eyes remained passive as he perused the letters laid out before him. He cleared his throat before raising his eyes to meet Aaron's.

"I would say you present a fine argument, Mr Price," he said tapping his finger on the desk. "I would be most happy to oblige you and forward my recommendation along with your petition and these letters."

Aaron heaved a sigh and nodded. "Thank ye, Captain. I appreciate your support."

"I wish that was all you required," he said folding the letters. "I cannot influence the outcome any more than by providing my recommendation."

"I understand."

"Good, well I wish you every success, Mr Price. Was there anything else?"

"Actually, Captain. I wonder if I might make a request, not for myself, but for the benefit of my wife?"

"By all means."

"We now have four children, and she could greatly benefit from some assistance. An assigned servant to help her in the garden would be most appreciated."

"I see no reason why she can't be accommodated," he said reaching for a quill and parchment. "Take this note to Mr Forster. I'm sure he can recommend a suitable man."

"Thank ye."

Aaron felt like a great weight had been lifted as he left the barracks. He'd done all he could to obtain a successful outcome – now he had to wait. He imagined Jessie surrounded by her family in her own house up on the river. He wanted that for her and their children. He prayed he could make it happen.

He stopped by the Commissariat to submit his request for a manservant. He found Will Forster, the Superintendent of Convicts sitting at his desk on the second floor of the store. He peered over his spectacles at Aaron and gestured to him to sit.

"I could do with a distraction, Mr Price. What business are ye here on?"

"I'm here to have a servant assigned," he said drawing the note from his pocket and handing it to him. "I want someone trustworthy. They'll be working for my wife."

"Hmm. I've got a couple of men that would fit the bill," he said running his fingers through his whiskers. "Do ye know Henry Marsh?"

"Aye, I know of him."

"He's earned some freedoms and he's well-behaved. I expect he'd work well in your wife's garden or whatever. Shall I have him report to ye wife in the morning then?"

From what he could recall Henry Marsh was around his age and a man who kept to himself. He would suit fine. "Aye, thank ye, Mr Forster."

"Very good. Good day then, Mr Price."

He left the store and started on the short walk home. He was pleased with his day's work and excited to surprise Jessie with a servant. Since Matthew had been born she barely had time for anything. He hoped Henry Marsh would not only take care of the garden but also chop wood and fetch water. Jessie had enough to do without those heavy chores. It would be good if he could be trusted with the children…no, he wasn't that trusting.

"A moment, Mr Price."

He stopped and turned to see who had called him. Captain Hulme was hurrying down the road towards him accompanied by three other soldiers. He'd replaced Captain Bordes several months ago and Aaron thought he was an improvement over Bordes.

However, he was a rather serious fellow and right now he looked to be in somewhat of a hurry.

"Captain. How can I help ye?"

"We've got intelligence that three men have distilled some rather intoxicating spirits. I sent two constables to deal with the matter but they appear to have partaken of the stuff."

Aaron suppressed a smile. If the good Captain couldn't control his constables there was nothing he could do about it. Hulme didn't look to be in the mood to be poked so instead Aaron adopted a serious expression. "How can I help?"

"I thought ye might know where they'd have gotten the equipment to make such a thing. It's all very well for me to bring the three to justice, but I'd like to root out the evil entirely. Ye've been here a long time, Mr Price. Do ye have any idea?"

Aaron had a very good idea, but he wasn't sure he wanted to share that with Hulme. He glanced at the soldiers accompanying the Captain – they were young privates by the look of them, and none of them were familiar to him. He put his hand on Hulme's shoulder and urged him to take several steps away from his companions. "Aye

I do," he said in a voice barely above a whisper. "Well, at least I suspect I know where the still came from."

The Captain's keen brown eyes locked with his. "And where would that be?"

Aaron hoped he wasn't about to regret his decision to help him. "Charles Ormsby."

It was clear by the look on the Captain's face that he was none the wiser.

"Mr Ormsby was the Superintendent of Agriculture. He's no longer here but he had a penchant for distilling spirits from sugar cane. I suspect the men have found his still rather than made one themselves."

"Thank ye, Mr Price. Ye've put my mind to rest."

"Good day, Captain."

He watched as the Captain turned on his heel and the four began marching down the road before turning for home. He was a little sorry he'd told him about Ormsby's still. He'd partaken of his rum on many occasions and now the still would likely be destroyed.

***

Chapter 15

1843

Jessie put five-month-old Matthew in the pram and parked it outside the front door. It was a gorgeous sunny day with a light breeze blowing. She tucked her knitting in beside him and hurried back inside.

"Ellen, Aaron, Moses," she called as she went into their bedroom. "Come on hurry up."

She didn't want to be late. Some of the ladies had formed a regular morning once a week, and it was the highlight of her week. It gave her a chance to catch up on gossip and spend a few hours talking to grown-up women rather than children. She loved it.

"Coming Mamma," said Ellen sticking a straw hat on her head. She tilted her head back while Jessie tied the ribbon under her chin.

"You've nearly done it, darling," she said smiling at two-year-old Aaron. He had his boots on the wrong feet, but at least he had them on. She deftly pulled them off and put them on the right feet before tying them firmly. "Where's Moses?"

"Here Mamma," he said appearing in the doorway.

She eyed him suspiciously. He appeared to be dressed and ready to go, but she was always suspicious of what he'd been up to. "Good, come on then."

She bustled them out the door and sighed as she began pushing the pram up the path. Henry was on his knees weeding a flower bed and he glanced up at her as she passed him. "I'll only be a few hours, Henry. I'll be back in time for luncheon."

"Aye, ma'am."

She smiled and turned her attention back to her wayward children. "Come along, Moses," she said over her shoulder.

He'd stopped and bent down beside Henry and was inspecting the weeds like he knew what he was doing. A moment later he came skipping along beside her. She smiled at him. "Are you looking forward to playing with James?"

"Aye."

It was only a short walk to Alicia Hutchins's house. She was hosting this morning and her son James had become best friends with Moses and Aaron. The pram caught in a rut in the road and Jessie groaned as she hauled the thing free. Wiping her brow she drew in a breath. The house was only a few minutes walk and she sighed when she spied the well-tended wooden house, very similar to her own.

"Go and knock on the door, Ellen," she said putting the brake on the pram. She lifted Matthew into her arms and looped her knitting bag over her arm.

The door opened and Alicia Hutchins stood on the threshold smiling. "Jess, I'm so glad you could come."

"I wouldn't have missed it," said Jessie greeting the other woman with a kiss on the cheek. "Come on boys."

"Mary Vowell's already here and so is Mrs Fletcher," she said closing the door behind them.

Jessie glanced around the small sitting room. Mary and Mrs Fletcher were both sitting with handiwork in their hands. They murmured greetings and smiled. Another woman who Jessie hadn't met before was sitting with a young child on her knee. "Good morning, I'm Jessie Price."

"Oh you haven't met," said Alicia coming to stand beside her. "This is Mrs Drummond. Her husband's only recently been appointed an Overseer."

"Oh, well welcome," said Jessie putting Matthew down on the rug on the floor.

She excused herself and went to get the children organised. Fifteen minutes later she was finally able to sit and talk with the ladies. The boys were outside playing in the yard with James Hutchins and Ellen had settled herself in the bedroom with Hannah Vowell and Laura Hutchins. Peace would probably reign for all of ten minutes before there was some squabble or other. Matthew was gurgling happily and inspecting the rug.

Jessie pulled out her knitting and sighed. "So any news ladies?"

Mrs Fletcher paused with her needle in midair. "Did ye hear about the men that slaughtered the bullock? I think Captain Maconochie's lost control over this one."

"Aye. I can't believe he ordered them to three hundred lashes," said Alicia shaking her head. "And only reduced the sentence if the man agreed to tell who his accomplices were."

Jessie swallowed. She'd heard about the bullock being killed by some of the prisoners but hadn't believed the rumour that Captain Maconachie had ordered three hundred lashes. "Did he tell?"

"Aye. After two hundred he gave the Commandant the name of his partner in crime, and then he in turn was given three hundred," said Mary putting her sewing aside. "At least that's what I heard."

"Ye heard right," said Mrs Fletcher nodding. "They didn't expect such severe punishment I'm sure."

"Agreed," said Alicia rising to her feet. "Captain Maconachie's known for his leniency, but not this time."

"I think he's had enough. They've abused his kindness," said Mrs Fletcher. "Some of them were caught distilling liquor and I heard another lot made a boat and were nearly successful in their escape."

"Tea ladies?" said Alicia glancing around at them.

They all nodded. "Would you like some help?" said Jessie.

"No. I'll be fine."

Mrs Drummond had been sitting quietly the whole time and she now put her daughter on the floor. “I heard they plan to replace Captain Maconachie because of his leniency.” She was softly spoken and for a moment Jessie wasn’t sure she’d heard her right. “He’s become rather unpopular with the Colonial Secretary.”

Mrs Fletcher stared at her. “Where did ye hear such a thing?”

Mrs Drummond’s face reddened as all eyes in the room turned to her. “I cannot say. But believe me, it’s true. They plan to replace him with someone more suitable.”

“Ye mean with someone with a firmer hand,” said Mary looking both shocked and appalled. “I don’t like the sound of it.”

The rest of the morning was taken up with speculation about Maconachie’s replacement. Jessie was anxious to discuss the matter with Aaron. Did he know about this? The implications weren’t lost on her. Aaron may have Maconachie’s favour, but he wouldn’t have the ear of a new Commandant. She prayed his pardon would be granted and then it wouldn’t matter.

***

The Governor Phillip arrived in early March. Jessie tried to busy herself and not think about what news it might bring with it. It had been months since Aaron's letters had been sent to Sydney and she prayed if there was news, it would be good news.

She settled the children down for the night and fed Matthew. He was such a good baby and he snuggled down into his crib without complaint. Supper for her and Aaron was simmering on the stove and she hoped he wouldn't be too long. A small anxious knot had formed in the pit of her stomach which had grown as the day went on.

He arrived home a short time later clutching several letters. He put them on the sideboard and gathered her into his arms. "How was ye day?"

"Hmm, good."

He nuzzled her neck and then pulled her closer and pressed his lips to hers. She sighed and drank him in as she breathed in his familiar scent. It was good to be safe in his arms and she felt the tension begin to leave her body. She moaned softly when their lips parted, and he grinned at her.

"Ye'll have to wait I'm afraid," he said picking up the letters. "I'm famished and we have news."

Her eyes widened at the sight of the letters. "Come and I'll fetch you some supper and you can read to me."

"Aye," he said following her out to the kitchen. "There's one from the convict department – I want to read it and then again I don't."

"I know what you mean," she said pushing him towards a chair. "Eat first and then open the letter."

She dished them up supper of beef stew and vegetables. It was delicious even if the beef was a little on the tough side. She was sure she'd cooked it long enough and it should've been falling apart. All through supper, they both eyed the letter sitting on top of the pile. Would it be the answer to their prayers?

"Open it, Aaron. I can't stand it another minute."

"Aye," he said putting down his fork and reaching for it. "This is it then." He tore the envelope open and carefully unfolded the letter within. He drew in a breath before he started reading it aloud.

We refer to your letter and that of Captain Maconachie concerning your petition for a Conditional Pardon. We have given the matter much consideration in respect of your loyal service and continued good behaviour.

We note, however, that you are yet to take advantage of your Ticket of Leave, issued for the state of New South Wales on the 30th of April, 1840. It is, therefore, our desire that you spend one year in the colony of New South Wales on your Ticket of Leave.

We will consider your petition for a Conditional Pardon once this condition has been met.

He let the letter slip from his fingers and compressed his lips. “Well, that’s that then.”

Jessie reached out and squeezed his hand. “I’m so sorry. I know how much we both wanted this.”

He nodded and drew in a deep breath. “I can’t do it, Jess. I wish I could, I really do, but I’ll end up a dead man if I go to New South Wales on my ticket.” He ran his fingers through his hair and shook his head.

"I just don't know if I can convince them of it."

"You could try." She stared into his troubled eyes. "But you better do it quick before Maconachie goes."

"I'll need to get more letters of recommendation, but aye, I might be able to convince Maconachie of the danger my life would be in…and he might be able to convince them."

"It's worth a try."

"Aye, it is."

***

Chapter 16

Take Two

With May came the realisation that Jessie was pregnant again. She wasn't panicked about it exactly, but she did wonder how she would cope with five small children. She put the last of the laundry in the basket and carried it outside and down to the line. She dropped it and glanced about. She'd expected to see Henry digging over the sweet bucks, but there was no sign of him.

"Damn," she muttered.

The ache in her lower back refused to budge even when she stretched and ran her fingers down her spine. She eyed the basket of laundry and groaned. Where was Henry? She wanted him to hang the washing.

She wandered up the side path to the front yard where she fully expected to find him bent over a garden bed. Once again there was no sign of him. She stood with her hands on her hips while she pondered where he might be. He'd never left the yard before without telling her. It suddenly dawned on her that it was very quiet. No sounds of children playing and squabbling. Her heart leapt into her throat as she hurried inside.

Ellen looked up as she entered the sitting room, a frown creasing her young face. "What's wrong Mamma?"

"Have you seen Henry lately?"

She nodded, returning her attention to the pile of blocks in front of her. "I saw him. He went down to the beach."

It was now Jessie's turn to frown. "The beach? Are you sure?"

"Mmm," she said adding another block to her pile. "He went to fetch Aaron and Moses." She swung around and her blue eyes locked with Jessie's. "They're bad."

Jessie sighed. Ellen was right, they were naughty sometimes, but surely they wouldn't have gone to the beach. They knew better than that. She hurried into her bedroom – Matthew was still asleep in his crib. She grabbed her bonnet and hastily tied it on as she returned to the sitting room.

"Stay here, Ellen. I'm going to find the boys and Henry. Don't go anywhere."

"Aye, Mamma."

She raced out the front door and down the path. What would've possessed her sons to go to the beach? She hurried down the road – keeping her eye out for any sign of Henry or her twins. She was passing the parsonage when she saw Henry coming up the road towards her with Aaron and Moses. She quickened her pace as relief flooded her.

"Henry, thank God. Where did you find them?" she said coming to a halt in front of him.

"They were nearly at the beach before I caught up to them," he said glancing down at the pair.

"You know better than to go to the beach," she said kneeling down and glaring at her sons. "That's very naughty."

"Papa," said Aaron looking over his shoulder and pointing. "Papa."

She looked to where he was pointing. There was no one there, not even the launch was docked. "Papa's at work," she said before straightening. "Thank you, Henry. How did you know?"

He shifted his weight. "They were with me in the garden and then they disappeared. I looked in the house, but they weren't there. I remember Mr Price saying this morning he was working on Nepean

Island. I thought they may have gone after him."

"Well you were right," she said taking Aaron by the hand. "I hate to think what might've happened without your quick thinking. Thank you."

"I had two boys meself once," he said as they began walking towards home.

"Did you?" she said tilting her head to the side. "Where are they now?"

"With their mother I 'spect. I dunno." His voice was flat and there was a desolate look in his dark eyes. "I haven't seen them in years."

"I'm sorry." She meant it. She couldn't imagine being separated from her children like that. She wondered briefly how long Henry had been on the island but decided not to pry any further. It was clearly a painful subject.

***

The Governor Phillip docked at the island at the end of July and Jessie could barely contain herself. Surely, there would be a letter from the Reverend for Aaron and he could once again apply for his freedom.

She was on edge all day waiting for him to come home.

When he finally arrived – he was empty-handed apart from a letter from her brother George. “I was sure there’d been enough time for him to reply,” said Jessie stepping into Aaron’s arms.

“Aye so did I,” he said enfolding her in his arms and nuzzling her neck.

“There’s still time,” said Jessie tilting her face upwards. “We don’t even know for sure if Captain Maconachie’s going to be replaced. It could just be rumour.”

“No, it’s no rumour,” he said with a sigh. He let her go and ran his fingers through his hair. “Time’s running out.”

“So Mrs Drummond was right?”

“Aye. I had it confirmed by Tom Sellers,” he said leaning against the sideboard. “Ye know him - he’s the Foreman of Works.”

“Yes, I know who you mean. But how would he know any more than we do?”

“Well, apparently he has an acquaintance who works for the Colonial Secretary in London. And according to him, Lord Stanley intends to replace Maconachie as soon as possible. He's sending a man out from England to take over the command."

"Well, that will take time."

"Perhaps. But I get the feeling the man may already be on his way," he said with obvious frustration. "If I'm honest, Jess, I'm starting to feel like it's never going to happen."

"No," she said embracing him again and pulling him close. "We can't give up," she whispered.

His hazel eyes flecked with grey gazed down into hers and she drew in a breath as her heart quickened. Time stood still for a moment while they lost themselves in each other. Then his lips met hers, firm and demanding as his tongue flicked along her upper lip. She moaned and melted into him, thrilling at the feel of his solid form hard up against her. Their lips parted and he scooped her into his arms.

"I need ye, Jess."

He strode into their bedroom, closing the door with his boot before depositing her onto the bed. He leaned over her and grinned before kissing her again as he began to raise the hem of her skirt. His warm fingers rubbed against her thighs as he pushed her skirts up. She clung to him and arched her back as he pushed her thighs apart and grasping her hips pulled her towards him. She gasped as her skirts rode up to her waist and her bottom rested precariously close to the edge of the bed.

He leaned over her and she wrapped her legs around his waist as he undid his breeches with one hand. “I love ye so much,” he whispered as his hungry lips met hers.

Jessie grasped his shoulders and pulled him closer as she explored his mouth with her tongue. She was so ready for him and urged him on by thrusting her hips towards him. She licked her lips when the kiss ended and he pulled from her embrace. Grasping her thighs he entered her and she moaned with sheer relief as he filled her. Their lovemaking was fast and frantic as he poured his frustrations into her.

Jessie’s climax didn’t come before Aaron let out a groan and he stopped thrusting. She didn’t care. Her husband had needed her this evening and she was content. He withdrew and pulled up his breeches before turning his attention back to her. Jessie pushed down her skirts and sat on the edge of the bed.

"I'm sorry," he said taking her face in his hands and kissing her.

"It's alright," she said shaking her head. "Next time though…"

He gave her a lopsided grin as he took her hands in his and pulled her to her feet. "I promise I'll have ye making those little mewling sounds next time."

"I do not make mewling sounds." She slapped his arm playfully as her eyes widened.

"Aye, ye do." He wrapped his arms around her and pulled her close. "And ye moan a lot."

His lips met hers suppressing her retort. Jessie melted into him and relished the kiss. She was happy his mood had lightened and he'd put his worries aside, even if it was only briefly.

***

27 November 1843

Aaron's heart was racing as he approached home. He prayed the letter clutched in his hand would include a recommendation from Tom Sharpe. It was addressed to Jessie from Ellison Sharpe, but surely the Reverend would've included a letter for him as well.

He opened the door and stepped into the sitting room. It was quiet - far too quiet. There were no sounds of children playing and he paused. Whispering voices wafted to him from the bedroom and he made his way there. He paused in the doorway as he took in the scene. Mrs Fletcher was reclining in the chair and Jessie was sitting up in bed with a small bundle lying beside her.

She looked pale and tired but she smiled when she spied him. "Aaron…we have a new son."

"Aye, so I see."

He approached the bed and gazed down at him. He was smaller than he remembered Matthew being when he was born, and instead of a mop of dark or brown hair, his head was covered in pale, almost white fuzz. "Are ye alright?" he said turning his gaze to Jessie.

"Yes. Tired but I'm fine."

Mrs Fletcher rose to her feet and straightened her skirts. "Well, I'll be off now that ye're home, Mr Price."

"Thank you for all your help, Mrs Fletcher," said Jessie. "It's always a great relief to me to know that you're there for me and my babies."

She smiled – looking pleased with Jessie's words. "Aye, well I'm happy to help ye. I'll call in a day or two to see how ye are." She picked up her bonnet and left the room.

Aaron eased himself onto the bed beside his wife. He leant forward and kissed her as he studied her. "Are ye really alright?" She looked very frail and clammy. Small beads of perspiration dotted her forehead and he was concerned she may have a fever.

"Yes," she said with a sigh. "I'm tired is all."

He nodded as he held out the letter he'd been holding. "I hope ye not too tired to open this then. It's from Ellison, but I'm hoping Tom has put my letter in with it."

"Open it."

He didn't need to be told twice as he ripped the envelope open. A single page of parchment slipped from it and he opened it, knowing it would be a letter from Ellison. There was nothing from Tom. He handed it to Jessie and blew out his breath. There seemed to be only one explanation and that was that Tom hadn't received his letter requesting he write him another recommendation. He'd lost so much time, and it was fast running out. A pang of fear stabbed him in the stomach. What if it was too late? He'd probably already missed his opportunity to press what advantage he still may have with Maconachie. His frustration and anxiety had a firm grip and he could feel it writhing in his belly.

Jessie looked up and a wide smile spread across her face. "They have a son. Finally, they've been blessed with a baby. Ellison says he's strong and healthy. I'm so pleased for them."

"Aye," he said in a short clipped tone.

"What's wrong?"

He ran his fingers through his hair. "There's no letter from Tom. I can only think he never received mine."

"I'm sorry," she said reaching out and taking his hand. She squeezed his fingers. "I should've realised."

"No – there's no need," he said shaking his head. "I'm just so afraid that we've run out of time."

"We can't give up, Aaron. Write to him again."

"Do ye think there's time?"

"We can hope."

"Aye." His gaze rested on his new son for a moment before turning back to Jessie. "Ye're right – we can't give up."

***

Chapter 17

Is it too late to appeal?

With Christmas came official notification that the new commandant, Major Joseph Childs had been appointed. The news spread through Kingston like wildfire, and Jessie prayed his arrival would be delayed. She'd done her best to convince Aaron to submit his letter for a pardon without the Reverend's recommendation, but he refused. He thought he had little to no hope without it.

It was towards the end of January when the Governor Phillip moored off the island. Jessie was on edge all day as she waited for word that Major Childs was on board or not. She prayed the Reverend's letter would be amongst the mail and it wouldn't be too late to present their appeal to Captain Maconachie.

Eight-week-old Mark was fussing and equally unsettled. "Hush now," she cooed putting him over her shoulder.

She gently rubbed his back as she paced the sitting room. She was thankful the boys were occupied outside with Henry. He'd turned out to be a godsend and was happy enough for the twins to dog his footsteps. Ellen was spending the night at Hannah Vowell's house. They'd become inseparable and Jessie was delighted her daughter had a playmate. She glanced at Matthew who was occupied making a tower of blocks. He was tall for his age but such a placid child which was just as well. Moses and Aaron always seemed to find trouble and were full of curiosity. She feared it could well be their downfall one day.

Mark quietened and she cradled him as she walked through to the bedroom. She placed him gently in the crib and continued to pat him until she was sure he was asleep. She stretched her back and sighed. Not knowing their future was starting to gnaw at her, and she knew Aaron was equally anxious. She was so desperate for her children to have a normal life, and the MacDonald River beckoned.

She got the other children fed and into bed early so she could give Aaron her undivided attention when he got home. She expected there would be much to discuss.

Aaron arrived home clutching several letters – and on top was one from Tom Sharpe. “It’s here,” he said grinning like a loon. “I cannot tell ye how relieved I am.” He grabbed her around the waist and swung around before kissing her briefly.

“And what news of Major Childs?” she said.

“Ah…well, it’s not all good news. He’s arrived,” he said letting her go. He put the other letters on the sideboard. “I expect he’ll be taking command immediately.” He turned to face her as he opened Tom’s letter.

Jessie felt her heart somersault. “What will you do? Are we too late do you think to approach Maconachie directly?” She prayed not, but if he was no longer in command then surely they would need Major Childs's recommendation.

He shook his head as he scanned the letter in his hands. He nodded as he slipped it back into the envelope and gazed at her. “We have no choice. We need Maconachie’s recommendation as well. I’ll write my letter to him after supper. I believe he’ll attend to it for us.”

Jessie prayed he was right.

After supper, he spent an hour writing his carefully worded letter to Maconachie. Jessie sat with her mending motionless on her knee. Her mind was a whirl of thoughts and emotions and she could feel a knot of panic forming in the pit of her stomach. If only they'd gotten Tom's letter sooner and were not forced to make their appeal at the eleventh hour.

Aaron sat back and stretched. "Well, I've written it, and I pray it's enough. Will ye read it?"

"Yes, of course." She put her mending aside and joined him at the small writing desk.

Sir,

I'm feeling anxiety for the welfare of my family, and the recovery of my freedom is something for which I have long exerted myself to attain, and by which I am induced at this late hour to address to you. I, therefore, trust I shall be excused.

You have already kindly applied to His Excellency the Governor for my emancipation and the reply was, that prior to receiving that indulgence it was necessary for me to serve twelve months with a Ticket of Leave in the colony. I cannot help thinking that if an official communication written by you was left with Major Childs, again urging this most important object, particularly on you leaving this command, His Excellency would acquiesce your wishes.

It should be borne in mind that my service here, particularly in past years has been accompanied with very considerable personal danger, and that the duties I then performed rendered me extremely unpopular with the majority of the prisoners here. Most of these are now in the colonies, and if I were to attempt to serve the year specified in the colony, in all probability, I should from treachery, or malice, either soon infect my Ticket of Leave, or receive some serious personal injury which might be attended even with the loss of life.

I earnestly press these circumstances on your favourable consideration, and beg as a last favour, that you will be pleased to address His Excellency once more on my behalf.

Sir, your most obedient servant,
Aaron Price.

"It's good," said Jessie nodding. She placed her hand on his arm and squeezed. "I pray it's enough."

He covered her hand with his and grimaced. "Aye, so do I."

***

March 1844

Aaron slipped through the front door into the balmy moonlit night. He breathed deeply and stretched his arms out wide feeling some small amount of tension leave him. The knot of despair between his shoulder blades had become a constant companion and nothing he did gave him any relief. He headed up the path with no particular destination in mind and turned towards the beach.

His mind was constantly employed with thoughts of his situation, and he couldn't bear to share them with Jess. She was full of hope and optimism that they would succeed in their bid for freedom – he knew it was hopeless. His legs walked on without needing any direct input from him, and so his despair consumed him, as it did most nights.

Like a drummer's tattoo, the words repeated in his mind over and over again. The island was now attached to Van Diemen’s Land. The act had already passed Parliament and it was just a matter of the administration catching up. His application for a pardon had been a complete waste of time – he imagined his letters sitting atop some clerk’s pile of papers waiting to be discarded. The Governor of New South Wales would hardly bother with an application for a pardon that no longer came under his jurisdiction. He couldn’t bring himself to tell Jess that it had all been for naught.

He stopped and looked towards the pier as someone yelling rent the air. " Don't ye see the boat, why don't ye fire and give the alarm?" There was no reply.

Aaron hastened towards the beach and very soon came across a man hurrying towards the settlement. “What’s amiss?” said Aaron taking in the man’s appearance. It was only then that he realised it was Smith the overseer. He had a hut down near the boat shed.

"They've stolen a boat - six of 'em and soldiers too. I'm going to raise the guard," he said panting.

"I'll go," said Aaron looking past Smith as he scanned the dark water for any sign of the boat. He couldn't see anything. "Go raise the guards at the boat shed."

"Aye." He turned on his heel and hurried back towards the beach.

Aaron turned and ran towards the barracks as fast as he could. It had been some time since any of the prisoners had tried to escape in a boat, and he wondered if it had anything to do with the two whaling ships moored off the island. One was an American whaler, and the crew had been on the island gathering provisions. He reached the barracks and wrenching open the door raced inside. "Sergeant. Sergeant get ye men to arms."

A moment later a door opened and Sergeant Hughes appeared. "What is it?" he said shrugging into his jacket and staring bleary-eyed at Aaron.

"Some prisoners have stolen a boat, down at the boat shed. Get your men."

"The buggers," he said before racing down the hall and seizing a door pulled it open. "Jones, Watkins, Harris on ye feet." He then raced to the next door and swung it open. "Shit!"

"What is it?" said Aaron.

"Three of my men are missing. There'll be hell to pay when I find them." He disappeared into another room and came out carrying four muskets. "Hurry ye, sluggards."

A moment later the three soldiers appeared. They were still getting dressed but they were looking alert. Giving them each a musket, Sergeant Hughes wasted no time in running from the barracks followed closely by his men. Aaron paused briefly before chasing after them.

They arrived at the beach in time to see a single whaling boat being rowed seaward. Three pairs of oars were dipping frantically in and out of the water and Aaron stared – appalled at the sight. Three soldiers in uniform were visible amongst the prisoners. Two were manning the oars and rowing with all their might.

"Fire!" yelled Hughes before discharging his musket.

Only two of the muskets fired, and Sergeant Hughes cast an angry glare in the direction of his men. Before he could say anything, Harris interjected.

"It's not my fault." He looked aghast at his weapon.

"Reload," said Hughes handing Harris his musket and taking his.

After a brief inspection, he swore. "There's no primer. The bastard's." He looked exasperated as Watkins and Jones reloaded their weapons. "Fire God damn it!"

Smith appeared on the scene accompanied by two soldiers from the boat shed. They were armed with muskets and wasted no time in firing at the fast-receding boat. Aaron saw a man fall from the boat into the water as the men onboard kept rowing as fast as they could.

"Don't shoot," the man in the water yelled. "It's me, Brady."

"Fire," yelled Hughes again urging his men to ignore the traitorous soldier in the water.

Aaron thought there was little hope their musket balls would hit their mark. The boat was now too far away and was receding fast. It looked like Brady wasn't the only one in the water. He was sure he could see two others – possibly dead.

"Sergeant, ye should launch a boat and give chase. Ye will not stop them from here," said Aaron watching the silhouette of the boat getting smaller. "Leave Brady to me."

"Aye," he said looking momentarily annoyed before letting out a deep breath. "Hold ye fire. Get a boat onto the slip."

He watched as the soldiers all headed for the boat shed before marching down to the water's edge. Brady was lying panting on the wet sand with blood oozing from a wounded shoulder.

"Here, let me help," said Smith coming to stand beside Aaron.

"Thank ye," said Aaron as the two grabbed Brady and hauled him to his feet.

"Who was with ye?" said Aaron glaring at him.

"Clinton," he said gasping for breath. "I think he's been shot, and Bryan."

"And the prisoners?"

He shook his head. "I dunno for sure. Monds and Sullivan, I don't know who else."

Aaron scanned the dark water for any sign of Clinton, and soon spotted two men being tossed by the waves – they both looked to be dead.

"I'll get them," said Smith following Aaron's gaze.

"Alright," said Aaron taking a firmer grip on Brady. "I'll take him to the hospital and then I'll come back and help ye with the other two."

Smith nodded as he released his hold on Brady. He slumped against Aaron who shoved him forward as he began the walk to the hospital. The events of the evening had been a wonderful distraction but as he marched Brady ahead of him, his thoughts returned to his troubles. A deep despair settled in his bones and he yearned to hold Jess in his arms. She alone could chase away his demons and give him respite, albeit temporarily.

***

Chapter 18

Times are Changing

Spring came and so did news from family and Ellison Sharpe. Jessie read her letters over and over again, savouring every morsel of news and gossip. She still had a few days to write her replies before the Governor Phillip was due to sail, and so she'd settled in her chair to read the latest newspaper from Sydney. She rarely got to read the newspaper before it was quite ragged from much handling and often unreadable. However, Aaron had left it on the sideboard this morning and it looked like it had hardly been touched.

There was the usual news and then there was an article that grabbed her attention. As she read her heart began to race and her breathing changed to short shallow breaths. Administration of the island would now come under the authority of the Governor of Van Diemen's Land. The implications of such a change did not escape her. Did Aaron know about this?

She let the newspaper go limp as her mind whirred. He must know. It was likely he'd know well before it was public knowledge. Her heart sank as realisation dawned on her. He'd known for months…and he hadn't told her. Several conflicting emotions surfaced all at the same time and hot tears pricked her eyes. Did he not trust her? She could think of no other reason that he'd keep such important news from her.

She folded the newspaper and rose to her feet. She walked to the sideboard and put the paper down smoothing it with her fingertips as she did so. She stood there drawing in deep breaths as she tried to steady herself. There was no escaping the feeling of hurt that her husband didn't trust her, nor the anger that was beginning to broil inside her.

All these months she'd been sure his pardon would be arriving any day, and now it was very clear there was no hope of that happening. She stamped her foot. "Damn it."

"What is it Mamma?" said Ellen wandering over to her side with her rag doll under her arm. "Bad news?"

"No sweetheart," she said shaking her head. "Just a beetle."

She peered at the floor and shuddered. “I don’t like beetles.”

“Neither do I.”

Ellen wandered back over to the chair she’d been sitting on and resumed her conversation with her doll. Jessie watched her and smoothed her hands down over her waist, leaving them on her hips. Mark’s squawks reached her ears and glancing at Matthew who was happily occupied on the floor she headed for the bedroom. Mark was lying on his back kicking his legs furiously and yelling. He stopped as soon as he saw her and a wide grin spread across his face. Her heart melted as she lifted him into her arms.

“Hello my baby,” she cooed kissing his forehead. “Did you have a good nap? Hmm.”

She put him down on the bed while she grabbed a clean clout and swiftly changed him. He giggled as she lifted him into her arms again. Going through to the sitting room she put him on the floor beside Matthew. He would play happily with his little brother and keep him occupied until supper. Heading back into the bedroom she grabbed the dirty clout and overalls.

"You be good boys," she said as she passed them on her way to the washhouse.

As soon as she stepped out the back door she heard Moses and Aaron's happy voices chatting away. She smiled. At least her children were content.

Jessie suppressed her feelings as she went about her afternoon chores. But the hurt gnawed at her and her anger at Aaron's treatment of her boiled away unchecked. She couldn't remember ever feeling so betrayed, not even by her stepmother. She'd treated her badly but she grew to expect it and so it was never accompanied by feelings of betrayal. This was different. He'd let her continue to hope for something that was never going to happen. He'd lied to her and she never expected that from him.

She fed the children their supper earlier than usual and got them ready for bed. She wanted them to be asleep when their father got home. Moses complained about going to bed before seeing his Papa but was soon placated with the promise that Jessie would take him to the beach the following day. She closed the door of their bedroom and leaned against it and sighed.

She settled herself at the kitchen table with a glass of wine with the newspaper by her elbow while she waited for Aaron. Their supper of poached fish and vegetables was keeping warm above a simmering pot and could wait until they were ready to eat without spoiling. She took a sip of her wine and sighed. She had an awful nervous feeling in her stomach and the wine wasn't helping. She took a large gulp and swallowed as the door to the kitchen opened and Aaron's smiling face appeared.

"Good evening," he said walking over to her and placing a kiss on her forehead. "Mmm, something smells good. Are the children abed?" A slight crease marred his brow as he surveyed her.

"Yes," said Jessie compressing her lips. "We need to talk."

"What about?" he said seating himself.

She drew in a deep breath and locked eyes with his. "About you…lying to me," she said pushing the folded newspaper across the table in front of him. "I know about the island's administration changing, and I know you've been lying to me about it for months."

He shook his head and stared at the newspaper. “I never lied to ye.” He turned his gaze to her and licked his lips. “I couldn’t tell ye.”

“What because you don’t trust me?” she said rising to her feet and placing her palms flat on the table. “Because you wanted me to believe you were doing everything to gain your freedom when you wanted the very opposite.” Her voice rose several octaves and she glared at him with a furrowed brow.

“No. Don’t be ridiculous.”

“Oh, so I’m ridiculous now. You’re the one who won’t leave this damn island, and it’s obvious to me that you don’t want to. Stop pretending Aaron and be bloody honest for once.”

“Ye have no idea how many sleepless nights I’ve had,” he said running his fingers through his hair. “I didn’t tell ye because I couldn’t bear to see the disappointment in your eyes, not because I don’t trust ye. God, I trust ye with my life, Jess.”

“Forgive me if I don’t believe you.” She continued to glare at him while her heart raced and thumped madly against her ribcage. “You let me believe and hope when you knew. You knew they weren’t going to give you a pardon. Did you ever intend to tell me? Or were you just going to go on lying to me and treating me like an idiot?"

He rose to his feet and scowled at her. "I have not lied to ye. I did it to protect ye. I didn't want ye to be filled with despair like I've been."

"That may be what you told yourself, Aaron, but I have never been so hurt." She straightened and twisted her fingers in the folds of her skirt "You're supper's on the stove," she said before marching to the door and throwing it open.

She walked blindly through the house and out the front door. She had no idea where she was going - she just needed to be alone. He didn't understand, he didn't see what he'd done or how it had made her feel. Hot tears splashed down her face as she marched along the road towards the beach. Before she knew it her feet were sinking into the soft sand. Gathering her skirt in one hand she made her way along the sand to the black rock.

It had been an age since she'd been down here. She used to come here a lot before she was married. Firstly to watch the soldiers fish and later, she'd meet Aaron here secretly at night. She licked her lips and swallowed as she made her way through the rocks to the private nook they used to share. It was lonely and silent here without him and not the place of solace she thought it would've been.

She sat down and wrapped her arms around her knees and sighed as she wiped her tears aside. Her mind was a whirl of different thoughts and emotions but overriding everything was the realisation that this was their first real disagreement. He'd always supported her and a small voice in the back of her mind wondered if she was being a child. Was she? The hurt was real but what about Aaron?

She knew he'd had sleepless nights. Knew he'd leave their bed and wander at night but it hadn't occurred to her it was because he couldn't tell her the truth. She blew out her breath and then gasped.

"Jess."

Tears came unbidden as she stared at her husband. He was standing there with his hair ruffled by the breeze. He wasn't scowling anymore, but a crease across his brow told her he was here out of concern. She sighed as she rose to her feet and stood in front of him, gazing into his worried face. A pang of guilt shot through her that she'd caused him to worry.

"I'm sorry. I never meant to hurt ye."

"I know," she said doing her best to blink away her tears.

"I knew ye'd be disappointed that we'd wasted months getting our letters together. I've been overcome by despair and I didn't want that for ye. I thought I could find a solution before I had to tell ye." He looked imploringly at her and held out his arms.

She looked at him for a moment before stepping forward and into his embrace. She sighed as he wrapped his arms around her and some of the tension left her. She felt so safe in his arms and hated feeling so apart from him.

"There's only one solution," she said pulling from his arms and looking up at him. "We must get more letters and apply to the Governor of Van Diemen's Land, or else give up."

"Aye," he said pulling her close again. "You're right. I'll start gathering them right away."

She sighed – glad to have their disagreement come to an end. He smiled and looked down at her and then his lips were on hers and she pressed herself against him until she could feel the full length of his solid form. The kiss deepened and she was gasping when their lips finally parted.

"I love ye so much," he whispered.

She knew it was true. She could see the love in his eyes as he gazed at her and she smiled. "I love you too."

***

Chapter 19

Future Plans

Over the next few days, Aaron and Jessie were both busy writing letters. Jessie to her grandmother, George and Ellison, while Aaron penned yet another letter of request to Tom Sharpe. When the Governor Phillip sailed, it went with all their hopes and dreams on board. Aaron prayed he wouldn't have to wait too long for Tom's reply.

In the meantime, he had several other people to solicit letters of recommendation from. Lieutenant Hamilton was an obvious choice, and one that he was sure would be forthcoming. This time around he wouldn't be able to get the Commandant's help. Major Childs was a very different prospect than Maconachie. He was confident the man would forward his request but was not so confident he would add his recommendation to the pile.

He walked purposefully down the road towards the settlement. His swagger belied the confidence he was feeling inside. The Foreman's office was a small wooden hut situated near the boat shed. Thomas Seller was the foreman of works and Aaron had worked closely with the man on several projects. In that time, they'd developed a good relationship based on mutual respect, and Aaron was sure he'd lend his support.

"Aaron," said Tom Seller's as soon as he entered. He was a middle-aged balding man with a pair of spectacles perched on the end of his nose. His friendly brown eyes surveyed Aaron as a smile played around his mouth. "I wasn't expecting you. Is the stone ready?"

"Ah…no, not yet," said Aaron approaching his desk. "It will likely be another three weeks."

"Hmm, that'll be fine. So, you must be here on another matter. How can I help you then?"

"Well, Tom I have a favour to ask of ye."

"Go on."

Aaron drew in a deep breath. "I would ask ye to add your weight to my appeal for a pardon. A letter of recommendation if ye will. I feel we've got to know one another quite well in recent times, and I thought ye might assist me."

"I'd be happy to," he said removing his spectacles and looking thoughtful. "I wonder if you need such a thing though. You have a ticket don't you?"

"Aye, but I've made a lot of enemies, Tom. I wouldn't feel comfortable going to the colonies with just my ticket."

"Hmm, I understand. Your concern no doubt is for your family. Which is why my wife isn't here with me, but rather safe in Sydney." He put his spectacles back on. "Perhaps you should do the same."

Aaron thought for a moment, imagining himself here without Jess and the children. Life wouldn't be bearable without them. And anyway, would they be safe all alone in Sydney? No, but they would be on the MacDonald River with her family. A pang of guilt shot through him which he shrugged aside.

"They wouldn't be safe without me," he lied.

"Ah well, perhaps you're right to apply for a pardon. At any rate, I'm more than happy to help. I'll have the letter written for you in a day or two. Come on by and collect it when you're ready."

"Thank ye, Tom, it's much appreciated."

He left the foreman's office and wandered down to the pier. He could see the launch slicing through the water on its way back from Nepean Island - it wouldn't be long. He leant against one of the upright posts while he waited. Thoughts of Jess and the children at the MacDonald River swam around in his mind. He couldn't bear to send them away. It had been several years since Jess had seen her family, and he did feel guilty about that. He sighed – he had to admit- he was selfish where his wife was concerned.

***

November 1844

Jessie's stomach heaved again and she swore as the last of her breakfast erupted from her. Drawing in a deep breath she wiped her mouth with the back of her hand. Well, that confirmed it, she was definitely pregnant. She'd suspected for some weeks that she was. She smiled as she made her way back into the house. If she thought five children were a handful, how was she going to manage with six? She knew she'd manage somehow but the house might not.

Their house only had two decent size bedrooms. Ellen's room was more like an added-on lean too – it was tiny. And the four boys shared the other room and there was no room to add another bed.

She poked her head into the boy's room to check on Aaron and Moses. They were both sitting on the floor drawing on their slates. She smiled to herself. They would be five in a few weeks and off to school after Christmas. She was looking forward to that. Ellen was already at school and thoroughly loving it.

Matthew and Mark ignored her as she crossed to the sideboard and picked up the letters which had arrived yesterday. She picked up the top one and settled herself in the chair to read it again. It was from George and he had lots of news to share.

Dearest Jess,

I hope you and Aaron and the children are all keeping in good health. When I last saw Grandma she was quite blind, but Grandpa Joe was in fine form.

William is taking care of them both, now that I have left the MacDonald River.

That's the big news I have to share. I've moved up to Wollombi where I'm managing the Traveller's Inn. I know that doesn't sound like something I'd do, but I've met this wonderful woman. Her name is Mary Crothers, and her father owns the inn. He's teaching me everything there is to know about running the business with the hopes that Mary and I will take over from him when we get married next year.

That's the other big news. Mary and I are getting married. Jess, it would be wonderful if you could come and celebrate with us. Grandma and Grandpa Joe have promised to travel up for the occasion, and of course, William will be there. I do hope you can convince Aaron to let you come as well. We'll be married on the 28th of March, and it wouldn't be the same without you.

Please do your best to convince him.

Your dearest brother, George

She folded the letter and slipped it back into the envelope. Oh, how she would love to be there for George's wedding. Not only that, but she could see everyone again.

She sighed as she got to her feet and placed the letter on the sideboard. She would wait and talk to Aaron before replying to George – there was a slim chance he would let her go.

Several days passed before she found the opportunity to discuss George's letter with Aaron. She'd decided to lead with the good news, and then broach the subject of going to Wollombi.

"I have news," she said wrapping her arms around his waist. She tilted her face upwards and smiled.

He gazed at her with one brow arched upwards before bending down and kissing her. "Good news I hope."

"Yes, well I think it is." She smiled and squeezed him. "We're having another baby."

"Oh, that is good news," he said grinning as he wrapped his arms around her. "Although, I don't know if we've got room for another one."

"I know what you mean. Do you think we might be able to add another room?"

He shook his head. "I don't know. I'll talk to Tom Sellers about it."

Jessie nodded, satisfied with his response to her news and adding to their house. "I have another matter I'd like to discuss."

"Hmm what is it?" he said letting her go and eyeing her critically.

"Well, I got a letter from George…and he's getting married next year…in March."

"Oh well done, George. You must pass on my congratulations when you write to him."

"I will," she said nodding. "Anyway, he's invited me to come to his wedding. I know you won't be happy about me going alone, but I'll be with family. Grandma and Grandpa Joe are going as well."

"Ye can't go alone, Jess," he said shaking his head. "It's too dangerous."

"I knew you'd say that," she said with a sigh. "But, Aaron…"

"I'll come with you." He gathered her in his arms again and grinned. "I've been thinking it's about time we visited your family."

"Really? You mean it?" she exclaimed as warmth and joy exploded within her. A wide smile spread across her face - she never imagined they'd all go together.

"Aye. Well if I can manage it," he said looking serious. "I've never taken time away before, but I expect Lieutenant Hamilton will agree. Of course, it'll be three or four weeks without any salary, but we've got enough money to cover us."

"Oh, Aaron, thank you."

She grabbed his face between her hands and pulled his head down before kissing him. He pulled her hard up against him and probed her lips apart with his tongue. She wrapped her arms around him and thrilled at the feel of his solid form in her arms. She was panting when their lips parted and feeling happier than she had in a while.

***

Chapter 20

The Surprising Major Childs

By February Aaron had gathered three letters of recommendation which he presented before Major Childs. He sat nervously on the edge of the chair, his left knee bouncing up and down of its own accord. The Major was a stern man in many respects, at least that was his reputation. Aaron surveyed his whiskered face with heavy lines around his mouth which made him look perhaps more serious than he was. He'd had little to do with the man since his arrival and was quite unsure of him.

"Well, I see these men think quite highly of you, Mr Price," he said raising his head and piercing Aaron with a stare.

"Aye." He drew in a breath and did his best to calm his racing heart. If Childs refused to present his appeal to the Governor, there was nothing he could do. The man was unreadable.

"I must say since taking over command here I've heard no complaints about you, and Captain Maconachie certainly held you in high regard," he said as he folded the letters and slipped them back into the envelope.

"Thank ye," said Aaron, relaxing just a little at the reassuring words.

He ran his fingers through his whiskers and Aaron thought a smile was playing at the corner of his mouth. "Mr Price I have every faith in adding my weight to your appeal. I'll pen my own letter of recommendation before forwarding these to His Excellency."

It was more than he'd hoped for, and he stared at him for a moment before getting himself under control. "Thank ye, Major. I believe with your recommendation I have every reason to hope His Excellency will indulge me."

"As do I," he said and this time his thin lips went taut for the briefest moment showing his yellowing teeth. "You will need to be patient, Mr Price. However, I expect His Excellency will give your case due consideration."

He nodded. "Aye. Well, I thank ye once again for your indulgence."

He rose to his feet and with a brief nod from the Commandant he turned and left his office. Once outside he heaved a sigh. That had gone far better than he'd imagined and he almost felt hopeful that this time he would succeed. The taste of freedom would be sweet.

***

March 1845

Jessie's excitement was palpable as she boarded the brig Agincourt. She could hardly believe they were really going to New South Wales, and she would soon see her family. With the change in administration, the Governor Phillip no longer sailed to Sydney. They'd managed to get passage on the Agincourt, but the return journey was far from certain.

"Wait for your Papa," she called to Aaron and Moses who had boarded ahead of her.

She had Mark on her hip and Aaron had Matthew in his arms. Ellen was clinging to her skirt as she walked across the deck to the railing. Her skirts billowed in the stiff breeze and Ellen let go and raced towards her brothers. A wide smile spread across

Jessie's face at the sight of her children – this was going to be such an adventure for them.

Aaron came and stood beside her before putting Matthew down. He toddled after his older siblings and Aaron put his arm around her growing waist. "Happy?"

"Deliriously so," she said leaning against him.

She never imagined today could happen. Not only was she going to see her family, but Aaron was accompanying her. It hadn't been easy for him to get time away from his work. They were working on cutting stone for the extension to the barracks and Lieutenant Hamilton had been loathed to let him go. Surprisingly, it was Major Childs's support that led to him finally agreeing to give him leave.

The trip to Sydney was short and uneventful. They had fine weather and a good breeze which saw them land eight days later. Sydney was bustling as usual, and Jessie was glad to have her husband by her side. They remained on board while he tracked down a conveyance to take them to the MacDonald River.

Jessie had written to both her grandmother and George advising them of their plans. They'd go to the MacDonald River first and possibly stay a few days if there was time, and travel up to Wollombi with Grandpa Joe, Grandma and William. She privately hoped they'd be able to spend a few days there on the way back as well.

They arrived at the MacDonald River two days later. The children were so excited and chatted away like parrots about Uncle William and Grandma. Jessie doubted any of them remembered their last visit. The twins were only babies, and of course, Matthew and Mark weren't even born. Ellen, however, was the font of all knowledge, although Jessie suspected she was just repeating what she'd overheard, and not truly remembering.

Jessie climbed down from the wagon and stretched. Her bottom was quite numb from hours of bumping along on a hard wooden seat, but nothing could suppress her joy at being back here.

"Aaron and Moses – go knock on the door," she said as Aaron put Mark in her arms.

Taking Matthew by the hand she walked to the veranda and up the steps. Aaron and Moses hadn't needed to be told twice and had scampered up the steps and were now banging on the door.

"Grandma, it's us," yelled Moses as he peered in the window. A moment later he spun around and grinned. "Grandpa Joe's coming – I saw him."

Their excitement was contagious and Jessie found herself grinning like a loon as the door opened and Grandpa Joe's wrinkled face peered out. A wide smile spread across his face showing several missing teeth. He turned his head and yelled down the hall. "It's them. It's Jess and Aaron and the children."

"Well, let them in," came a muffled reply.

"Grandpa Joe," said Jessie putting Mark down. He promptly sat down and shoved his fist in his mouth. She hugged Grandpa Joe and kissed his cheek. "It's so good to see you."

After many hugs and greetings, they all went into the house. Aaron and Grandpa Joe were loaded with bags as they disappeared down the hall. Jessie made her way to the sitting room, where she fully expected to find her grandmother. She could hear children's footsteps behind her and a glance confirmed that Ellen, Matthew and Mark were following her. She presumed the twins had gone with Aaron.

She found Grandma sitting in her favourite chair. Her eyes were closed, but Jessie knew she wasn't asleep. "Grandma."

"Jessie," she said with a sigh and opened her blind eyes. "I was just sitting here imagining what ye might look like now. I expect ye've grown into a young woman since I last saw ye. Come let me see ye."

She crossed the floor and knelt in front of her grandmother. Maggie took her face in her gnarled hands and ran her thumbs across her cheekbones. "Ye too thin child," she said shaking her head. "Ah, but ye've grown into a fine-looking woman."

Jessie smiled and took her grandmother's hands in hers. "You're too kind." She kissed them before letting them go. "You must meet my two youngest boys…Matthew and Mark," she said turning and beckoning them to come closer.

Maggie smiled as Jessie lifted Mark onto her knee. She wrapped her arms around him. "He's a fine boy."

"He's tall for his age and sturdy," said Jessie eyeing her youngest. "He's got very blonde hair, Grandma and a cheeky smile."

"Oh I can just imagine," said Maggie running her fingers through his hair.

"No," said Mark frowning brushing her hand away.

"Jess," said William appearing in the doorway. "I heard ye'd arrived."

Jessie swung around and grinned. "William...oh my."

Her baby brother had grown at least another three inches and had his dark hair tied in a queue at the nape of his neck. He was sporting a thin moustache and he looked so handsome.

"Aye, I expect I've changed since ye saw me last," he said crossing the room. "Tis good to see ye." He swept her into his arms and hugged her tight. "Are ye expecting another one?" His eye widened as he let her go.

"Yes," she said running her hand over her stomach. "In a few months. I'm hoping for a sister for Ellen."

"I missed that," said Maggie with a frown. "Good Lord, Jess that'll be six."

"I know," she said with a laugh. "Our house will need to expand to accommodate us all."

"Where's Aaron? Ye said he was coming with ye," said William scanning the room.

"He's down the hall with Grandpa Joe."

The conversation over supper that evening was constant. Everyone had so much news to catch up on and so many questions that needed answering. Jessie collapsed into bed exhausted from the busy day and fell asleep in Aaron's arms – content and happy.

The following day was full of making plans to travel up to Wollombi. They would need to take the spring cart and the wagon to accommodate everyone. Grandpa Joe and William would hitch the horses early the following morning, and load the luggage. Jessie wondered how it would all be accomplished, but had faith that they knew what they were doing.

Everyone was up early and Jessie got the children breakfasted and dressed before seeing to her own needs. She was twisting her plaited hair into a bun when Aaron entered the bedroom. Jessie glanced at him and smiled. “All ready to go?”

“Aye. Your brother and Grandpa Joe have everything in hand,” he said coming up behind her and wrapping his arms around her waist. He kissed her neck and breathed in. “Hmm, ye smell good.”

“I can’t imagine how,” she said turning around to face him.

She put her arms around his neck and standing on tippy toes she kissed him. “I love you.”

“Aye. I love ye too,” he said before gathering her to him and pressing his lips to hers.

Their kiss deepened as Jessie pressed herself against him and drank him in. She sighed with contentment when their lips parted. “Come, we have a long day ahead of us.”

“Not yet…they can wait a minute.”

He ran his hands down her spine until they pressed against her bottom as he pulled her closer. Her protruding stomach pressed into him and he grinned. “Ah, for a moment I forgot about our little one.”

“It will be hard to forget about her in another few months,” she said smiling up at him. "One more kiss, then we really must go."

***

Chapter 21

The Wedding

The trip to Wollombi was slow but uneventful. They arrived in the early evening, hungry and exhausted after a long day on the road. Jessie hoped George would have a nice hot supper and a comfortable bed for them all.

Jessie took Grandma's arm as they made their way inside the Traveller's Inn. It was a two-story stone building with a veranda running along the top floor with turned timber railings. The interior was cool with tin-lined ceilings and timber-panelled walls. Voices wafted to them from what she presumed was the dining room or the public bar as they passed.

"I thought George would be here to greet us," said Maggie in a disgruntled tone.

"I'm sure he'll be along in a moment," said Jessie squeezing her grandmother's arm.

"Any sign of George?" said William coming up behind them. "Looks kinda fancy don't it."

Jessie smiled to herself – yes it did look rather fancy.

"Grandma," came George's voice before he appeared a moment later at the end of the hall. "I've been trying to keep an eye out for ye," he said hurrying towards them. "Jess. Oh my God, it's been an age."

He swept her into his arms before releasing her and turning his attention to Grandma. "It's so good to see ye, Grandma."

"George. Come closer," she said reaching for his face. "Ah, ye haven't changed a bit."

"It hasn't been so long," he said placing an affectionate kiss on her cheek. "Oh my goodness, are all these yours Jess?"

Jessie swung around and grinned at her five children and her husband making their way down the hall towards them. "Yes. You would remember Ellen, Moses and young Aaron. And these two scamps are Matthew and Mark."

"And ye husband," he said with a grin. "Good to see ye again, Aaron."

"Likewise George."

"Grandpa Joe, give me those bags," said George rushing forward and relieving him of several bags. “Come, I’ll show ye up to ye rooms.”

“I’ll take Grandma through to the dining room,” said Jessie taking her grandmother’s arm once again. “Point me in the right direction, George.”

“The end of the hallway, turn left,” he said over his shoulder as he disappeared up the stairs, followed by Aaron, William and Grandpa Joe.

“Did he look well?” said Maggie as they meandered down the hall. “And happy do ye think?”

“Yes, Grandma. He looks very happy and I think the hotel business suits him.”

“Hmm, perhaps more so than farming?”

”Perhaps.”

They reached the end of the hall and Jessie pushed open two double doors and guided Maggie through. A cosy dining room with a large ornate fireplace opened before them. Jessie stared around the room with its many paintings and cluttered furniture. Most of the tables were occupied with diners who paid them no heed. She was just beginning to wonder if there was a table large enough to accommodate them all when a young woman hurried across the room. She was smiling widely and threw her arms out wide as she approached them.

"Ye must be Grandma Maggie and Jessie. Who else would ye be?" she exclaimed throwing her arms around Jessie. "I'm Mary, and soon to be ye sister. I'm so very pleased to meet ye."

"Likewise," said Jessie rather taken aback by the young woman's enthusiasm.

"Are these all yours?" she said stepping around Jessie and grinning at the children. "I'll soon be ye Aunty Mary."

"This is Ellen, Aaron, Moses, Matthew and Mark. Say hello."

"I don't expect I'll remember all their names," she said turning her attention back to Maggie and Jessie. "Come, let me show ye to a table. Ye must be starving. Would ye like to take my arm, Grandma?"

"Thank ye," said Maggie looping her arm in the young woman's. "George didn't mention ye were so vivacious."

Mary giggled. "Me Pa always says I'll put the chickens off their laying with me chatter."

Jessie ushered her children ahead of her and watched Mary as she made her way between the tables. She could see why George had fallen in love with her. Grandma was right, she was engaging and pretty. Her blonde curls bounced as she walked and her hips swayed below her slim waist. She was pleased for George. Not only with his choice of wife, but she could see he was making his way in the world. Isn't that what she'd done?

Supper was a chaotic affair, with everyone talking at once. Voices were raised in an effort to be heard and Jessie gave up trying to hear anyone. Mary's parents Thomas and Anne also joined them for supper along with several of her young brothers and sisters. Jessie quite lost track of who was who and hoped Aaron might be doing a better job of remembering their names.

Her younger sister, Jane however was rather memorable, and she couldn't help but notice that William was rather taken with her. She was not vivacious like her sister, but rather more reserved, but one of the most striking young women Jessie had ever seen. She couldn't take her eyes off her. Her pale blonde hair was a startling contrast to her olive complexion and dark eyes. She could see her young brother was quite smitten with her.

Aaron and Jessie retired to their rooms straight after supper. Jessie was quite exhausted and looking forward to an early night. Tomorrow would be busy with George and Mary's wedding in the morning, and a large gathering was expected at the Inn in the afternoon. As soon as the children were settled she slipped into her nightgown and brushed out her hair. It hung long and golden down her back and she relished the feel of it. Like a silken shawl around her shoulders.

"Ye are so beautiful," said Aaron coming up behind her.

She put down her brush and turned to face him. He was wearing only his shirt and his grey-flecked brown hair hung loose around his face. "You're not so bad yourself." She gathered her hair between her fingers and began to weave it into a single plait for the night.

"Here, let me do that."

She sighed as he pulled on her tresses and subdued it into a long plait. "George's new in-laws seem like nice people, and most generous," he said.

"Yes. I think they've taken George into their family already. I'm pleased for him."

"Aye." He secured the plait and spun Jessie around to face him. "I'm sorry I have no family to give ye."

She shook her head. "You're enough for me, Aaron Price."

He bent his head and kissed her, softly without demand, and gathered her to him. "Ye are more than enough for me, Jessie Smith." He lifted her into his arms and carried her to bed.

***

The day dawned overcast with a cool breeze blowing, but by mid-morning the sun had poked through the clouds. Jessie dressed in her best pale grey skirt and jacket. The skirt was layered with a small sprig pattern of blue flowers over it. She eyed herself critically in the mirror as she tied her bonnet. There was no disguising the dark smudges around her eyes - she looked tired and drawn. She sighed and pinched her cheeks. She was tired. Two days' travel from Sydney with barely a day's rest in between had left her more exhausted than she liked to admit.

She turned as the door opened and Maggie came in, tapping her cane as she went. "Are ye ready, Jess? William an' Joe have the children in hand, an' Aaron's helping George to hitch up the spring cart."

"Yes, I'm ready."

"Are ye alright?"

"Of course. What would make you think I wasn't?" Jessie took her grandmother by the shoulders and kissed her wrinkled cheek. "I'm fine."

"Hmm. Ye were quiet over supper last night, an' I cannot help think this has been too much for ye in ye condition."

Jessie smiled and looped her arm in Grandma's. "I'm tired is all."

Maggie patted her hand and smiled. "Well, it's no wonder, but ye must take some rest, Jess, for the sake of ye baby."

"I will."

They all just fitted in the wagon for the short drive to the church. William drove the cart with George on board, and Grandpa Joe drove everyone else in the wagon. It was cramped and uncomfortable, and Jessie was thankful it was only a short way. Ten minutes later they pulled up out the front of the small stone church. Jessie waited while Grandpa Joe helped Grandma to alight and Aaron lifted the younger children down.

He took her hand and steadied her while she climbed down. “Thank you,” she said slipping her arm through his.

“Come,” said Aaron over his shoulder to their children.

“Coming Papa,” said Ellen hurrying to his side.

She was dressed in her best Sunday dress and matching bonnet. He smiled down at her. “Ye look lovely today, Ellen.”

“Thank ye, Papa.” Her face beamed as she walked beside him.

Aaron and Moses, who were also in their Sunday best tore passed them and disappeared into the church. Jessie groaned. She prayed they wouldn’t make pests of themselves.

“Come, Mark,” said Aaron coming to a halt and twisting around.

Jessie watched him toddle towards them and smiled. He was such a delightful child and brought her so much joy.“Here, darling take my hand,” she said gesturing to him.

Moments later they entered the church and Jessie scanned the pews to see where they might sit. It looked as though most of the residents of Wollombi were here this morning. Then she noticed Tommy Crothers. He was at the front and waving to them to join him. Jessie nudged Aaron who glanced and then commenced walking down the aisle.

"Good morning to ye," said Tommy as soon as they reached him. "We've saved ye seats down the front here."

He gestured to the pew second from the front. The front one was taken up with the entire Crothers family - Anne and her six children. They ranged in age from about sixteen to seven. Anne Crothers stood up and greeted them both.

"It's so nice to see ye again," she said kissing Jessie on the cheek. "How's George this morning?"

"He's fine and well," said Jessie smiling. "He's out front with William. I expect he'll be along in a minute."

She nodded before turning her attention to Maggie and Grandpa Joe, who had just arrived. After more greetings and small talk, everyone seated themselves.

Jessie found herself seated next to Grandma and she tucked her hand in the crook of her elbow.

A few minutes went by before the Reverend appeared at the rostrum and the congregation quieted almost immediately. George and William came walking up the aisle and joined him – standing to one side. George looked so handsome, although Jessie thought he looked a little anxious. She smiled – he would soon be happily married and all nervousness would be gone.

The organ started playing and the crowd turned to watch as Mary came down the aisle on her father's arm. She looked beautiful in a creamy dress with her blonde hair piled high on her head with a small hat perched on top. She was radiant.

Jessie clasped Aaron's hand as the ceremony commenced. This was the first wedding she'd attended since her own. The memory of that day came flooding back. Aaron had still been a prisoner under guard then, and no sooner were they married than he was marched from the church. How very different George's wedding would be. Later, they would be celebrating with family and friends and then tonight they would lie in each other's arms. She was happy for her brother, but the day was tinged with a pang of sadness for her wedding which was so stark in comparison.

The Reverend pronounced them married and the happy couple kissed before turning to face their family and friends. They were both beaming, and Jessie rose to her feet with the rest of the congregation as they walked from the church to enthusiastic calls of congratulations. She noticed William take Jane Crothers' arm as they followed the happy couple down the aisle. Perhaps there would be another Smith and Crothers wedding in a few years.

Jessie and Aaron followed Grandpa Joe and Grandma from the church before gathering their children to them.

"Ye go and congratulate your brother, I'll watch the children," said Aaron urging her to join her family members.

She smiled and nodded before making her way through the throng to George and Mary's side. She waited while the couple ahead of her gave them their congratulations.

"Congratulations, George." She hugged him and kissed his cheek before letting him go and embracing Mary. “I’m so happy for you two.”

“Thank ye,” said George slipping his arm around his bride’s waist. “I only hope we can be half as happy as ye and Aaron.”

“I’m sure you will be,” said Jessie smiling. “You look so beautiful, Mary.”

“Thank ye,” she said blushing.

“I hope ye’ll be staying a few days,” said George gazing beyond Jessie to where Aaron was waiting.

“I’m not sure.” Jessie shook her head and pressed her lips together. “We must be back in Sydney by next Monday. We daren’t miss our ship.”

“That will surely give ye a few days here.”

“Perhaps,” said Jessie stepping aside as Mary’s sister Jane approached. “I was hoping to spend a day or two with Grandma.”

“Excuse me, Jessie. It’s time to go,” said Jane.

“Aye. We’ll talk about this later,” said George urging Mary forward. “We’ll see ye back at the inn.”

Jessie nodded and watched them walk towards the waiting spring cart. She sighed. How she wished she had more time.

***

Chapter 22

Return to Sydney

The wagon was loaded with bags and the children were settled. William was driving while Grandpa Joe and Aaron would take the spring cart with Grandma. They'd spent several days in Wollombi after the wedding and Jessie was loath to leave, but they had to get back to Sydney.

The day trip from Wollombi to the MacDonald River was cool and overcast, and it started raining as they turned down the track to the river. Jessie pulled a blanket out from under the seat and covered the children as best she could. However, by the time the wagon pulled up outside the homestead, she was shivering and chilled to the bone. She waited for Aaron to come around her side of the wagon and help her down.

"You're freezing," he said wrapping his arms around her.

"I'll be alright."

He kissed her and released her before gathering Matthew in his arms. "Go inside with ye grandmother, I'll get the children and bags."

"Thank you."

She stamped her feet as she walked over to the spring cart. Grandpa Joe had just helped Grandma down when she arrived. "I'll take her," she said tucking her hand in her elbow.

"Thank ye," said Grandpa Joe kissing Maggie's cheek. "Get her in outta the cold."

Grandma grasped her arm in a vice-like grip. "Thank ye."

The two women walked to the veranda and up the steps. "The door'll be open," said Maggie reaching for the knob. "Ned an' Eliza were keeping an eye on things while we were gone." She pushed open the door and they entered and walked down the hall.

"I'll go and tell her we're home. I hope she's got something for supper," said Jessie.

"Aye. Take me to my room first will ye child," said Maggie relaxing her grip.

"Of course."

Jessie glanced sideways at her. It was only then she noticed how tired and drawn her grandmother looked. The trip to

Wollombi and back had taken its toll. Grandma wasn't alone. Jessie would like nothing better than to go straight to bed and skip supper altogether. She guided Grandma down to her bedroom and helped her out of her wet travelling clothes and her stays until she was just wearing her shift. Pulling back the counterpane and quilt she climbed into bed and sighed as she relaxed against the pillows.

"Would you like a nice hot cup of tea?" said Jessie smoothing the counterpane and kissing her forehead.

"No...I'll wait." She closed her eyes and breathed out slowly. "Be a dear an' bring me supper in bed."

"Yes, Grandma."

Giving her one final concerned look she left the room and made her way back towards the front door. She hoped she'd be alright. Seeing her lying there in her bed scared Jessie just a bit. She stripped off her wet cloak and hung it on the hook in the bedroom as she passed. She sighed as she made her along the hall and stopped at the children's room. She peered in and smiled. Aaron had the five of them in various states of stripping off wet clothes and putting on warm dry ones. She continued on and nearly ran into Grandpa Joe.

"Where's Maggie?"

"In bed," said Jessie with a crease marring her forehead. "I'm worried about her."

"Don't lass. It's been a big trip for her, but she'll be alright in a day or two."

Jessie nodded. "She wants supper in bed."

"Will ye go and see what Eliza can rustle up?"

"Yes, that's where I'm going now."

"Good," he said over his shoulder as he continued down the hall with his load of bags. "Tell her not to fuss."

Supper was a quiet affair. The children were nearly asleep but managed to stuff a few mouthfuls of cold ham with potatoes and peas into their mouths. Jessie fell into bed and went straight into a dreamless slumber. She awoke at dawn feeling refreshed but her legs were stiff and her back was aching. She was thankful they were staying one more night before heading for Sydney tomorrow. That would get them to Sydney on Saturday evening, in plenty of time to meet the Lady Isabella. They had to be onboard by Monday morning – they would have ample time should anything go awry with their plans.

***

The following morning William hitched up the wagon and helped Aaron to load the bags. The children were settled and with a heavy heart, Jessie said her goodbyes.

She clung to her grandmother. "I don't know when we'll see each other again," she said kissing her cheek. "I'm missing you already."

Maggie smiled and patted her cheek. "I know, but we have to be glad of the time we've had child."

"I am….it's just that I don't know when we can come back. I'm praying that Aaron gets his pardon soon, but I just don't know."

"Have faith, Jess. You'll be free and back here before ye know it. Now go. An' take care of yeself an' ye new baby."

She ran her hand over her stomach and felt her baby kick in response. "I will, I promise."

"Take care lass," said Grandpa Joe grabbing her in a tight hug. "It's been so good having ye stay a few days."

"Thank you, Grandpa Joe." She hugged him in return. "Take care of Grandma," she whispered.

He smiled and nodded as he let her go, and she sighed. Of course, he'd take care of Grandma, but she couldn't shake the feeling that she would never see her again. She climbed into the wagon and William wasted no time in urging the horses to walk on. Jessie's eyes were glued to her grandmother until they turned the corner and she disappeared from sight.

She settled herself with her cloak wrapped around her. The morning was cool, but she expected the day would be rather pleasant once the sun broke through the clouds. By late afternoon they would be back in Sydney, and her thoughts turned to their return to the island. They'd been gone nearly three weeks already and wouldn't land for another ten days or so. She wondered how much longer they'd be there before Aaron got his pardon. Surely this time it would be granted and they would finally be free. She imagined the joy of leaving for the last time and settling on the MacDonald River or somewhere close to it. She glanced around at her children - they all looked rather glum and resigned to the long day ahead. How different life was going to be for them – and Aaron. Her gaze rested on his back for a moment. He hadn't known freedom for so long that she couldn't imagine how he was going to feel when it finally happened.

They arrived in Sydney late in the day and William drove them straight to the docks. Jessie had no idea which of the three ships docked at the wharf was the Lady Isabella and she hoped Aaron knew.

He leapt down from the seat and stretched. "I'll go check with the Captain. Wait here."

Jessie watched him as he walked across the wharf to the ship moored at the far end. He disappeared up the gangplank and Jessie sighed.

"Are we going?" said Moses leaning out of the wagon.

"In a minute. You heard your Papa – he said to wait here."

He gave her a disgruntled scowl and sat back. William jumped down and grinned at him. “Ye can help carry the bags when he comes back, hey? Ye too Aaron.”

“Aye,” said young Aaron with a sigh.

Aaron returned a few minutes later wearing a wide smile. “Come on, down ye get. Take a bag if ye can.” He gathered Matthew in his arms and swung him down to the ground. He staggered when his father let him go and Aaron grabbed his arm. “Are ye alright?”

He nodded. “Aye, Papa.”

“The captain has our cabins ready for us,” said Aaron as he helped Jessie down. “I’m glad that worked out.”

“Yes so am I.”

Aaron had booked passage on the Lady Isabella before they left Sydney to go to Wollombi, but neither of them had been certain the ship would be in port when they returned. Jessie was pleasantly surprised that their plans had indeed panned out.

“I’ll say goodbye then,” said William hugging each of the children. “I’ve got errands to run for Grandpa Joe, and I’ll need to get lodgings for the night.”

“Thank you so much, William. We couldn’t have done it without you,” said Jessie.

"Glad to help," he said wrapping his arms around his sister. "Take care until we see each other again."

"I don't know when that'll be."

William grinned. "I trust it won't be long."

"Goodbye, William and thank ye," said Aaron shaking his hand. "Safe travels."

"Aye, ye too."

Gathering their bags and herding the children between them, Aaron and Jessie made their way across the wharf and onto the ship. The second mate showed them to two cabins. One for them and one for the five children. The cabins were opposite one another, but Jessie was still a bit concerned the children would wander – particularly Moses and Aaron. The pair were prone to finding trouble.

"I'll go see if the cook can give us supper," said Aaron depositing the last bag in the corner of the cabin.

"Good. I'm starving," said Jessie kissing his cheek as he passed.

There wasn't much for Jessie to organise. The children's cabin had two beds and two hammocks had been hung. Ellen would have a bed to herself and Matthew and Mark could share. She eyed the two hammocks. If Aaron and Moses didn't kill themselves trying to get out of them, they'd be quite fine sleeping in hammocks.

"I'm hungry, Mamma," said Ellen slumping down on one of the beds.

"I know sweetheart." Jessie smiled and kissed her forehead. "Papa will be back soon with supper."

It was at least twenty minutes before he returned, by which time Jessie was not only starving but rather disgruntled at his tardiness. "Good, Lord, Aaron where have you been? How long does it take to find out if the cook will have supper for us?" she said in an annoyed tone which Aaron appeared to ignore, only adding to her irritation.

"I'm sorry. I ran into Captain Walker and his wife. They've invited us to dine with them."

"Oh." His words deflated her and she was left with nothing else to say. Well good, at least they would have supper before bed.

It was barely eight o'clock when Jessie crawled into bed and snuggled up to Aaron. She sighed as he wrapped his arms around her. He kissed the top of her head. "I love ye."

"I love you too," she said breathing in his familiar masculine scent. "Do you think we'll sail tomorrow?" Now that she was here on board she was anxious to be underway.

"No, it'll be Monday at the earliest," he said with a shake of his head.

She sighed and buried her head in his shoulder. Monday couldn't come soon enough.

***

Chapter 23

Their Last Night in Sydney

The following morning Jessie awoke to discover Aaron was already up and in the midst of getting dressed. The dawn light was coming in through the window, but Jessie thought it was still early.

"What are you doing?" she said propping herself up on one elbow.

He grinned and leaning his hands on the bed, bent forward and kissed her. "I'm getting dressed." He continued tucking his shirt in his breeches. "Go back to sleep. I'll take the children for breakfast while ye get some more rest."

"Really? Oh, that would be wonderful." She smiled as she lay back down and snuggled under the covers. She was tired and some extra time in bed without having to worry about what the children were doing was heaven. "Thank you," she murmured.

She must've gone straight back to sleep because she awoke with a fright. Blinking she glanced around the cabin. There was no sign of her husband and a thin beam of sunshine was coming in through the window. She stretched before swinging her legs over the side and sitting up. She had no idea what the time was but knew it must be late.

Taking her time she fossicked through the bags until she found a warm skirt and a clean blouse. Her stays and chemise were in a crumpled mess on the floor. She retrieved them and slipping from her nightgown she put on her undergarments. She was sorry they weren't getting underway today and sighed as she donned her skirt and blouse. It wasn't that she hadn't enjoyed her visit with her family and George's wedding – but now she was ready to go home.

Her brown jacket was hanging on a hook on the door and she shrugged into it before turning her attention to her hair. It was in a long plait and she deftly twisted it and pinned it to her head. It would do for now. She'd have to brush it out later. Tying on her bonnet she opened the door and peered out into the corridor. It was devoid of anyone. She opened the door opposite and peeked in – there was no sign of the children. She smiled as she made her way along the corridor to the salon. It was so nice of Aaron to take care of the children for her. She pushed open the double doors and went inside.

The salon was typical for ships of this size. Tables were strung from the ceiling with benches for seats that lined both sides. The only illumination came from several lamps which were also hanging from the ceiling. A rotund middle-aged woman wearing a mob cap was sitting at one of the tables. She looked up and smiled which only made her already round face rounder.

"Good morning, Mrs Price," she said gesturing to her to sit opposite. "I trust ye slept well. Would ye like some tea? Cook's just made a fresh pot."

"Yes, thank you," said Jessie seating herself.

"Yushan. Yushan," she called before turning her attention back to Jessie. "I trust ye don't mind another day in port, we won't be sailing until tomorrow at best."

"I don't mind in the least" she lied.

"Yes honourable wife," said Yushan arriving on the scene.

He bowed and stood with his hands folded behind his back. Jessie had never in her life been so close to a Chinaman and couldn't stop staring at him. His hair was as black as coal and pulled back into a long plait that hung straight down his back.

"Mrs Price will have tea, and tell cook to bring her some breakfast as well."

"Yes, Mrs Walker."

He bowed and hurried off on his slippered feet. Jessie was mesmerised.

"I must say I'm rather curious, Mrs Price," said Mrs Walker sipping her mug of tea.

Jessie swung her head around to face Mrs Walker and smiled. "How so?"

"That ye and yer husband continue to live on Norfolk Island when ye don't have to. I must say, I couldn't imagine it myself. They say the devil himself won't have anything to do with the place."

"Well, my husband has a well-paid job and it's not as bad as you might think."

Yushan arrived carrying a tray which he placed on the table before pouring a cup of tea and putting it in front of Jessie. "Breakfast coming Missus," he said in his Mandarin accent. He bowed and retreated once more.

Jessie reached for the tea and took a sip. It was strong and sweet – exactly how she liked it. “We really don’t have anything to do with the prisoners. Well, Aaron does, but I rarely notice them to be honest.”

Mrs Walker’s eyebrows raised but she smiled. “Well, I must say it does sound intriguing.”

After an enjoyable breakfast chatting with Mrs Walker, Jessie went to find Aaron and the children. She found them on the deck watching the comings and goings on the dock.

“Good morning,” said Aaron putting his arm around her growing waist. He kissed her cheek and pulled her close. “How are ye?”

She smiled and turning her face to his kissed him softly. “I’m well rested thank you.”

“Good. I have an errand to run,” he said letting her go. “I’ll be back afore ye know it.”

“An errand?” She raised her brows and looked at him. What errand could he possibly have to run?

He'd already taken several steps when he turned and grinned. "Aye. Well, it's a surprise so ye'll have to be patient."

She watched him go down the gangplank and disappear into the throng. A surprise - for her or the children? She shrugged as she leaned against the railing and watched the gulls soaring on the breeze.

***

Jessie finished applying the final touches to her hair and peered at herself in the small mirror. She smiled with satisfaction. The dark smudges beneath her eyes had disappeared and some colour had returned to her cheeks. She'd piled her honey-blonde hair on top of her head, and several strands framed her face, softening the whole look.

"Are ye ready?" Aaron opened the door and his face appeared in the mirror behind her.

She heard his intake of breath and smiled inwardly. It was nice to know her husband still appreciated her.

"Ye look beautiful." His voice was barely a whisper.

She turned to face him. "Thank you…and yes I'm ready."

He held the cabin door open and proffered her his arm, which she took. "Will I need my cloak do you think?" she said pausing for a moment.

"I don't think so."

She shrugged as they left the cabin and made their way to the top deck. Aaron's big surprise had been revealed this afternoon when he returned from his errand. He'd procured tickets to the theatre to see the musical Kate Kearney. He'd arranged everything. Mrs Walker was keeping an eye on the children, who'd had supper and were all now tucked in their beds.

Jessie could feel the excitement thrumming through her veins. She'd never been to the theatre – well you couldn't call the pantomimes put on by the prisoner's theatre. It was only a short walk to the Royal Victoria Theatre on Pitt Street, and in no time they'd joined the queue to find their seats.

Jessie's eyes swivelled in every direction as she tried to take it all in. The women dressed in their finest evening attire and the theatre with its ornate ceilings and velvet seats. She clung to Aaron as they were finally shown to their seats and she settled herself, still clinging to his arm.

"Have you ever been to the theatre?" she said glancing at him.

"No…tis a first for me."

"Me too."

It took at least another twenty minutes before all the patrons found their seats. The chatter came to an abrupt end as the curtain lifted and the music started. Jessie was enthralled by the costumes and the dance. The whole was like nothing she'd ever seen or heard before and she got totally immersed in the experience. When the final curtain fell she jumped to her feet and applauded with gusto. She wasn't alone – almost the entire theatre gave the players a standing ovation.

Aaron grinned at her when she sat back down. "When we're finally free, I'll take ye to the theatre often."

"Really? Oh, Aaron, I'd love that." If they hadn't been in such a public place she would've thrown herself in his arms and kissed him. As it was, she simply reached out and squeezed his arm.

They sat and waited while their row emptied of patrons before making their way out of the theatre. It was a lovely evening, and she grasped Aaron's arm as they walked down George Street towards the docks. After a wonderful night out she was anxious to see her children. She prayed they'd been well-behaved and would be all in their beds fast asleep.

"Are ye happy, Jess?" said Aaron glancing sideways at her.

"Very," she said looking up at him. "Thank ye so much."

He stopped walking and wrapped her in his arms. "I am only sorry we may not be able to do this again for some years."

"Don't be," she said shaking her head. "I am forever grateful."

He bent his head and pressed his lips to hers. It was only a brief kiss, but it was full of promise and if they had not been standing in the middle of the street Jessie would've pressed herself against him. She sighed as their lips parted and they began walking again. They turned when several voices rang out.

"It's him I'm sure of it," shouted one of them.

"Grab the wee mongrel," yelled another.

Fear gripped Jessie and she clung to Aaron as she peered into the gloom. The street was dimly lit with one brazier alight on the corner, but the other end of the street where the voices had come from was in darkness. Jessie could feel her heart thumping against her ribs as she stood there waiting to see who would emerge from the darkness.

"Run," said Aaron pushing her roughly towards the other side of the street.

Seconds later two men lurched out of the darkness. One made a beeline for Jessie and she froze as his large hands reached for her. Aaron stepped between them, but the other man's meaty fist slammed into Aaron's face and he staggered. Blood oozed from his nose and he wiped it with the back of his hand.

"Run," he screamed at her before lunging at his attacker.

She gathered her skirt in her hands and turned to run. She'd barely taken two steps when rough hands clawed at her waist. Her heart jumped into her throat as adrenaline coursed through her. God no, this couldn't be happening. The man pulled her hard up against him as his fingers reached for her bodice. She heard it rip as she pushed with all her might to escape his grasp.

"Not so fast my sweet." His hot breath was on the back of her neck as his hands squeezed her breasts hard.

She screamed as she tried once more to escape. She hoped Aaron was alright and that he'd soon subdue the man who'd hit him. Jessie sucked in a breath and brought up her knee before slamming her booted foot down as hard as she could onto the man's foot. He howled and his grip loosened slightly.

"Ye bitch."

He spun her around so she was facing him before pulling her hard up against him once more. She could smell his foul breath tinged with ale and turned her head to the side as she pushed against his chest with the palm of her hands. "Get off me."

He momentarily let her go, before grabbing her and dragging her to the other side of the street. He shoved her up against a wall knocking the breath out of her. She groaned as he pressed himself against her and began pulling the hem of her skirt upwards. Gasping for air she struggled to stop him. “No. Get off me.”

The back of his hand made contact with her cheek whipping her head to one side. She groaned as her cheek stung and warm sticky blood oozed from her nose. Realisation dawned on her that she couldn’t stop him and any second now he’d have his way with her and there was nothing she could do.

He pushed his knee roughly between her thighs, forcing them apart as his fingers fumbled with the buttons on his breeches. She screamed but she couldn’t get him off her – he’d pinned her to the wall and she could do nothing to stop him.

And then he was gone. She looked up as her skirts fluttered down to see Aaron’s enraged face pressed into the man’s frightened one. A second later his fist smacked into the man’s face and his knee slammed into his groin. He groaned and slumped to the ground. Aaron swung around and raced to her side. Her legs gave way and she slumped to the ground.

“Are ye hurt?” He took her face in his hands, wiping the blood away as he searched her face.

“I don’t think so,” she said letting out a sob as he gathered her into his arms. “Who were they?”

“I don’t know, but we’d best get out of here.”

He helped her to her feet and removing his jacket wrapped it around her shoulders. Putting his arm around her waist they hurried down the street to the docks. A few minutes later they reached the wharf where the Lady Isabella was moored. They crossed to the gangplank and were about to step on board when Jessie let out a loud moan as pain shot through her abdomen. Hot tears came unbidden as she clutched her stomach.

“The baby,” she said gasping as another sharp lightning bolt of pain went through her. “Oh no…it’s too soon.”

She could see the fear etched on Aaron’s face as he scooped her into his arms. She buried her face in his shoulder and let her tears go as he ran up the gangplank. “I need the surgeon,” he yelled.

A crewman on guard looked up in alarm. “I’ll fetch him, Mr Price.”

"Thank ye," said Aaron who without missing a stride disappeared down the hatch to their cabin.

He kicked open the door open with his boot and deposited Jessie on the bed. "What can I do?"

Jessie gasped as another contraction gripped her. She drew in several breaths and did her best to breathe through the pain. "Nothing," she said once it had passed. "Check on the children," she said drawing in another breath.

"Aye…but not yet. Not until the surgeon gets here."

He grabbed her foot and unlaced her boot and pulled it off before doing the same with the other one. He gently took hold of her ankles and lifted her feet onto the bed.

Jessie lay back against the pillows and closed her eyes – she didn't want to see the fear in his eyes. "Go, Aaron. I'll be fine. Please I need to know the children are safe." She sucked in another breath as pain gripped her once more.

"Alright, but I'll be back."

She nodded and wiped aside the tears that leaked from her eyes. Her poor baby, it was too soon and she knew it would be born tonight.

***

Chapter 24

Homeward Bound

Jessie's eyes widened at the knock on the door.

"Come in," said Aaron and without waiting he wrenched the door open and stared at the small greyed haired man.

"Good evening, I'm Mr Whitby the ship's surgeon," he said doffing his hat. "How may I…what ever happened to ye, Mr Price?"

"We were set upon, but it's not me that needs ye, it's my wife," said Aaron stepping aside and gesturing to the surgeon to enter. "She's gone into labour."

"It's too soon," said Jessie with a sob.

"Aye, leave us, Mr Price. I'll need to examine your wife."

Aaron nodded. "I'll go check on the children," he said placing a kiss on Jessie's forehead. "It'll be alright."

She breathed in heavily through her nostrils and nodded. She wanted to reassure him, but she knew her baby shouldn't be coming and she couldn't stop the tears that leaked out of the corner of her eyes.

***

Aaron paced up and down the narrow corridor. It had been hours and he had no idea what was going on with Jess. Muffled moans and grunts came to him through the panelled walls - was she alright? Would their baby be alright? He blamed himself. He knew Sydney was dangerous for them and yet he'd let his guard down, and now his wife and child were in danger. He ran his fingers through his hair and sighed. The knot in the pit of his stomach was making him feel ill and his chest tightened as he tried to draw in a deep breath.

He swore this would never happen again. Never would he endanger his family again. He slumped against the wall and slid down it until he was sitting on the floor. He closed his eyes and prayed.

Time passed slowly and Aaron sat with his head in his hands berating himself for his stupidity. It must've been near dawn when the door to the cabin opened and Mr Whitby poked his head out. His grey hair was plastered to his balding head and his shirt sleeves were rolled up. Aaron noticed the front of the man's shirt was blood-spattered and his stomach contracted.

"My wife?" He leapt to his feet and stared at the surgeon.

"She's fine, Mr Price. Ye have a daughter." He said it in a flat tone without smiling. "She's not likely to live…I'm sorry."

Tears welled in Aaron's eyes as he stared at Mr Whitby. This was all his fault and he couldn't see how he could ever forgive himself. "May I see them?"

"Aye. I'll give ye a few minutes." He stepped out into the corridor and put his hand on Aaron's shoulder as he passed. "Mrs Price's labours have left her exhausted. She needs to rest."

"Aye," said Aaron nodding.

He drew in a breath as he entered the dimly lit cabin. Jessie was tucked under the quilt with a small bundle in her arms. She looked up and her clear blue eyes locked with his.

"Mr Whitby says she'll not live." Tears streamed down her face as she returned her gaze to her new daughter.

Aaron swallowed and took the two steps that brought him to her side. He eased himself onto the bed and put his hand on her shoulder. "I'm so sorry." He leaned forward and kissed her damp cheek.

"It's not your fault," she said turning to face him. "There was nothing you could've done."

He groaned. "I should've done much more."

She put her hand to his face forcing him to look at her. "Do not blame yourself, Aaron. Please, you couldn't have done more." She pressed her lips to his and kissed him softly. "I thought we might name her Mary for my mother...she'll take care of her in heaven."

His heart contracted and he nodded. "Aye."

It was only then that he turned his attention to his daughter lying in her mother's arms. She was tiny and perfect. Her dark fuzzy hair and long eyelashes contrasted against her pale skin. Too pale he thought – and too small.

"She's beautiful," he said running his finger down her tiny cheek. "Do ye think maybe Mr Whitby's wrong?" He glanced up at Jessie as his daughter let out a feeble squawk.

She shook her head. “No. She won’t suckle. Mr Whitby said I can try again, but he doesn’t think she will.”

Aaron had never felt so helpless in his life. If Mary wouldn’t feed then there was no hope. “Mr Whitby says ye need to rest,” he said sliding from the bed. “I’ll go sleep elsewhere. Try and get some sleep too.”

She nodded. “Are the children alright?”

“Aye, they were all asleep last time I checked. I’ll check again,” he said kissing her forehead. “Rest.”

“Get Mr Whitby to have a look at that gash on your cheek.”

He ran his finger over his cheek and winced. “Aye.”

He left the cabin and leaned against the closed door. He should’ve stayed and given Jess some support, but he couldn’t. He couldn’t bear to look at either his wife or their daughter. His guilt at failing to protect them was squirming in his stomach like a living thing and he needed to be alone with it.

The following morning Aaron rose early. He'd spent an uncomfortable night slumped against the bulkhead in the salon with only his guilt for company. He bypassed their cabin and made his way onto the deck, where the crew of the Isabella were getting the ship underway. The ropes had been loosed and the foresail raised. He braced himself as the wind filled the sails and the ship lurched.

He stood by the rail and watched the men at work as the ship sliced through the waves. He'd never been one for the sea but had to admit it held a certain appeal. His twin sons seemed to love being on board ship. He stayed on deck for as long as he could without Jessie noticing his absence and finally with a sigh he went down below.

For the next few days, he rose early and left their cabin before Jessie was awake. He spent the days alone on the top deck as he tried to bury his feelings of guilt and remorse. On the morning of the third day, he'd just stepped from the cabin when he heard Jess let out an awful moan. With his heart in his throat, he opened the cabin door and stepped back inside.

She looked up as he entered and let out another awful wail. His eyes went to the still bundle in her arms – he knew before she said anything. Knew his daughter was dead and the realisation cut through his heart like a dagger.

"She's gone…our baby's gone," she said pressing her dead baby to her breast as tears streamed down her face.

Aaron stood frozen to the spot as he watched her clutching Mary to her. It was his loss too, and he felt it acutely, but his pain was less important than the obvious anguish that Jess was in. He went to her and wrapped his arms around her and their child. She buried her face in his shoulder and howled. It broke his heart to hear her grief so raw. They clung to each other for how long he didn't know. Their tears intermingled with their grief, and somehow their shared pain brought him a small measure of relief.

He finally released her and took Mary in his arms. She was so small, so perfect and yet she was not to be. Jessie's tear-stained face looked from him to their daughter and back again.

"What will we do?" she whispered smoothing Mary's dark hair with her hand before kissing the top of her head.

He drew in a breath and slowly let it out. "What must be done," he said in a quiet voice.

She stared at him for several seconds with her mouth agape and he stared back at her. Was she going to resist? He hoped to God not. "I'll ask Captain Walker to say a few words," he said locking eyes with her.

For one horrible moment, he thought she was going to snatch Mary from him. Time stood still as he watched several emotions flit across her face. Fresh tears welled in her eyes and she nodded.

He sighed as he walked to the door and slowly opened it. "I'm so sorry, Jess."

She nodded again and sucked in a deep breath. "I know."

***

The day was grey and overcast which only added to Jessie's mood. She clutched Mark in her arms as her eyes rested unmoving on the small shrouded body lying on the plank. The Captain's words washed over her without her hearing any of them except his final ones – *we now commit her body to the deep*.

Two of the crew picked up the plank and turning it lengthways rested it on the railing before tipping it upwards. Mary's tiny enshrouded body slipped from the plank into the sea. Jessie looked over the side of the ship in time to see her make a small splash and disappear beneath the waves. She knew she should've felt something but she didn't. It was like this was happening to someone else's child, not hers. She wondered if her heart had stopped working and feeling as she stepped away from the railing. It was a very odd feeling - not feeling.

Aaron slipped his arm around her shoulders and squeezed her close. She glanced at him and at the tears running unheeded down his face. Her own eyes were dry.

Captain Walker and Mrs Walker were the first to embrace Jessie and Aaron and express their sympathy. Several of the crew also murmured words of comfort to them. Jessie nodded and thanked each of them for their kind words – but their words gave her no comfort – she just felt numb.

Yushan had stood a distance away during the ceremony and was the last person to approach her. He bowed and his dark almond eyes pinned her with a serious stare. "When a parent dies they are buried in the ground," he said. "When a child dies they are buried in their mother's heart." He smiled. "She will always be in your heart honourable, Mrs Price." He bowed and quietly walked away.

Jessie's breath caught in her throat and she swallowed. Mary would always be in her heart and in heaven with her mother. She pressed her lips together as they began walking across the deck to the main hatch. Like lighting a lamp that slowly brightens as the wick impregnates with oil the numbness began to leave Jessie. The pain of losing her daughter and the circumstances that had caused her to be born too soon hit her like a tidal wave. Never would she set foot in Sydney again.

***

Chapter 25

Life goes on

Six days later the Lady Isabella anchored off Norfolk Island and Jessie couldn't believe the feeling of relief that flooded her. The verdant green island with its tall cliffs and pines beckoned to her and she was anxious to be home.

No sooner had they landed than Sergeant Hughes accosted Aaron. "Lieutenant Hamilton requires ye as soon as ye can."

"I've only just returned, Sergeant. Tell the Lieutenant I'll see him in the morning unless it's of the utmost urgency."

Sergeant Hughes rubbed his fingers through his whiskers. "Well, I cannot say how urgent it is."

Aaron groaned inwardly. How he'd ever been promoted to Sergeant he didn't know. The man had no intellect or ability to make decisions as far as he could see. "Give my message to Lieutenant Hamilton, and if the matter is urgent he'll tell ye soon enough." He turned his back on the Sergeant and proceeded to load their bags onto a cart. "Come, we'll walk home and they'll bring our luggage later."

Jessie had to agree it was a lovely morning for a walk and it wasn't far. She breathed in the fresh air and sighed as they walked along the road. The island seemed to welcome her and embrace her. It was unchanged in the month since they'd been gone but Jessie realised she'd changed. She watched Aaron as he walked ahead of her with the twins. Had Aaron changed too? She didn't think anyone could lose a child without it changing them. She only hoped Aaron would stop blaming himself.

They settled back into the rhythm of life in no time. There was something soothing about the regular schedule and tending to her children that eased Jessie's pain. Her only worry was Aaron. He'd thrown himself back into work and came home tired and withdrawn at the end of the day. She'd tried talking to him, but he'd assured her he was fine. She knew he wasn't. They'd barely made love in recent months and she was missing the closeness they usually had.

"Jess…Jess are ye there?" came the muffled voice of Mary Vowell before she burst through the front door.

Jessie tossed her mending aside and leapt to her feet. Her friend looked pale and dishevelled and her eyes were as round as saucers. "Mary, what's happened? Are you alright?"

"I'm fine…I'm fine," she said holding her hand to her bosom and gasping for air. "It's Aaron. Oh, God Jess, he's hurt bad."

Jessie stared at her as fear cut through her and her heart leapt into her throat.

"He was stabbed…he's in the hospital now." She burst into tears and hugged Jessie. "I ran into Lieutenant Hamilton and he asked me to come and tell ye. He says he might not live."

Jessie felt her knees buckle and she clung to Mary while a million different thoughts raced through her mind. At the forefront was the thought of her unborn child. She hadn't told him yet that she was expecting another baby. She'd only realised herself about a week ago and was waiting for the right time to tell him. She hoped another child would bring them back together and strengthen their love. Now he might die before she could even tell him. Hot tears pricked her eyes which she brushed aside – now was not the time for tears.

She pulled from Mary's embrace and looked at her. "I must go to him, Mary. Can you stay with the children? I don't know how long I'll be."

She nodded. "Of course. Go, Jess. I'll be praying for him."

"Thank you, Mary. Ellen and the twins are at school and will be home soon."

Without another thought, she grabbed her cap from the hook and slapped it on her head and raced out the front door. She ran all the way to the hospital, and she was gasping and had a stitch in her side when she arrived. She didn't care – Aaron was the only thing that mattered right now.

***

The day had started like any other for Aaron. He'd gone out to the quarry to get his gang of men working. They were a lazy lot and without constant prodding from him would do the bare minimum of work. They were already behind schedule and Tom

Sellers had been badgering him for a load of stone for weeks.

He noticed Jackson was sitting on a rock doing bugger all. He was sick to death of the men's lack of work. "Back to work, Jackson," he yelled as he marched towards him. He gestured with his hands for the man to get up.

Jackson slowly rose to his feet. "I'm not feelin' well boss."

"Ye look fine to me. Get back to work," said Aaron eyeing him. He looked perfectly fine to Aaron and he didn't believe his claim of being unwell.

Jackson stared at Aaron - his pale blue eyes narrowing. "I can't." He sat back down on the rock and dropped his chisel.

"Get up, Jackson. Perhaps a few days in the lockup will make ye feel better."

He glared at Aaron but slowly rose to his feet again. Aaron prodded him in the back to get him moving before calling out to overseer Smith. "I'm taking Jackson to the gaol, I'll be back."

"Aye," said Smith looking his way and nodding.

Aaron continued to prod Jackson as they walked to the landing and climbed into the waiting launch. Young Bobby pushed off as soon as they were aboard and took up the oars. Jackson sat there scowling at Aaron who paid him no heed. This was the last thing he needed this morning and as the launch sliced through the water, his thoughts returned to his gang at the quarry. Without him there he was sure they'd slack off and he'd have to explain the delays to Sellers'.

The launch seemed to take forever to reach the pier and Aaron's anxiety was growing. He'd deliver Jackson and then get back as soon as possible. Finally, the launch bumped up against the pier and Aaron wrenched Jackson to his feet and shoved him.

"Wait here," said Aaron to young Bobby as he climbed out. "I'll only be ten minutes."

"Aye, Mr Price."

Aaron and Jackson were approaching the main road when Lieutenant Hamilton intercepted them. "What's going on? I need you out at the quarry," he said to Aaron. He eyed Jackson who looked back at him with a belligerent stare with his hands in his pockets.

Aaron sighed. "I know, and I'll be getting back there as soon as I've delivered Jackson to gaol."

"What have you done?" said Hamilton addressing Jackson directly.

"Nothin'."

"He's refusing to work," said Aaron.

"Indeed. Take your hands out of your pockets when I address you," said Hamilton glaring at him.

Jackson continued his belligerent stare and ignored Hamilton's request.

Lieutenant Hamilton looked down his long nose at him before speaking to Aaron. "Make him take his hands out of his pockets, Mr Price."

Aaron glanced at Jackson who continued to scowl. The man really wasn't worth the trouble and he'd be glad to be rid of him. "Ye heard the Lieutenant, take ye hands out of ye pockets." He grabbed him by the wrist and pulled in an attempt to force him to remove his hand from his pocket.

A second later Jackson pulled his other hand from his pocket. He was clutching a knife which he plunged into

Aaron's abdomen before pulling it out and turning on Hamilton.

"Aargh," yelled Aaron clutching his stomach as a dark stain of blood spread across his shirt. His knees crumpled beneath him and he landed in the dirt.

"Shit – you bloody blighter," said Hamilton.

Jackson circled Hamilton and tried to stab him as well. Aaron watched as Hamilton backed away and Jackson lunged at him. Hamilton grabbed his wrist and twisted his arm up his back as Jackson tried to wrestle free of him. Jackson let out a loud grunt as the bloody knife fell from his fingers, and Hamilton hit him in the stomach knocking the wind out of him. He crumpled to the ground moaning and holding his middle.

Hamilton rushed to Aaron's side. "Are you alright?"

"No," he said breathing heavily. "I don't think so." He knew his lifeblood was draining out of him but he couldn't feel anything. The sound of rushing blood filled his ears and he could feel it, warm and sticky between his fingers as he pressed his hand to the wound – but that was all. And then everything went black and all thought abruptly ended.

***

Jessie wrenched open the door to the hospital and hurried inside. She stopped and held her hand to her bosom while she caught her breath. Looking down the corridor she hoped someone would appear who would know where Aaron was. She waited a few seconds but no one appeared.

Breathing heavily she walked down the aisle, listening for any sound that would tell her where he was. She passed several closed doors and then one opened and George Chapman came running out and nearly knocked her over.

He wasn‘t looking where he was going and so he didn’t immediately recognise her “Oh…ah sorry,” he stammered as he grabbed hold of her to stop her from falling. His eyes finally met hers. “Mrs Price.”

“Where’s Aaron?” she said without the usual formalities as her eyes searched his face. “Lieutenant Hamilton said he might die.” The words caught in her throat and she covered her mouth with the back of her hand. "Forgive me, Mr Chapman."

"Forgiveness is not necessary, Mrs Price. Your husband's badly hurt, but he's alive and in the care of Doctor Graham."

Relief flooded her at those words – he's alive. "And where is he, exactly."

"Aye. Well, down the hall here. Ye can't go in, but I'm sure Doctor Graham will not mind if ye wait. There's a couple of chairs in a small alcove on the left, Mrs Price. Ye can wait there."

"Thank you, Mr Chapman."

He nodded, and she continued to walk down the hall until she found the small alcove he'd mentioned. She was just about to sit down when the door opposite, where she presumed Aaron was being attended to, opened and Lieutenant Hamilton stepped out. He closed the door behind him and only then did he notice her.

"Mrs Price."

"Lieutenant. How's my husband?"

"Badly injured I'm afraid," he said removing his hat. "Doctor Graham is sewing his wound."

"He's alive though. Mr Chapman said he was."

"Aye." He took her by the arm and walked a couple of paces. "Mrs Price, the wound is serious and Doctor Graham fears he may be bleeding inside."

Tears welled in her eyes and an ache stretched across her throat. "But…he's alive."

"For now…I'm sorry I couldn't stop it from happening."

She drew in a deep breath and swallowed. "Who did this?"

Hamilton shook his head. "It's not important, Mrs Price. But, rest assured he's in gaol and will face the magistrate in due course."

"I would have his name."

He took a step back and put his hat on. "Truly that's not important."

"I would have his name, Lieutenant." Her voice rose by several octaves and ended on a shrill note. Her breast was heaving as she stood with her hands balled into fists and her eyes boring into Hamilton's.

He gave her a long look and finally nodded. "John Jackson. He'll hang for it."

***

Chapter 26

He's Alive

Jessie rung out the cloth and wiped the beads of perspiration from Aaron's forehead. She'd been sitting by his bedside for five days while fever raged through his body. She'd run out of tears and her prayers were all she had left.

She put the cloth back into the basin and sat down with her head in her hands. Surely today the fever would break. A moment later Aaron's eyes opened and he groaned as he reached for his bandaged stomach.

"Hush now," said Jessie leaping to her feet and pulling his hand away. "You've got a fever and you must leave your bandage."

His eyes rolled back in his head and he moaned again. "Water," he croaked as he closed his eyes again.

She reached for the mug of water and lifting his head put it to his lips. "Slowly."

She held him while he drank several sips and then gently put his head back against the pillow. She sighed as she placed the mug back on the side table. Jessie watched him for several minutes before sitting back down. She'd need to go soon. Mary was taking care of her children, but she needed to eat and take care of herself. Aaron would also need some broth when this fever finally broke. She glanced at him – surely it would be soon.

The door to the small room opened and Doctor Graham smiled as he entered. "How's our patient?"

"He's been awake and had some water," said Jessie shaking her head. "But he's no better."

"Hmm," said Doctor Graham examining Aaron. He pressed the back of his hand to his forehead before putting his stethoscope to his ears.

Jessie sat silently watching and hoping.

"Good news," he said removing the instrument and smiling at Jessie. "The fever's breaking and his heart's strong."

"Really?" said Jessie drawing in a deep breath. She could barely believe his words. "You're sure?"

"Aye. The beads of perspiration on his face are a good sign he's winning against the infection. I expect it'll break afore long." He patted her on the shoulder. "You should get some rest, Mrs Price. I'll send young Bobby in to watch him overnight."

"Thank you, Doctor."

Aaron's eyes opened and he grasped the Doctor's arm. "Will I live?" he said in a rasping voice.

Jessie saw the fear in his fevered eyes and tears welled in her own.

"Aye, Mr Price I believe you will." He removed Aaron's hand and smiled. "Rest."

She rose to her feet and kissed her husband's forehead. "I'll return in the morning. Do as the Doctor says and rest."

"Aye." His eyes closed and he drew in a shallow breath.

***

For the next two days, there was no change in Aaron's condition that Jessie could see. She doubted Doctor Graham knew what he was talking about. Her anxiety was growing with each step she took down the road towards the hospital. Was he even right about the wound? He'd said the blade had missed any vital organs and he was able to stop the internal bleeding – but did he? She groaned as she opened the door to the hospital; she hated the unknown.

She made her way down the hall to Aaron's room and paused with her hand on the knob. Drawing in a deep breath she opened the door and went in. Her eyes lit on Aaron who was reclining against the pillows. He opened his eyes and gave her a lopsided grin.

"Jess."

His voice was barely above a whisper but it was the most wonderful sound she'd ever heard. Tears came unbidden as she stared at him. "Aaron…oh my God." Two steps brought her to his bedside and she sat on the edge of the narrow bed and took his face in her hands. "Oh, Aaron." She kissed his forehead, which was cool and unfevered, before pressing her lips to his several times in quick succession. She drew in a breath and smiled. "How are you?" she said sitting back and feasting her eyes on him.

"Weak, but I'll live." He smiled as he reached his hand out and cupped her face. "Kiss me again."

She leant forward and kissed him, probing with her tongue until he opened himself to her. She drank him in – relishing the feel of his lips on hers. It had been too long since they'd kissed like this and she wished she could press herself to him and feel his solid form beneath her. When the kiss ended he gasped and drew in a deep breath.

She grinned. "Perhaps it was too soon."

"Perhaps." He took her hands in his and brought them up to his lips and kissed them. "I'm sorry, Jess."

"What?" She pulled her hands free and stared at him. "You've nothing to be sorry for."

"Aye I do," he said with a frown. "I know I've been withdrawn from ye since we got back from Sydney. I'm sorry and it will not happen again."

"Let's not talk about it," she said swallowing the lump in her throat. "I'm just so glad to have you back…considering we'll be having another baby in the autumn." She ran her hand across her stomach and smiled at the surprised look on his face.

"That's wonderful news, Jess…it gives me even more reason to get back on my feet."

"Good." She leant forward and brushed her lips briefly against his. "I love you so much."

The door opened and Doctor Graham came in. "Good morning, Mrs Price," he said with a smile. "As you can see your husband's much improved. I'm sure he'll make a full recovery in no time."

"Good morning," said Jessie standing and smoothing her skirt. "Yes, he's so much better. Thank you, Doctor."

He nodded before turning his attention to Aaron. "I'm discharging you into the care of your wife. Continue to rest and don't overdo it. That wound will need time to fully heal."

Aaron grinned and looked at Jessie who smiled in return. "That's wonderful news," said Jessie. "When will you send him home?"

"Today, just as soon as I can get a litter organised to take him."

"Thank ye," said Aaron.

"Well, I best get home and get ready for you," said Jessie kissing Aaron's forehead. "I've got lots to do."

He grinned and squeezed her hand. "Thank ye."

***

Jessie took one last look at the bedroom. The bed was freshly made with clean linen and she'd found some extra pillows for Aaron. It was all in readiness. She paused in the sitting room before heading out the back door. Matthew and Mark were down the yard with Henry, and she smiled at the sound of their happy voices. Mark would need to go down for a nap soon but she'd let him play a little longer.

She entered the kitchen and breathed in the aroma of fresh bread and vegetable soup. Lifting the pot lid she stirred the soup and smiled with satisfaction. Another hour and it would be ready. A fresh loaf of bread was cooling on the table and her stomach grumbled at the aroma.

She returned to the sitting room and paced up and down for several minutes before settling in her chair. She picked up her mending and did her best to distract her thoughts – without much success. She was so relieved that Aaron was going to be alright, but the whole incident had been so frightening. It made her realise how tenuous life was, even here on the island. She stabbed her needle into the shirt she was mending. Would they ever be truly safe? She jumped with fright at the knock on the door and tossing her mending aside leapt to her feet and wrenched open the door.

"Good afternoon," said Lieutenant Hamilton removing his hat. "We have your husband."

"Lieutenant," said Jessie peering passed him to see Aaron lying on a stretcher being carried by four men. "Please, come in." She stepped aside allowing the Lieutenant and the men carrying Aaron to enter. "This way," she said gesturing to the bedroom.

She followed them into the room and watched while they helped Aaron from the stretcher to the bed. He groaned as he lay down.

Jessie rushed to his side and pulled the covers over him. "Are you alright?"

He gasped and closed his eyes as he relaxed against the pillows. “I will be.”

She kissed his forehead. “I’ll be back in a minute.”

She followed the men from the room and arrived in the sitting room as they were heading out the front door. Lieutenant Hamilton closed the door behind them before turning to her.

“I trust your husband will recover,” he said looking towards the bedroom. He then turned back to Jessie and looked at her down his long nose. “I thought you’d like to know, Jackson’s been tried and found guilty of attempted murder.”

Jessie nodded. She was glad.

“He’s been sentenced to hang.”

She swallowed and licked her lips. “Thank you, Lieutenant.”

He nodded and opened the door. “I thought you’d like to know.”

“Yes.” She didn’t know what else to say. She was glad he was going to hang, but she wasn’t sure she wanted to know anything else. It didn’t matter when and she didn’t want to be there. The fact that he would hang was enough.

Lieutenant Hamilton stared at her as if he was trying to read her mind before finally bidding her good day.

She closed the door behind him and leaned against it. There was only one thing that truly mattered now – and that was getting Aaron back on his feet. She smiled as she went through to the bedroom – she was certain of one thing - she had her husband back in more ways than one.

***

Chapter 27

Thank Goodness

Aaron spent the next month recovering from his wounds, and Jessie watched as he grew stronger every day. He'd be back at work soon and that did scare her just a little. She snuggled into him and ran her fingers down his chest relishing in the feel of him beneath her fingers.

A soft moan escaped his lips and she smiled, pulling the covers aside so she could follow her fingers with kisses. He was warm and solid and she shivered as he ran his fingers down her spine. They hadn't been together for so long that Jessie almost felt feverish at his touch. She raised her head and looked into his eyes which were filled with desire.

She drew in a breath and kissed him. "I love you."

"Aye, I love ye too."

He wrapped his arms around her and she relaxed a little against his chest, well aware of the fresh scar on his abdomen. He pulled her closer and she stiffened. “I don’t want to hurt you.”

“Ye won’t.”

Smiling she threw her leg over him, straddling his hips and pressing her palms to his chest she lowered her face to his. “How’s this?”

She kissed him, softly at first and then firmer, demanding he respond to her. His tongue probed her mouth and she sucked softly drawing it in. His warm hands grasped her thighs and she felt the cool air as he lifted her shift. Breaking off the kiss she sat upright and pulled her nightshift over her head.

“Mmm I like the view from here,” he said grinning at her as he cupped her breasts and lifted his head to meet them.

Jessie moaned and arched her back in response to his attention. After a few moments, he reclined back on the pillows and ran his hands down her sides to her hips and she bent over him, her long honey-blonde hair forming a curtain around them. A long sigh escaped her lips when his fingers found her moist womanly cleft. Their bodies were ready and Jessie was impatient for their lovemaking to begin. Taking him between her fingers she eased herself onto him until he filled her. She groaned from sheer relief to finally have him inside her.

She thrilled at being on top and in control but was acutely aware of her husband's frailty and the nasty red scar on his side. Their lovemaking was slow at first as Jessie tentatively tried her new position, but soon enough they were both urgent in their need.

Later, she lay curled against Aaron with her head on his shoulder, feeling complete contentment. Right now, nothing could touch them. Aaron squeezed her and kissed the top of her head.

"Afore I fall asleep there's something I need to say," he said in a voice barely above a whisper but full of determination. "I know I've been denying there was anything wrong after what happened in Sydney, and ye know that wasn't true. I've been blaming myself, and rightly so, but I know now that's not important." He paused and Jessie drew in a breath "I promise ye, I'll always be here for ye, Jess. Never again will ye have to wonder if I still love ye or not." He kissed her forehead. "I'll love ye to the end of time."

She relaxed against him and let out her breath. She was glad he was no longer blaming anyone for what happened and overjoyed to have his solid form beside her. Neither of them would ever forget Mary. She tilted her head back and kissed his cheek. "It gladdens my heart to hear you'll not shut me out again." She pushed herself up on her elbow and stared down at him. "I'll hold you to that promise, Aaron Price."

He grinned and pushed her hair aside. "I expect ye will."

She lowered her lips to his and sealed his promise with a long slow kiss.

***

January 1846

Supper time was always a busy affair, and now that the children were older they ate supper with their father and her. It meant Aaron and she had less time for themselves, but he had more time with them, and they adored him.

"How's school?" said Aaron looking at Ellen.

"Good. I'm learning to read," she said with her fork poised ready to take another mouthful. "And I can write my name."

"That's wonderful," said Aaron smiling at his daughter.

Jessie ate her supper, enjoying the conversation between Aaron and the children.

"What about ye, Moses?" he said taking a mouthful of ale.

Moses shrugged.

"I can do numbers," said young Aaron unable to contain himself. "I'm better at them than Moses."

"Ye are not," said Moses glaring at his brother.

"Ah…so ye learning your numbers," said Aaron before taking another mouthful of his supper.

"Don't you dare do that, Mark," said Jessie who'd just noticed Mark was about to toss his plate on the floor. She scooped some vegetables onto his spoon and shoved it in his mouth. "Now eat."

Supper conversation continued to focus on the children and their schooling, which gave both Jessie and Aaron a chance to discover how their offspring were progressing in their studies. On the whole, Jessie was satisfied with the school. It was open five days a week under the supervision of one of the Superintendents with several prisoners acting as teachers. She'd been surprised to learn that quite a few prisoners were well-educated men.

After supper, Aaron joined Jessie in the kitchen. He didn't usually help with the dishes, and she raised a brow at him as he entered the small kitchen.

He picked up the tea towel and absently dried a plate. "Um…I have to warn ye there may be trouble."

Jessie stopped washing the dish in her hand and stared at him as her heart jumped into her throat. "For us?"

"Not specifically," he said shaking his head. "Major Childs's issued a proclamation, and I expect there'll be trouble. By public order, he's taken the prisoner's garden plots from them."

"Why would he do such a thing?" said Jessie her mouth agape.

The prisoners had so little, but their garden plots supplemented their meagre diet of beef and maize with sweet bucks and other vegetables. She could see no logical reason why he'd take them away. The prisoners worked in them on their own time – not that they had much of that – but still, it didn't cost the Government anything to let them have gardens.

"There's been unrest among the men for months now, and I think this is his way of asserting his power over them." He shrugged and put the tea towel down. "I don't want to scare ye, but I need ye to be on your guard when you're out and about – just in case."

She nodded. "Don't worry, I will be." She wiped her hands on the towel and turned to face him. "Is it safe for the children to go to school do you think? Should I keep them home?"

He shook his head. "I cannot think that the children would be harmed." He wrapped her in his arms and kissed her. "And I would not deprive them of it."

She smiled and buried her face in his shoulder, breathing in the familiar scent of him, of lye soap and the sea. She squeezed him close. She was sure they'd be safe – she and the children, but what about him? She pulled out of his embrace and looked up at him.

"I fear you're in more danger than us. Promise me you'll be careful."

"I'll do my best," he said smiling. "I doubt I'm in any more danger than usual." He kissed her again before releasing her. "But I'll take extra care."

For the next few weeks Jessie, along with the rest of the free population of Kingston were on edge. There were extra patrols by the soldiers and the whole feeling was one of waiting for something to happen. For the most part, Jessie did her best to put thoughts of unrest aside and go about her usual business, including her weekly visit to Mary Vowell's house.

Jessie glanced at her two youngest sons who were happily playing on the floor with Johnny Hutchins. She returned her attention to Mrs Drummond who had been saying something, and Jessie was now trying to catch up on the conversation.

Mrs Fletcher sighed and stopped clicking her knitting needles together. "I'm thinking it can't be too long before the man's replaced. He's made a complete botch of things."

Mrs Drummond smiled sweetly, but Jessie sensed she wasn't in agreement.

"Major Childs has done his best with what Captain Maconachie left him. Let's not forget what a mess he left behind."

Mary Vowell nodded her approval and rose to her feet. "I'll fetch us all some refreshments, ladies. Jessie, would ye like to assist me?"

"Of course," said Jessie putting her sewing aside.

She was relieved to have a break from the conversation and followed Mary out to the kitchen.

"I'll pour the tea," said Mary pushing the kettle back onto the hearth. "Fetch the cups and saucers will ye, Jess?"

Jessie nodded and proceeded to take the crockery from the dresser and put them on a tray. She sighed. "Do you think they'll replace the Major?"

"I expect so," said Mary filling the pot with tea leaves. She put the lid on the caddy and turned to face Jessie. "What else can they do? The prisoners are refusing to work, even after he promised them more rations of flour and peas to replace their lost gardens."

"I thought they'd gone back to work."

"Some have, but their resentment of the Major is so great I fear for the worst."

Jessie swallowed and stared at her friend. "You mean mutiny?"

"Aye. I've never known their insolence to be as bad as it is right now. Surely Aaron's told ye?"

"Yes he has," she said with a nod. "I just thought things would surely return to normal soon. What else can they do?"

"Well, something has to give, and it won't be Major Childs ye can be sure of that," said Mary as she poured the boiling water into the teapot. She placed the kettle back on the hearth and put the sugar bowl on the tray with the cups. "Come on, let's have a cup of tea. We'll feel better." She hugged Jessie briefly and kissed her cheek. "Don't worry. Your husband and mine will keep us safe."

***

Things didn't change over the coming months and Jessie felt like they were sitting on top of a powder keg that might go off at any moment. The prisoners hadn't done anything specific, but there was a general feeling of resentment and more and more of them refused to work. Floggings had become an almost daily occurrence.

Jessie's labour pains began on the morning of the twenty-second of May and she was grateful to Henry for fetching Mrs Fletcher. It was a comfort to have her by her side, even though it didn't seem that her baby was in a hurry to arrive. Her contractions didn't settle into a closely timed pattern for hours, and then all of a sudden her baby was coming. After one final push, she lay back on the bed in a lather of perspiration, panting and gasping for air.

"What is it, Mrs Fletcher? A boy or a girl?"

Mrs Fletcher smiled as the slippery bundle in her arms let out a loud wail. "A girl. Ye have a fine healthy daughter."

"Oh…a girl," said Jessie between drawing in large gulps of air. "I felt sure she would be another boy." She hadn't dared hope for another daughter - not after losing Mary last year.

Ten minutes later Mrs Fletcher placed the small bundle in her arms and she gazed at her for the first time. She was only a little thing with a wrinkled up face and a head covered in gold fuzz. Jessie kissed her and ran her finger under her chin. “I think you take after your Mamma…hello Jessie.”

***

Chapter 28

The Cooking Pot Saga

Aaron's heart was racing as he hurried up the road towards home. The worst was about to happen, he could feel it in his bones, and Childs the idiot had just pushed the prisoners beyond their tipping point – he was sure of it. Over recent months he'd increased their work hours and reduced their rations, but this last insult wouldn't go unanswered.

Aaron pushed open the front door and rushed inside. "Jess…Jess are ye there?" he called as he glanced around the sitting room. There was no sign of her and he'd taken two steps towards the back door when she appeared.

"Hush, what is it? I've just got Jessie down for a sleep."

"Sorry," he said drawing in a deep breath. "Lock the doors and stay inside. Are the children home from school yet?"

"Yes. They're out in the yard playing. What's happened?" she said searching his face.

"Nothing yet, but I fear it's about to. Childs the idiot has just posted a new proclamation – one I fear will tip them over the edge. He's confiscated their cooking kettles and pans and from now on they won't be getting individual rations."

Jessie stared open-mouthed and then seeming to come to her senses she nodded. "I'll go gather the children now. What will you do?"

"Wait and watch…and pray the soldiers can stop anything from happening before it starts." He kissed her and turning on his heel marched out the front door.

He was glad he'd have no part to play in confiscating their cooking pots but was acutely aware that he'd be expected to play his part in quelling any uprising. He was sure Jess would follow his instructions and lock herself and the children in the house. He'd done all he could. His work gang was working down at the Cascade docks and he made his way directly there– casting furtive glances over his shoulder from time to time.

The day ended without any disturbances and Aaron was relieved. That night he lay awake, listening for even the slightest sound of trouble. Jess was cradled in his arms, safe and secure while every muscle of his was tensed and ready to leap into action. He must've dozed off in the early hours and he woke with a fright as Jessie's weight left the bed.

He sat bolt upright and stared at her. "It's alright…Jessie's awake." She padded across the floor to the crib and lifted her daughter into her arms. She cradled her and cooed at her as she walked back to the bed and lowered herself onto it. "Go back to sleep, Aaron."

"No." He swung his legs over the side of the bed and ran his fingers through his hair. "I can't."

He fumbled for the tinder box and moments later the lamp sprang to life, spreading a soft glow around the room. He retrieved his breeches from the floor and hastily pulled them on before fastening his belt. He could feel Jessie's eyes boring into his back and he swung around. His daughter was making soft sucking noises and Jess was staring at him – her eyes wide with fear.

"Aaron you'll be careful won't you?" she whispered.

He drew in a breath and nodded. "Aye. I don't plan on getting myself in the middle of it if I can help it." He stood and grabbed his shirt from the back of the chair and shrugged into it. "Try not to worry, and keep the doors locked. Nothing may yet happen."

She grimaced. "I'll stay here, but you don't truly believe nothing will happen."

He leaned forward, placing his hands on the bed to support himself and kissed her. "No. I've seen mutiny here before and ye know the tension's been building. Still, it may not happen today."

She nodded and tilted her face towards him. He obliged by pressing his lips to hers again before pulling away and buttoning his shirt. "Lock the door behind me."

He slid open the top drawer of the tallboy and paused. His musket was lying there with a powder horn and a pouch of musket balls. He took them along with a long knife which he slipped into his belt. Grabbing his jacket and cap he walked from the bedroom without another word.

The chilly July air hit him as soon as he stepped outside. He welcomed it. He needed every sense to be alert this day. It was early yet – barely dawn and the men would no doubt still be at the barrack yard for morning prayer. Nothing would happen there. Aaron took his time as he walked down the road towards the barracks. He should mind his business and go out to the quarry, but if there was trouble, and he was almost sure there would be, he didn't want to find himself stuck on Nepean Island and not able to protect his family.

He didn't see any prisoners on his way to the military barracks. That gave him some comfort, although he expected the real trouble would start after muster when they went to get their breakfast. Their pots were confiscated last night and he thought their anger would hit boiling point this morning.

He reached the barracks and nearly ran into Captain Conran as he entered. "Ah…sorry, Captain, I didn't see ye in my haste."

He clicked his heels and bowed. "Mr Price."

Previous dealings with Conran had left Aaron with the impression he was a military man through and through. He was tall, with neatly trimmed whiskers and his dark hair pulled back in a queue. His deep-set eyes were alert and intelligent.

"Captain, I presume you're aware of the Commandant's latest proclamation," said Aaron removing his cap. "I'm concerned there may be trouble with the men this morning."

"Aye I'm aware of it, and ye can rest assured we'll deal swiftly with any troublemakers."

"Aye, I wouldn't expect any less of ye," said Aaron licking his lips. "It's just that perhaps it would be wise to post some extra men down at the lumber yard."

Conran drew in a breath and nodded. "You're a good Overseer, Mr Price, better than most, but I'll thank ye to go about ye business," he said with a tight smile.

Several thoughts went through Aaron's mind all at once. He could order the Captain to send men down to the lumber yard, but he thought better of it - he might be wrong. "Aye. Well, I just wanted to be sure that ye knew about it, Captain."

"I thank ye, Mr Price."

Aaron nodded and slapping his cap back on he left the barracks. He'd done all he could.

***

Patrick Hiney wasn't a nervous man by nature, but this morning he could feel the tension in the air, and the adrenalin pumping through his veins. He finished muster and scanned the sea of men assembled in the lumber yard. The Commandant's latest proclamation was pinned to the wall and a large crowd of men had gathered around it.

Several of them looked his way before breaking away from the main group and marching over to him. "What's the meaning of this, Hiney?" said the ringleader.

Patrick Hiney recognised him. He was known as Jackey Jackey by the men and Hiney knew him. He had a reputation for being a gentleman and having an even temperament.

"They've taken our bloody cooking pots. What are we supposed to do now?"

Hiney drew himself up to his full height. "Get ye bowl and get in line."

Jackey Jackey glared at him before retreating. Hiney gave him one final look before slipping from the yard. He hurried next door to the cookhouse and sighed with relief when he spied the overseer, Stephen Smith.

"Mr Smith, thank God I found ye. Trouble's brewing up at the yard."

"Morning Mr Hiney," he said looking alarmed. "To be expected I suppose."

"Aye. All well and good, but I fear they'll mutiny this time." His agitation was obvious as he glanced over his shoulder and back again at Smith. "Be on ye guard, Mr Smith."

"Aye, I will, thank ye."

With a final nod, Hiney turned and marched back to the yard where he found the prisoners in an even more agitated state. They were milling about and yelling their complaints to anyone who wanted to listen. Jackey Jackey was at the centre of it all and Hiney, drawing in a deep breath, approached him.

"Come now, Jackey get ye breakfast," he said in a cajoling tone. "The men will listen to ye."

Jackey Jackey glared at Hiney. "Not this time."

Before Hiney could say another word the men, as a whole raced from the yard with Jackey Jackey at the lead. "Wait," called Hiney. They paid him no heed and he watched them run up the road towards the barracks. “Shit,” he swore under his breath.

His heart was hammering in his chest as he stood there wondering what to do. He was unarmed and he doubted he could stop them even if he was armed. The minutes passed while he paced the yard in a state of indecision. To his amazement, they returned not ten minutes later armed with the cooking pots that had been confiscated the night before.

They set about lighting fires and preparing their breakfasts. Peace and calm was restored and Hiney breathed a sigh of relief. Giving the men one final look he left the yard to fetch the work gang overseers and constables. The men would be finished with their breakfast soon and the day’s normal routine would be restored. He would demand more constables be stationed at the lumber yard in the future.

Passing the gates he paused at the guard hut where Constable John Morris was on duty. “The men are having breakfast but be on ye guard – they’re still in a state.”

Morris looked towards the yard and spat on the ground. “I’m not worried about them buggers.”

Hiney was well aware of Morris's reputation among the prisoners, and perhaps he ought to worry. A man who was all too eager to hand out punishments should take care. The prisoners in their current state may take their revenge upon him.

"Suit yeself," said Hiney and he continued on to the military barracks.

***

The peace was broken when somebody yelled, "Come on, we'll kill the bastards."

The men needed no more encouragement as they began arming themselves with pieces of wood, pitch forks or whatever they could find.

"Now, men," said Jackey Jackey grabbing an axe. "I've made up my mind to bear this oppression no longer. But I'm for the gallows. Those who want to follow me – come on!"

Jackey's face was infused with rage as he charged towards the gate. He saw the look of horror on Morris's face as he swung his axe and struck him on the head with it. He fell to the ground and was immediately set upon with knives and sticks until he was dead. Adrenaline was pumping through Jackey's veins making him feel more alive than he had done in years. If he was going to hang, he'd make it worth their while.

He ran from the yard towards the cook house with at least sixty men at his back. He didn't blame the others for staying at the yard. He knew many of them were scared but he was beyond that. He saw Smith the overseer leaning against the porch of the cookhouse and raising his axe above his head he ran at him.

Smith straightened and stared aghast at Jackey Jackey. "For God's sake don't hurt me, Jackey!" He held up his hands in surrender. "Think of my wife and children."

"Damn your wife and children," said Jackey as he brought the axe down on his head.

Smith fell to the ground, senseless and Jackey stepped over him and went into the cookhouse. It was deserted and sneering he went back outside in time to see the others beating Smith. They hacked at him with knives and within minutes he was a mutilated corpse. Gathering the men together Jackey ran from the cookhouse and up the road to the barracks. They pushed aside a sentry and an overseer, intent on getting to Government House.

Passing the lime kiln Jackey forced open the door to the guard hut. He paused as he surveyed the interior. Two men were asleep – he knew them - bastards the pair of them. They were prisoners just like him who'd lagged on the lads and bettered their position. He raised his axe and brought it down onto the skull of Dinon – he thought he'd killed him with one stroke. He then turned to the other man, Saxton, who woke up seconds before he smashed the axe into his skull as well. He felt nothing, no pity no remorse – nothing. The bastard's deserved it.

***

Aaron glanced nervously in every direction as he walked down towards the barracks. It was quiet, too quiet. He expected to see the work gangs, supervised by the overseer's, to be on the road by now. He saw a lone man walking towards him and he stopped. As the man came closer he recognised him. It was Patrick Hiney, the Assistant Superintendent of Convicts.

"Good morning, Mr Hiney."

"Mr Price," he said with a nod. "There's trouble down at the lumber yard on account of the cooking pots. They went to the barracks and retrieved them."

Aaron rubbed his hand along his forehead. "I knew there'd be trouble. I've just come from the military barracks where I tried to convince Captain Conran to send the soldiers down to the yard."

"I plan on ordering him to send troops down there, just to be sure."

"I'll join ye if ye don't mind."

"I don't mind at all, Mr Price. I welcome your support."

The two hurried back up the road to the military barracks. Aaron was sorry he hadn't ordered the Captain himself now that he knew for sure that the men had broken the Commandant's proclamation. He prayed they wouldn't be too late with a show of force to settle the prisoners down.

Mr Hiney opened the door and the two went inside. Patrick Hiney marched down the corridor, looking left and right, followed by Aaron. They found Captain Conran at the end of the corridor and he glanced first at Hiney and then at Aaron.

"Captain, get your men down to the lumber yard," said Patrick Hiney without preamble. "The prisoners have stolen the pots back and ignored Major Childs's proclamation."

The Captain, who had been reclining in a chair jumped to his feet. "How many?"

"All of them," said Hiney in an exasperated tone. "There's no time to lose, Captain. They were a bit calmer when I left them, but there's no telling what they'll do next."

"Aye." He put his hat on his head as he hurried down the hallway. "Corporal Higgins," he bellowed as he went.

A young man, no more than twenty appeared in the hall. "Aye, Captain."

"Gather twenty of our best men. I want them armed with muskets and bayonets. Go."

"Aye, Captain," he said again as he ran out into the yard yelling for men.

The door to the barracks opened and Overseer Henry Miller ran inside. He was gasping for breath and his eyes were bulging. He caught sight of Captain Conran and fell to his knees. "They've killed Stephen Smith and several guards. They're on their way here – and to Government House."

Aaron's heart leapt into his throat and started hammering like a mad thing. So it had happened. All because that idiot Childs thought to deprive them of cooking pots of all things.

"How many?" said Captain Conran bending down to talk to Miller. "How many are coming?"

He shook his head. "I don't know – maybe fifty or so. They're armed with knives and pitchforks and such."

"They'll be no match for us," he said straightening.

Glancing out into the yard he bellowed again for Corporal Higgins who arrived moments later accompanied by twenty soldiers.

"Good. Form a line and have your muskets primed and ready to fire." He marched out the door followed by his men.

Aaron paused for a brief moment before he followed the soldiers out into the street. He had no intention of joining their numbers, he was confident the Captain could deal with the mutineers. But he intended to be behind them, ready to fire if the need arose.

Under Captain Conran's direction, his men formed a double line of defence across the road. The prisoners would have no choice but to engage the soldiers if they hoped to reach Government House. Aaron's heart was thumping and adrenalin was coursing through him as he took up a position behind the soldiers.

He kept his eyes planted firmly on the road leading up from the convict barracks and didn't have to wait long before the mutineers came into view. They were rushing up the road in a rough formation and he could see they were waving makeshift weapons. He licked his lips and shifted his gaze to Captain Conran. He was marching up and down behind his men, stopping occasionally to speak to one.

The prisoners, at least sixty came to a halt, and Aaron was surprised to see Jackey Jackey leading them. He'd always been rather mild-mannered but it was clear he was the ringleader. The soldiers raised their muskets, ready to fire on the Captain's command, and the mutineers appeared to falter. Their bravado quickly faded in the face of musket fire and they retreated.

Captain Conran wasted no time in pursuing them. “Formation,” he yelled as he marched out in front of his men. “March.”

Aaron watched as the soldiers quickly formed three columns and went in pursuit of the prisoners. He waited until they were out of sight before he started down the road for home. Conran would no doubt round up the mutineers and put an end to their riot. He needed to see Jess. Needed to reassure himself that she was safe and that no harm had come to her.

***

Chapter 29

Magistrate John Price

Sixty murderous rioters were rounded up by Captain Conran and secured in the boat shed. The gaol wasn't large enough to hold them, and as the new gaol was still under construction he had little choice. It wasn't ideal, but each prisoner was in leg irons and chained together and then secured to the wall of the shed. This very fact had eased Jessie's fears, but with news that they'd removed stones from the walls and attempted to break out had left her feeling nervous and on edge.

"They'll not escape," said Aaron pulling her into his arms. "Ye need not worry."

Jessie put her head on his shoulder and melted against him. His solid form beneath her fingers gave her strength and reassurance. She pulled out of his arms so she could look into his face. "You truly believe they won't?"

"I do," he said kissing her briefly. "And a commission to investigate the uprising has already commenced. Lieutenant Hamilton, Major Harold and Mr Barrow are gathering evidence and questioning witnesses. They'll be tried in coming weeks and dealt with."

"It cannot happen fast enough," she said and a shudder went down her spine. She didn't wish for men to be hung but she would be glad when it was done. She smiled and stood on tip toes as she pressed her lips to his. "I'm just so glad you weren't involved this time."

"Aye, so am I," he said releasing her and slapping his cap on his head. "I must to work. I'll be home in time to have supper with the children." He gave her a peck on the cheek.

As soon as he was gone Jessie turned her thoughts to the day ahead. She put baby Jessie in the pram and sat Mark on the seat. Four-year-old Matthew was more than capable of walking. Ellen gave her an odd look as they set off down the road while the three boys raced ahead without a care.

"Why are ye taking us to school today?" she enquired, her nut-brown pigtails swinging in the breeze.

"Well, I'm going visiting, so I thought I'd walk with you," said Jessie smiling. She hoped her tone was casual enough that she wouldn't question her further.

"Hmm," she said turning her blue eyes on her. "Who are ye visiting?"

"Mrs Vowell."

"Oh."

Jessie was relieved that her daughter's interrogation was at an end. She hadn't actually intended to visit Mary this morning, but after dropping the three eldest children off at school she thought better of it. She could do with a cup of tea and some company.

Mary welcomed her in with open arms. "I'm so glad ye decided to drop by. I've been wanting to ask ye about Aaron. He wasn't hurt in all that was he?"

"No, no," said Jessie with a shake of her head. "He was hardly involved at all and he hasn't been called to give evidence."

"Well that's a relief," said Mary pouring them both a cup of tea. "I'm wondering how long it'll take to replace Childs. The man's made a right mess of things."

"That he has, but news of the uprising won't have reached them in Hobart Town yet, so I expect it'll be a while before they replace him." Jessie took a sip of tea and sighed as the hot sweet liquid ran down her throat easing the tension as it went.

"Hmm, you're probably right. I'm just thankful Magistrate Barrow's in charge of the trials. He won't spare them the noose that's for sure."

Jessie grimaced. She didn't like to think of those men being hung, although she was in agreement with Mary, and was glad Mr Barrow was in charge. He didn't shy away from handing out punishment. "No, he won't. Let's talk about something else, Mary."

Mary raised a brow and looked at her enquiringly. "Good Lord, Jess the whole settlement's talking of nothing else but the uprising. I haven't got any other gossip to share."

She looked slightly affronted and Jessie hurried to explain herself. "I'm sorry, Mary. It's just that I've been rather scared. You know they tried to escape."

Reaching out Mary grabbed her arm - she smiled and squeezed. "I know. I'm sorry,

I forgot that your Aaron was in the thick of it. Of course, you've been scared." She sat back in her chair and sipped her tea. "I heard they've been behaving like animals down there in the boat shed."

Jessie was relieved her friend understood. "I heard the same. I wish they'd hurry up and get the trials over with."

Jessie finished her tea and bid Mary a good day. She was anxious to be home and doing her normal chores. Matthew ran ahead, picking up stones and tossing them. She called him back and he stopped and grinned – waiting patiently for her to catch up to him. She was thankful he was an obedient child, unlike the twins.

In the following days, Mr Barrow held preliminary trials of the men imprisoned in the boat shed. The main perpetrators were reduced to twenty-seven in number and they were transferred to the gaol. Jessie was more relieved than she thought she'd be.

It seemed their usual quiet life on the island would be in a state for some time yet. A week later the brig Governor Phillip arrived from Hobart Town with news that Major Childs had been replaced. The new Commandant, John Price would arrive on board the Lady Franklin the following week with his wife and family. Jessie was surprised – he'd obviously been replaced even before the riots had taken place. Of course, there were letters too which she put aside until she had a quiet moment to enjoy them.

"Do you know anything about this man?" asked Jessie quirking a brow upwards.

Aaron shook his head. "Not really. He's not military so it's hard to know what to expect." Aaron paused and sipped his wine. "He's a wife and children from what I understand."

"And they're accompanying him?" Not all the civil superintendents brought their wives and families with them. Thomas Sellers' wife still remained in Sydney, and he'd been the Foreman of Works for a number of years. She visited him several times a year, but Jessie didn't think that was any way to run a marriage.

Aaron had put a mouthful of his supper in his mouth and he hastily chewed. "I think so," he mumbled as he reached for his wine again. "At any rate, he cannot possibly do a worse job than Major Childs."

Jessie nodded as she chewed her supper. Aaron was right he couldn't do a worse job. But a civil man was an unknown quantity and she couldn't help but be concerned. She swallowed and sipped her wine. "Well, I hope he can bring order back to the island without pushing the prisoners to their limit."

"Aye, so do I."

***

The inhabitants of Kingston were in a state of jubilation when news spread that sails had been spotted on the horizon. It was no doubt the Lady Franklin with the new Commandant on board. Jessie found herself humming happily as she went about her chores. Surely all the strife and trouble was behind them now and life would soon return to normal.

Two days later the Lady Franklin dropped anchor and Mr John Price along with his wife and five children stepped foot on the island. Jessie left Matthew and Mark at home under Henry's care and with Jessie in the pram she went down to the Cascades. She joined the throng of people who had come to greet the new Commandant. There were soldiers everywhere and Jessie recognised Lieutenant Hamilton and Tom Sellers amongst the official greeting party.

Mary Vowell sidled up beside Jessie and looped her arm in hers. "I've never known a new Commandant to get such a reception."

Mrs Fletcher and Mrs Drummond accompanied her and greeted Jessie as the four women formed a small cluster. "Neither have I," said Jessie smiling.

"Everyone's desperate to be reassured," said Mrs Fletcher pulling her shawl tight around her shoulders. "I just pray he can get the place under control."

"He will I'm sure," said Mary with a confident smile. "He's recently been the Police Magistrate in Hobart Town. I expect he'll have a firm hand, but fair."

Jessie hoped she was right. She watched as he was greeted by the official party. He wasn't a large man - in fact, Jessie thought he was rather short. His dark wavy hair blended with bushy side whiskers. He had a hook nose that didn't detract from a rather kind-looking face. His wife was short and plump and surrounded by five children, the youngest only looked to be about two years old.

Another large man accompanied him who Jessie overheard him introduce as Judge Burgess. She swallowed. There could only be one reason a Judge would accompany him.

Mary nudged her. “Did ye hear that? He’s a Judge.”

“Yes,” whispered Jessie with a nod. “It would seem they’ll hold the trials here.”

“And the hangings,” quipped Mrs Fletcher with a smile.

Jessie shuddered. She didn’t share Mrs Fletcher’s delight in hangings and floggings. The women waited until the new Commandant and the officials had started for Kingston before they followed.

“Will ye come for tea?” asked Mary as they neared the settlement.

“No,” said Jessie with a shake of her head. “I best get back. I’ve left Matthew and Mark with Henry.”

Mary hugged her and kissed her cheek. “Well, until Wednesday then.”

"Yes." Jessie hugged her in return and sighed when they parted. Mary was such a good friend.

***

Chapter 30

August 1846

No sooner had the trials begun than they ended with Judge Burgess taking ill. There was some fear that the illness would prove fatal, and so ten days later he returned to Hobart Town on board the Lady Franklin. Justice would have to wait until another Judge could be despatched.

Major Childs sailed for Sydney on board the Mary at the end of August, on his way back to England. Aaron doubted anyone was sad to see him go. However, the new Commandant's rule was felt almost immediately, as he implemented a range of new restrictions. It was obvious from the start he intended to rule with an iron fist. In the wake of the recent uprising, Aaron couldn't entirely blame him for his hard stance.

Aaron stepped from the launch onto the landing on Nepean Island and stretched. He began the short walk to the quarry with a myriad of thoughts going around in his head. He had to get a good load of stone to the mainland this week for the new gaol. Tom Sellers was hounding him for it. He was also anxious for his family right now. Jessie had been terrified by the uprising and was still loath to let the children out of her sight.

As soon as he arrived at the quarry he was accosted by Lieutenant Hamilton. He looked down his long nose and grimaced. “A private word if you would,” he said gesturing to him to step into the work hut.

Aaron nodded and complied although he frowned as he entered. It was unlike Hamilton to require a private word with him. Anything they had to discuss involved the quarry and the work gangs and there were no secrets to be had in that.

Hamilton closed the door and cleared his throat. “I’ll get straight to the matter at hand. Certain allegations have been levelled against you and several other persons by Henry Pasley.”

Aaron’s eyebrows raised in surprise which he didn’t try to hide. “What sort of allegations?”

“Lieutenant Pasley alleges that you’ve been profiting from selling stores to the prisoners.” He paused and drew in a breath. "He particularly accuses you of profiting from tobacco."

Aaron stared at Hamilton as he tried to fathom where such an accusation would come from. He shook his head. "I deny it absolutely." He barely knew Pasley but he'd certainly had dealings with him. Dealings that he suspected had ruffled the man's pride.

"I thought you might, but you can expect to be investigated," he said running his finger down his nose. "I thought you'd like to know. And for the record, I believe these are baseless allegations."

"Thank ye, Lieutenant, I appreciate your confidence in me."

"I've known you a long time, and I believe I have the calibre of the man you are." He opened the door and gestured to Aaron to go before him. "Be on your guard."

Aaron drew in a deep breath as he stepped out of the hut. It was the last thing he'd expected or needed. He had every hope of gaining the trust of the new Commandant, but not if he was being investigated for impropriety. He would indeed be on his guard in future dealings with the soldiers. He was confident there was no evidence to support such claims, and he was also convinced this was a case of sour grapes. The soldiers didn't like the fact that they took orders from overseers such as him, who they saw as inferior.

He pushed all thoughts of Pasley aside as he turned his attention to the consignment of stone that he needed to get loaded onto the punt.

***

Towards the end of September Judge Fielding Browne arrived on the island. He wasted no time in conducting trials of the men involved in the uprising. The number to be tried for murder and aiding and abetting murder was reduced to twelve. A temporary courthouse was set up in the prisoner's barracks, with a jury made up of seven military officers. It seemed the entire settlement was waiting with bated breath for the verdict to be handed down.

It was a sunny October morning, and Aaron eyed the newly erected scaffold outside the new gaol. He would be glad when the executions were over and done with. Surely then, life could return to some level of normalcy. Although, hanging over his head was the investigation into his profiteering. He had no idea if the matter had yet been investigated, and for the most part, put it out of his mind.

He watched as the condemned men were marched out of the old gaol and assembled before Commandant Price, the soldiers and those present. The first six were taken in chains to the scaffold and a noose put around their necks. A few words were said and with a loud clunk the trapdoors were sprung and the six men were launched into oblivion. Aaron's stomach churned and he swallowed the rising bile in the back of his throat.

They were left to hang for several minutes before being cut down and six fresh nooses fixed to the scaffold. With the trapdoors reset the next six men were led to the scaffold. Aaron grimaced as the lever was pulled and they swung freely from their necks. It was over and he hoped he'd never be required to attend another hanging.

He waited until the men were cut down and those gathered began to disperse before putting on his cap and walking purposefully from the gaol yard. He was determined to get out to the quarry and get some work done. He was near the gate when someone called out to him. He turned and waited while a young red-faced Private hurried towards him.

"You're Overseer Price? Mr Price wants a word with ye," he said gasping for air. "In the Foreman's office."

"Now?"

"Aye," he replied nodding.

Aaron nodded and swore under his breath. It was odd that he wanted to speak to him in the Foreman's Office, but he started walking in that direction. At least it was on the way to the pier. He was thankful he had a few minutes to think about what he was going to say in his defence. Surely, there was no evidence and Mr Price would see that. His heart was thumping against his ribs as he opened the door to the Foreman's Office and went inside. He stopped and stared around the room in surprise.

There were at least two dozen men there, who all turned and looked at him as he entered. He took a few steps and found an empty spot to stand beside the wall. He recognised most of them – they were all Overseers or Principal Overseers like himself. So, whatever this was about it wasn't about the profiteering allegations. At least he didn't think so.

He shifted his weight from one foot to the other while he waited. In the ensuing ten minutes, several more Overseers arrived, but it was a good fifteen minutes before Mr Price finally made an appearance. He strode across the crowded room and took up his position on the other side of Tom Seller's desk. The room fell silent almost immediately.

"Good morning, gentlemen, and thank you for taking time out of your day." His eyes moved slowly from man to man, seeming to take them all in with his gaze. He grimaced. "You're all well aware of the recent uprising and it falls to me to ensure that it never happens again. I intend to handle the prisoners with a firm but fair hand, and you are my deputies."

He paused and pressed the palms of his hands down firmly on the desk, leaning forward slightly he pierced each of them with a steady eye.

"To that end, I expect every misdemeanour no matter how minor to be reported. It's not your job to decide if a prisoner deserves punishment only if they have transgressed. This includes insolence, refusing to work, being late, lazy or not keeping their huts in order.

"I don't expect you to take time out of your day to deal with these matters. Soldiers will be posted with every work gang and will ensure such prisoners are escorted to gaol for examination."

He straightened and putting his hands behind his back paced up and down behind the desk. He stopped and turned to face them again. "With your help, gentlemen, we will soon have this settlement in order." He smiled and nodded. "Thank you." Giving them all one final look he marched across the room and out the door.

Aaron let the breath go that he hadn't realised he was holding. So, they were to be spies for the Commandant. He'd seen many Commandants in his years on the island and in his opinion, Maconachie had been one of the best. Treating the prisoners like animals would only result in them behaving like animals. Maconachie had treated them with fairness and given them a chance to better their situation.

As he left the hut he couldn't help but be thankful he had a ticket – but would that be enough? He was yet to receive an answer from Hobart Town on his request for a pardon. As long as there was no reply there was hope that it would be forthcoming. If he lost his ticket for some transgression like profiteering he could find himself back amongst the prisoner population and that scared him more than anything. He paused and drew in a deep breath as he tried to still his racing heart. His situation all of sudden seemed precarious at best.

***

Chapter 31

The New Regime

Jessie snuggled closer to Aaron, wrapping herself around him. She lay there listening to his rhythmic breathing, feeling his chest rise and fall steadily. His solidness beside her gave her reassurance that she was safe and secure. She wondered if he felt the same in her arms. The last few months had been difficult for him, she knew that. Mr Price's directives had become extreme in recent times and Aaron had struggled with that.

She knew he didn't want to see men chained to the triangle and flogged in the gaol yard. It had become a daily occurrence and while even she thought the island needed to be purged after the uprising, there seemed to be no end to it. Aaron had told her that on some days the yard ran red with men's blood – she shuddered at the thought.

She squeezed him gently and pressed her lips to his bare shoulder. Fear was a strange bedfellow and one that she didn't like, but until Aaron was granted his freedom it would be with them. It had seeped into every corner of their lives and into the crevices and quiet places like an unwelcome guest.

Aaron stirred and opened his eyes. He smiled when they lit on her – rolling over he gathered her close and breathed in. “Are ye alright my love?”

“Yes,” she whispered burying herself into him. “I just can’t sleep.”

“Hm.”

He ran his hand down her spine and stopped on her hip momentarily before moving it back up to her shoulder. She could feel it warm through the thin cotton nightshift and she sighed.

“Why can’t ye sleep?”

She pulled her head out from his shoulder and looked at him. In the early morning light, she could see his eyes were half closed but a crease on his brow told her he was awake and concerned. “I’m uncertain is all.”

“Aye…I know how ye feel.” He kissed her briefly. “Ye need not fear, Jess…we’re safe, nothing will happen.”

“What about Pasley? That matter’s not yet settled and it scares me.”

He opened his eyes and they locked with hers – full of love and fierce protection. “It will come to naught. In the meantime, I’m doing all I can to prove myself invaluable to Mr Price, just in case.”

She shuddered and he gathered her hard up against him and kissed the top of her head. She drew in a deep breath and pulled from his tight embrace so she could once again see his face. “Be careful, do not lose yourself, Aaron.”

He smiled. “I won’t.”

He kissed her again, passionately this time and she pressed herself against him, feeling the whole length of him, hard and solid against her. Their lovemaking was slow and tender and erased all other thoughts. She fell asleep curled up against him.

When she awoke again he was gone. She stretched and ran her hand over the indentation and felt the coolness of the linen. He’d been gone for a while. Jessie’s mewing sounds reached her ears and she sighed as she swung her legs over the side of the bed. No sooner had she stood up than her stomach contracted and retching she raced to the basin. She wiped her mouth with the back of her hand and straightened, sucking in a large lungful of air. Well, that confirmed it, she was expecting again. She ran her hand over her stomach and smiled – they were definitely going to have to put another room on the house.

***

January 1847

Eight-month-old Jessie was a chubby cherubic baby. Her honey-gold hair was thin and wispy still, but it curled around her ears making her appear pixie-like. Jessie tied a bonnet on her head and lifted her into the pram. Leaving Matthew and Mark under Henry's watchful eye she headed for the Foreman's Office and the Commissariat Store. She had a list of supplies they needed, and she hoped to speak with Tom Sellers about adding another bedroom onto the house.

It was a warm morning with the promise of getting hotter by the afternoon. She was anxious to get all her messages done before the day heated up. She was just leaving the Commissariat after depositing her list with Mr Forster when she saw Mrs

Price coming towards her. She had hold of a young girl by the hand and she smiled at Jessie, inclining her head in greeting.

"Good morning, Mrs Price," said Jessie coming to a halt and smiling widely. "How nice to see you." Jessie had been introduced to the Commandant's wife several months ago but had only had one or two brief conversations with her since. "And who's this little one?"

"This is Emily. Say hello to Mrs Price," she said urging her daughter forward with a prod between her shoulder blades.

"Hello, Emily. What a pretty name," said Jessie bending down until she was eye-to-eye with the little girl. She was a pretty thing with big brown eyes and a riot of curls.

"Hello," she said in a sweet voice.

Mrs Price smiled. "I must say, your husband is proving to be a godsend. John's mentioned him more than once as being one of the most reliable men at his disposal."

"Oh, well I'm so pleased that he's proven so useful," said Jessie with a continued smile on her face. She hoped Mrs Price couldn't read her. Aaron only did enough to keep the Commandant satisfied and turned a blind eye to any transgressions that he didn't consider grave.

"I worry so much about John. He's in a most difficult position, and the decisions he has to make have given him many sleepless nights. He truly hates the many floggings. I wish the prisoners would just behave in a proper fashion." She took a step closer to Jessie and put her hand on her arm. "I'm so glad you and your husband can be relied upon. It gives me great comfort."

Jessie swallowed and gripped the handle of the pram until her knuckles shone white. "I'm so pleased, Mrs Price. If there's anything further I can do, please you must call upon me."

"You're too kind. Well, good day, Mrs Price."

"Good day," said Jessie.

She waited until Mrs Price had disappeared into the Commissiart before she continued walking down the road. She felt rather weak at the knees as she headed for the Foreman's Office. They were at the mercy of the Price's and she prayed they could stay in their good graces until Aaron received his pardon. And then what? She had no idea and didn't want to think about it.

She hurried down to the Foreman's Office and parked the pram in the shade outside before going inside. She satisfied herself by keeping an eye on Jessie through the window. Tom Sellers looked up at her from behind his desk and smiled.

"Good morning, Jessie. How can I help ye?"

"Hello, Tom. I had asked Aaron to speak with you, but he's been so busy," she said eyeing him. He looked rather harassed and she wondered if she should perhaps come back another time.

"Aye, we've all been put upon lately. What seems to be the problem?"

"Well, it's about our house," she said tentatively. "Our family's growing and I was wondering if we might be able to add another room. It's awfully small."

He drew in a breath and nodded. "I understand. How long have ye been in that house?"

"Since we were married." She walked to the window and looked out, before turning back to Tom. "So, about nine years."

"Hrm, well we might be able to do something. Leave it with me, Jessie."

"Thank you."

He gave her a brief smile before going back to his ledgers. Jessie drew in a breath and slowly let it out. She doubted he'd be successful in getting permission for them to add to the house. Perhaps she should've raised the subject with Mrs Price? It was too late now.

She left and slowly made her way back home. She was rather dissatisfied with her morning out, and not at all confident in the outcome. She was also a bit nervous about her conversation with Mrs Price. She'd prefer not to have come to the attention of Mrs Price for fear that she would say the wrong thing. If she had already done so, well it was too late.

***

Chapter 32

1847

Aaron stretched as he climbed from the launch onto the pier. It had been a trying day and he'd had no choice but to report Lawson for insolence. If Private Hickey hadn't witnessed it he could've dealt with Lawson himself. As it was, Lawson would no doubt find himself chained to the triangle and flogged in the coming days. His own back flinched at the very thought.

He knew he wasn't the only one finding Price's rule unforgiving, but there were others who he knew found pleasure in the misery of others. Sadists perhaps, although he suspected they just liked to see others suffer as they'd once done. He did his best to push further thoughts of Lawson aside as he made his way to the forge.

He found the Smith as he was finishing for the day and dropped his bag onto the workbench. The Smith was a thin wiry man with a weathered face and he sauntered over to Aaron with an inquisitive look. Aaron couldn't recall the man's name – everyone just called him Smithy.

"What's this then?"

"Chisels," said Aaron upturning the bag and tipping its contents onto the bench. "I need them sharpened as soon as ye can."

"Aye," he said picking one up and inspecting it. "Give me a day or two."

"Thank ye. I'll call back for them on Thursday then." He turned to leave, and that's when he noticed a steel cage large enough to fit over a man's head. He stared at it before walking over for a closer look. "What's this ye making?"

"A special order for the Commandant," he said wandering over to join Aaron. "He wants some sort of contraption to stop a man from speaking."

Aaron licked his lips as he studied the thing. It was a metal cage with a leather strap that would go under a man's chin, but it was the prongs screwed to the side of it that made his blood run cold.

"The prongs there will hold the tongue ye see." Smithy demonstrated by turning the prongs until they almost met in the middle acting like a pincer. "It's not finished yet, I've still got a few bits to work out."

Smithy appeared nonplussed by the tortuous device he was making which shook Aaron to the core. "Aye," he managed to say as he stepped away from the ghastly thing. He sucked in a deep breath and turned his gaze back to Smithy. "Until Thursday then."

The sun was setting as he left the forge and headed for home. The image of the metal cage and prongs was seared into his brain and he couldn't get it out of his mind. Surely Price had lost all sense of propriety to be imagining such a device to be used as punishment. It scared him – that and the realisation that there wasn't anything he could do. They were all at the mercy of Price.

Jessie greeted him with a warm smile and a passionate kiss. "Ellen's spending the night at Hannah Vowell's, and the twins have not yet returned from their frog hunt. Matthew, Mark and Jessie are all abed. So," she said wrapping her arms around his neck, "we can enjoy a quiet supper just the two of us, and…" She pulled from his arms and picked up a creamy envelope from the sideboard. "This came for you today…it's from Hobart Town. The Lady Franklin lay anchor this morning."

He took the envelope and turned it over in his hands. Was it what he thought it was? Did he hold his freedom in his hands? His heart started hammering at the mere thought of it.

"Come," she said taking him by the hand. "Let's open that over supper."

He let her lead him out to the kitchen where the aroma of roast beef filled the air and his stomach grumbled.

"Sit." She poured two glasses of red wine and put them on the table along with what was left in the bottle. "Open it, I cannot wait another minute to hear what it says."

"Aye."

He sat at the table and gulped down half a glass of wine before slitting the envelope open. His eyes first scanned the bottom of the letter – it was signed Robert Pringle Stewart, Magistrate. That wasn't what he'd been expecting, and this wasn't from the Convict Department. His eyes returned to the top of the letter.

I write to inform you that I have completed my report into the accusations made by Lieutenant Henry Pasley and that no further action will be undertaken.

He tossed the letter aside.

"What is it?" said Jessie putting his supper down in front of him. She reached for the letter and perused it as she sat down. "Oh, well that's a relief but not what I thought it was."

"No. Not what we were hoping for." He sighed and ran his fingers through his hair. "It's been two years for God's sake. I can only think my appeal has been forgotten."

She folded the letter and slipped it back into the envelope before taking a large mouthful of wine. "We can't lose hope." She reached across the table and took his hand in hers. "Anyway, are we not happy here?" She picked up her cutlery and sliced off some beef and popped it into her mouth.

Aaron watched her for a moment before diving into his supper. She hadn't seen what he'd seen and without a pardon what guarantee did he have that he would not be plunged back into the hell hole? He needed that pardon, now more than ever.

***

Over the next few weeks, an uneasy feeling settled on Aaron that he couldn't shake. Price's regime was creating mistrust even among the Overseers and while he knew he could trust Hamilton, he thought his loyalties lay with Price. He was distracted and was therefore surprised when a Private who he recognised as being a clerk for Price called out to him to wait.

He stopped and waited for him to reach him. "Good morning."

"Good morning, Private Wilson at yer service," he said doffing his hat. "Mr Price requires your attendance in his office in the barracks."

"Aye…I'll go directly then."

"Aye," he said doffing his hat again. "Good day, Mr Price."

Private Wilson continued on his way and Aaron turned in the direction of the barracks. An audience with Mr Price didn't bode well – he presumed it would be another mass meeting and Price would be handing out further orders. What more he could expect of them he didn't know and only hoped he could continue to make him believe he was following his orders to the letter.

He entered the barracks and without delay knocked on the Commandant's office door. He was surprised to hear Price's muffled command for him to enter. Removing his cap he opened the door and entered. He glanced quickly around the room which was empty except for Price who was sitting behind his desk. He looked up before smiling and gesturing to Aaron to sit down.

"Thank you so much for joining me, Mr Price," he said leaning his elbows on his desk and pushing the tips of his fingers together.

"How can I help ye?"

He smiled, which didn't quite reach his eyes and sat back in his chair. "Straight to the point…very well. There's a man assigned to one of your gangs – Daniel Smith. Do you know who I mean?"

"I do."

"I gave him the opportunity to spy for me and to better his position, which he refused."

Aaron nodded. He'd suspected Price had spies amongst the prisoners but was still surprised to hear it was true. "Perhaps ye could choose another?"

"Indeed, but that is hardly the point now is it?" He leaned forward on his elbows again and pinned Aaron with a cold stare. "I want you to break him. You understand?"

"Aye." He swallowed as his breath quickened and his heart started thumping.

"Good." He smiled with satisfaction and relaxed back in his chair again. "I expect you to report him for even the most minor infringement and leave the rest to me. I don't even mind if you lie about it, just so long as he comes to heel."

Aaron felt sick but managed a tight smile. "Leave it to me, Mr Price."

"Excellent, and please pass on my regards to your wife," he said rising to his feet.

Aaron stood up and inclined his head. "Aye, thank ye."

He left the barracks and wandered down the road in a bit of a daze as he replayed the conversation with Price over in his mind. How the hell was he going to live with himself if he did as the Commandant wanted? But how could he disobey? *Shit*…he made his way down to the beach and walked along to the black rock. He hadn't been here in a long while and he moved between the rocks until he came to the sheltered nook. He eased himself down, pulled off his cap and put his head on his knees.

A small voice in the back of his head whispered to him *you've lagged before – you did it to drag yourself out of the pits of hell, but you did it at the expense of others*. His head snapped up with a jolt at the memory of it.

He'd been a prisoner on the island for a few years, and both of his old bushranging mates were gone. Paddy was dead and Lawrie had been sent to Cockatoo Island and he knew he'd be next if he didn't do something. It started off as almost unnoticeable. A word to an Overseer here and a comment there, nothing too serious, and then he'd fully snitched on Tommy Watkins.

They'd been working on building the new barracks. It was tedious work but not arduous. Aaron settled the next stone in place and tapped it with his hammer until he was satisfied. He straightened and stretched and his eyes just happened to light on Tommy Watkins as he disappeared through the bushes.

His eyes narrowed as he glanced left and right before making his way over to the spot where he'd disappeared. There was no sign of him – so he hadn't gone to relieve himself. Surveying where the Overseer and the soldiers were; he waited until he thought he'd be unnoticed before slipping through the bushes after him. He went a few paces before he stopped and scanned up ahead for any sign of Watkins. A moment later he spied him, gathering cherry guava from a laden tree as fast as he could.

Aaron hurried back to the building site and stepped from behind the bushes without being noticed. He was about to cross the line and he drew in a deep breath. He had no choice if he hoped to survive this hell hole and so without another thought, he approached the nearest soldier.

"Watkins has done a runner."

The soldier turned and glared at him. "What? Explain yeself."

His heart was thumping hard in his chest. "Tommy Watkins. He's gone and he's stealing guavas just through there." He pointed in the direction he'd just come. "Ye best hurry."

"Williams, come with me," he yelled to another soldier who turned and hurried over to him.

The two soldiers disappeared through the bushes and Aaron calmly walked back to where he'd been working and picked up the next stone. His outward calm belied his inner turmoil as he laid the next stone and tapped it gently into place. He'd turned on his fellow prisoners and there was no going back.

Aaron wrenched himself back to the present and ran his fingers roughly through his hair. There was no going back – he'd be a dead man.

***

Chapter 33

Walk the Line

Aaron could only imagine what Jess was thinking right now. He knew he'd been solemn and withdrawn for the past week, but he didn't want to share his problem with her. If he was honest with himself he didn't want her to think less of him. He thought less of him and he didn't need to see that reflected in her eyes. He'd wrestled with the Commandant's demands and there was only one solution that he could see whereby he could still look at himself in the mirror.

He deliberately waited until the end of the day when the men were downing tools and going back to their huts.

"A word if ye please, Smith," he called out to Daniel Smith as he was about to head off with a group of men.

He glanced up and with a look of resignation bid the lads go ahead without him. He waited for Aaron to come to him which rankled Aaron but he immediately let it go. He had bigger concerns on his mind than Smith's insolence.

Smith's face was unreadable but Aaron recognised caution when he saw it. "Would ye step into the work hut for a moment?"

"Aye."

Aaron walked ahead of him into the small work hut. He glanced around and grimaced. It was hardly a work hut – there were a couple of crates that acted as a desk and that was it. The hut had been hastily erected to service the new gaol work site without much thought.

"I'll get straight to the point," said Aaron closing the door behind Smith. "I believe the Commandant's asked ye to spy for him, and I believe ye said no."

Smith appeared to relax slightly and he drew in a deep breath. "Aye."

"As ye can imagine he's not well pleased by that, and I recommend ye change your mind."

"I won't," said Smith jutting his chin out and shaking his head. "I'm no lagger."

Aaron sighed. "Ye cannot win. Price intends for ye to spy for him or he'll break ye. Better to lag than to be at the receiving end of that man's ire."

Smith stared at Aaron for a few moments before once again shaking his head. “If he’s asked ye to convince me I can tell ye now yer wasting yer time.” He paused before taking a step towards the door. “If that’s all ye wanted I’ll be on my way.”

“Wait. Listen to me,” said Aaron with a desperate tone in his voice. “If ye don’t do it I’ll break ye. I’ve got no choice.” He shook his head and blew out his breath. “For God’s sake man, just do it.”

“Do what ye must.”

He turned and scraping the door open disappeared through it leaving Aaron to stare after him. Smith had no idea what Price had in store for him and it made Aaron sick to his stomach. His heart was thumping loudly in his ears as he left the hut and headed for home. He could do nothing more except do Price’s bidding and the thought of it nestled in the pit of his stomach like a writhing serpent.

No sooner had he walked into the house than he was bombarded by his three eldest sons, who literally threw themselves at him. All screeching ‘Papa, Papa’. He grabbed them to him and found solace in their small squirming bodies against his. Not that they were small anymore. Aaron and Moses, who were nearly identical and tall for their ages would be seven this year. Matthew was half a head shorter, and looked nothing like his brothers –he was about to turn five. He was a quiet lad with his nut-brown hair and soft brown eyes.

He let them go and ruffled Matthew's hair. "Where's Mark?"

On hearing his name he came running out of the bedroom and launched himself at Aaron, who caught him and threw him into the air. He giggled.

"Papa."

Aaron kissed him before putting him down. He was the least like his siblings with his blonde hair and round face.

"Come, supper won't be long," he said herding them ahead of him as they went out to the kitchen. The boys settled themselves at the table and Aaron greeted his wife and daughters. Supper was loud with the children chatting about school and other matters. Aaron let it wash over him enjoying the chatter and banter. It helped to wash away some of the stress of the day.

It was later when the children were tucked in bed and Jess crawled into bed beside him that his problems could no longer be ignored. She pressed her small warm body against his, curling around him. He could feel her pregnant belly pressing into him and he smiled. Before long they'd have another one.

"You made me a promise once," she said in a low voice.

He stiffened. It wasn't her words so much as the accusation behind them. He shifted so he could see her face. She stared back at him unblinking and he swallowed. "Aye," he whispered.

"Do you remember?"

Once again he swallowed. "Tis not the same."

She shuffled backwards and he felt the cool night air replace her warm body. "You clearly don't remember." There was no doubting the accusing tone. "You promised never to shut me out – and you are – and you know it!"

He rolled onto his back and stared at the ceiling. It wasn't the same. He'd promised her that she'd never have to doubt his love. "I've kept my promise to ye."

She rose up on her elbow and stared down at him, pushing her plaited hair to one side. “I know something’s troubling you and that you’re not telling me.”

“Let it go, Jess.”

“No. You’ve been distant for weeks and I’ve given you time enough. What’s going on?”

She was now glaring at him with a furrowed brow and he groaned as he sat up and swung his legs over the side of the bed. “Leave it,” he said rubbing his hands through his hair. “I can’t tell ye.”

“Was your pardon denied? Is that it? You’ve had word and you’re not telling me.”

He felt the bed shift beneath him as she sat upright. He looked at her over his shoulder and at the hurt in her eyes. He ran his hands over his face and stood up, turning to face her. “I would not keep that from ye.” His voice was low but he couldn’t keep the hurt tone from it. How could she think that of him?

Grabbing his breeches and shirt he turned and walked from the room. He had no idea where he was going or what he was doing – he just had to clear his head. He hauled on his breeches as he opened the front door and went out into the night.

***

Jessie stared at the empty doorway and was about to dive out of bed and go after him when she heard the front door clunk closed. She blew out her breath and pressed her lips together as hot tears welled in her eyes. She knew he was keeping something from her, something important and she'd be damned if she'd allow it to tear them apart.

She settled back under the covers and ran her hand over the still-warm spot where he'd been. He was a stubborn proud man – God were all men like him? Thinking they were the only ones who could shoulder problems and deal with them. She was more than capable of sharing whatever it was that was eating him. She curled her legs up, resting her pregnant belly against them. Nothing more could be achieved tonight. She sighed and closed her eyes, praying he'd return soon – it was cold out and he'd catch the death of him.

***

2nd July 1847

Two weeks later Aaron arrived home from work to find the household in a state. He was met by Mary Vowell who promptly directed him to the kitchen to feed the children their supper.

"Where's Jess?" he demanded.

Mary looked at him as though he was a complete imbecile with her hands on her hips. "She's rather occupied giving birth to your child. Now go."

It was only then that he became aware of a long low moan coming from the bedroom. He took one step towards the bedroom door and then thought better of it. "Aye," he said before heading out the back door and into the kitchen.

Mrs Drummond turned and stared at him, clearly surprised by his sudden entrance. "Mr Price good evening. Everything's well in hand."

"Good evening, Mrs Drummond." He glanced around the kitchen at his six children all with their eyes firmly fixed on him. "Mrs Vowell sent me out here to feed the children."

"It's all in hand, Mr Price," she said smiling patiently. "Why don't ye sit and I'll fetch ye some supper

"Aye."

He sat down at the head of the table and the children wasted no time in taking up their previous conversation. Who wanted a brother and who was getting a new sister, in between face-pulling and throwing insults.

"You're stupid anyway,' said Moses to Ellen screwing up his face. "We're getting a little brother."

"Are not," she shot back at him along with her tongue which she poked out in his direction.

"Enough," said Aaron glaring them into silence.

Mr Drummond smiled as she placed bowls of steaming stew and potatoes on the table in front of the children. "Mind it's hot."

She put one in front of Aaron and then joined them at the table with some for herself, which she shared with Jessie, who was thumping the table with her chubby fists in anticipation. Apart from Jessie smacking her lips and thumping her fists, supper was a quiet affair which suited Aaron. His thoughts were with Jess and her labours – he prayed they would both be alright. Childbirth was a risky business.

He was halfway through his supper when Mary's beaming face appeared at the kitchen door. "It's a boy. A fine healthy boy."

Aaron leapt to his feet pushing his chair back to the wall in his haste. "And Jess?"

"Rather exhausted I'm sure, but in fine spirits." Mary walked over to him and leaning against him kissed his cheek. "Congratulations, Aaron. Ye can go see them if ye wish."

"Thank ye."

He glared at Moses who was pulling a face at Ellen then turned and raced from the kitchen. He slowed when he reached the bedroom and peered through the doorway. Jess was sitting up, resting on pillows with a small dark fuzzy head at her breast. His heart contracted at the sight of them.

"Jess."

It was barely a whisper, but she looked up and smiled before beckoning him to join her. He eased himself onto the bed beside her and leaning forward kissed her before turning his gaze to his new son.

"He's perfect," he said smiling. "Luke?"

"Yes."

Luke let go of her nipple with a slight popping sound and Jess lay him down beside her, rubbing his back in a rhythmic motion. "How are you?" she said raising her eyes to meet his as she took his hand in hers and squeezed. "Please, Aaron I know something's very wrong and I hate that it's between us."

"Not now."

She ignored him and pushed on. "It's Price isn't it?"

He swallowed and nodded. "Aye...but I don't want to talk about it."

She let go of his hand and compressed her lips. "Whatever it is it's eating you alive, Aaron."

He put his face in his hands and groaned. "I know…but I can hardly bear to look at myself," he raised his eyes to hers. "I can't bear to see how ye'll look at me."

She held his gaze and shook her head. "I cannot promise you anything except I love you and nothing will change that."

He nodded and drew in a deep breath. "Ye remember I told ye Price demanded we, the overseers report prisoners for even minor misdemeanours?"

She nodded and took his hand in hers, rubbing her thumb across the back of it.

"Well, we aren't the only ones reporting to him, he's got, spies."

"Spies?"

"Aye. He called me to his office a few weeks back and told me that one of the men in my work gang, Smith, had refused to spy for him. He was none too pleased as ye can imagine." He paused and swallowed and looked away. "He ordered me to break him."

"Break him?"

She hadn't tried to disguise the shock in her voice and he glanced back at her. She stared at him, her eyes wide and her mouth slightly agape. "What did you do?"

"I begged Smith to reconsider. I told him Price had ordered me to break him, and I'd do it. He refused."

Jessie paled visibly and swallowed. "You had no choice, Aaron. Surely you know that."

"Perhaps," he rubbed his fingers through his hair. "Price has lost all reason…he's a madman." He swallowed as tears welled in his eyes and a sharp ache stretched across his throat. "I've not seen Smith in a week and I fear for him." He couldn't tell her about the ghastly contraption the smith was making.

Jessie leaned forward and wrapped her arms around him as tears rolled down his face. "It's not your fault. God, I cannot believe you thought I'd think less of you for this."

He pulled from her embrace and wiped his face with the back of his hand. "I think less of me for God's sake, how can ye not?"

"Because I see this for what it is. Price is the monster, not you."

"I've been a monster," he whispered. "I've used men for my own purpose. I've lagged on men to elevate my position and degrade theirs. I've done things I'm ashamed of."

She sucked in a breath and swallowed as tears filled her eyes. "You did those things because you had to, not because you wanted to hurt those men. It's not the same."

He could see that…she was right…but it didn't sit any better on him.

Smith could be dead for all he knew and no matter what Jess said, that was on him.

***

Chapter 34

Debts Repaid

Aaron paused, with his hand resting on the handle of the Commandant's office. He'd already been announced but his heart was thumping against his rib cage, and he was afraid of what news lay on the other side of the door. Drawing in a deep breath he pushed it open and went inside. John Price was standing with his back to him with his hands clasped behind his back, gazing out the window.

"Take a seat, Mr Price we have much to discuss," he said without turning around.

"Good morning," said Aaron as he settled himself on the chair opposite the Commandant's desk. "I pray all is in order."

Price swung around and smiled. "Yes indeed." He eased into his chair and shuffled through a pile of papers littering his desk. "Good news for you…now where is it." He flipped through the papers on his desk again – finally extracting one. "Ah…here it is." He pushed it across the desk towards Aaron. "I'm delighted to congratulate you, Mr Price.

You've received the greatest indulgence from His Excellency."

Aaron's heart leapt into his throat as he reached for the parchment. "Thank ye." He could scarce believe what he was reading – but there it was – he'd been granted a conditional pardon. So many thoughts and emotions raced through his mind all at once – elation, dread and joy. He was free. He could go wherever he wanted except return to England – and he didn't want to go there anyway. He sucked in a deep breath and folded the parchment. He would celebrate this with Jess, not Price. "I can hardly believe it," he said grinning.

Price had been watching him carefully and he smiled again. "Take the rest of the day off and celebrate with your family."

"Thank ye, Mr Price, that's most generous of ye."

"Not at all." He sat back in his chair with a wide grin on his face. "I believe further congratulations are in order. You have a new son I believe."

"Aye, thank ye."

"And I've given Mr Seller's the final approval for your new house. I hope you'll have sufficient incentive not to leave the island, Mr Price. You're one of my most reliable overseers."

"A new house? I thought to add another room is all."

"I hardly think your present abode suitable, Mr Price. You're now a free man and it's high time you joined the settlement proper, instead of residing on the outskirts. The house next to the parsonage has been vacant since Mr Ross departed. It's sufficiently larger and its position far superior."

Aaron was flabbergasted and was sure the surprise was written on his face. "I don't know how I can thank ye. You've been most generous."

"Continue to assist me in keeping order is all the thanks I require. We must remain vigilant and show the devils they can't beat us."

"Aye." He didn't know what else to say. He knew exactly what Price required of him and he wasn't sure he could deliver. He prayed he wouldn't have to do to another man what he'd done to Dan Smith.

"Well, I think that covers everything. Good day to you, Mr Price."

Aaron rose to his feet and smiled – it was a disingenuous smile that didn't reach his eyes. "Good day." He reached the door and swung it open.

"Oh…I nearly forgot to thank you for your not-insignificant part in bringing Smith to order."

Aaron swallowed and turned to face the Commandant. He prayed his face was impassive and unreadable. "Glad to be of assistance." The lie rolled from his tongue like honey.

"You can have him back in a week or so once he's done with his current task," he said with a grin. "A couple of thirty-six-pound weights chained to him and a saw will see to the end of his insolence."

Aaron nodded. "Aye."

He felt sick to the core as he left the barracks and made his way home. The elation of obtaining his freedom soured in his mouth at the thought of his part in punishing Smith. He knew what Price was doing to him – what he'd done to countless others. Chained with weights and forced to cut coral was one of his more innovative punishments.

As he neared home he pushed all thoughts of Price and Smith aside and plastered a smile on his face. There was no need for Jess to know what Price was doing. He knocked softly on the door so as not to alarm her, before opening it and entering. She was sitting in her chair with Jessie on her knee and the pair of them looked up and smiled at him.

Jessie wiggled from her mother's lap and toddled over to him with her arms outstretched. He scooped her into his arms and kissed her. "How's my girl?"

She giggled and patted his face with her chubby hands. "Papa."

"She's good," said Jessie rising to her feet and smiling. "What are you doing home?" She arched one brow as she walked over to him and kissed him.

"Ah…I have the afternoon off, and I have news." He put Jessie down and swept Jess into his arms. "We're free."

"Free?"

He grinned and hugged her tight. God, it felt so good to hold her in his arms. Her familiar scent and the feel of her small body against his were enough to soothe him. "Aye." He released her slightly and gazed down into her enquiring face. "I've been granted a conditional pardon. We're free."

"Oh my, God, Aaron," she exclaimed and wrapped her arms around him again. "I can hardly believe it."

He brushed his lips against hers and sighed. "I know, we've wanted it for so long that it's hard to believe – but it's true."

He pushed her from him and stared down into her face. "What's wrong?" He'd expected to see excitement or joy and that's not how she looked at all.

"Nothing," she said shaking her head. "It's just unexpected is all."

"Aye, I'll grant ye that. But ye don't look pleased about it."

She let out a sigh and pulled from his arms. "It's not that, Aaron. I'm pleased, really I am. I'm so happy you've got your pardon, it's just that…well it's a bit scary too."

"It is…but we don't have to decide anything right away," he said taking her hands in his and squeezing them softly. "We can take our time deciding where we want to go." He smiled and cupped her face in his hand. "There's no need to be scared."

She swallowed and nodded. "What if we want to stay?"

He took a step back and nearly stood on Jessie who was sitting on the floor behind him. “Oh, are ye alright?” He picked her up and she smiled happily, quite unhurt. “Well, we might want to stay for a while…I have other news.” He kissed Jessie’s forehead and put her down on the floor. “The Commandant’s approved a new house for us. Mr Ross’s old place down near the parsonage. We can move as soon as I’ve arranged it with Sellers.”

“A new house?”

She stared at him with her lips slightly agape and he grinned. “Aye, a new house.” He grabbed her by the waist and pulled her into his arms. “So, we might want to stay for a bit longer then.”

He bent his head and kissed her - a soft kiss full of love rather than passion. He’d expected her to want to leave the island right away and was rather glad she didn’t. He had mixed feelings and needed time to think as well. Their lips parted and she sighed as she melted against him.

“As long as we’re together I don’t care where we live.”

***

Two days later Aaron and Jess loaded Luke into the pram and with Jessie seated on the seat in front went to inspect their new house. The three eldest children were in school, and Henry promised to watch Matthew and Mark for an hour or so. It was a chill winter's day and the two babies were rugged up with hats and mittens. Jessie wrapped her cloak around herself as they strolled down the road together.

Since Aaron had brought news of his pardon she'd thought of little else. After ten years on the island though she was loath to leave, but if Aaron wanted to then of course she'd go with him and be happy about it. She glanced sideways at him. They hadn't spoken of it since and she had no idea what he was thinking on the matter.

Ross's old place was anything but old. Jess remembered the house well from when she lived in this part of the settlement. It was a timber house, like most of the others. The exception was the row of beautiful stone cottages along the main road, elevated above the barracks. They were reserved for the civil engineers and such, and those in higher positions than Principal Overseers.

The front garden was overgrown, but what was peeking through the weeds looked retrievable. Aaron went ahead of her to the front door and slipped the key in the lock. Jessie followed him inside, parking the pram beside the fireplace. Luke had fallen asleep during the walk but Jessie held her arms out to her.

"Mamma."

She lifted her into her arms before glancing around the sitting room. It was large and would more than suit their needs. She followed Aaron into the first bedroom which led off to the left side.

"Our room, what do ye think?" he said with raised brows.

"Mmm…I think so."

It would be a sunny room in the summer and it was large enough for their furniture. The three other bedrooms were much larger and Jess thought the twins could have the smaller room, the girls in one and the younger boys in the other. It was going to be so much better than their current home.

The washhouse and out-kitchen were unremarkable, although there was far more room in the new kitchen. Jess grinned as she looked around the house for the second time.

They were not going to know themselves. Henry on the other hand had a lot of work ahead of him to get the kitchen garden in order.

"The field next door's ours as well," said Aaron as they strolled up the front path.

Jess walked over to the fence for a closer look. It was a medium-sized paddock that looked like it had been planted with sweet bucks. She turned to Aaron and smiled. "I can hardly believe how generous Mr Price has been. You must be doing everything right where he's concerned."

Aaron grimaced and nodded. "Aye."

She tilted her head to the side and scrutinised her husband. She hadn't imagined it –he'd grimaced when she mentioned the Commandant. Well, that wasn't surprising. She knew he didn't agree with Price's methods or the severity of his regime. She sighed, perhaps they should seriously think about leaving.

***

Chapter 35

Resettled

With the New Year came the sad news that the Vowells were leaving for Sydney. Mary had been Jess's closest friend and she couldn't imagine how her life was going to be without her. Jess also realised she was expecting again and was thankful the new house was more than large enough to accommodate another one.

The Lady Franklin had anchored off the island yesterday and brought letters from both Grandma and George. The latest newspaper from Hobart Town was also sitting on the sideboard waiting until she had a spare moment to devour the latest news.

George and Mary had another daughter, who they'd named Victoria (for the Queen) and Margaret which was obviously after Grandma. Big sister Ann was apparently delighted. George was busy but enjoying the innkeeper's life. Jess smiled as she folded his letter and slipped it back into the envelope. How she wished she could visit and see them again. She pushed the thought aside – Sydney was out of the question.

Grandma's letter was full of news about the farm. It was clearly written by Grandpa Joe and Jess longed to hear her grandmother's words. It saddened her to hear that she was spending more and more time in bed. With a sigh, she folded the letter and reached for the latest newspaper. She smiled as she spread it open. Not that many years ago she didn't get to read the news until it was well-read by just about everyone else in the settlement. The paper would be frayed and dog-eared and scrunched so badly in places she couldn't read it. Today, she'd received it straight from the ship with the mail.

The front page was full of news about Hobart Town which didn't interest her too much. A new play was starting at the theatre which brought back memories of the last time she attended the theatre. She quickly turned the page and pushed any further thoughts of that night to the back of her mind. The headline on page three caught her attention – *The State of Norfolk Island.*

In Friday's Herald, we published, amongst other documents respecting Norfolk Island, a despatch from Earl Grey to Lieutenant Governor Sir William Denison, directing that the penal establishment of Norfolk Island should be at once broken up, and the whole population of the settlement withdrawn to Van Diemen's Land.

Jessie licked her lips as she read the entire article. Apparently, this all had to do with some report by Reverend Naylor concerning the state of things. He was no longer on the island, and she believed he'd resigned and left of his own accord. She put the newspaper aside and sucked in a deep breath. It would appear they'd have no choice in the matter if this article was to be believed.

Aaron and she had been avoiding further conversation about whether to leave or stay. She had the distinct feeling that he wanted to stay and she was quite undecided. She certainly didn't want to go to New South Wales but Van Diemen's Land would be like going home. She had some happy memories from her childhood living in Launceston. She left the newspaper open at page three on the sideboard – Aaron would no doubt want to read it. She smoothed the newsprint with her finger as she wondered if he already knew about this.

***

Later that night, Jessie lay snuggled against Aaron who was drowsy from their lovemaking. He'd read the news that the Government planned to close down the island, and he wasn't all that surprised. Rumours had been circulating for several months – unsubstantiated until now. He'd had time to think about what they might do if that happened – he'd thought of little else in fact.

Jessie let out a soft sigh as she pressed herself closer to him. He smiled and kissed the top of her head. She'd shared the happy news that they would have another child, and he was delighted. Their family was growing and life was good here except for Mr Price. He sighed and pulled her closer.

"Hmm," she whispered as she tilted her face to his. "Have you thought about what we might do?"

He nodded. "I've thought of little else," he said. "And I'm no closer to knowing for sure."

"Hmm." She kissed his cheek. "If they're truly going to shut the island down, then perhaps we should go now before that happens?"

"Perhaps…but it might be better to wait." He pushed himself into a sitting position and rubbed his hands over his face. "I've been here a long time, and if I wait until we're forced to leave it could be beneficial. I'd likely be pensioned off, which means we'd have money." He paused and looked down at her. "When we finally leave, Jess we'll have to get our own house – pay for it I mean." He shook his head. "I don't think we've got enough money to do that. Where would we live while I get settled in a new job? It's not as simple as us deciding to leave or stay – there's much more to it."

She frowned and rolled onto her back. "I agree there's much to consider…but what do you want?"

He drew in a deep breath and slowly let it out. "If ye want the truth..."

She sat up and put her arm around him. "I do."

He turned his head and gazed into her clear blue eyes full of love and trust. He swallowed and compressed his lips. "The thought of leaving here scares me to the core," he whispered. "I've known nothing but this for twenty-five years…freedom…I'm not sure I can do it," he said shaking his head.

He saw the tears well in her eyes and the tremble of her lip.

"Don't," he said. "If ye want to go we'll go."

She shook her head. "No. It's not that," she said wiping her eyes. "I'm so sorry I didn't see how hard this was for you."

He put his arm around her and pulled her close. He was surprised at how relieved he was that she understood. It wasn't perfect here – far from it, but the thought of leaving brought him out in a cold sweat of illogical fear. "So ye don't mind if we stay?"

She smiled and kissed him. "I don't mind at all. But one day, Aaron it's going to happen whether you want it or not. You must be ready when that day comes."

He sighed as he tightened his arms around her. Would he be ready? “I will be.”

***

With the departure of her dear friend Mary Vowell, Jess found herself in dire need of a new confidante. She had never become that close to Mrs Drummond or the other ladies, and so the arrival of a new Reverend and his wife posed a possible opportunity. Caroline Batchelor was a young woman – a couple of years younger than herself, or so she thought.

The Batchelors had taken up residence in the parsonage next door, and Jessie intended to take full advantage of having a potential new friend right on her doorstep. Balancing the tea cake she’d made in one hand she knocked firmly on the door.

“Me Mamma,” said Mark.

Before she could stop him he started thumping loudly on the door. She was in the midst of wrestling with him when the door opened and Caroline Batchelor rescued the cake which was teetering precariously. She smiled and stepped aside gesturing to Jessie to enter.

"I'm so sorry," said Jessie. "And thank you for rescuing the cake." She lifted Jessie down from the pram seat and gathered Luke in her arms. She brushed a loose tendril aside and did her best to smile as she followed Caroline Batchelor into the house.

She found herself standing in an all too familiar sitting room. Tears stung her eyes as the memory of the Reverend Sharpe and Ellison flooded her mind. It was so long ago and yet right now she felt the loss of her dear friend more than she imagined she would after all these years.

Caroline Batchelor stared at her and patted her arm. "Are you alright?" Her voice was soft and kind and full of concern which completely undid Jessie and she dissolved into tears. "Oh dear me, whatever's the matter?" She peered at Jessie and continued to pat her arm. "Here, let me get you a cup of tea and we can talk about it," she said.

"No, no…I'm so sorry," said Jessie as she tried to dry her tears. "I used to live here, a long time ago, and I never expected those memories to be like that."

Caroline nodded with a knowing smile. "Sometimes things can hit us when we least expect it. Come, I'll make us some tea and I'm sure the children would like cake."

"Yes they would," said Jessie with a laugh as she dried her eyes. "Thank you, Mrs Batchelor you're too kind."

"Nonsense, and please call me Caroline."

"You must call me Jessie then."

She nodded and the two women made their way out to the kitchen with Mark and Jessie toddling along behind. In no time the children were settled with cake and milk and Jessie found herself relaxing in the old kitchen. It held so many memories, but they were all good, and Caroline Batchelor oozed a calming influence over everything.

"I expect you miss your old friend very much," said Caroline as she placed tea cups on the table. "I've only been here a few weeks and I'm so homesick." She paused and ran her hand over her stomach. "I'd be grateful for a friend when my baby comes." Her dove grey eyes swam with tears and Jessie's heart wrenched for the younger woman.

"Oh, Caroline you can rely on me," she said leaping to her feet and without a second thought she wrapped her in a tight hug. “We’re all in need of close friends and allies here, and I’d be honoured to call you friend.”

Caroline pulled from her embrace and took her handkerchief from her apron pocket. “Thank you, Jessie. I’ve been meaning to come over and introduce myself and I’m so glad you came today.” She wiped her eyes and blew her nose. “How do you not miss your family?”

“I do,” said Jessie with a rueful smile. “And you’ll soon be like the rest of us.” She poured the tea and returned her gaze to Caroline. “Every time the sails are sighted my heart skips a beat – I know tomorrow I’ll hold letters in my hand from my brother and grandmother.” She sighed and patted her arm. “You’ll learn to appreciate that more than anything.”

Jessie sat beside Luke who was busy shoving a fist full of cake into his mouth with gusto. She smiled and shook her head before reaching for her tea.

“I miss my family more than anything,” said Caroline sitting opposite and picking up her tea cup. “I never imagined I’d be moving so far away from them, but when

Francis was offered this position we couldn't say no."

"Do you have a large family?"

"Not really," she said shaking her head. "But we're close. My mother and sister are like my best friends."

"Well, I'm sure they'll write and maybe you can visit them on occasion."

Caroline's brows raised and she put her cup down with a clatter. "I hadn't thought of that. Although, we probably won't be here that long – there's talk they'll send all the prisoners to Van Diemen's Land soon."

Jessie smiled. "That's true – but I hear the people of Van Diemen's Land are none too happy about the decision. So that may not happen for a while yet."

Caroline looked crestfallen at that and Jessie was sorry she'd said anything. She reached out and touched her hand. "Your sister and mother could visit when your baby's due. Tom Seller's, he's the Foreman of Works – well his wife resides in Sydney and only visits him on occasion. But, there's never any problem with her visiting. I'm sure it could be arranged."

"I'd like that."

After another hour of chatting Jessie gathered the children and headed for home. She felt lighter than she had in weeks and was sure Caroline and she would be fast friends in no time.

***

Chapter 36

The Beginning of the End

Jessie found Reverend Batchelors Sunday service, not unlike the Reverend Sharpes used to be. He had a rather melodic voice which he used to great effect. She left divine service feeling calm and content with her lot. The Batchelors had invited them back to their house for the midday meal, and the aroma of roasting meat hit Jessie as soon as she entered the kitchen. Her stomach grumbled in response and she smiled at Caroline.

"Hmm, I'm obviously hungry."

"Well, it won't be long," said Caroline grinning as she sliced the beef and set it on a tray. "Could you dish the potatoes?"

Jessie set to dishing up the potatoes and other vegetables for the children. The kitchen was too small for them to all eat together, so Caroline had set a table out in the garden for the children. Jessie frowned as she placed the plates down in front of her tribe.

"Now, not one argument," she said staring at Moses and Aaron who were apt to tease Ellen until she snapped.

"Yes, Mamma," said Aaron with a sideways glance at Ellen.

"I mean it. Your father will be out to deal with you if there's any misbehaving."

"We'll be good," said Moses with an angelic smile in his mother's direction.

Jessie groaned inwardly as she sliced young Jessie's meat and vegetables for her. Gathering Luke in her arms she headed inside. Ellen was a sensible nine-year-old girl, unlike her young brothers and Jessie knew they'd cause mischief as soon as her back was turned. She left the kitchen door wide open so she could hear any squabbles and Aaron could deal with them.

The conversation over luncheon was dominated by Aaron and Francis with talk of the latest news from Hobart Town.

"How many did you say they were removing?" said Francis eyeing Aaron with his alert blue eyes.

Francis Batchelor was not yet thirty by the looks of him with a thatch of dark wavy hair. He had a wide mouth that upturned at the corners which gave Jessie the impression he was a jovial man. Caroline and he appeared well suited.

Aaron swallowed a mouthful and nodded. “Eight hundred…it’ll leave barely five hundred here. I cannot see how things will continue to function.”

Francis shrugged and sipped his wine. “Does it matter? I don’t mean to be flippant, but surely the Governor isn’t profiting from works here…well, that’s the whole point really isn’t it? It’s become too costly.”

“Aye, essentially that’s the problem,” said Aaron. “Which is why I think it would make more sense to close it down entirely.” He paused with his fork halfway to his mouth. “I believe that’s what Governor Denison’s been ordered to do.”

Jessie had been listening intently to their conversation and was surprised that so many prisoners were to be removed. “I read in the newspaper that he was to close the island, and yet he hasn’t,” she said eyeing Aaron across the table.

“No…well not yet,” said Aaron.

“I think His Excellency is relying on his distance from London,” said Francis with a grimace “He’ll have to capitulate eventually, but I believe he'll delay as long as he can."

"Aye," said Aaron nodding. "I agree wholeheartedly."

"Why?" said Caroline entering the conversation. "What difference would it make to him?"

"Well, my dear it's a question of the colonists of Van Diemen's Land who don't wish to be inundated with scoundrels from Norfolk Island," said Francis. "The Governor has many he must appease."

Caroline nodded.

"They're fearful," said Aaron with a sigh. "The prisoners here have been portrayed not as men but as monsters and they don't want them in their midst…ye cannot blame them."

Francis sipped his wine and nodded. "Do you know how many soldiers are going? I hope they don't leave us without sufficient to keep the peace."

Aaron compressed his lips. "I heard they'll leave us with a hundred and fifty." He grimaced. "Ye need not worry our Commandant will ensure the peace is kept."

At that moment their peace was interrupted by squeals and cries coming from the garden. Jessie raised her brows at Aaron who excused himself and went to sort out the commotion.

"Sorry about that," said Jessie rolling her eyes. "It was only a matter of time before there was a squabble."

"Please don't worry," said Caroline reaching for her husband's hand. "I love the sound of children in the house."

"We'll have ours soon enough, my dear," he said.

"I can't wait," she said sitting back in her chair. "You're so blessed, Jessie."

"Well, yes – children are a blessing, but they're also a trial."

"A trial I welcome," said Caroline.

Aaron returned a few minutes later and they finished luncheon without any further interruptions. Afterwards, Jessie and Caroline cleaned up the dishes while the men retired to the sitting room. Ellen was put to work with a tea towel while the boys started a game of hide and seek in the yard. Luke had fallen asleep and was wrapped in a rug in the corner of the kitchen. Jessie sighed when the work was finally done and they joined the menfolk. Life was good here – her children were happy and healthy and she'd found a new friend in Caroline Batchelor. She had much to be thankful for.

***

Three weeks later the barque Pestongee Bomangee lay anchor off the island. It had been specially chartered to transport eight hundred prisoners from the island to Van Diemen's Land. The first two hundred and fifty boarded and she set sail a week later.

The quarry work gangs were virtually unaffected by the exodus. The majority of prisoners had been taken from Cascades and Longwood and so works in Kingston continued unabated. Aaron found Commandant Price, if at all possible, more determined than ever to maintain discipline.

Eighteen men were flogged this morning and Mr Price had now made it an offence for salve to be applied to their wounds. Aaron kept his own counsel and his thoughts to himself. He'd considered sharing his concerns with Francis Batchelor. He seemed like a fair and reasonable man with enlightened views, but something stopped him.

Aaron came out of his reverie as the punt thumped against the pier. He watched while it was secured before turning his attention to his gang. “Harris and Thomas, go fetch the cart and bring it down here,” he said waving his arms in the general direction of the boat shed. “The rest of ye start unloading.”

Harris and Thomas wasted no time in following his orders. They leapt from the punt and hurried up to the boat shed. The rest of them started unloading the stone blocks onto the pier. He noticed Dan Smith and his stomach clenched. Since returning to the work gang Aaron noticed he kept to himself. He moved mechanically – lifting one stone block and slowly walking down the plank onto the pier. He carefully placed it and straightened – gazing about like he was disorientated. After a moment he took several steps along the pier towards the shore.

“Back to work, Smith,” yelled Aaron stepping from the punt.

Smith turned and looked vaguely in Aaron’s direction. His shoulders slumped and without a word, he ambled back to the punt and up the gangplank. Aaron pushed aside his feelings of guilt and returned to the job at hand.

It was several hours before the stone was unloaded and the punt prepared to depart for the quarry. Aaron was supervising the men who would pull the cart to the worksite. He wanted to be sure the load was secure and the men unlikely to lose control of it. Satisfied, he stretched and twisting around he noticed Smith was still on board the punt which was already too far from the pier for him to do anything about it.

He swore under his breath before glancing at the cart – the men were already in position and ready to start hauling. "Alright, get going I'll meet ye at the site," he said. "Harris, you're in charge of the load."

Harris was one of the more reliable men in his work gang, and Aaron trusted him. With a final glance at his men, he began hurrying up the road to the barracks. The soldiers on guard at the quarry hadn't accompanied him on the punt or else he would've sent one of them after Smith. Damn the silly blighter – what was he playing at?

He wrenched open the door to the barracks and hurried inside. In his haste he ran straight into the surgeon, Mr Bedford, knocking his spectacles from his nose and sending him staggering into the wall.

"My apologies," he said scooping the spectacles from the floor and handing them to the surgeon. "Are ye alright?"

"Fine, fine," he said with a wave of his hand. "No harm done." He put on his spectacles and straightened himself. "I cannot say the same for the Commandant, and I've ordered him to rest. Whatever you want to see him about will have to wait."

"Ah…oh…sorry to hear it," said Aaron gathering his thoughts. "Actually, I'm not here to see him, but I hope it's nothing serious."

"I fear the man's losing his..." He stopped abruptly and cleared his throat. "Right then, well good day, Mr Price."

He disappeared through the door without another word or a backward glance. Aaron stared at the door for several moments while the surgeon's words reverberated in his brain. *I fear the man's losing his…*what? Aaron could think of several things Price was losing and one of them was not his stomach for excessive punishment. His thoughts returned to Smith and turning on his heel he walked down the hall and spied Captain Conran.

"Captain," he called as he approached him.

Captain Conran looked up and on seeing Aaron leapt from his chair and grabbed his hat. "What is it?"

He sounded alarmed and Aaron smiled to himself recalling the last time he'd come in search of him. He shook his head. "Nothing urgent. One of my men has stowed himself on the punt and gone out to the quarry and I'd like ye to send a soldier after him. Dan Smith's his name and he's not himself."

"The soldiers stationed at the quarry will surely round him up when he gets there."

"Perhaps, but as they'll not be expecting him and he may not make himself known to them, I'd rather ye send someone after him."

"Aye, leave it to me I'll send Williams."

"Thank ye."

He left the barracks and made his way to the work site with thoughts of Smith swimming around in his head. He didn't like the idea of him wandering around on his own.

***

Chapter 37

Kingston - Spring 1848

The children always enjoyed spending an hour or so down at the beach. It was early September and the chills of winter were long passed and Jessie lifted her face to the warm ocean breeze. She sighed, before turning her attention back to the sandcastle that Jessie and Mark were busy building. She grabbed Luke, who was about to squash the west side of it and pressed him into her lap.

He moaned as he wriggled to be free of her.

"No you don't," she said kissing his cheek. She looked up the beach towards the black rock and spied Ellen and Matthew. There was no sign of Moses and Aaron, and she groaned. They knew not to go beyond the black rock but that meant nothing to them.

She wasn't alone on the beach. Several people were promenading up and down and Alicia Hutchins and Mrs Drummond had only recently departed. She'd half expected she might see Aaron.

Not that he'd be at the beach, but the pier wasn't that far away and she was sure he was bringing a load from the quarry today. In reality, he'd probably done that already – it was late in the day.

"Ellen, Matthew," she called letting Luke go and getting her feet underneath her. "Time to go."

They immediately started running towards her and she smiled as she stretched her aching back. Two more months before this baby was due and it couldn't come fast enough. She waited for the two to reach her before asking them about their brothers.

"They went down by the rocks," said Ellen.

"Alright, wait here all of you while I go find them."

She wasn't annoyed with her twins exactly, just exasperated. Aaron and Moses always pushed the limits and were far too adventuresome for their own good. She'd curtail them for a few days and hope they got the message to do as they were told. Or maybe she'd ask Aaron to deal with the wayward pair – they were more than a little scared of him. She grinned as she imagined the stern look on Aaron’s face as he dealt with his sons.

“Mamma…Mamma,” came a fearful cry from behind the rocks up ahead of her. It chilled her to the bone. “I’m here,” she called as she lifted her skirt with both hands and hurried past the black rock. She scanned the area for any sign of her sons. “Where are you?”

Moses’s head popped up from behind a rock. “Here Mamma.” His wide eyes stared at her, full of excitement and fear. “There’s a man.”

“A man? What do you mean? Has he hurt you?” It was something that was always at the forefront of her mind. Aaron was disliked by so many of the prisoners and she feared one day one of them would take revenge on her children.

He shook his head. “Aaron says he’s dead.”

“Show me where.”

She scrambled over the rocks as she followed Moses down to the ocean edge. Aaron was kneeling beside the body of a man who was lying face down in the sand, half in the water and half out.

"Get away from there," she yelled grabbing him by the arm she dragged him away. She was breathing heavily as she stared at the man. He was a prisoner by the look of his clothes and he looked dead.

"Come on. You two shouldn't be here. You know very well you're not to go beyond the black rock," she shoved them both gently ahead of her as the three made their way back to the beach.

They rejoined the other children and Jessie told them all to stay put until she returned. Hiking her skirt up around her knees she walked as fast as she could up the beach, all the time scanning for any sign of a soldier or overseer. She wasn't far from the boat shed when she spied two soldiers. She called out to them and beckoned them to come to her. She was relieved that they wasted no time in responding to her.

"What is it, ma'am? Are ye hurt?" said a fresh-faced Private.

She was panting and gasping for air, but she managed to shake her head. The two stared at her for a moment while she gathered herself. "There's a man…washed up on the beach…I think he's dead."

The other soldier's eyes darted from his companion to Jessie and back again. He licked his lips. "Where is he then?"

"I'll show you…just the other side of the black rock," said Jessie still trying to catch her breath. "He's half in the water still."

"I'll go with the lady, ye go fetch Captain Conran," said the young one.

With a quick nod, the other soldier set off in the direction of the barracks.

"Lead the way, ma'am."

Jessie nodded and turning began to walk back towards the beach. She prayed her children were waiting patiently for her without getting into any mischief. She was slightly concerned that Moses might've gone back to look at the man, and taken the younger children with him. It was just the sort of thing he'd do.

She needn't have worried. They were all sitting on the sand right where she'd told them to stay, and Francis Batchelor was with them. As she drew closer she could see that he was in a state, pacing up and down the beach. When he saw her coming he hurried towards her.

"Jessie, oh thank heavens I found you…it's Caroline…the baby's coming," he said. "I've sent Mrs Fletcher to attend to her, but I know she'll want you there." His normally upturned mouth was compressed into a thin line. "I don't like to hurry you, but can you go now?"

"Of course," she said taking hold of his forearm. "Don't worry it'll be alright." She turned back to the young private and drew in a breath. "I'm sure you can find him by yourself…he's just the other side of the black rock, maybe fifty yards."

"Thank ye, ma'am." He doffed his hat in the Reverend's direction and set off down the beach.

She gathered Luke in her arms. "Come on, we have to go home," she said urging the rest of them to get to their feet. "Francis, you go on ahead, I'll be there as soon as I can."

"Thank you, Jessie."

Jessie smiled to herself as he took off at a run towards his house. This was Caroline's first baby and it would probably be several hours before it was born. Still, she didn't want Francis or Caroline to fret because she wasn't there. She hurried the children home as fast as they would go and gave Henry strict instructions to come and fetch her if necessary. Aaron would be home before too long and Henry promised to stay with the children until then.

The parsonage door was opened almost as soon as she knocked and Francis literally grabbed her and hauled her inside. “I’m so glad you came.”

In his agitation, he’d obviously been running his hands through his hair and it was now standing on end. Jessie patted his arm and smiled – of course, he was in a state. “Why don’t you go and put the kettle on?”

“I’ve already done that. Mrs Fletcher’s been ordering me around for the past half hour.” He looked indignant for a moment before his face went back to one of a man who was about to have a baby and had no idea what to do about it.

“Right, well I’ll go check on Caroline then.”

Leaving him to his own devices she knocked softly on the bedroom door and entered. Caroline was standing by the bed in her night shift with her face etched with pain. “Jessie, thank goodness you came.”

"Of course, I'm here. I promised you I would be."

"Walk a little more," said Mrs Fletcher placing her hand firmly on Caroline's lower back and prodding her.

"What can I do?" said Jessie directing her attention to Mrs Fletcher.

"Here, keep her moving," said Mrs Fletcher stepping aside. She lowered herself into the nearest chair and sighed. "It's going to be a while yet."

Jessie nodded and urged Caroline to walk to the end of the bed and then turn and walk back. "Francis is so excited about becoming a father."

"Is he alright?" said Caroline and then she grabbed her belly and bent over slightly. "Oohhh…aargh." Panting she straightened and sucked in a deep breath.

"He's fine," said Jessie rubbing Caroline's lower back as she urged her to keep moving. "You're doing just fine."

"I don't feel like I am."

For the next few hours, Caroline oscillated between walking and resting as her labour slowly progressed. Mrs Fletcher was calm and appeared unconcerned as time wore on and there was no sign that

Caroline's contractions were intensifying. Jessie did her best to reassure her friend that everything was perfectly fine – but she wasn't sure. Her labours never lasted so long but this was Caroline's first baby, surely that made a difference.

"Go and fetch some tea, Jessie," said Mrs Fletcher rising to her feet. "Lie down, Caroline and let me see what this baby's doing, hmm."

Jessie nodded and left the room. It was dark, and she was grateful Francis had lit a lamp in the sitting room, although there was no sign of him. She made her way to the kitchen where she found him sitting at the table with his head in his hands.

He looked up, alarm etched on his face. "What's happened? Is Caroline alright?"

"She's fine…your baby's just taking its time," she said reaching for the teapot.

"Surely it won't be long now," he said.

Jessie shrugged. "Babies have a way of coming when they're ready. We just have to be patient."

She made a pot of tea and loaded a tray with cups and saucers and the sugar pot.

She knew Mrs Fletcher wanted to distract Caroline and she was glad of the distraction as well. Leaving Francis alone in the kitchen she went back to the sitting room and rested her tray on the sideboard while she opened the door.

"Breathe Caroline…that's it breathe," she heard Mrs Fletcher say as she entered. "Don't push yet."

Caroline was red-faced and panting and Jessie was surprised. It looked like things had progressed rapidly in her absence. She placed the tray on the dressing table and looked enquiringly at Mrs Fletcher.

"Is it time?"

"Not quite," she said with a shake of her head. "But, it won't be too much longer. Pour the tea, my dear."

Jessie obliged, although she wasn't too sure how Caroline was going to balance a teacup. Her contractions were definitely coming closer together now. She placed a cup of tea on the dressing table and Caroline padded over to her and smiled.

"Thank you. I'm not sure if it will help, but it will certainly calm my nerves."

"You're doing fine," said Jessie placing her hand on her forearm. "It won't be long now and you'll be holding your new baby."

Caroline let out a long moan as another contraction ripped through her. Panting she gripped Jessie's arm as the pain eased. "Oh my…"

It was another hour before Mrs Fletcher deemed it time for Caroline to bear down and push. She had hold of Jessie and every time a contraction gripped her she tightened her hold. Jessie thought her hand would be crushed before the baby arrived but she did her best to encourage Caroline. After the last contraction she managed to free her hand – she stretched her fingers as the blood flowed back into them.

"Aaargh…OOMPH." Caroline strained and pushed. She was red-faced and lathered in perspiration, but Jessie recognised the determination on her face. She wasn't giving up.

"Push hard on the next one, we're almost there," said Mrs Fletcher who was kneeling between Caroline's thighs, ready to ease her baby into the world.

Caroline nodded and sucked in a deep breath.

Jessie wrung out a cloth in the basin and gently wiped Caroline's face. She smiled and then grimaced as the next contraction came.

"Push…NOW," said Mrs Fletcher.

A few moments later the squawk of an indignant child being forced into the world reverberated around the room. Caroline let out a triumphant. "Yes," followed by tears as she relaxed back against the pillows. "Oh my God, is it alright?"

"Yes, yes, perfectly alright," said Mrs Fletcher as she deftly cut the cord and set to cleaning and swaddling the baby. "It's a girl, Caroline. Ye have a fine daughter."

Jessie was grinning as she went to take a look at the new arrival. She peered over Mrs Fletcher's shoulder at the small squirming bundle with a mop of dark frizzy hair.

"Oh, Caroline she's beautiful," she said turning to face her. "Wait till you see her."

Caroline was beaming. "I can hardly wait."

"Here, take her to her mother," said Mrs Fletcher handing the swaddled baby to

Jessie. “Now, Caroline you’re not quite done yet.”

Jessie smiled as she put the baby in Caroline’s arms. “What will you name her?”

“Margaret…we already decided to name a girl after Francis’s mother,” she said taking her in her arms. “Oh…she’s so perfect.”

***

Chapter 38

The Cycle of Life

Jessie crept into the house and was pleased to see Aaron had left the lamp burning in their bedroom. He was asleep on his side of the bed with one arm flung out on her side. She sighed as she began undressing. She was tired and couldn't wait to crawl in beside him. It had been a long day and she supposed it was now after midnight. She slipped her nightgown over her head and pulled her hair out of its bun. Sitting at the dressing table she picked up her brush and began brushing out her long tresses.

She was surprised when Aaron's warm fingers closed around her hand. "I'll do that," he whispered kissing her neck.

"Aaron," she said smiling at him in the mirror. "I'm sorry…I didn't mean to wake you."

"I was trying to stay awake to see ye," he said running the brush through her honey-blonde hair. "Is Caroline safely delivered then?"

"Yes…a girl, they've named her, Margaret."

"I must congratulate them when I see them next."

Jessie sighed as he brushed her hair and then began plaiting it. It was so nice to have someone do that at the end of a tiring day. He tied off the end and kissed the top of her head. "Done…come to bed, ye must be exhausted."

She nodded as she got to her feet and padded to the bed and climbed in. Aaron got in the other side and immediately gathered her into his arms. She sighed as she melted against him, feeling safe and protected.

"Before ye go to sleep there's one thing I need to know," he said rubbing his thumb against her arm. "I believe the boys found a man's body on the beach today."

"Yes…he looked to be a prisoner. I left it to a couple of soldiers to investigate," she said. "Francis arrived about that time to fetch me to assist Caroline in her labours."

"Were the boys alright?"

She shook her head. "I think so. Honestly, I haven't had a chance to see if they are or not. Moses looked excited and a little scared, but you know them, I'm sure they thought it was just a big adventure."

He nodded and squeezed her. "Do ye know who it was?"

"No."

He sucked in a deep breath. "It was Dan Smith."

It took a moment for the name to register. "Dan Smith? Isn't he the one…"

"Aye."

"Oh…you don't think he was murdered do you?" she whispered, almost afraid to say it out loud. "The Commandant wouldn't have, would he?"

"No," said Aaron with a shake of his head. "I'm almost certain the poor bastard took his own life."

She didn't know which was worse. "It's not your fault you know…you can't blame yourself."

"Can't I?"

"No. If it's anyone's fault it's Commandant Price's. Please don't do that to yourself."

He squeezed her and kissed her forehead. "Thank ye. I know you're tired and I'm sorry to burden ye with it, but I needed to talk to ye about it tonight."

"I'm glad you did." She was delighted he'd spoken to her about it tonight. He was sharing his thoughts and not shutting her out as he'd done in the past. She closed her eyes and sighed. She was sorry poor Dan Smith had not been able to see another option.

***

November 1848

Jessie's labour pains started early Monday afternoon, and by supper time she was holding her new son in her arms. He had a ruddy complexion and a few wisps of dark fuzz on his head.

Aaron took him and stared down at him. Jessie thought he looked good with a babe in his arms, although his greying hair was making him look a bit old to be holding a newborn.

"Shall we name him John?" he said.

Jessie smiled. "Of course. That gives us Matthew, Mark, Luke and John…perfect don't you think?"

He grinned as he lowered him into her arms. "I love ye." He pressed his lips to hers before retreating. "I must go attend to the rest of them."

"Send them in to meet their little brother."

He nodded before leaving the room. Jessie sighed as she relaxed against the pillows. She never would've believed that she could be so content with a brood of children and a loving husband. Never once in the last ten years had she had cause to regret marrying Aaron – and she didn't think she ever would.

***

Aaron adjusted his stride to match Lieutenant Hamilton's slightly shorter one. They'd both been summoned to the Commandant's office and Aaron was cautious. One never knew what was on the man's mind or what he may demand next. They entered the barracks and were immediately ushered into the Commandant's office by a young soldier.

"Close the door, gentlemen," said Mr Price turning to face the two before easing himself into his chair.

Aaron closed the door and drew in a breath as he perched himself on the edge of the last remaining chair. He glanced briefly at Hamilton, who was sitting ramrod straight with a passive face, which revealed none of his thoughts.

Price leant forward on his elbows and pressed his fingertips together. "I've asked to see you both because I'm reducing the workforce out at the quarry." He removed his elbows from the desk.

Hamilton said nothing and Aaron shifted in his chair as he waited for Price to continue. The silence stretched between them as the Commandant appeared to lose track of his thoughts. He shuffled through some papers before piling them neatly and pushing them to the edge of his desk. He swept away some imaginary dust and looked up, surprise clear on his face.

"Lieutenant Hamilton, Mr Price…right," he said. "I'm reducing it to just one gang. So, Mr Price, you won't be needed out at the quarry. I'm relocating you to Orange Vale."

Aaron nodded and hoped his face didn't portray his feelings. Agricultural work was the most hated on the island with many of the men forced to work in chains. Hence, the gangs were far more disgruntled than those that worked out at the quarry. He'd been an overseer out there before for a number of years and wasn't keen on going back. He glanced at Hamilton, who was stoney faced.

"Understandable," said Lieutenant Hamilton with a nod.

"Good... report there tomorrow, Price." He leaned back in his chair and rubbed his fingers through his whiskers. "Hmm."

Aaron's eyes flicked from the Commandant to Hamilton, who continued to sit there like a statue. He was hiding his feelings so well that Aaron had no idea what his thoughts were. Commandant Price appeared distracted again and it was several moments before he looked up and noticed them.

"Dismissed gentlemen.'

"Aye thank ye," said Aaron getting his feet under him. He'd been wondering about the Commandant's ability to govern for several months, and today's meeting had left him thinking there was something definitely not right about him.

He waited until they were well clear of the barracks before broaching the subject with Hamilton. “The Commandant doesn’t seem himself.”

Hamilton glanced sideways at him. “I don’t know what you mean.”

That wasn’t the response he’d hoped for and he sucked in a deep breath. He had no intention of sharing his thoughts with the Lieutenant if he didn’t share them. “Only that he seemed distracted.”

“Well, he’s a busy man,” said Hamilton with a shrug. “At any rate, it’s not surprising we don’t need as many men out at the quarry. They’ll be closing everything down before too long.”

Aaron nodded. He agreed with the Lieutenant on that point.

***

Happy New Year

The Lady Franklin lay anchor on the 5th of February and Jessie was on edge waiting for letters and news to be unloaded. It had been months since the last ship had visited and she'd already written letters to both Grandma and George.

She paced the sitting room with John cradled in her arms. At three months old he was rather chubby and growing fast. But he was a fussy baby and getting him to sleep was a chore. She stopped and peered out the window – there was still no sign of anyone with mail deliveries. She sighed and began pacing again, jiggling John as she went. He was nearly asleep and she daren't stop until he was. She glanced at Luke who was playing happily on the floor with Jessie. She was thankful the pair played well together. She walked out to the back door and poked her head out and listened. Mark's voice wafted to her on the breeze and she closed the door and returned to pacing. He was probably driving Henry to distraction with his constant chatter, but at least he was occupied.

Ten minutes later John was fast asleep and she placed him gently in his crib and tip-toed out of the room. She sighed as she closed the door and leaned against it. She had any number of chores to get done while he slept and she wasted no time in heading for the washhouse.

By early afternoon she had her mending in hand with her needle poised. Every few minutes she glanced out the window, hoping to see someone coming with the latest news from Hobart Town and letters. Surely there were letters for her. She was frustrated and anxious by the time they turned up at her door.

She did her best to smile as she took the mail and bidding them good day she closed the door behind them. There were two letters for her and three newspapers. She put the papers on the sideboard and sat down with her letters on her lap. She ran her thumb over Grandpa Joe's scrawled writing and compressed her lips. She wanted to read it so badly, but then once it was read it would be months before she would get another letter.

After several minutes, she gave up trying to savour it and tore the envelope open and devoured its contents.

Dearest Jessie, Aaron and family,

I hope this letter finds you all in the best of health. My sight has failed me completely and I find myself spending more and more time in bed – but I am content.

Please do not worry on my account. Joe takes such good care of me.

I must confess that we are missing William now. He's moved to Wollombi – he says George needs his help with the Inn, but I suspect there is much more to it than that. Do you remember Mary's younger sister Jane Crothers? You would've met her at George and Mary's wedding. Well, it turns out young William has been courting Miss Crothers and they've recently announced their engagement. I'm sure he'll write to you very soon with news of his impending marriage. I won't be able to attend, but I do wish him well.

Of course, we are delighted for him – it is the way of things. It's just that we are really missing him. He was such a wonderful help to Joe and in recent years was virtually running the farm. I keep telling Joe it's time to sell off the livestock and retire. I'm sure we'd have enough money, but he says no. (I hope he's writing what I'm telling him.) Your Uncle Joseph has also tried to convince him. (Jess, I'm not retiring, I love your Grandma but what would I do if I retired?)

Speaking of your Uncle Joseph, he and Mary are expecting another baby next year. There's no such news concerning your brother, George. He and Mary have the two girls but I thought they might've had more by now. No matter. I hope you safely delivered – I expect your baby will be born next month, and by the time you receive my letter, you'll be holding your new little one.

I've had no word from your sister Mary. The last I heard she and Charles were living in Maitland, but she rarely writes. As for your eldest sister, Charlotte - I've not heard a word from her in a number of years, but she was also living in Maitland, so I like to think your two sisters are together.

Well, my dear, that's all the news I have for now. Do take good care of yourself, and kiss the children for me. Please also don't forget to give my love to your dear husband.

All my love Grandma and Grandpa Joe

So, William was getting married. She still thought of him as a gangly youth, but of course, he was a man now. Could she go to his wedding? Oh, how wonderful it would be to see her two brothers again. She crushed the letter to her bosom as she imagined seeing them one more time.

***

Chapter 39

Time Flies

The closure of the island appeared to stall as the colonists in Van Diemen's Land complained loudly at the prisoners from Norfolk Island being dumped on them. New prisoners had been sent to the island to serve their sentences and Jessie wondered at the indecision of the Lord's in London.

She'd spoken to Aaron at length about whether to stay or go, and they were no closer to a firm decision. Aaron wanted to wait and see, and Jessie thought he hoped to be pensioned off if they were forced to leave. She was more than happy to wait and see if that eventuated.

Commandant Price was indisposed and it was rumoured he would be replaced due to his continued ill health. Jessie hoped it was true. Not that the poor man was so ill, but that he'd be replaced. Surely they couldn't do any worse.

All in all life on the island was going smoothly for Aaron and Jessie. Her friendship with Caroline was blossoming and

Aaron had settled into his position at Orange Vale. She'd hoped to attend William's wedding in July but as the time neared she realised that travelling all that way with nine children in tow was impossible. She wrote to him and wished him all the best – there was nothing else she could do.

Early in the New Year Jessie discovered she was expecting again. Ten children were going to be a handful but at least Ellen and the twins were older now. Ellen in particular was a great help with her younger siblings, the twins, not so much.

"We'll be having our babies together," said Caroline beaming at Jessie over the rim of her teacup. "According to Mrs Fletcher, I'm only just – and should birth in October. What about you?"

"September, I think. I did my own calculations, but I'm generally right." Jessie drained the last of her tea. "Will your mother or sister visit do you think?"

"Maybe," she said with a shrug. "I think my mother's expecting us to be back by then – you know with the whole island being closed down." She rolled her eyes. "I wonder if it will ever happen."

"I wonder the same thing," said Jessie shaking her head. "It all seems to depend on the Governor right now. I read that the colonists are rather unhappy with him. Something about broken promises."

"Yes, I heard the same thing. Apparently, he made certain promises about the prisoners from Cockatoo Island and then went back on his word. No one trusts him in regards to Norfolk Island."

"Well, whatever's going on, Aaron and I are just going to wait and see what happens."

***

Over the next few months, nothing much changed. Life went on as usual with no official word on when or even if they would need to leave. In early September Jessie gave birth to a daughter who she named Caroline. She was a tiny little thing and Jessie worried she'd come too soon. Memories of losing Mary came flooding back and Jessie fussed over her new daughter, anxious lest something happen to her.

The following month her dear friend Caroline Batchelor gave birth to a fine healthy boy. They named him Francis after his father – and after his father and so on. From what Jessie understood, the eldest son in the Batchelor family going back generations was named Francis, no exceptions.

After Sunday Service Jessie returned home with Ellen and the younger children. Aaron, the twins and Matthew went down to Cascades to meet the Lady Franklin which had arrived yesterday morning. Young Aaron and Moses had spent most of yesterday down at the dock watching the goings on. They had become quite fascinated with the comings and goings and with ships in general.

Jessie was anxious for the latest news and letters from Grandma and George and hoped Aaron would bring letters home with him.

By the time the children were changed out of their Sunday best Jessie was exhausted. She hadn't recovered so quickly from having Caroline as she had with her previous pregnancies. She removed her Sunday best dress and eyed herself critically in the mirror. She was painfully thin although her breasts were full – she had plenty of milk. She twisted herself around so she could see herself from all angles. Sighing, she stepped into her everyday skirt and put on her blouse. Her clothes hung on her and she quickly tied on her apron, covering herself. Her apron hid how thin she was, and with a final glance, she left the bedroom.

Aaron and the boys didn't arrive home until it was nearly dark. They were full of exciting stories which had been regaled by the sailors. Jessie's brow arched as she listened to her son's talk of whales and pirates.

"Well, that's all very exciting," she said shaking her head. "Go and wash up for supper."

Aaron laughed as they ran off, still chatting about their day. "How are ye?" He pulled her into his arms and kissed her.

"I'm fine…tired."

"Why don't ye sit down and I'll get the children fed. What's for supper?"

"There's beef pie in the oven," she said smiling.

He kissed her again before letting her go. "I have a letter for ye." He pulled a battered envelope from his pocket and handed it to her. "Sit and read it. Once I've fed the children ye and I will have supper together – what do ye say?"

She sighed as she pressed the envelope to her bosom. "I say you're a wonderful husband."

She kissed him before sinking into the nearest chair to devour her letter. At least that was her plan but instead of tearing the letter open she sat and watched as he gathered the children and headed for the kitchen. It was so good to just sit for five minutes and have someone else worry about everything. She closed her eyes, savouring the few minutes she had to herself.

She could hear Aaron calling her name, and someone was prodding her, which was rather annoying. It took several seconds before her eyes fluttered open and she realised she'd been asleep. She yawned and blinked until her eyes focused on Aaron. His brow was furrowed and he cupped her face with his hand.

"Are ye alright? I've been trying to wake ye for a good minute."

"I'm fine," she said shaking her head as she tried to clear the last fog of sleep. "I'm sorry, I…"

"Fell asleep?" He was grinning at her as he took her hands in his and pulled her to her feet. "Come, supper's ready, and the children are occupied for at least the next ten minutes."

She grasped his arm to steady herself as she came fully awake. "My letter?"

"Here," he said retrieving it from the floor. "Come, Jess, I'm starving."

They went out to the kitchen and Jessie slid into a chair and breathed in the aroma of beef pie. Her stomach grumbled as she reached for her cutlery. "Thank you for taking care of the children and for serving my supper."

"You're welcome," he said kissing the top of her head as he passed her. "Wine?"

"No," she said shaking her head. "I'm afraid it'll just put me to sleep. But you have some."

He sat opposite her and poured himself a liberal glass of red wine. "How was your afternoon?"

"Fine. Although I think you and the boys had more fun."

They ate supper while they discussed the day, which focused more on what Aaron and the boys had done all afternoon. Jessie didn't mind. It was good to hear her sons and their father had enjoyed their time together down at the landing. She put the last mouthful of pie in her mouth and finally reached for her letter. She slit the envelope open and unfolded the single sheet of parchment. She frowned, and as the words leapt off the page at her and hot tears filled her eyes.

I'm sorry I cannot tell you this in person, Jess. I can only hope Aaron is there with you. Your Grandma passed away in her sleep on Sunday night.

Jessie sucked in a breath, which caught in her throat as the enormity of those words struck her. She was gone. Her most kind and wonderful grandmother was gone. Tears rolled down her face unbidden and blurred her vision.

"What is it?" said Aaron taking her hand in his. "What's happened?"

Jessie compressed her lips and shook her head. She couldn't get the words out – couldn't say them out loud. She wiped her tears aside as she read the rest of the letter.

I am beyond grief-stricken and although I have expected it for some weeks, I wasn't ready. I would never have been ready to lose her, of course. She was my rock my steady hand and the love of my life.

All my love Grandpa Joe

"It's Grandma."

She let the letter slip from her fingers as she reached into her pocket and retrieved her handkerchief. Life would never be the same. Aaron wasted no time in snatching the letter from the table and reading it.

Jessie wiped her eyes and blew her nose. "It won't be the same without her. I never thought I'd seen her the for the last time…if only I'd known."

"I'm so sorry, Jess," said Aaron sliding the letter across the table towards her. "I know how much she meant to ye."

"She was so wonderful."

Tears rolled down her cheeks as her loss truly hit home. She felt Aaron's arms go around her and she buried her face in her hands and allowed her grief to wash over her. She'd lost her mother and Papa and now the last person that connected her to her wider family was gone. She felt so alone all of a sudden…she knew she wasn't, but there was an ache in her heart that she didn't think would ever heal.

***

Chapter 40

June 1851

Jessie cuddled against Aaron as she tried to steal his warmth. It was the end of June and a colder winter than usual. She pressed her cold feet against him and he gasped.

"Jesus, Jess you're freezing."

She snuggled closer and wrapped her arm around him. "You're so warm and cosy."

He rolled onto his side and pulled her chilled body against his. She tilted her face towards him and he obliged by pressing his lips to hers - probing with his tongue until her lips parted. She moaned as she drank him in, relishing the feel of his arms wrapped tight around her.

He ran his hand down her spine, resting on her rounded hip. He moaned as she flicked her tongue against his lips and ended the kiss. She could feel his desire and she melted against him, feeling the heat from his body seeping into her bones.

"I love you," she murmured as his hand slipped lower and she felt him tugging at the hem of her nightgown. She needed no further encouragement and pushed her hips into him, feeling him pressing against her, hard and insistent.

"Jess, I love ye so much," he whispered as he rolled her onto her back and began kissing her neck, moving lower to her breasts as he pulled her nightgown upwards. She raised her bottom and he pushed it higher and then over her head.

He ripped off his nightshirt and pressed his naked body against hers. She moaned at the feel of his warm flesh. It was intoxicating and she thrust her hips upwards, impatient for him to take her. The chill had left her and now she felt fevered. She burned for him and groaned when he did not immediately oblige her.

He continued his kisses down her belly and then spread her thighs. She moaned with delight when his tongue found its mark and she arched her back in response. She got lost in the sheer pleasure he was giving her and let out a massive sigh when he finally entered her. Their lovemaking was slow as Aaron took his time until Jessie exploded.

Later she lay wrapped in his arms. Her whole body felt like molten lead as it moulded to his. If only she could spend eternity right here, right now. Aaron shifted and she curled herself around him, not wanting the moment to end. They fell asleep, content and secure in each other's arms.

***

Life has a way of rudely interrupting. Caroline's loud squawking brought Jessie out of her slumber and she sat bolt upright. She instinctively reached out for Aaron, but he'd gone. The bed was cold to the touch and disappointment flooded her. Sighing she swung her legs over the side of the bed and spied her nightgown, scrunched in a pile on the floor. She retrieved it and slipped it over her head. She shivered as the cold fabric hit her skin.

Caroline let out another loud indignant scream. "I'm coming," called Jessie reaching for her dressing gown and hastily slipping into it. The day had begun and the memory of the previous night in her husband's arms was quickly fading.

No sooner had she got her feet under her than her stomach lurched and she gagged on rising bile. She reached the basin in time to dry reach but nothing more. She was panting as she straightened and poured water into the basin. She rinsed her mouth and grimaced. She'd suspected that she might be pregnant again and now she was certain. Good Lord another child…she had not yet fully recovered from having Caroline last September.

A long insistent squawk from Caroline rent the air and Jessie quickly wiped her face. "Coming."

Her morning sickness persisted, and by the time she sat down with her mending in the early afternoon, she was feeling washed out and weary. She would've gladly closed her eyes and slept for a few hours. A knock on the door brought her to her feet and she glanced at John, Luke and Jessie before wrenching it open. She smiled at Caroline who was standing on the threshold with Francis in her arms and Margaret clinging to her skirt.

"I hope you don't mind, Jessie, but I needed some company."

"No, come in. I could do with some company myself" she said. "Caroline's asleep, but Margaret and Francis can join the others. They won't mind as long as Francis doesn't upset their game." She smiled as Margaret toddled over and plopped herself down on the floor.

"I can't promise that," said Caroline with a laugh. "He's becoming rather mischievous."

"Boys are like that," said Jessie with a roll of her eyes. "Come, I'll make us a pot of tea. We'll keep an ear out for the children from the kitchen."

The two women settled themselves in the kitchen with a pot of tea between them. Jessie sighed as she sat down and poured.

"Did you hear the Lady Franklin arrived this morning?" said Caroline. "It seems there's a great deal of talk about abolishing the transportation of prisoners to our shores."

Jessie arched a brow. "Really? I haven't seen a newspaper yet."

"I wouldn't ordinarily have, but Francis went down to meet with several new prisoners and received our newspapers and letters earlier than usual."

"So what did the newspaper say?" said Jessie with genuine interest.

"Only that the colonists have petitioned the Queen to end transportation. It doesn't mean she will agree, of course."

"Perhaps not, but it's probably only a matter of time. And if they do stop sending prisoners…well there's no need for a penal colony here is there?" said Jessie. She took a sip of tea and sighed as the hot liquid slid down her throat. "Was there any talk of when they will finally shut the island down?"

"No," said Caroline with a shake of her head. "Although…I'm sorry I didn't bring the paper with me. There was an article about them relocating the Pitcairn Islanders here. So maybe they will close us down sooner rather than later."

"The Pitcairn Islanders? Aren't they the descendants of the mutineers?"

"The very ones," said Caroline leaning forward. "It would seem to be a rather generous reward to give them a whole island wouldn't it?"

Jessie nodded. She was surprised that the Government would consider giving them such a reward, after all some of the mutineers were probably still alive and amongst them. It seemed rather unlike the Lords of London to reward such people.

"Well, I just wish they'd make up their mind and be done with it," said Jessie with a sigh. "I hate not knowing when we'll be forced to leave."

Caroline quirked a brow upwards. "So, you'll wait until then? Until you're forced to go?"

Jessie put down her cup and sighed again. "Honestly, I don't know. But I think Aaron will wait it out. What about you and Francis?"

Caroline shook her head. "That's not really up to us. Francis could apply for a new position, but I don't think he will. So, we'll be here until either the Commandant dismisses us or we're called to another parish," she said. "Either way, I think we'll be here until they close it down for good."

Jessie picked up her cup and smiled. "Well, I'll be pleased if you stay until the end."

***

By the following day, the entire island was full of gossip and rumours about the end of transportation and the Pitcairn Islanders. Speculation was rife about when Governor Denison would capitulate and order the last of the prisoners to be sent to Van Diemen's Land. Aaron wasn't of that opinion.

His Excellency had many colonists to please, and he was clearly not doing a very good job of doing so. Why else would they have taken matters into their own hands and petitioned the Queen directly? Aaron didn't envy Denison in the least. It didn't matter what he did in regards to prisoners – he would feel the wrath from some quarter.

He smiled as he walked up the road towards home. As for the Pitcairn Islanders – that was wishful thinking on someone's behalf. He considered it nothing more than a rumour and gave it no credence. Even when the British Government finally decided to vacate the island he could see no reason why they'd give it away – particularly to mutineers who by all accounts had never been brought to justice. No, the idea was absurd.

He called out to Jess as he opened the front door and went inside. He barely had time to place the letters and newspapers on the sideboard when he was bombarded by half a dozen children.

"Papa, Papa," they chanted as they wrapped themselves around his legs and begged to be hugged.

"One at a time," he said with a laugh. "Matthew, ye first my lad. How are ye?"

"Good, Papa."

"And what about ye Mark? How was school?"

He shrugged. "Alright."

"Jessie, did ye have a good day?"

"Aha…"

Aaron and Moses were more forthcoming – they'd been down to Cascades after school to watch the ship at anchor. Luke was content to have his hair ruffled as he clung to Aaron's legs. He scooped John into his arms, and he giggled with delight.

"Where's Ellen?" he asked.

"She's in the kitchen with Mamma and Caroline," said Moses.

"Well then," he said putting John down. "Go and wash up for supper."

He ushered the children ahead of him as he went out the back door. He opened the kitchen door and was met with the aroma of supper in the air. Stew?

"Hmm, that smells good."

Jess was at the stove stirring a pot and she swung around and smiled. "Good. Go wash up."

He kissed her briefly. "Aye. I've brought letters for ye. From Mary Vowell, your brother and one from Ellison Sharpe."

"Ooh, I'll enjoy those later."

He grinned as he left the kitchen. The sound of squabbling children met his ears well before he reached the washhouse. He groaned as he entered.

"Enough arguing. Your mother's got supper ready, now wash up and get going." He glared them into silence but he couldn't help grinning to himself.

***

Chapter 41

A Temporary Arrangement

Whenever Aaron was called to the Commandant's office it came with a feeling of dread in the pit of his stomach. However, he did have some sympathy for the man. He'd been plagued with bouts of illness for the past year and although no one knew what ailed him, he was periodically indisposed. Aaron suspected he was suffering some sort of lunacy, but he kept his thoughts to himself.

He was relieved to discover he wasn't the only one summoned. The office was crowded with the likes of Tom Sellers, Lieutenant Hamilton and at least a dozen Principal Overseers. He found a spot to stand against the wall and waited.

"Any idea what this is about?" said Tom Sellers sidling up to him.

"None," said Aaron with a shake of his head. "Although it would seem with all of us here he may have another announcement about the prisoners."

“Aye, I tend to agree. Perhaps there’s some truth to the rumours.”

“Perhaps.” On the other hand, perhaps he’d gathered them together to quell the rumours and speculation. Either way, Aaron didn’t particularly care as long as he wasn’t singled out.

Five minutes later Commandant Price arrived with his clerk in tow. He stood behind his desk and glanced around the room. Aaron thought he looked more haggard than usual. What was left of his thinning hair was plastered to his head and there was an air of neglect about him.

“Gentlemen…good morning, and thank you for attending upon me at short notice.” He clasped his hands behind his back and raised himself up on his toes. “I’ve called you all here to advise you of the immediate change to the transportation laws. There has already been too much rumour and innuendo concerning this matter, and I would put an end to it.

”Initially, the number of prisoners on the island won’t be affected, nor the number of soldiers stationed here. It will, however, affect the ongoing viability of this settlement.” He paused and paced up and down behind his desk, coming to halt and placing his hands on the back of his chair. "The Home Office in London has reached the decision to cease the transportation of male convicts to our shores for a period of two years.

"This takes immediate effect and is, as I understand it, a temporary measure. However, I believe in all likelihood that no prisoners will be sent directly from England to our island in the future." He drew in a breath and eased himself into his chair. "As to the rumour concerning the Pitcairn Islanders, this is no rumour." He leaned his elbows on his desk and stared down his hook nose. "The Home Office has agreed to relocate these people to our island. I believe this will hasten the closure of Norfolk Island as a penal settlement, but as yet, I have no firm orders on when that might occur.

"So, gentlemen, I hope this will bring further speculation to an end on these matters, and we can get on with the job at hand. Thank you and good day."

Aaron, like his counterparts, waited until they'd vacated the Commandant's office before voicing an opinion on what he'd heard.

“What do ye think?” said Tom Sellers running his fingers through his hair before putting on his cap. “Tis the beginning of the end I would say.”

“Aye,” said Aaron nodding. It was. If no more prisoners were going to be sent to the island then it was only a matter of time. However, he imagined the island would slowly wind down. “I don’t expect there’ll be a mass exodus though.”

“Agreed,” said Lieutenant Hamilton joining their conversation as the three walked side by side down the road. “It would seem we are a long way from closing the island for good, although the Pitcairn Islanders may add some urgency to the situation.”

“That it might,” said Tom. “Quite frankly I’m surprised that the Home Office has agreed to it.”

Aaron had to agree. It was surprising. The British Government wasn’t known for its generosity, particularly to lawbreakers – and they were mutineers for God's sake.

***

11th of January, 1852

Jessie's labour pains started around midday and she was grateful to Henry for fetching Mrs Fletcher to her. The older woman had felt her stomach and declared it would be an easy birth.

"Ye need not fuss, Jessie. This one will be here afore ye knows it."

She was right - barely two hours later she was nursing her new son in her arms. He had blonde wispy hair and a pale complexion. He was perfect.

"What shall ye name this one?" said Mrs Fletcher peering at him.

"Sylvester Theophilus," she said smiling. "He's named for his great grandfather's."

"Aye, they're fine names to be sure," she said getting to her feet. "Well, if you're settled I'll be off. Send word if ye need me, but I think you'll be just fine."

"Thank you, Mrs Fletcher."

Jessie put Sylvester beside her on the bed and lay back against the pillows. She'd wanted him to have Theophilus for his first name but had conceded to Aaron. Her grandfather was Theophilus, and she'd loved the name since she was a girl. She remembered how she always liked the sound of it.

"Theophilus," she whispered and smiled – she still liked the feel of it on her tongue.

Her grandfather had gone away and never came back and had died before she was born. She remembered having a conversation a few years ago with one of Reverend Sharpe's parishioners. What was her name? She frowned as she tried to remember. She was a funny old thing and she'd told her about her husband, and how her grandfather most likely went to Ceylon with his regiment and died over there.

She closed her eyes and sighed. She couldn't imagine someone she loved going away and never coming back. Imagine never truly knowing what happened to them. She reached out and patted Sylvester – reassuring herself.

***

While the Commandant may have quelled some speculation, the inhabitants of Kingston talked of little else. When would the island be vacated and the mutineers and their families arrive? There was an air of anticipation every time a ship arrived from Hobart Town. What news from London? Had Governor Denison been able to appease the colonists?

As the year drew to a close there were still no definite answers to any of these matters and there was barely a person who didn't have an opinion. Aaron had thought more prisoners would've been evacuated by now – but while they rarely received new prisoners, the number on the island had not reduced any further.

He'd just come from a meeting with Lieutenant Hamilton who had given him some surprising news. He still wasn't sure he believed him. During Commandant Price's tenure, he'd always invited Aaron to his office to deliver any important information. Not just him, he was of the habit of bringing all his overseers together and informing them of any changes. So, it seemed rather odd to Aaron that on this occasion he hadn't.

According to Hamilton, the Commandant would be leaving for Hobart Town on the next ship and would not be coming back. His request for leave had been granted and he was retiring to a farm near New Norfolk. His continued ill health could certainly account for such an outcome, however, Aaron still wasn't sure if he believed it.

The Lady Franklin lay anchor in early January with the latest news from Hobart Town and beyond which was devoured without delay. There were letters for Jessie, but they would wait until she'd read the latest news. After a week of taking on cargo, the Lady Franklin set sail for Hobart Town. Commandant Price and his wife and children were on board.

"What will happen now?" said Jessie.

She was sitting at the dressing table brushing her hair in readiness for bed. She swung around to look at Aaron who was still in the midst of undressing. She took a moment to admire his trim torso and still round bottom as he removed his breeches.

"It's hard to say," he said hanging his breeches over the back of the chair. "But one thing is certain, without a Commandant things will be different."

"I still can't believe they're not replacing Mr Price. Are you sure?"

He climbed into bed and pulled the sheet over himself as he relaxed against the pillows. “That’s the official word. Governor Denison will govern the island from Hobart Town until its closure.”

“Well, surely that can’t be far away now,” she said twisting her hair into a plait. “Oh…I wish they’d just make up their minds and be done with it. It is agonising not knowing when we are to leave.” She tied a ribbon at the end of her plait and climbed into bed beside Aaron. “You don’t think they’ll send the Pitcairners here before we leave do you?”

“No, I don’t think so.” He wrapped her in his arms and kissed the top of her head. “Try not to worry about it.”

“It’s not that I’m worried exactly, it’s just constantly on my mind. Everyone talks of little else, so even if I wanted to forget it I can’t.”

“We need to be patient, Jess. I’m sure they’ll offer me a generous pension if we can just wait it out.” He sighed and pulled her closer. “It won’t be long. If Governor Denison thought it would be a drawn out affair I’m sure he would’ve appointed a replacement Commandant. The fact that he didn't makes me think we'll receive our orders to leave very soon."

She smiled and snuggled closer to him. "I hope you're right."

***

Chapter 42

The Resolution 1853

By March the settlement was at a fever pitch when the latest news arrived. Transportation of prisoners had been completely abolished to all colonies except for the Swan River. Jessie was sure the next news from Hobart Town would include a date for their departure. She paused, with the newspaper open in her hands. What would happen to the furniture? It wasn't theirs. Like the house, it had been provided by the government and she couldn't imagine them carting it all the way back to Hobart Town.

She glanced at Sylvester who was sitting on the floor at her feet, doing his best to shove his big toe in his mouth. She smiled and tilted her head to the side, listening. The sound of happy children playing reached her and she spared a moment's thought for Henry. They were probably driving him to distraction.

She went back to her newspaper and an article concerning the Pitcairners – as they were now commonly referred to, jumped out at her.

'It is probable that the inhabitants of Pitcairn's Island, the descendants of John Adams, Christian, and others (the mutineers of the Bounty), will be removed to Norfolk Island. That place will no longer be occupied as a place of punishment. We think it certain, that all prisoners will be removed to Tasman's Peninsula.'

There was no mention of when all this might occur, and Jessie groaned with frustration. Everything was still probably will happen, most likely this will occur. She needed something solid under her feet and at the moment she felt like she was walking on quicksand.

There was no improvement over the coming months. The newspapers were full of stories of what would possibly happen, not what had been definitely decided. As far as Jessie was concerned it was all just speculation, not news.

In October Jessie came to the realisation that she was once again pregnant – this would make number eleven. She shared her news with Caroline, who also announced she was expecting her third child. After several miscarriages, she had almost despaired of having more children. It gave Jessie some comfort that she and Caroline would have their babies at around the same time.

Two weeks before Christmas Aaron arrived home for supper accompanied by unexpected guests. The barque Resolution had called at the island to effect repairs to its foremast. Aaron had met the Captain at the lumber yard and invited him and his wife home for supper.

"Ye remember Captain Walker?" he said by way of introduction. "And Mrs Walker of course."

"Of course," said Jessie with a smile. "How very nice to see you again."

She was genuine in welcoming them to her home, but she couldn't help but recall the last time she'd seen them. He'd been the Captain of the Lady Isabella and had conducted the funeral for her dear baby Mary. It was far from a happy occasion and one she'd rather not be reminded of. However, she also recalled the kindness afforded her by Mrs Walker during that fateful voyage.

"I'll have supper on the table soon," she said wiping her hands on her apron. "I'm just getting the younger children fed. I'm afraid we don't all fit in the kitchen at once anymore."

Mrs Walker smiled and her already round face became rounder. "Let me help ye."

"Aye," said Aaron. "Can I offer ye a drink while we wait Captain?"

"Thank you, Mrs Walker," said Jessie. "I'd welcome your assistance."

"A dram if ye have it," said Captain Walker.

The two women went out to the kitchen and were greeted by a table full of six noisy children. They stopped and stared at Mrs Walker, who smiled warmly.

"Less talk and more eating," said Jessie with a stern look at her offspring.

With disgruntled looks, they went back to eating their supper, although they all kept their eyes on the visitor. Jessie indicated to an empty chair and lifted Sylvester onto Mrs Walker's lap.

"Would ye mind feeding him?" she said placing a bowl of mashed vegetables down in front of her.

"I'd be happy to," she said taking the spoon and setting to work. "My, how many children do ye have, Mrs Price."

Jessie sighed as she went back to stirring the pot of gravy. "Ten…the three eldest will eat with us."

"Ye truly are blessed," she said spooning a mouthful of food into Sylvester's mouth.

"What about you? Do you have a large family?"

"Well, they're all grown now and living their own lives. But I've got three sons and two daughters."

She sounded wistful and Jessie turned and quirked a brow upwards. "Do you see them often?"

"Not as often as I'd like. I hope when George finally gives up the sea I'll see more of them and my grandchildren."

As soon as the children were fed Jessie ushered them out of the kitchen and put ten-year-old Matthew in charge to keep them quiet and occupied. Ellen, Moses and young Aaron joined the Walkers for supper in the kitchen and Jessie heaved a sigh as she finally sat down. Meal times were always so chaotic.

"Wine?" said Aaron with the bottle poised.

"Please," said Jessie.

"So, once your mast is repaired where are ye bound?" said Aaron as he poured the wine for Jessie and his guests.

"China and Manila," said Captain Walker taking a large mouthful of wine."Hm, very nice."

"Are ye a real Captain?" said Moses, his eyes wide in astonishment.

"Aye, I am." Captain Walker smiled before cutting his beef. "Ye may not remember me, but ye were on board my ship a few years ago."

Moses's face didn't show any recognition and he shook his head. "I don't remember."

"No matter," said Aaron ruffling his son's hair. "Captain Walker was telling me earlier that he needs a new cabin boy."

Young Aaron's head snapped up and he hastily swallowed. "What like a boy like me?"

Captain Walker chuckled. “Aye, you’d be about the right size.”

“What about me?” interjected Moses. “I’m about the right size too.”

“Aye ye are.”

Jessie’s brows had risen to the hairline as she stared from Aaron to her sons. “What are you suggesting, Aaron?”

Aaron finished chewing and took a mouthful of wine which he swished around in his mouth before swallowing. “I was talking to Captain Walker earlier and I asked him if he’d consider taking the boys with him.”

“I’d be more than happy to, Mrs Price. After our trading voyage, we’ll be docking in Hobart Town, and I’ve assured your husband I can drop your sons off there…unless, of course, they’d like to stay on.”

Jessie stared at her son’s excited faces. Their enthusiasm for the idea was unmistakable. She turned her gaze to Aaron who was smiling at the twins and nodding. She couldn’t believe he’d done this without discussing it with her first. Of course, Aaron and Moses would want to go – they were besotted with ships and sailors. "I think they're a bit too young yet."

"Not at all, Mrs Price," said Mrs Walker eyeing the boys. "How old ye? Twelve - thirteen?"

"We'll be thirteen soon," said Moses sitting up straight in his chair.

"They're twelve," said Jessie.

"They'll be thirteen in a few weeks," said Aaron. "And more than old enough to know if they'd like to sign on for a voyage. What say ye lads?"

"Aye," said young Aaron. "I want to go."

"Me too," said Moses.

"Well it's settled then," said Aaron raising his glass to his lips. "I thank ye, Captain."

"You're welcome, Mr Price. I think the lads will do well," said Captain Walker raising his glass. He clinked it against Aaron's. "To new ventures then."

Jessie put down her cutlery and compressed her lips. She was about to interject when she felt Mrs Walker's hand on her forearm. She turned her face towards the older woman who smiled kindly. "I promise I'll take care of your sons like they were my own, Mrs Price. Ye need not fear for their welfare."

Jessie drew in a breath. "It's not that, I…I just wasn't expecting to lose my sons like this."

Aaron reached out and squeezed her hand. "It will do them good, Jess. They need to see the world and there's no better way."

She sighed and nodded. "Of course…I'm sure you're right." There was no point in arguing any further. The decision was made and everyone seemed happy with the outcome except for her. How could she kiss them goodbye in a few days and be happy for them? She didn't know.

As soon as Ellen and the twins finished their supper Jessie sent them off to check on the younger children. Aaron poured more wine as Jessie cleared the table and stacked the dishes. She sat back down beside Mrs Walker and reached for her wine.

"Captain, you mentioned that you'd drop our sons off in Hobart Town at the end of the voyage. I'm not sure how we'd get them back from there," said Jessie. She wanted to be sure her sons would be returned to her and this plan seemed sketchy at best.

“Aye. I know a Mr Murray of the Wellington Hotel. He’s a most trustworthy man, Mrs Price and he’ll see your sons returned to ye. As Mr Price has said, ye’ll likely be in Hobart Town yourselves by then.”

“Yes I expect we will,” said Jessie. She wasn’t convinced of the plan, and she wasn’t happy about sending her sons away, but it was done.

Aaron’s gaze rested on her and she swallowed as she locked eyes with him. “I know you’re not happy about this, Jess,” he said evenly. “But, it will do our sons good to see something of the world out there before they’re forced into it.”

She nodded and sighed. He was right about one thing – none of their children knew anything of the world. Life on the island had not prepared them for living in the real world.

***

A week later Jessie stood on the shore at Cascade and watched as the launch sliced through the water towards them. Her eldest two sons stood waiting with their bags slung over their shoulders. Their young faces were alive with anticipation and their hazel eyes, so like their father's, were locked on the launch.

"Come, give me a hug goodbye," said Jessie grabbing Moses and pulling him tight up against her. "Be good and don't do anything foolish. You hear me?"

"Aye, Mamma."

Tears welled in her eyes as she pushed him away keeping hold of him. "I'm going to miss you."

He nodded and wrapped his arms around her. "I'll miss ye too."

She swallowed the ache in her throat as she let him go. "Aaron." She grasped her eldest son and hugged him close. "Take care of yourself and Moses."

"I will Mamma," he whispered wrapping his arms around her. "I promise."

She let him go and watched as they bid farewell to their father and siblings. Over the past week, she'd come to terms with her sons leaving. She'd berated Aaron for not consulting her, but in the end, had forgiven him. He was only doing what he thought was right and she couldn't fault him for that.

The launch bumped against the pier and Aaron and Moses bid their final goodbyes before hurrying down to get in. Aaron sidled up beside Jessie and put his arm around her. "They'll be fine ye know. It's going to be a grand adventure for them."

"I know," she said nodding. "They're leaving boys and they'll return as men. I guess that's hard for a mother."

"Aye…and a father."

***

Chapter 43

By Order of Council

News arrived in early February that repealed all previous orders. It was now official; Norfolk Island was no longer to be used as a penal settlement. Aaron set the newspaper aside and drew in a deep breath. A small party was to remain on the island to care for the farms and livestock and to hand over to the settlers from Pitcairn's Island.

"I expect they'll start to relocate the prisoners any day now," said Aaron running his fingers through his hair. "And I'm yet to receive any indication of a pension."

Jessie looked up from her mending and nodded. She knew Aaron was frustrated – so was she – but he'd obviously not read about the Lady Franklin. "Did you see the piece about prisoners taking over the Lady Franklin?"

"What? No." He reached for the paper again and spread it out.

"Page three I think. Twenty-five prisoners overpowered the guards."

She watched while he found the article and folding the paper began reading. She returned her attention to her sewing. "I doubt they'll start taking prisoners for another month or more."

"Aye," he murmured as he read the article.

Jessie watched Aaron's face as several emotions flitted across it. At least Captain Willett had managed to regain control of his vessel.

With a sigh, he folded the paper again and set it aside. "It would seem it may be months before they're transferred. And in the meantime, there's no direction from His Excellency."

Jessie paused with her needle poised. "Have faith, Aaron. We've waited this long, we can't give up now."

"You're right," he said standing and stretching. "We have no choice but to wait it out and pray they provide for us. I cannot see how we can resettle in Van Diemen's Land without some support."

She sighed and returned to her sewing. Their financial situation was, she thought, better than Aaron imagined. However, once they left the island they'd need to get a house and furniture and that would no doubt take all the money they had. In the meantime – she glanced at her husband who was pacing up and down the sitting room – the situation was causing them both a lot of anxiety.

Aaron was right about it being months before the prisoners would be moved. As April gave way to May there was still no sign that the prisoners would be relocated.

Jessie was stirring a pot of soup when the first contraction shot through her. She gasped and bending over grasped her stomach. By the time it passed, she was panting and gasping.

"What is it Mamma?" said Ellen peering at her. "Is it the baby?"

"Yes. Run and fetch Mrs Fletcher for Mamma."

"She's gone," said Ellen with a shake of her head.

"What? When?" said Jessie drawing in a deep breath. She hadn't heard that she'd left the island, although many had gone already. Still, she would've thought Mrs Fletcher might've told her and said goodbye. Ellen must be wrong.

Ellen stared thoughtfully into space. "I don't know."

"Go and see if Mrs Fletcher's at home," said Jessie. "Go."

She watched her hurry out the kitchen door before easing herself into the nearest chair. She could feel a small knot of panic forming in the pit of her stomach. She couldn't call on Caroline to assist her. She'd had her third baby only two days ago. A boy who they'd named William.

She groaned as another contraction hit her and breathing heavily she got her feet under her. As soon as it passed she moved the pot of soup from the stove and waddled through to the sitting room. Caroline and Sylvester were playing some sort of imaginary game together and they both gave her inquisitive looks.

She smiled. "It's alright – keep playing your game."

She settled herself in her bedroom after stripping off her apron and day dress. She was pacing the room in her shift when Mrs Fletcher arrived on the scene.

"Mrs Fletcher, thank God you're here. Ellen thought you'd left the island already," she said as relief flooded through her.

Mrs Fletcher smiled and set her bag on the floor. "Aye well I will be leaving as soon as the Lady Franklin gets here, but who knows when that will be," she said. "I wouldn't have left without telling ye."

"I didn't think you would," said Jessie and then gasped as another contraction gripped her.

"Lie down and let me see how far along this babe is," said Mrs Fletcher guiding her to the bed with her hand on the small of her back. "There ye go."

Joseph Horatio Price was in quite a hurry to be born, and barely half an hour later he came squawking into the world. Jessie was reclining against the pillows with her new son cradled in her arms when Aaron arrived home from work. He took the tiny bundle in his arms and kissed Jess on the forehead.

"A boy," said Jess.

Aaron smiled and ran his finger down his new son's cheek. "I was hoping for another girl for ye."

Jessie smiled and shook her head. "I don't need another daughter. I'm just happy he's all in one piece and healthy."

"Aye," he said kissing the baby's forehead before placing him back in his mother's arms. "I'm more thankful that you're in one piece." He bent down and kissed her again. "I could not live without ye."

"Nor could I live without you," she said as she sank back against the pillows. "There's soup for supper. You best feed the horde before they start to complain."

"Aye." He chuckled as he left the room. "I'll bring ye a bowl," he called over his shoulder.

***

It was nearly August before the Lady Franklin lay anchor off the island. The first launch was slowly making its way towards the landing. Aaron rocked back on his heels as he waited on shore with Lieutenant Hamilton. He prayed the despatches from Governor Denison would be forthright with clear instructions.

After waiting for months in the hopes he would be offered a retiring pension, he'd taken matters into his own hands. His application for consideration was addressed directly to His Excellency and would go with the Lady Franklin when she sailed. He hoped he had time to wait for a reply before being ordered to leave.

Captain Willett was first out of the launch and Lieutenant Hamilton greeted him cordially. "I'm sorry for our delay," said Captain Willett handing the Lieutenant a well-worn satchel. "I suppose ye heard about the pirates trying to take my ship?" His eyes flicked between Aaron and Hamilton with a look of indignation.

"Aye we did," said Aaron.

"And we're most pleased to see you did not come to any harm," said Hamilton with a nod.

"Aye, well it would take more than a few miscreants to take me down." He glanced around and scratched his chin. "Cargo? I was expecting ye'd have coffee and arrowroot ready for loading."

"Ah…while you were indisposed the Governor sent the Lady Delia to us and she took most of the cargo we had waiting," said

Hamilton nonplussed. "We've got a few expirees for you, however."

"Very well," said Captain Willett with a shrug. "Well, I'll leave ye, gentlemen, to your despatches. I have a few calls to make." He doffed his hat. "Good day."

Lieutenant Hamilton and Aaron retired to the barracks with the satchel of despatches. None of them would be addressed to Aaron, but he knew Hamilton would not only share the Governor's letters with him but would want his opinion as well.

Aaron waited somewhat impatiently for Hamilton to read the first of the despatches. The Lieutenant rubbed his chin and mumbled under his breath which only added to Aaron's annoyance. After several minutes he lay the letter aside and sighed.

"Well, it seems the final push is to start," he said leaning back in his chair. "The Governor has confirmed the settlement is to be broken up immediately. He's ordered us to send the first lot with the Lady Franklin."

"May I?" said Aaron indicating to the letter sitting on the desk between them.

"Of course."

Aaron scanned the letter quickly – picking out the important points which were that the expirees and the first fifty prisoners were to go with the Lady Franklin. "He's sending them to work in the mines at Port Arthur?"

"Aye…well it was to be expected." Hamilton reached for the next letter and spread it open before him. He grunted and nodded while Aaron once again waited with bated breath. "Well," said the Lieutenant as he placed the letter in front of Aaron. "He's leaving it up to us which fifty we send so long as they're not in the agricultural gang."

That made sense. Aaron read the letter and nodded. The agricultural gangs would be the last to be evacuated meaning the crops would be tended until the last possible moment. He set the letter aside. "He says he'll charter a ship to take the three hundred or so that are still here," said Aaron with a frown. "I wonder why it doesn't just use the Lady Franklin?"

Lieutenant Hamilton shrugged. "I expect he will use her as well. More to the point, however, is which fifty should we send with Captain Willett?"

"Hmm, that is not my decision to make," said Aaron getting his feet under him.

Hamilton eyed him. “Perhaps not, but I’m making it yours.” He got to his feet and straightened his jacket. “I leave it to you.”

Putting his hat on he departed leaving Aaron to stare after him and groan. He’d have to make a list of prisoners to give to Captain Willett. Their name, the ship they were transported on, length of sentence etc and it would take him at least a week to do it. Surely the Lieutenant didn’t mean to leave it to him entirely. He poked his head out the door, expecting to see the Lieutenant in the hallway. It was vacant - there was no sign of Hamilton.

The Lady Franklin sailed ten days later with sixty-eight prisoners accompanied by twenty-six soldiers. Dr Downing and Mrs and Mrs Warner and their children were also on board. The final closure of the island had finally begun and Aaron felt some small measure of relief.

***

Chapter 44

The Southern Cross

By Christmas, the Lady Franklin had delivered over a hundred prisoners to Port Arthur and the evacuation of the island was well underway. The additional vessel chartered by the Governor had not yet been seen but was expected almost daily.

News arrived in early January per the Lady Franklin that Governor Denison had taken up a new position in New South Wales. His replacement, Sir Henry Fox-Young appeared to be in a no greater hurry to clear the island than his predecessor had been.

Aaron rubbed his fingers through his hair and tossed the newspaper aside. "I don't expect I'll be getting a reply from His Excellency now."

His frustration was obvious and Jessie rose from her chair and walking up behind him wrapped her arms around his waist. "You can apply again…it's not too late," she said pressing her face to his shoulder.

He turned around and she saw it was more than mere frustration in his eyes. “What is it?”

He sighed. “Nothing.” He pulled her into a tight embrace and kissed the top of her head.

She pulled from his arms and stared into his eyes. “Don’t shut me out, Aaron.”

“It’s truly nothing,” he said shaking his head. “It’s just that I’ll have to find work when we get to Van Diemen’s Land. What will I do?”

She smiled and couldn’t stop the laugh that followed. He gave her an indignant stare and raised his brows. “Aaron, you’re a stonemason are you not?

“Aye.”

“Well then, I’m sure they need stonemasons in Van Diemen’s Land.”

He smiled and pulled her into his arms before pressing his lips to hers. Jessie relished the feel of him and explored briefly with her tongue. She was glad he’d been so easy to appease.

He ended the kiss and shook his head. “I was thinking that without prisoners what would I do.”

She laughed again before taking his hand and pressing it to her belly. “Well, you’ll definitely need to work with another mouth to feed.”

A smile slowly spread across his face as realisation dawned. “You’re pregnant?”

“Yes, we’ll be having another before the winter is out.”

“That’s wonderful news, Jess,” he said grinning. “I just hope we know what we’re doing by then.” He swept her into his arms again and kissed her briefly.

***

Over the next few weeks, Aaron had little time to dwell on his situation. The barque Southern Cross finally arrived with orders to begin transporting livestock to Hobart Town. The Government had called for tenders to purchase several hundred head of cattle and nearly three thousand sheep which were currently on the island. Aaron spent the next few weeks overseeing the muster and loading of the first lot of livestock. When the Southern Cross set sail he heaved a massive sigh of relief. He’d have a few weeks to muster the next lot before the barque returned.

The Lady Franklin arrived in early February with despatches from the new Governor. Aaron had been expecting Lieutenant Hamilton to seek him out for a couple of days now, and yet he hadn't. He wondered if there was some ominous reason, and then he did his best to set aside such thoughts. There was no reason to think so – he trusted Hamilton.

He was leaving the Commissariat when he just about ran straight into the Lieutenant. "My apologies," he said sidestepping and nearly falling off the step.

Hamilton grabbed him by the arm and righted him. "Mr Price, just the man I wanted to see."

"Thank ye," said Aaron as his brows quirked upwards. He couldn't help but notice the Lieutenant looked weary and a little unkept. "Is everything alright?"

"Oh, aye," he said with a sigh. "I'm not sure the new Governor fully appreciates the situation, but that aside, you'll be leaving on the Southern Cross when it returns."

"What? Really?" His heart started thumping madly at the news. He knew he'd have to leave one day, but that day had seemed never to come and he'd been more than happy with that. A small knot of fear was quickly forming in the pit of his stomach and he drew in a deep breath.

"Aye. By the time you leave here there'll only be about fifty prisoners remaining with a small guard," Hamilton went on. "Your services will no longer be required. It's been a pleasure, Mr Price."

"Likewise. Thank ye, Lieutenant."

Hamilton doffed his hat and disappeared into the Commissariat leaving Aaron standing on the steps. He stood there for several minutes with a million different thoughts running wild in his head. He couldn't imagine how he was going to navigate life in the real world, and it scared him to the core.

After several minutes he gathered himself together and began walking home. He had to tell Jess as soon as he could. His legs felt like jelly beneath him and his heart was still racing. He sucked in several deep breaths and breathed out through his nostrils. How long before the Southern Cross returned? He thought they probably had two weeks, three at best to pack and say their goodbyes.

He had such an odd feeling as he walked down the path to the front door of his house. He paused and looked towards the beach framed by several tall pines. How long had he been looking at that view? Thirty years? He shook his head and sighed -.a lifetime.

He called Jessie's name as he opened the door and went inside. She was coming out of the bedroom and she put her finger to her pursed lips and shushed him. "I just got Joe down," she whispered before standing on tip-toe and kissing him. "What are you doing home already?"

"Ah…I have news, big news," he said blowing out his breath. "We'll be leaving on the Southern Cross when she returns in a few weeks."

"Oh, Aaron." She gasped and stared at him. "Are you alright?"

"No, not really," he said shaking his head. "I thought I'd be ready – but I'm not." He had a queasy feeling in the pit of his stomach and he grimaced.

"It'll be alright." She squeezed his arm and smiled. "We'll do this together."

"Aye…but, Jess." He swallowed and breathed in heavily through his nostrils.

Jessie took hold of him by his shoulders and stared intently into his eyes. "It's not Sydney…we're not going to Sydney."

Her voice held a note of finality to it as she gazed directly into his eyes. "No." He shook his head and wrapped his arms around her. He felt tears prick his eyes and he squeezed them shut and breathed in Jess's familiar scent. It wasn't Sydney, but that knowledge didn't reduce his fear. And it was fear. He was leaving all that was familiar and all that he'd known for thirty years. The big wide world was a terrifying thought.

She pulled from his embrace and kissed him. "We have much to do. How long do we have do you think?"

"Two weeks, maybe three."

She cupped his face and pressed her lips to his. "I promise you, my love, I'll be by your side. You have me."

"Thank God, for I couldn't do it without ye."

***

Jessie balanced Joe on her hip as she knocked on the door. Sylvester was standing quietly by her side but Caroline was still wandering down the path behind her. Jessie glanced at her and gestured to her to hurry. She grinned and skipped the rest of the way to the door and arrived just as Caroline Batchelor opened it.

“Jess, what a lovely surprise. Come in.” She kissed Jess on the cheek before stepping back to allow her to enter. “Francis come and see who’s here,” she called.

A moment later a dark-haired little boy with a cheeky grin arrived. He squealed with delight at seeing Caroline and without a word to Jessie grabbed Caroline by the hand and the two disappeared into the bedroom.

“Be good,” Jessie called after her daughter.

“They’ll be fine,” said Caroline with a smile. “Why don’t you go and play with them, Sylvester?”

He nodded and ran off after them. Jessie hoped Caroline and Francis would let him join in whatever game they were playing. He was a quiet boy and would often get left out.

"I've left Willie in the kitchen. Come, I've got a batch of biscuits about to come out of the oven."

The aroma of biscuits baking assaulted Jessie as soon as she entered the kitchen. She breathed in and grinned. "They smell wonderful."

"Tea?"

"Yes, thank you." Jessie put Joe on the floor to play with Willie before seating herself. She sighed as she watched Caroline prepare the tea. "I'm going to miss this."

"What?" said Caroline swinging around to face her. "I knew it. You're leaving aren't you?"

Jessie nodded. "Yes, in a few weeks when the Southern Cross returns. I can hardly believe it's finally happening and I've got such mixed feelings. Of course," she paused. "We have no choice in the matter."

"None of us do," said Caroline with a sigh. "I'm going to miss you so much. We have no idea when we'll be leaving but Francis thinks they'll leave us to the very end – whenever that is."

"Aaron thinks that could be six months away," said Jessie. "There's still so much livestock to move and the Government wants some return from."

"Understandably so," said Caroline putting the pot of tea on the table along with two cups and saucers. "Oh the biscuits," she exclaimed grabbing the nearest tea towel and pulling the tray of golden treats from the oven. "Just in time," she said prodding one with her finger. "Oh, they're hot."

Jessie grinned as she poured the tea. "They would be."

"Yes, we'll give them a few minutes to cool before calling the children in to have one."

Jessie and Caroline spent the next hour or so chatting and enjoying one another's company. There wouldn't be too many more opportunities for them to spend time together, and Jessie savoured every moment.

Time has a way of playing tricks when you least expect it. Sometimes it slows down at the most inopportune times and in other situations, it speeds up. This was one of those times in Jessie's life when time had sped up and was disappearing at a rapid rate. Aaron had acquired a large sea trunk from the Commissariat Store and she'd packed it with linen and as many clothes as it would take.

By the end of February, she was as organised as she could possibly be. All that was left to pack was the one set of clothes she'd left out for everyone. She stretched and rubbed her hand over her growing belly. This baby would be born in Van Diemen's Land and she couldn't help but wonder where. She'd been pushing her fears aside ever since Aaron told her they were leaving. She knew he was scared enough for both of them and she'd tried to assure him that all would be well. Had she succeeded? She didn't think so.

Two days later Aaron arrived home white-faced and breathing heavily. Jessie was immediately concerned he was coming down with some malady.

"Sails were sighted this morning," he said swallowing. "It'll be the Southern Cross…Jesus, Jess."

She went to him and pulled him into a tight embrace. She could feel his heart thumping madly against her. "Hush…it will be alright." Her stomach clenched as a surge of adrenaline coursed through her. They stood there for ages, lost in each other's arms. Jessie finally pulled free and taking his face in her hands kissed him. “I love you and we will face this together. We’ll be alright.”

He nodded, but she could see the fear hadn’t left him. It broke her heart to see him reduced to such a state but she was sure they would be alright. He would see once they arrived in Van Diemen’s Land – they would be alright.

Three days later they stood on the deck of the Southern Cross. A squally wind was blowing and Jessie gripped the railing as the ship lurched beneath her. The sails filled and she swallowed as the ship began to slice through the water. Her eyes were glued to the tall cliffs and pines until they disappeared from view. Aaron put his arm around her and squeezed her, nuzzling her neck. She turned her face to the side and he obliged her with a kiss.

“Are you alright?” she said with her voice full of doubt.

“Aye. As long as you’re by my side I’ll always be alright.”

She smiled. “I always will be.”

The End

The Fight for Freedom

I've always looked upon Aaron and Jessie's life on Norfolk Island as a struggle to be free. He applied three times before he finally succeeded in obtaining his pardon, and I spent many years trying to understand why they stayed once it was granted.

While writing this book I had to think long and hard to find a reason, and fear became the most logical answer. Aaron wrote about his fear in his second letter to Captain Maconachie. Fear for this family and for his safety if he was required to go to New South Wales on his Ticket of Leave. I imagine that even after his pardon was granted that he would've feared leaving all that he knew.

When they finally left the island they settled in Rokeby. Aaron was successful in his application for a pension, and in 1855 was granted an allowance of thirty pounds and ten shillings per year. He also found himself a job at Kangaroo Point.

The second Norfolk Island penal settlement was a place of the harshest punishments, short of death. However, my focus was not so much on the convicts as on Aaron and Jessie and their story. I hope I haven't disappointed those of you who would've preferred more of the grisly details.

The events that Aaron was involved in on the island as Principal Overseer are based on factual events. He went to Sydney several times to give evidence in court, however, the attacks on him and Jessie in Sydney are fictitious.

Aaron was severely injured on one occasion and his life was threatened. I believe the fear he felt was real and he'd earned the hatred of many prisoners.

From convict to bushranger and as a prisoner for many years on Norfolk Island, he had to find a way to survive and ultimately to thrive. He turned on his fellow prisoners and gained the trust of Commandant's that eventually led to him achieving his greatest goal – freedom.

C J Bessell

Aaron and Jessie's Children

Ellen Ann Price

Ellen was born in December 1839. She married George Wheeler in 1861 and they had ten children.

Aaron Price

Aaron was born in December 1840. He never married and was a whaler.
In 1870 he signed on with the whaling barque Japan out of Melbourne as Fourth Officer.

Moses Price

Moses was Aaron's twin brother. The last mention I have found of him in the records is when he set off on board the Resolution in 1853 with his brother.

Matthew Price

Matthew was born in August 1842. He married Alice Maud Mundy in 1863 and they had eight children.

<u>Mark Price</u>

Mark was born in November 1843. He married Margaret Dunn in 1864 and they had eleven children.

<u>Jessie Price</u>

Jessie was born in 1846. She married Alfred Harrington in 1865 and they had four children.

<u>Luke Price</u>

Luke was born in July 1847. He married Mary Ann Nunn in 1869 and they had ten children.

<u>John Price</u>

John was born in about 1848. He married Rachel Richardson in 1868 and they had eleven children.

<u>Caroline Price</u>

Caroline was born in 1850. She married John Gilley in 1870 and they had six children.

<u>Sylvester Theophilus Price</u>

Sylvester was born in 1852. He married Maria Haywood in 1884.

Joseph Horatio Price
Joseph was born in 1854 and died the following year in Hobart Town.

James Price
James was born in 1855 and only live for a few days.

Jessie died of a fever on the 9th of April 1856 in Rokeby. She was only thirty two years old.

Some evidence suggests that Aaron remarried following Jessie's death. Aaron died on the 24th of April 1882 at Cambridge and was buried at St Matthew's in Rokeby.

One newspaper notice stated he was in his eighty seventh year, but the age given on his death certificate is ninety one. I have no idea if either one of them is correct. He lied so often about his age that it's almost impossible to know for sure.

***

Margaret

From Bredgar House to Van Diemen's Land.....

Margaret Chambers never imagined she'd be forced to flee her family home and country to escape a hideous old man and an arranged marriage. Pretending to be a general servant she boards a ship bound for Hobart Town. It's 1837, and in order to get free passage out to Van Diemen's Land, she's agreed to work for Mrs Hector. There's just one problem, she's never done a day's menial work in her life and her lie is soon discovered.

Taken into the household of the Reverend Davies and his wife Maria, she not only finds kindness but friendship, and is employed as Maria's companion. She couldn't have hoped for a better situation, but when convict and scoundrel William Hartley crosses her path will it all come tumbling down? Seduced by the young and charming William she finds herself unable to remain with the Reverend and his wife. Maria doesn't want her to go but Margaret can see the conflict between Maria and her husband. Not wanting to be the cause of any rift between them she leaves.

William still has five years of his seven-year sentence to serve and he's not free to marry her. However, he stands by her side by stealing food for her and his unborn child until he gets caught. Sent away to work on the chain gang Margaret's left to fend for herself. Somehow she finds a way to survive until William's free to join her and when he gets a Ticket of Leave and permission to marry her, the future's looking hopeful.

Available from Amazon

Pioneers of Burra

From Cornwall to an untamed South Australia...

Based on the true story of the Bryar family, who left their homeland in search of a better life. Richard and his son Thomas secure free passage to South Australia, where they dream of a new beginning working in the copper mine of Burra.

After months at sea and a perilous journey from Adelaide to Burra, their families are finally reunited. Can they overcome the hardships of living in a dugout on the Burra Creek to carve out a better future for their children? Will a disaster in the mine finally bring them together with hope for the future?

Out Now

Printed in Great Britain
by Amazon

57857288R10300